Praise for

"A grabber from pag[e] [...] adventure and revenge sprinkled with echoes of our own dangerous times. James Maxey's world of dragons and humans at war is so solidly and engagingly rendered that I never wanted to leave."

—**John Marco**

"Bitterwood is an unlikely hero in a rich world, with a rich history that holds many surprises. James Maxey tells his story with a sure hand. Enjoy the journey!"

—**Carrie Vaughn, author of *Kitty and the Midnight Hour* and *Kitty Goes to Washington***

An inventive fantasy tale inhabited by a cast of satisfyingly complex characters. Maxey's fantasy world is well-rendered and limber enough to serve as a metaphor for our own, and the author effectively weaves into the narrative social commentary on topics as varied as right rule, religious zealotry and genocide. For the sake of humanity, join in Bitterwood's revolt."

—*Kirkus Reviews*

"The dragons are wonderfully written, as is the tormented hero; it is almost a shame that the story is so self-contained, as many readers will pine for a whole series of Dragon Age titles."

—*Publishers Weekly* (Starred Review)

JAMES MAXEY

DRAGONSEED

SOLARIS

First published 2009 by Solaris
an imprint of BL Publishing
Games Workshop Ltd
Willow Road
Nottingham
NG7 2WS
UK

www.solarisbooks.com

ISBN: 978-1-84416-754-8

A CIP catalogue record for this book is available from the British Library.

Designed & typeset by BL Publishing.
Printed and bound in the UK.

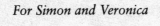

For Simon and Veronica

...I shall appoint over you terror,
consumption, and the burning fever,
that shall consume the eyes,
and cause sorrow of heart:
and ye shall sow your seed in vain,
for your enemies shall eat it.

Leviticus 26:16

CHAPTER ONE

HOPE OF THE SLAVE

CLOUDS THE COLOR of bruises stained the winter sunset. Shay hoped that the yellow-brown sky meant they were near the foundries of Dragon Forge. He wasn't certain Hemming would make it if their journey lasted another day. Shay, Hemming, and Terpin were at the edge of a pine forest on a steep hill leading down to a slow muddy river. On the other side of the water a broad, flat field had been trampled to muck. Shay wondered if this was evidence of the retreat of Shandrazel's army. Thousands of earth-dragons had fled on foot. The ground would surely bear witness.

"I don't think I can go on," Hemming whined as he slid down the bank, landing on a bed of gravel beside the river. Hemming was the oldest of the three slaves, a stooped, white-haired man in his late sixties. In a perfect world, Hemming's age and experience would have endowed him with wisdom and toughness, but in actuality it had left only a fragile shell of a man

9

with an unceasing passion for complaint. "My blisters have popped," Hemming moaned. "My boots are filled with blood."

"All the more reason to keep moving," said Terpin, sliding down beside him. Unlike Hemming, a house slave, Terpin had worked the grounds of the College of Spires. He was a short man, but heavily muscled. His wispy hair clung in a band around his ears, as white as Hemming's more ample mane, though he was at least twenty years younger. Terpin's face was a mass of wrinkles and he only had teeth on the left side of his jaw. His voice was authoritative and gruff as he said, "Walk while you still can, old man. If you can't go on, we're not going to carry you."

Hemming's lower lip quivered. "Y-you'd leave me behind? After we've come this far together?"

Shay cleared his throat. He still clung to a skinny tree on the steep slope. The last ten feet down to the river looked particularly treacherous. He couldn't get the memory of the horse's broken leg out of his mind. He announced, "We're not leaving anyone behind. I'll drag you both if I have to." He was the youngest of the slaves, only twenty-two. He was lanky, tall despite his hunched posture, with a thick head of orange hair bright as the scales of a sun-dragon. Unlike the drab, threadbare outfits of the older men, Shay was dressed in a long red coat with shiny brass buttons. His black boots were scuffed and muddied from walking, but the upper parts still showed their former polish.

Shay had led a more privileged life than either of the older slaves. He'd been the personal attendant to Chapelion, the sky-dragon scholar who oversaw the College of Spires. Few humans knew how to read, but Shay's precociousness had been recognized at an early age and encouraged by Chapelion, who'd seen advantages in having a literate slave. Chapelion had thought that his bright-eyed favorite had been smart enough to recognize the benefits of life in his service. Instead Shay's relatively easy life in the face of the hardships of his fellow men had only made his status all the more intolerable. Not that his life had been easy—as a slave, he'd been subject to beatings for minor mistakes. His back bore scars from the bite of whips. When news of a human rebellion at Dragon Forge had reached the College of Spires, Shay instantly knew that he belonged there. He'd persuaded Terpin to accompany him, because he liked Terpin and thought the tough, worldly slave knew a thing or two about surviving in the world. They'd taken Hemming because the older man had eavesdropped on their plans and asked to come, and they'd both been certain he would betray them if left behind.

"Hemming, I'm as tired as you," Shay said. "I want nothing more than to stretch out on the ground and drift to sleep. But look at those clouds. That has to be the smoke from Dragon Forge. I've heard the sky above it is always tinted this way at sunset. We're close."

"It's Terpin's fault we don't have horses," Hemming grumbled.

Shay sighed to hear this argument brought up again.

"Oh lord," Terpin groaned, throwing his hands up.

"If you'd listened to me, we'd be there already," Hemming said.

This was arguably true, but Shay didn't think it mattered. They'd left with two horses, with Hemming and Shay sharing a mount. On their first day out, they'd pushed too far. Terpin had assured them the horses could go another mile, then another, and he'd beaten the horses with branches to keep them moving. After hours of rough treatment the horse that carried the two of them fell dead, its heart burst. The next morning, they'd taken turns with the last horse, and as Terpin rode down a ravine the horse had stumbled and broken its leg. Shay knew they had made mistakes that cost them dearly, but he couldn't see any advantage in dwelling on them, not when they were so close to freedom.

"What's past is past," said Shay. "We're all cold and hungry. Dragon Forge will have fireplaces, and food to fill our bellies, and it wouldn't surprise me if there's whiskey as well. It's worth another hour of walking, even in the dark."

"Whiskey gives me heartburn," Hemming grumbled. "And you think they're just giving out food? You think they're going to welcome three runaway slaves with open arms?"

"It's a rebellion. They need soldiers, and workers, and cooks, and any other talents we can bring," said Shay. "They'll feed us. Especially once they see what I'm carrying."

He tapped the leather pack slung over his shoulder. It had been a heavy burden to tote all this way, but he thought the contents were the most precious thing in the world. He held onto the faith that Dragon Forge would welcome them with the same certainty that dawn would follow the night. Hemming didn't look convinced.

"You youngsters think you're immortal," Hemming said. "But if we're stumbling around out here in the dark with numb feet, we're likely to break our legs. You remember the horse, don't you? You remember the way that bone jutted through the hide, the way that blood shot out in a fountain?"

Shay did remember this. Any time he closed his eyes, he could see it. This was one reason he was still clinging to the tree instead of jumping down to the gravel.

Perhaps sensing he was touching Shay's fears, Hemming went on: "None of us can see worth a damn in the dark, but the slavecatchers can. They'll find us while we're lying there in the open field with broken legs. Those bastards have eyes like cats."

"Our ears are rather sharp as well," said a voice overhead.

Shay looked up, his heart in his throat. Perched in the gnarled branches of a towering pine, he spotted a pair of golden eyes glowing in the last rays of the sun. The blue wings of a sky-dragon unfurled against the dark sky as the beast rose and glided down to the gravel bed, landing ten feet away from Hemming. The old man trembled. A high-pitched cry erupted from his lips, a sound like a rabbit shrieking in the jaws of a hound.

The slavecatchers were frequent visitors to Chapelion's chambers, and Shay recognized this one as Galath, a fairly young and inexperienced member of the trade. Perhaps they still had a chance. Hope faded as a second sky-dragon glided down to join Galath. This was Enozan, a much older and more experienced slavecatcher. Still, it was two against three; not all hope was lost. In the air, sky-dragons were much larger than men, with their twenty-foot wingspans and long whip-like tails. On the ground, however, standing on their hind-legs like oversized blue jays, the two slavecatchers were no taller than Hemming. Perhaps this gave Terpin courage because, as Hemming fell to his knees to beg for mercy, Terpin grabbed a fallen tree branch and wielded it like a club.

"Stay back!" he shouted. "Or I'll knock your brains out!"

There was a rustling in the tree behind Shay. A third dragon had landed in the branches. Shay recognized him immediately—Zernex, one of the most feared slavecatchers employed by the College of Spires, second in cruelty and cunning only to Vulpine, the infamous Slavecatcher General.

Zernex spread his wings wide and stretched his neck as he stood on the swaying branch, perhaps for balance, perhaps to emphasize his size. While sky-dragons were small compared to sun-dragons, they were still fearsome beasts. Their heads were the size of a large ram's, with jaws that could open wide enough to close around a human throat and sink into it with gleaming rows of saw-like teeth. Their talons may have been little larger than a man's hand, but they were tipped with sharp-hooked claws that could slice through flesh with ease. Zernex raised the fringe of long feather-scales that ran along the back of his neck as he snarled at Terpin. "Drop the branch, slave! I'm paid the same whether I bring you back alive or dead. I won't hesitate to gut you."

Shay shouted at Zernex. "If you don't care if we're alive or dead, why bring us back at all? Leave us alone! The College of Spires won't miss three slaves!"

Zernex glared at Shay. "Do you think we're fools, boy? You're running off to join the rebellion. You think we're going to let you go get armed with a bow and arrow so you can kill dragons? Besides, we both know you aren't merely escaped slaves... you're thieves as well." His eyes fixed on Shay's leather backpack.

Despair welled up within Shay like a black fog. He looked at Hemming, groveling on the damp gravel, his hands clasped behind his head. A small hard knot formed in Shay's belly. He'd never been in a fight in his life. He'd never even thrown a punch. But he'd been running away to become a rebel, hadn't he? He spotted another fallen branch on the slope below him. He let go of the tree and slipped the leather pack from his shoulders. He jumped down to the gravel, grabbing the branch. He stood back to back with Terpin and shouted, "You'll never take us alive!"

"Take me alive, please," whimpered Hemming.

The branch that Shay had grabbed was damp and half-rotten. He cast his eyes about for another weapon, but it was too late. Apparently emboldened by Shay's defiance, Terpin lunged, hacking out with his more sturdy club. It was a powerful swing, but easily anticipated. Galath, the target of the blow, flapped his wings once and darted backward as the club passed through the air where he'd stood.

Terpin, off balance, didn't show a similar talent for evasion. Enozan's toothy jaws shot toward him in a serpentine strike, clamping onto the bald man's windpipe. Terpin unleashed a gurgling yelp as the dragon shook his head back and forth. Enozan kicked out with a hind-talon, sinking his hawk-like claws deep into the man's belly. In seconds the fight was over, as the dragon dropped Terpin's lifeless body from his jaws.

Shay fought to keep from dropping to his knees as the older man fell.

"Oh god oh god oh god," prayed Hemming, his head pressed into the gravel.

Galath hopped forward and opened his reptilian jaws wide. He snapped them shut on Hemming's skull with a horrible *crunch*. Hemming's whimpers suddenly went silent.

"Why?" Shay shouted, dropping his useless branch, clenching his fists. "Why'd you kill him? He wasn't fighting you!"

From the branch above, Zernex answered. "It's a long way back to the College of Spires. It's easier to carry just the heads."

Zernex dropped from the branches onto the bank, grabbing the leather pack Shay had dropped. He held it up, his eyes fixed on it hungrily as if he appreciated the importance of its contents. "This is what Chapelion cared about most. And while I won't hesitate to kill you, Shay, I think your master would prefer to see you alive. I imagine he'd like the satisfaction of watching you flayed. Honestly, you've known Chapelion your whole life. Did you truly think he'd let you get away with even a single book from his private library?"

"I know the truth about those books!" Shay protested. "They were written by men! For men! In a time before the Dragon Age! They shouldn't be part of a dragon's library!"

"If dragons can own men, why can't they own their books as well?" Zernex asked in a condescending tone.

"You can't own us!" Shay shouted, reaching down and grabbing a smooth river stone the size of his fist. "You can only enslave us!"

Shay hurled the stone with all his strength at the hated slavecatcher. Zernex lifted the leather bag in his fore-talons, blocking the stone before it collided with his chest. Shay knew he had no chance in a fight. He turned toward the river. He didn't know how deep it was. Could he dive and swim downstream? Lose his pursuers in the dark? Or would he only freeze to death in the icy water? What choice did he have? Better to drown a free man than ever to face the lash again. He darted toward the water.

Behind him, there was a hiss as a dozen feet of leather sliced the air. His charge was brought to a sudden halt as the tip of a whip curled around his neck like a noose. His feet flew out from under him and he slammed to the ground on his back.

Zernex loomed above him. The other two slave-catchers drew close, forming a rough triangle as their golden eyes looked down. Above their shadowy forms, a few dim stars glowed through the haze of clouds. Shay clawed at the loop of leather around his windpipe, trying to pry it free. He couldn't breathe. The gravel beneath him was ice cold as dampness seeped through his coat.

"Hmmph," Zernex sneered, looking down. "Chapelion should have known teaching a human to read was a waste. Even if your kind is smart enough to recite the words, you plainly lack the capacity to understand them. A truly educated being would have known that nothing but death awaited him if he stole from his master. I think there's a famous quote from a human holy book about this, isn't there? 'The wages of sin are death?'"

Shay had heard the quote, but wasn't in a position to discuss its significance. His eyes bulged and his lips felt numb as he found the tassel at the end of the braided leather around his neck and tried to untwine it. No matter how he pulled, it only grew tighter.

The dragons chuckled softly as they watched his struggles. He could barely hear them over the pounding of his heart. When a new voice from the trees spoke, he heard the words almost as if they were part of a dream. Unlike the reptilian voices of the dragons, the new speaker was plainly human, a male, his voice chill as the winter wind.

"Nothing true in this world has ever been written in a book," the man said. The three dragons whirled toward the slope, looking for the source of the voice. Black spots danced before Shay's eyes as he suddenly found a way to tug the whip that produced slack. He fumbled with trembling fingers and worked the leather loose, until he drew a long gasp of damp air.

"Death has nothing to do with sin," the man continued, still invisible in the shadows of the trees. "Death claims the righteous as surely as the wicked. It awaits the slavecatcher as certainly as the slave."

"Who's there?" Zernex growled. "Show yourself, human."

"These have been the last words of many of your kind,"' answered the voice.

"Spread out," Zernex commanded Galath and Enozan. "Search the hillside. I would like to meet our mysterious philosopher."

Galath spread his wings, flapping, rising up ten feet. A whistling sound rushed through the air and his wings went limp. He fell to the gravel bed, unmoving. The bloody tip of an arrow jutted from the back of his skull, having come all the way through after entering his eye.

Shay kept still, wondering if the dragons even remembered him.

Enozan leapt into the air. There was a second whistling sound, and he, too, fell to the gravel, though he was still alive. He was only a few feet away from Shay, down on all fours. An arrow was buried deep in his left breast.

"*What?*" Enozan gasped, looking confused as he twisted his neck to study the shaft that jutted from him. Perhaps it was a trick of the light, but the fletching on the arrow looked to Shay like living leaves. They were bright green, as if they had been plucked in spring. It was the dead of winter. What tree had fresh green leaves this time of year?

Enozan spasmed. He coughed and pink saliva sprayed from his toothy jaws. His strength failed him and he collapsed, one of his broad blue wings draping over Shay. The dragon shivered; blood gushed from his wound with each heartbeat.

Zernex snarled. Shay was dismayed to discover he hadn't been forgotten after all. The slavecatcher reached down and grabbed him by the collar of his bright red coat. He yanked Shay to his feet, pulling him around to serve as a living shield.

"You obviously care about this slave!" Zernex shouted, his fore-talon pressed against Shay's jugular. "Show yourself, or I'll slit his throat!"

From the dark hillside there was no sign of movement.

"I mean it!" Zernex screamed. The dragon's claws hooked more deeply into Shay's flesh. A bead of blood slid down Shay's throat.

Zernex's demands were met with silence. Cold sweat trickled down Shay's face as Zernex's eyes darted back and forth, searching the shadows. "Come out," he said, fear reducing his voice to a trembling whisper. "Your surrender is this slave's only hope."

In the branches of tall pines, a shadow separated itself from the others rising, taking on the form of a man.

"Do not speak to me of hope," the dark figure said. "I am not the hope of the slave. I am the shadow on the stone. I am the black unbroken silence. I am the Death of All Dragons."

"Bitterwood?" Zernex whimpered, sounding as terrified as Hemming had moments before. His claws began to tremble. His grip slackened. Seeing his chance, Shay grabbed the talon and pushed it away, dropping down, freeing himself. He leapt away as Zernex spread his wings to take flight. The slavecatcher let out a pained grunt. Shay tripped on the gravel and rolled to his back. Zernex had an arrow in his left leg, buried in the meatiest part of his thigh.

"Bitterwood?" Zernex whispered again, sounding like he was in shock. Terror flashed into his eyes. He craned his neck heavenward, and beat his wings in a mighty down thrust. He lifted from the ground, his tail swinging around toward Shay. Acting on pure instinct, Shay grabbed the slavecatcher's long tail and yanked hard, with his full weight. Zernex was thrown back to the gravel bed, landing on his left wing with a sickening snap.

Shay rose to his knees and saw a smooth river stone before him nearly as large as a skull. With both hands, he lifted it above his head and hurled it at the slavecatcher, who was struggling to stand. The heavy rock caught the dragon in the side of his jaw. Zernex's head was knocked back to the gravel. He still wasn't dead. He lifted his long, serpentine neck, his jaw bleeding and broken, and looked toward Shay with murder in his eyes.

In a flash, there was an arrow sprouting between those eyes, the green, leafy fletching shuddering from the sudden halt of its flight. Zernex's golden eyes crossed as they tried to examine the object between them. Then they fluttered shut, and the slavecatcher's head dropped. Shay grabbed another good-sized rock and lifted it, holding it for a moment above his head, waiting for any sign of life. At last, he dropped the stone before him. Zernex wasn't breathing. The dragon would never catch another slave.

Shay rose on unsteady feet. He was breathing hard, his heart racing. The last five minutes of his life seemed disconnected and unreal. The bodies of three dragons and two men sprawled before him, their dark blood blending with the gathering shadows. He saw the leather satchel and lifted it, slinging it back over his shoulder.

He looked up toward the hillside, searching for any signs of movement among the black branches of the pines. The shadow he'd seen earlier was gone.

"A-are you really Bitterwood?" he asked.

No one answered.

"Are you... are you going to Dragon Forge? To join the rebellion? I've read about you. You fought at the last rebellion. At Conyers."

Shay listened hard, certain he heard movement.

It was, perhaps, only the rustle of trees in the winter night. Shay waited for several minutes, until the cold set his teeth chattering. He knew his only hope of surviving the night was to keep moving. He turned up the collar of his coat against the breeze. He rubbed his windpipe, feeling the indentations on his throat where the slavecatcher's claws had been. When he lifted his fingers, the tips were red and wet. He turned toward the west, and saw the clouds above the distant foundries glowing brightly, reflecting the furnaces of the rebellion.

Shay took one last glance at the pines, shifted the pack to better balance it on his back, and walked toward the glow on the horizon. The foundries of Dragon Forge burned like an eternal sunrise. This was the hope of the slave. With numb feet he staggered forward, freedom bound.

CHAPTER TWO

GOOD BOSS

THE EARLY MORNING light coming into the loft was tinted yellow by the sulfurous plumes that rose from the smokestacks. Jandra had been in Dragon Forge for a week now and still wasn't used to the stench, the rotten-egg aroma of coal burning continuously. One of the furnaces had been transformed into a crematorium, adding a black, oily soot that coated every exposed surface and smelled disturbingly like charred bacon. The bacon-stink of the crematorium swirling together with the egg-stink of the foundry left Jandra certain she'd never want breakfast for the rest of her life. She leaned against the window, looking out through the wavy glass, her forehead touching the cold pane as she gazed toward the low hills beyond the walls of the fortress. The last of the snow had melted off, leaving the landscape a mucky, reddish brown.

She was waiting on the second floor of the central foundry, in a high-roofed loft with exposed ceiling beams and baked brick walls. The floors were thick, oily timbers, worn smooth by centuries of constant use. Half a dozen tables had been lugged into the space and all were covered with sheets of parchment scribbled with Burke's notes and diagrams. Across the room, coals glowed cherry red in a large open fireplace. The room was chilly despite this. She sank her hands deeper into the pockets of her ridiculously large, ill-fitting coat. It was a dark green coat from an earth-dragon's formal guard uniform, designed to fit a creature three times as broad across the shoulders as she was. Beneath the coat she wore a man's cotton shirt and baggy britches. When she'd arrived at Dragon Forge, she'd been wearing a blood-stained blanket and a dress torn down the back from neck to waist. Everything she'd worn had been so ripped or filthy she'd wound up burning it all. The only things she'd kept were the large silver bracelet on her left wrist and her knee-high black leather boots.

Behind her the elevator chattered. The iron cage rattled as the lift chains locked into place. The door squeaked open and Burke the Machinist rolled his wheeled chair onto the thick oak planks of the floor. Burke's eyes were bloodshot; he'd obviously worked through the night. His long dark hair was normally pulled into a tight braid, but this morning his hair hung freely around his shoulders, revealing numerous streaks of gray. Burke wasn't ancient; he was only in his fifties, in reasonably good health despite his broken leg. A member of an ancient race known as the Cherokee, Burke possessed a sharp-featured face with a strong jaw that gave him an air of authority. The symmetry of his features was broken by three parallel scars along his right cheek. Behind a newly-fashioned pair of spectacles, Burke's eyes glimmered with excitement. In his lap, he carried an iron rod, the final product of the night's work.

"We've done it," Burke said as he handed the long rod to Jandra. He winced from the movement. Despite the mobility allowed by the wheeled chair, Jandra could tell his broken leg was a source of agony. He clenched his jaw and drew a long breath through his nose, then said, "It's a fully functioning prototype."

Jandra took the device from Burke. The rod was four feet long and quite heavy despite being hollow. One end was open, slightly flared, sporting a perfectly circular hole almost a half-inch across; the other was fixed to a triangle of wood that served as a handle. The steel was lightly engraved with a scale pattern at the open end.

"So this is a gun," said Jandra, turning the weapon every which way as she examined it. She stared down the shaft bored into the center of the tube. Could this weapon really change the world?

"More specifically, a shotgun," said Burke. "And I wouldn't look down that hole. It's loaded. I've got the safety on, but there's no reason to press your luck. Going forward, I'll remember to mention this before I hand it to people."

"So how does it work?" Jandra asked, examining the trigger.

"It's a flintlock," Burke explained, wheeling his chair around to get closer. He pointed at the small iron hammer that was pulled back, held in tension by a spring. A small sharp splinter of flint was held at the tip. "When you take off the safety and pull this trigger, the hammer snaps shut and the flint strikes a spark into the flash pan, here. That creates a small explosion and lights this fuse, which then triggers the black powder packed into the rifle itself. The black powder is loaded into the barrel from the front and jammed tightly with the ramrod beforehand." He tapped a thin iron rod attached to the underside of the barrel.

"Oh," said Jandra, not certain she could envision the process. She pulled out a small pad of paper from her coat pocket. "This sounds like something I should be writing down."

"I doubt you'll have the luxury of checking your notes in situations where you'd be using this," said Burke. He showed her two white cotton sacks, each about the size of her thumb. "To speed the loading process and to keep the powder compact, I've sewed up the appropriate amount of powder into these bags. Each charge provides a serious kick. The other bag holds small lead spheres and is jammed in front of the charge bag. The explosion will produce an expanding force of hot gas that propels the spheres down the barrel at great speed."

"How fast?"

"The balls of lead will come out of the barrel at about ten times the speed that an arrow flies off a bow. It's going to make a crack like thunder."

"Yowza," said Jandra.

"Yowza?" asked Burke. "I don't think I've ever heard that expression."

Jandra frowned. "I haven't either. It must be something she would have said."

"The goddess?"

Jandra nodded, then sighed. She already had enough problems connecting with other humans, having been raised by a sky-dragon. The fact that her most recent adventures had left her head jammed full of alien memories only added to her sense of isolation and loneliness. Of course, having the memories of a thousand-year-old woman from a far more technologically advanced society had a few benefits. She now knew the long-lost recipe for gunpowder, for example.

Burke looked concerned. He was a member of the Anudahdeesdee, a Cherokee clan dedicated to remembering the secrets of the once dominant human civilization that existed before the Dragon Age. His people had a long history of confrontations with Jasmine Robertson, the so-called goddess, the woman who had altered Jandra's brain.

"So, what are these scale marks along the barrel for?" She was eager to change the subject away from her jumbled memories.

"I often design my inventions to resemble creatures in the natural world, like my spy-owl, my chess monkey, the time-frog, etc. I was going to call the gun the Noisy Snake, but the scale pattern was taking too long, so I gave up halfway. It had no bearing on the function." He shook his head as he looked at the gun. "My grandfather used to scold me for being more concerned with making sculptures than machinery."

Jandra smiled. "Your daughter showed me the spy-owl. I liked the attention to detail in the feathers. You're a talented sculptor. The fact that you've only needed a week to design and build a shotgun from scratch shows that you're an equally talented engineer. "

Burke didn't look cheered by her words. "I'm putting a lot of trust in you, placing this in your hands and sending you outside the fortress. If the dragons capture this and figure out how it works, it could forever change the world. Are you certain you can get your powers back?"

"Nothing in this world is ever certain," said Jandra. "But, the sooner I leave, the better the odds are that no one has taken the genie."

Burke nodded. "Anza's anxious to leave as well. She says she's tired of the way this place smells. She should be here in a moment. Let me—" Before he could finish his sentence, shouting erupted outside the window.

"Get it!" someone yelled.

"Circle around!" a man called out. A dozen other excited voices chimed in.

Jandra went to the window. She raised the pane and leaned out. The action was taking place only fifteen feet below her. A crowd of men were chasing a tiny green earth-dragon. The earth-dragon was the smallest she'd ever seen, barely a foot tall, obviously a child. Unlike adult earth-dragons, wingless beasts who moved in a slow plod, the earth-dragon child was darting back and forth like a jackrabbit. Despite its speed, it was pinned in by the crowd, and quickly found itself with its back to the wall directly beneath Jandra.

The men gathered round, keeping a slight distance as the small dragon opened its turtle-like jaws wide and hissed. Its tiny claws flexed as it took up a defensive stance. Its long, skinny tail whipped back and forth like a cat ready to pounce.

Jandra recognized the leader of the men, a white-haired, bearded fellow named Frost, a blacksmith from the foundry. His eyes were wide and he was smiling, as if chasing this young dragon were great sport.

"Frost!" Jandra yelled. "What are you doing?"

The crowd looked up. Whispers ran among the men. Jandra caught the word "witch" among the murmurs.

"We found this lizard hiding in a cellar! We're going to cook it!"

In response, the earth-dragon yelled, "No eat! No eat!"

Jandra felt her stomach turn at the thought of what these men were going to do. A month ago, the drop to the street would have looked imposing. But, in a process similar to the reshaping of her memories, her body had also been retuned, leaving her with a physical prowess that rivaled even the legendary Bant Bitterwood. She leapt from the window, shotgun in hand, and landed in a crouch between the crowd and the dragon child.

"Back off!" she said. "The new rule is: if it talks, we don't eat it."

The men looked wary. Jandra knew it was due to her reputation as a witch... a reputation that, at the moment, was completely undeserved. Once, she'd commanded the elements, and would have been able to summon a ring of fire to shield her, or simply turn invisible to escape a fight. Unfortunately, she required a device known as a genie to use her abilities, and her genie had been stolen. Until she got it back, her "witchcraft" was nothing but bluff.

She stood, pulling back her shoulders. The green wool coat she wore hung down to her ankles. She hoped that the bulky coat and the thick heels on her leather boots helped hide the fact that the smallest of these men outweighed her by a hundred pounds.

Frost was the largest of them, broad-shouldered, barrel-chested, with biceps like hams. His face was speckled with a constellation of scars, pale white splotches from a life spent hammering hot metal. While some of the men looked nervous after Jandra's sudden appearance, Frost didn't show the least flicker of intimidation. He said, "Even if you are Ragnar's sister, you have no authority to declare what is and isn't food."

Jandra put the shotgun to her shoulder, imitating the firing stance she'd seen in Burke's sketches when he'd designed the gun.

"I think you'll find this gives me the authority," she said.

Frost didn't look impressed.

"Is this more of your *magic*, girl?" Frost mocked. "Where I'm from, we burn witches. Perhaps we'll cook the lizard over the fire we build from your bones."

The dragon child grabbed Jandra's coattails. He cowered behind her legs and yelled, "No eat! No eat!"

Frost took a step forward.

"Not one more step," Jandra growled.

Frost took another step.

Jandra raised the barrel of the shotgun, targeting the empty air above Frost's head. She pulled the trigger. Nothing happened. What had Burke said about a safety? She examined the intricate firing mechanism.

Frost reached out to grab the gun. Jandra slipped aside the metal latch that kept the flint from falling. She pulled the trigger again as Frost's fingers closed on the barrel. The hammer clicked down. For half a second, there was a flashing light and a sizzle, plus a lot of smoke.

Lightning struck.

At least, it seemed like lightning, with a bright flash and a thunderous boom. The butt of the shotgun slammed into Jandra's shoulder, knocking her into the wall. Everyone in the crowd jumped in unison, wide-eyed.

Frost released the gun and spun away, cursing. He raised his hand to his right ear. Jandra had meant to aim above his head, but the gun had fired in a more or less random direction after Frost grabbed it. When Frost lowered his bloodied fingers, his ear was gone. Only a few shreds of bloody flesh dangled where it had been.

Jandra was disoriented. She hadn't expected the gun to be so loud. She looked around, uncertain where the dragon child had gone. Her arm was numb from the impact of the shotgun.

She couldn't help but wonder why the goddess had worked so hard to rid the world of guns. Of what use was a weapon that crippled its user?

The crowd grew deathly silent as Frost recovered his wits. He narrowed his eyes in anger.

"Witch," he snarled. Jandra could barely hear him over the ringing in her ears. "The last time a woman scratched me, I tore her nails out!" He lunged toward her, arms outstretched.

Before Jandra understood what was happening, something human-sized dropped down from above, landing between her and Frost. The crowd sucked in its collective breath.

There was a loud *SNAP*. Frost shrieked.

Jandra blinked her eyes. The person who had jumped in front of her was Burke's daughter, Anza. Anza was dressed in black buckskins and had at least a dozen blades strapped to her body. It was said that Burke had trained Anza in the art of combat from the day she'd learned to walk. Frost fell to his knees in front of Anza. Anza shifted her body slightly and Jandra could see that she had Frost's middle and ring fingers in her grasp, bending them back much further than unbroken fingers could possibly bend.

Anza pushed Frost away and stood between Jandra and the crowd, drawing a long slender sword from the scabbard slung over her back. The razor-sharp edge gleamed like a mirror in the smoky light.

Men at the back of the mob looked around and wandered off, as if suddenly remembering other appointments. Some of the nearer men looked down at the ground as they, too, walked away.

Only two men remained behind to help Frost back to his feet.

Frost looked as if he were on the verge of spitting at the two women. Then, his eyes flickered upwards. Burke was at the window above, looking down sternly.

Frost growled, "Wait until Ragnar learns of this!"

"Why don't you go tell him?" said Burke. "He can come to me if he wishes to discuss the proper punishment for a man your age threatening teenage girls with violence. I'm disappointed in you, Frost. You're one of the best fighters I know. But there's a fine line between a fighter and a bully. I would advise you to learn where that line is."

Frost glared as he turned away, leaving the two women alone.

Anza gazed up at her father, a smug look in her eyes.

"Don't feel proud," Burke scolded. "You just ruined the hand of one of my most experienced blacksmiths. And Jandra, that was a damned stupid thing to do. Why didn't you let them eat the varmint? It may be small and cute, but it's still an earthdragon. We killed them by the thousands to take Dragon Forge. What's one more dead lizard?"

"This is only a child!" Jandra protested. "He's innocent! He's more frightened of us than we are of him."

"Where'd the lizard go?" Burke asked. He was still in his chair, and couldn't look straight down.

Jandra studied the area. Had the dragon slipped away while she was distracted? Finally, she noticed a shadow on the wall, and a peculiar outline. She knelt and reached toward the shadow.

The outline on the wall shifted color slightly. The eyes became visible as they looked at her. The chameleon-like camouflage vanished as the dragon shifted back to a deep green hue, almost black. It held a skinny arm toward her, the claw at the end outstretched like a human hand, though it had only three fingers. These digits ended in claws that any bobcat would have envied.

"No eat?" the dragon child asked.

"No eat," said Jandra, taking his hand. "I'll protect you." She lifted the dragon child up and hugged him to her chest.

"Good boss," he cooed.

It WAS LATE morning when Vulpine, the Slavecatcher General, drifted down to the rocky bank, his eyes drawn to the blue-scaled corpses being picked at by black-feathered buzzards. The buzzards hopped away as he landed, some taking to the air to perch in the branches of nearby pines, others, more bold, backing up only a few yards to glare at him. Even though the faces were mutilated, with the eyes torn away and the flesh around the mouths pecked and peeled, Vulpine recognized these dragons, fellow slavecatchers, good and honorable defenders of order. He shivered as a chill wind stirred his feather-scales.

There were human corpses as well, similarly mutilated by the buzzards. Vulpine recognized them as Hemming and Terpin. The world was no worse off without them. He noted that Shay wasn't among the corpses, nor was there any sign of Chapelion's stolen books.

Had Shay somehow managed to kill three slave-catchers? It made no sense. It was plain that all three dragons had been downed by arrows. He'd heard about the new bow that had caused the massacre at Dragon Forge, a weapon with more than twice the range of a longbow. Dragon Forge was barely ten miles distant. Had these slavecatchers fallen victim to a rebel patrol?

He noted something odd about the arrows. He reached out and plucked one from a corpse and held it to better catch the light. His eyes weren't playing tricks. These arrows were yard-long, perfectly straight shafts of living wood. The fletching at the end wasn't feathers, but fresh green leaves growing in perfect symmetry. Stranger still, the killing end of the twig showed no trace of an arrowhead. The wood simply narrowed down to a hard, thorn-like point. What tree grew such twigs? One final artifact of the arrow disturbed him. The shaft couldn't have been in the corpse for more than a day, judging from the condition of the bodies. Yet, the part of the arrow that had been buried in the body was covered with white, threadlike projections, as if the arrow had been taking root. The shaft sported several fresh pale bumps, like it was budding.

Vulpine snapped the shaft. The bark that peeled away from the jagged break was bright green and full of sap. He sniffed the wood. It was an unremarkable odor; he still couldn't identify the species. The biologians back at the College of Spires perhaps could assist, though his gut told him that this was something new under the sun, that no one had ever seen living arrows before. Most biologians were rationalists, but Vulpine was old enough and wise enough to suspect there were invisible forces beyond the comprehension of dragons. Most slaves believed in magic, in ghosts and witches, angels and demons, and Vulpine had some sympathy with these beliefs.

He felt a chill creep along his spine as a shadow passed over him. The long fringe of feathery scales along his neck stood on end. He looked up, then immediately let out his breath and chuckled. It was only Balikan, a young slave-catcher he was training, drifting down from the sky to join him. The vultures skittered back even further, but Vulpine was glad of his company.

Balikan wrinkled his nose in disgust at the odor. The corpses weren't rotting yet, but their bowels had emptied, and the gallons of blood that had seeped into the gravel had its own aroma. Vulpine had barely noticed; he'd been around corpses so often the odor had little effect on him.

"By the bones," Balikan said softly. "Who could have done this?"

"That, my young friend, is an excellent question."

"I don't see Shay's body. Could he—?"

"Doubtful," said Vulpine. "Shay's never held a bow in his life. Nor has he displayed much in the way of a spine. He probably groveled for mercy when the slavecatchers caught up to him. Someone else killed these dragons. They must have been hidden in the trees."

Balikan scanned the steep bank, his eyes darting from branch to branch.

"I don't think they're still around," said Vulpine. "These corpses are at least twelve hours old. Maybe sixteen."

"How can you tell?"

Vulpine nudged the twisted talon of the nearest corpse with a hind-claw. "They plainly didn't die today. The bodies are cold and stiff—it takes several hours to lose body heat, although one cold night on a damp bank can do it. Rigor mortis sets in little by little—the degree these limbs are contracted tells me it hasn't reached its peak. I also know it's not been more than a day because the buzzards haven't made much progress."

Balikan shuddered. "I've never been around this many dead bodies."

"Get used to it," said Vulpine. "You'll see many more in the coming days."

"Why, sir?"

"King Albekizan kept this kingdom stable for almost half a century. Now he's dead, and his son didn't last a month before a human assassinated him. The humans have taken advantage of all this instability and captured Dragon Forge, just to the west of here." He pointed to the brownish tint in the sky, evidence of the distant smokestacks. "I suspect that's where Shay is, along with Chapelion's books."

"Then he's escaped for good," said Balikan.

"Nonsense," said Vulpine. "I've had a few slaves vanish on me over the years. I can't claim a perfect record. But I've never let a slave go when I still had a lead simply because pursuing that lead was dangerous. Dragon Forge is a magnet for slaves. Shay and these two fools were among the first to hear the rumors and make a break for it, but they won't be the last. Our jobs are going to be much more difficult if the humans are allowed to hold on to Dragon Forge. It's imperative that we sky-dragons act now to strangle this revolution while it's still in its cradle."

"But, the humans defeated an army of sun-dragons!" said Balikan. "They slaughtered earth-dragons by the thousands. Why will we fare any better?"

Vulpine chuckled. "Besting an earth-dragon isn't so hard. In my experience, the average human is twice as smart as an earth-dragon. Sun-dragons might be as smart as the humans, but they're also bullies. They're used to winning fights due to their size, but if a few of them get hurt, the rest turn tail and run. They don't know the first thing about real courage—and next to nothing about strategy—because they don't need it. When evolution has left you with the deadliest jaws in the food chain, you get used to solving all your problems with your teeth. We sky-dragons are made of different stuff. Our brains might be half the size of sun-dragons, but we actually bother to use them. We study the world. We learn things. Brute force failed to break the rebellion at Dragon Forge. It's time for a more thoughtful approach."

"You have a plan in mind?"

"The rough outlines of one, yes," said Vulpine. "This isn't something we're going to be able to do alone, however. We should go consult with Chapelion."

"So it's back to the College of Spires."

"No," said Vulpine. "To the Grand Library of the High Biologian. That's where Chapelion will be by now. He's bringing some order to this chaos."

"How?"

Vulpine ignored him. "Our second priority should be reconnaissance. Let's study the area and gather the information we'll need to solve this problem once and for all. They say the new bows can reach out up to a mile... but there's a lot we can learn from over a mile away."

Balikan looked puzzled. "Our second priority? What's our first?"

Vulpine looked down at the bodies of the three slavecatchers. "We should build a pyre and cremate the remains of our brethren. I've known Zernex almost thirty years. He deserves a more noble end than to be pecked apart by buzzards."

"Of course," said Balikan, sounding embarrassed that this had required explanation. "What of the slaves?"

Vulpine shrugged. "Let the birds have their fill."

CHAPTER THREE

THE CITY AS A HEART

J ANDRA LOOKED DOWN at her notes on the thick oak table beside her. "Unlatch safety," was underlined. "One second delay between spark and shot," was underlined twice. "Keep butt of gun against shoulder," had four thick lines beneath it.

She looked back across the spacious loft at the target, a round wooden shield balanced atop a stool about fifty feet away, with a feather mattress behind it, and a thick brick wall behind that. She braced herself as she aimed, gritting her teeth as she pressed the butt of the weapon firmly against her bruised shoulder. She pulled the trigger. There was a flash, a hiss, a curl of peppery smoke, then *BOOM*. The force rattled every bone in her body, but she kept her balance. A cloud of thick white smoke in front of her hid the target for a few seconds. When it dispersed, she found the target gone, reduced to splinters jutting from the feather mattress. A few puffs of down floated in the air.

"Bull's-eye," said Burke. "That's how it's supposed to work."

Anza had her fingers in her ears. Her nose wrinkled as the acrid smoke reached her.

"Does it have to be so loud?" Jandra asked.

"Yes," said Burke. "The cannon I'm building will be even louder. It's the sound of the future, girl. Get used to it."

Jandra tried reloading the weapon the way Burke had shown her, stuffing the wad of powder-filled cotton down the barrel with the ramrod, then stuffing the shot bag in with it. She tapped some fresh powder into the flash pan, and inserted a new fuse.

"This isn't exactly a fast weapon to reload," said Jandra.

"I'm still working on a percussion-activated cartridge," said Burke. "In the Human Age, guns took centuries to refine. I had a week."

"I wasn't criticizing your work."

Burke sighed. "Sorry if I'm defensive. I've had almost no sleep in the last week. It's got me on edge."

"Is your leg keeping you awake?"

"That's part of it. The bigger part is trying to keep this town running. Ragnar's management skills are somewhat lacking. He had no plans for securing resources like food and water, let alone coal and ore. We've had some lucky breaks so far, but it's only a matter of time before the dragons reorganize and set up a blockade. It's what I would do. Holding onto the town isn't enough. We have to be able to project force."

Anza set up a new target, the top of a crate on which the crude outline of an earth-dragon had been drawn. Jandra looked toward the fireplace, where Lizard, the earth-dragon child, sat on the hearth, staring at the flames. The scales on his back shifted slowly through shades of dull orange and red. If Lizard had been frightened by the rifle shot, he didn't show it. She wondered if he'd even recognized the outline on the board. Once Anza was clear, Jandra pulled the trigger again. She clenched her jaw as the fuse sizzled... *BLAM!* Her shoulder felt bruised down to the bone. Again, though, she was pleased with the results. The target was shredded.

"Okay," Jandra said, lowering the gun. "This gives me the firepower I need if I get into a bad spot. And, I still have this if I need to turn invisible." She raised her left arm, sporting the silver bracelet, the ring of invisibility she'd created for her sun-dragon friend Hex. Her former friend, to be exact, now that Hex had stolen her genie, the source of her powers. Jandra had charged the bracelet with enough reflective nanites to work a half-dozen times. Hex had used it once, to her knowledge, meaning she had five chances to vanish from sight if needed.

Burke said, "Anza will be along to help remove obstacles. I'm also sending Vance."

"Vance?" Jandra asked. Anza glanced up from the stack of targets, looking as if she, too, was surprised by this news. "The short guy with the bad mustache? Why him?"

"He's the best archer we have with a sky-wall bow," said Burke. "Also, I like him. He's got a good heart. I trust him."

Anza made a flurry of hand signals toward her father. Burke frowned. "How can you say he's just a kid? I think he's the same age you are. He's definitely older than Jandra. He's going. I don't have the energy to discuss it further."

Anza scowled. Though Anza's feelings were easy to interpret at the moment, Jandra worried more about Anza as a companion than Vance. Anza didn't speak, and Jandra didn't understand her hand signals. Without Burke around to translate, she was worried about how they were supposed to communicate. Jandra was also worried about Burke's health. He was sweating despite the frigid drafts that cut through the loft. If she still had her powers, healing his leg would be a simple matter. She was frustrated that he had to be in such pain.

There was a knock on the floor. The trap door swung open, revealing the bald pate of Burke's chief foreman, a portly fellow everyone called Biscuit. "I know you said no visitors, Burke, but I think you're gonna want to talk to this guy. He says he's an escaped slave from the College of Spires. Used to work for Chapelion himself."

Burke raised an eyebrow. "Of course. Bring him up."

The man who followed Biscuit up through the trap door was dressed in a fine red coat with shiny metal buttons. The coat was mud-flecked and covered with brambles and small rips. Despite the poor state of the coat, it reminded Jandra of the finery she used to have access to growing up in the palace. Unlike many of the rough, rugged rebels who populated Dragon Forge, the new arrival looked as if he had at least a passing familiarity with soap. His bright orange hair was pulled back into a short braid with a black ribbon. He was young, in his early twenties perhaps, quite tall despite his atrocious posture, and too thin for his height. His face had a slightly feminine quality, perhaps due to the unusual fullness of his lips; his cheeks were dotted with freckles.

The new arrival cleared his throat. "You must be Kanati," he said, addressing Burke. "My name is Shay. I can't believe I've actually found you."

"Nobody calls me Kanati anymore," said Burke. "I left that name behind when I fled Conyers. I don't miss it. Call me Burke."

"By whatever name, it's an honor, sir," Shay said, crossing the room and extending his hand. Burke reached out and grasped it, giving it a good shake. "Chapelion wrote the history of the battle of Conyers. Even though Chapelion wrote from the perspective of the victors, you remain a sympathetic character in his narrative. Chapelion respects genius."

Burke cocked his head. "You can read?"

"Yes sir," said Shay. "Chapelion used me as a living quill. He would dictate his books while eating his dinner, or taking his bath, or simply walking the grounds of the College. I faithfully followed behind, recording his every thought. In the hours when his duties took him elsewhere, I had access to his private collection of books, some of the rarest manuscripts in the kingdom."

"How rare?" asked Burke.

"From the Human Age."

Shay slipped his leather pack from over his shoulder and sat it on the floor. "I stole several works from Chapelion before I escaped," he said, pulling out books one by one. The tomes looked ancient; Jandra noted the titles: *The Origin of Species*, *The Wealth of Nations*, *Harry Potter and the Goblet of Fire*, *Leviathan*. The fifth book was comparatively new— *A Glorious Victory: The Defeat of the Southern Uprising*. Shay held this book out to Burke. "I've marked the pages documenting your role in the rebellion."

Burke didn't reach to take the book. "Why would any man want to read a catalog of his failures? My sole claim to fame before Dragon Forge has been losing a rebellion." Burke shook his head, then glanced toward the fireplace. "Now I fear the next history written about me will say I learned nothing from my mistakes. They'll note how poorly planned our uprising was, and how little thought was given to what would come after we took Dragon Forge." He took off his spectacles and cleaned them on his shirt. "It's bad enough that people who don't read history fail to learn from it; how much worse is it that the men who lived it are unable to gain any wisdom?"

"The blow you struck here is still echoing through the kingdom," said Shay. "The dragon hierarchy is on the verge of collapse. Sun-dragons plot to seize advantage over other sun-dragons in this time of turmoil. And now, Chapelion has allied himself with the valkyries and plots to overthrow Androkom as High Biologian, risking a civil war among the colleges. The dragons are so busy with their intrigues, you may never face an attempt to retake Dragon Forge."

Burke shook his head. "We can't count on that. If it does work out that way, I still don't expect to wind up as a hero in anyone's history. Ragnar is going to get all the glory."

As if the sound of Ragnar's name had summoned him, a voice boomed from below: "All glory belongs to God!" The elevator that carried Burke's chair up to the loft rattled as the chains lifted it. The bushy, unkempt mane of hair that wreathed Ragnar's leathery face came into view. As usual, Ragnar was naked. He'd taken a sacred vow not to wear clothes or cut his hair until the last dragon was slain. His body was crisscrossed with scabs, souvenirs from the battle to capture Dragon Forge.

Jandra cast her gaze at his feet. Ragnar was her brother, though they'd been raised apart. As an orphan, she'd dreamed her whole life of finding a blood relative, someone who would instantly resonate as a member of her true family. Now that she'd found one, it had left her feeling even more orphaned than before.

Ragnar hadn't arrived alone. He was surrounded by eight burly warriors in armor he'd taken to calling his Mighty Men. The biggest of these, Stonewall, was a true giant—easily seven feet tall and thickly muscled. Unlike the other Mighty Men, veterans of battle whose grizzled faces were marred with scars, Stonewall's face was pristine, youthful, and clean-shaven, beneath wavy black locks.

Frost, the man she'd shot, stepped from behind Stonewall, looking furious. His head was wrapped in bandages, and brown blood stained the cotton gauze where his ear had been. Jandra felt a twinge of guilt; she'd only intended to frighten Frost. If she still had her powers, she could have grown him a new ear. Of course, she would likely have been denounced as a witch for the effort.

"Burke," Ragnar growled. "My tolerance has limits. Your usefulness as a weapon maker doesn't give you the right to shelter a witch. This is to be a holy city; turn over Jandra, that she may face the fitting punishment for her kind."

Jandra used the ramrod to slide a new bag of powder down the muzzle of the gun.

"I'm not a witch," she said, calmly. "And I'm not Burke's to turn over."

"If you're innocent you have nothing to fear," said Stonewall. His voice was as deep and smooth as a sun-dragon's. "There are tests we will apply to determine whether or not you've been touched by the devil."

Jandra pushed a bag of shot into the gun.

Suddenly, there was a heavy weight clawing up her back. Lizard, the dragon-child, scrambled onto her shoulder and flashed the same shade of green as her coat.

"No eat! No eat!" he hissed at Frost.

"And now you harbor dragons?" asked Ragnar.

"Where did that come from?" Shay asked, approaching Jandra. "Did it just change color?"

"He was sitting by the fireplace," said Jandra. "He blends into the background when he's not moving."

"Remarkable," said Shay. "The chameleon mutation is exceedingly rare; fewer than one in ten thousand earth-dragons display it. When he's fully grown, he'll become part of the assassin unit known as the Black Silence."

Jandra already knew more than she wanted to know about these assassins. She'd nearly died when one of them had slit her throat.

"If he's one of those monsters, it's all the more reason to kill him," said Frost.

"And all the more proof that you are a witch," growled Ragnar.

"Consorting with dragons doesn't make one a witch," Shay argued. "I've been a slave of dragons since birth, yet I'm not a witch. I've come to volunteer for the cause. I confess I'm lacking as a warrior, but I have other skills that may prove useful. I've brought books, great works from the Human Age." He held up a tome by Charles Darwin in one hand and by Adam Smith in the other. "If there are children here, I could set up a school. I want to lay the foundation for a new golden age of humanity."

Ragnar walked toward Shay, his eyes contemplating the books. He picked up the copy of *The Origin of Species*. The book was over a thousand years old. Shay held his breath as Ragnar opened the yellowed pages. Jandra's finely tuned eyes could see the dust that showered down from the book as it was opened, fine flecks of the ancient paper crumbling away.

"It's very fragile," Shay said softly, as if fearing that his own breath might damage the pages. "Please be careful. I intend to transcribe it before I—"

"The world needs only one book," Ragnar said, closing the pages with a violent clap. He flung the tome into the fireplace.

Shay sucked air, as if he'd been punched in the stomach. He dived for the fireplace, reaching into the bright flames to retrieve the book. He snatched it out, but it was too late. The ancient paper flared as quickly as gunpowder in a flash pan. In seconds, all that remained of the manuscript was a mound of black ash.

"You monster!" Shay, shouted, spinning around, his fists clenched. "Do you know what you just destroyed?"

"Useless old words by a man long dead," said Ragnar. His Mighty Men drew their swords, ready to strike if Shay approached.

Jandra raised her gun. Frost stepped back behind Stonewall.

"Stop this!" Burke snapped, wincing as he shifted in his seat. "Ragnar, you're not taking Jandra. She's brought us the secret to gunpowder. Right now, I'm designing and testing weapons that will make the sky-wall bows seem like toys. She and I are the only two people who know the secret. If you so much as lay a finger on Jandra, I'll have Anza slit my throat. I won't use my talents in the service of a man dedicated to launching a new dark age."

"Suicide will damn your soul to eternal torment," Ragnar growled.

"And it will rob you of the weapons that will let mankind rule this world. I'm a pessimist, Ragnar. I've anticipated that you'd ruin this since the day we met. I've been in constant, non-stop, pain since Charkon ruined my leg. Don't think I wouldn't welcome death."

Ragnar glared at Burke, as if trying to determine if the machinist was bluffing. Ragnar frowned; no doubt in his mind all heathens were unstable enough to kill themselves out of spite. The prophet turned his gaze toward Jandra. Lizard hissed at the hairy man. Glowering, Ragnar looked toward Shay, then to the pile of books beside the leather backpack.

"Take the books," he barked to Stonewall.

"No!" said Shay, rushing to grab the pile.

"Let him have the books," Burke snapped. Anza leapt forward, sword drawn, putting herself between Shay and the bag. She shook her head slowly as she eyed Shay.

"These may be the only copies of these books left in the world," Shay said, on the verge of begging. "You can't let him take them."

"Books aren't equal to human lives," Burke grumbled. "Ragnar, take the books. Use them to wrap fish for all I care. As for Jandra, she's leaving Dragon Forge before nightfall. You won't have to worry about her witching up any more of your men."

"I'll allow her to leave," Ragnar said, "provided she doesn't return."

"Fine," said Burke.

"But—" said Jandra.

"Drop it," Burke said, through gritted teeth. It was obvious that the stress of the encounter was causing him great pain.

Stonewall gathered up the books and went to Ragnar's side. Ragnar and his Mighty Men turned and went back to the elevator. He glanced back over his shoulder.

"Burke," he said. "Don't think I will tolerate your blasphemy indefinitely. I can be pushed too far."

"So can I," said Burke, narrowing his eyes. The elevator rumbled, lowering Ragnar and his men from view.

Shay fell to his knees in front of the charred remains of the book on the hearth. "This book survived twelve centuries, only to vanish at the whim of a fanatic. Why did you give him the books, Kanati? I would have thought you, of all people, would have valued those writings. Aren't you one of the Anudahdeesdee? The tribe that calls itself the Memory?"

"The Anudahdeesdee have copies of all the books you showed me," said Burke. "I've got a collection of over two-hundred manuscripts in the basement of my tavern. The physical books you lost were rare, but the information inside them is more than just the paper they're printed on. Information is essentially immortal with a little technological assistance. At my tribal home beyond the mountains, my people maintain an old press to preserve copies of essential works. We lost nothing here today."

Shay perked up. "There's a printing press in human control? That's fantastic! I wish I could see it."

"Maybe you can," said Burke. "You aren't going to be on Ragnar's list of favorite people. You should get out of here tonight. Go with Jandra and Anza. They'll be passing through Burke's Tavern, my adopted hometown. Assuming the town is still standing, and hasn't fallen victim to reprisals by retreating earth-dragons, there's a map in my basement that would be of interest to you. It contains instructions on how to go to my homeland. It's coded, but Anza can give you the key."

"But... but I only just arrived," said Shay. "I came to fight for the liberty of mankind."

"Stay here and you'll get your throat cut in your sleep by one of the Mighty Men," said Burke. "You've never held a sword in your life, have you?"

Shay lowered his head, looking embarrassed. "No, sir."

"You're lucky I've already forged the pieces to make a second shotgun," said Burke. "The beauty of a gun is the way it equalizes the slave and the warrior. Let me get the crew to assemble it and whip you up an ammo belt. I'll send you off with Anza, Jandra, and Vance."

Shay looked as if he were about to argue further, but held his tongue. Lizard, still on Jandra's shoulder, stared intently as Burke rolled his wheeled chair over to the elevator and pulled the lever to raise the cage.

"Strong boss," the little dragon whispered, sounding awed.

VULPINE DRIFTED ON the winds high above Dragon Forge, with Balikan a few yards off his left wing. Reports were that the sky-wall bows could reach a mile, and Vulpine took care to stay well beyond that range. He could see scores of humans armed with bows crowded onto the thick stone walls that surrounded the town. They watched him closely, though he knew at this distance he was little more than a speck.

"They look rather alert," said Balikan.

"Alert enough," said Vulpine. "This is why the brute strength, head-on approach of the sun-dragons was doomed to failure. Shandrazel was too eager to prove his strength and crush the rebellion in a grand slaughter, the way his father crushed the rebellion at Conyers. If he'd been more patient, he could have broken this insurgency without spilling a drop of dragon blood."

"I was thinking the same thing," said Balikan. "He had catapults in his army with a greater range than the bows. He could have lobbed in barrels of flaming pitch and burned the town to the ground."

Vulpine shook his head. "There's a difference between destroying Dragon Forge and reclaiming it."

Vulpine motioned with his head, inviting Balikan to follow his gaze. Dragon Forge wasn't a large town. The fortress was diamond-shaped, encompassing roughly one square mile of earth. Save for a few broad avenues, the interior of the fortress was cramped with buildings built on top of buildings, so that one dragon's floor was another dragon's roof. Three smokestacks dominated the skyline of Dragon Forge, belching plumes of ash high into the sky.

Outside of the walls there were hundreds of heaps of rusting metal dotting the low red hills, the raw material of the foundries. Amid these heaps were hovels where gleaners lived, among the poorest humans in the kingdom.

Threading through these heaps were four major roads. All were busy with traffic. In the absence of dragons, humans throughout the kingdom rushed to Dragon Forge. Some of this traffic, though, wasn't here for the rebellion. Mule trains hauling wagon loads of coal wound along the western road. They cared little who brought their wares, be it human or dragon.

Along the southern side of Dragon Forge there was a river; a canal had been dug long ago to divert water into the city, where a water wheel powered the bellows that fanned the foundries. The water also served to flush the gutters and sewers of the town—crude but effective sanitation. In addition to this water,

Vulpine could see a large well at the center of the town. The rebels wouldn't perish from thirst. "With the right eyes, you can see the city as a heart. The roads and rivers serve as arteries and veins, carrying in the lifeblood, carting off the waste. Choke off the roads and the city dies."

"But by now the rebels will have been stocking up on supplies. They could hold out for weeks, or months."

"And is the world suddenly in short supply of weeks and months?" asked Vulpine.

Balikan clamped his mouth shut, looking properly chastised.

"In any case, I don't think they will hold out for months," said Vulpine. "Humans lack the capacity for long-term planning we sky-dragon's possess. Presented with a blockade, with food and resources dwindling, they will likely turn on themselves in short order, especially once plague breaks out."

"*If* plague breaks out," said Balikan. "I must admit, it looks as if they are doing a fair job of keeping the town clean."

"This need not be something left to chance," said Vulpine. "Let's pay a visit to the Nest. It's only thirty miles away and a few dozen valkyries can easily blockade the western road and cut off the coal supply. The valkyrie engineers can also block off the canal feeding water into the town. After that, we'll follow the Forge Road back to the Palace to confer with Chapelion and get the authority to gather all the elements I need to truly solve this problem."

"Will he grant us this authority? We're slavecatchers, not soldiers."

"After I tell him his books are in the fort," said Vulpine, "he'll give me every last soldier in the kingdom."

CHAPTER FOUR

PHANTOMS

S HAY TOOK A sip of the steaming sassafras tea. The licorice bite of it opened his sinuses, clearing his ears so he could better hear Burke as he whispered to Anza. It wasn't Shay's intention to eavesdrop, but over the years he'd grown sensitive to hushed conversations. All the politics and intrigues that swirled around a dragon of Chapelion's station unfolded in whispers and nods. Thus, though he sat on a wooden stool by the fireplace across the loft from Burke and his daughter, he heard Burke's words as clearly as if he was standing between them.

"We had several groups of refugees report that the earth-dragons are raiding human villages." Burke slipped her a sheet of folded parchment. "It's only a matter of time before they strike the tavern. Take this to Thorny. There are tools in the hidden room I need, and my notebooks would also be useful. Have him bring them to me."

Anza scowled and made a hand gesture that Shay didn't understand.

Burke gave a weary shrug. "Thorny will just have to sober up. I need you to stay with Jandra and Shay. If anything happens to either of them, make sure their guns don't fall into the possession of dragons."

Anza's scowl faded.

"Thorny won't be coming alone. Tell the villagers it's time to join me here in Dragon Forge."

Anza nodded, looking serious. Shay found himself intrigued by the tall, dark-skinned woman dressed in black buckskins. He'd yet to hear Anza say a word. Ordinarily, he would have assumed she was deaf, or perhaps an imbecile. Yet she followed Burke's whispers easily enough, and she carried herself with an air that hinted of great intelligence.

Jandra sat cross-legged by the fire with Lizard in her lap. Lizard had numerous cuts and scrapes. She spoke to him in a soothing patter as she cleaned and bandaged his wounds. Shay knew Jandra by reputation—she was the human girl who'd been raised by the sky-dragon wizard Vendevorex. He assumed she'd been the dragon's pet. In general, slaves and pets despised one another. Both were legally the property of dragons, but slaves were regarded as little more than domestic animals, useful for certain labors, while pets were pampered and treated as children.

Having grown up as the pet of a wizard, it was said that Jandra had acquired supernatural powers. He'd heard she could turn invisible, and set things on fire by staring at them. Shay wondered if it was true. Chapelion had been a strict rationalist, dismissive of supernatural forces. Shay, however, had seen proof that magic had once been a powerful force in ages past. He was certain that Chapelion was too

quick to ignore evidence of things beyond his understanding.

Jandra was currently eluding his understanding.
She looked human enough, yet there was something
unmistakably alien about her. Perhaps it was her
voice; her words had an odd inflection, an accent that
made her sound more dragon than human. There
was also a strange quality to her posture, the way she
carried herself. Most humans tended to keep their
gazes toward the ground and walked with their
shoulders slouched. Jandra had the unnerving habit
of looking straight at people like Burke and Ragnar
when she spoke, even though they were obviously her
superiors. Finally, her fussing over the dragon child
struck him as wrong on some fundamental level, that
a human should be displaying such motherly behavior toward a creature covered with scales.

Jandra cradled Lizard in her arms and scratched
him beneath his chin. The little dragon's eyes rolled
up in his head and he made a soft humming noise.

"He doesn't need all that attention, you know,"
said Shay.

Jandra looked up. "What?"

"It's a waste to give him so much affection," Shay
repeated. "Earth-dragon children are never coddled
or cared for. They're regarded as little more than
parasites by adult earth-dragons. They live like rats
after they hatch, hiding in walls, eating scraps and
bugs and their smaller siblings. They absorb the
dragon language by spying. Earth-dragons raise
themselves until they're old enough to hold a tool or
a weapon, at which point they're put to work and
treated like any other member of the horde. They
don't get any mothering in their natural upbringing.
They aren't even clear on what the concept of a
mother is."

Jandra looked annoyed by his argument. "He's not a rat," she said. "He's an intelligent being who can talk."

"It's probably nothing more than imitation," said Shay. "I'd guess he's as smart as a parrot."

"If a parrot were injured, I'd treat his wounds too," said Jandra.

"Good boss," cooed Lizard, reaching up and stroking Jandra's cheek.

Shay turned away, shaking his head. He discovered their fourth companion climbing up through the trap door. This was Vance, a young man roughly his own age, with a wispy blond beard and close-cropped hair that looked as if it had been trimmed with a dull razor. Vance was dressed in the modest clothes of a farm boy; a simple brown wool coat and patched-up cotton britches tucked into boots badly in need of new soles. The only thing new in his possession was his bow—one of the now famous sky-wall bows, forged from steel, strung with wire, the tension tamed by a set of cams at each tip of the bow. Vance was short, barely five feet tall. A series of small white scars on his brow and around his lips, plus calluses covering his knuckles, gave Shay the impression that Vance was someone who'd survived many a tussle.

"Howdy, Shay," Vance said, with a nod in his direction. They'd met earlier at the eastern gate. Vance had been the guard who'd allowed Shay's passage into Dragon Forge.

Shay raised his hand in greeting. "I've heard that you're going to be our bodyguard. They say you're good with that bow."

"I'm not anybody's bodyguard if Anza's around," Vance said with a soft grin. He stepped close to Shay, and glanced nervously back toward Burke. He cleared his throat, and said, in a whisper, "I heard tell you came here with books. They say you wanted to teach people to read."

"Ragnar didn't approve of this plan, I'm afraid."

"Well, um…" Vance said, his voice growing even softer as he leaned in closer. "I've got a good head on my shoulders, but I don't have no formal learnin'. I did my part up on that wall fighting the dragons, but the battle was really won by Burke and his foremen. Them fellows are all the time looking over blueprints and books and sending notes back and forth. That's the kind of person I want to be. Can you teach me to read?"

Shay smiled broadly. "I'd be honored."

Before they could discuss the matter further, Biscuit came up through the trap door and announced, "The horses are ready at the north gate. I've got men I trust standing guard. They'll get you out without Frost and his friends bothering anyone."

Burke nodded. "There's no point in tarrying. I told Ragnar you'd be gone by nightfall. I'm not sure I have the energy to face him down again."

Anza leaned over to hug Burke. She gave him a silent nod as she grabbed her pack and headed for the elevator. Shay noticed the shiny steel tomahawks strapped to the pack. Anza was a walking arsenal, sporting swords, knives, darts, and a sky-wall bow identical to the one Vance carried. Shay picked up his own pack, and the shotgun with which he'd barely had an hour to train. He was impressed with the weapon, but if guns were as deadly as Burke claimed, why didn't his own daughter carry one?

He joined Anza and the others on the elevator. As it began to lower, he caught the grim, worried look in Burke's eyes. He had a feeling that there was some secret Burke was keeping from them.

Jandra waved and said, "Thanks, Burke."

Lizard waved as well, and said, "Strong boss."

Anza didn't wave. She stared ahead, her face unreadable, as the elevator carried them down.

BURKE SAGGED AS the elevator lowered Anza and her companions from his sight. He'd been in pain ever since his thigh had been broken, but the stress of his confrontation with Ragnar had pushed him to a new level of agony. It had taken all he had to hide his suffering from Anza. He'd always taught Anza to bear her wounds stoically and never surrender to pain. He was glad he hadn't broken.

Biscuit stood by the window, watching as the four adventurers left the foundry and marched toward the North Gate.

"They're on their way," he announced. "Let's get you started on the whiskey."

Burke flung back the heavy wool blanket that covered his lap. His right leg was thrust straight out before him, naked save for bandages securing it to a splint. The entire limb was blue-gray with bruises. Large chunks of his foot were now black, the flesh dead and stinking. Vicious red streaks ran up his hip into his torso. His fever had been rising every day. If he didn't act now, the infection would spread into his entire body.

"The whole leg has to go," Burke said flatly, as if he were discussing a broken wagon wheel.

"I sharpened the saw earlier," Biscuit said, handing Burke a brown ceramic jug. Burke uncorked it. The fumes made his eyes water. "Drink until the bottle falls out of your hands. It won't take me more than ten minutes once you're down."

Burke tilted back the jug. Even though it was ice-cold, it burned his throat going down. He wiped his lips after the swig, not looking forward to how many more times he'd need to do that before he passed out.

"This might take a while," he said, then hiccupped. "There's some paper on the desk there. I have something important I need you to take down."

"Sure," said Biscuit, grabbing a quill jutting from an ink bottle. The quill was fiery red and almost eighteen inches long, not a true feather but a feather-like scale from the wing of a sun-dragon. In the recent battle, the sky-wall archers had killed dozens of the great beasts as they'd attacked Dragon Forge. An unanticipated consequence of victory was that Burke always had a pen nearby when he needed one.

"You got some new orders for the boys on the floor?" Biscuit asked.

"No," Burke said, taking another swig. He belched in the aftermath. "I might not survive this."

"I appreciate the vote of confidence in my surgical skills," Biscuit said, a wry grin wrinkling the leathery skin around his eyes.

"There's something I know that shouldn't vanish from human memory. I don't want Ragnar to learn the secret—it's my only real leverage over him. But I also don't want this secret to die with me, or with Jandra should she not survive. So listen closely. I'm going to tell you how to make gunpowder."

THE FORGE ROAD ran through a landscape of rolling hills and farms, one hundred and eighty miles to the Dragon Palace. In normal times, it was considered a safe road, heavily trafficked by the king's armies. Human villages were abundant along the Forge Road. The one nearest Dragon Forge was Mullton, a hamlet of two hundred souls, only ten miles distant. Jandra was in the lead as she and her companions approached the town. In the weeks before Hex had stolen her genie, her senses had been fine-tuned by the device, so she still had excellent night vision. A cloudy sky without a hint of stars hung over them. They'd ridden slowly for the last few hours; it was too dark to ride a horse at a gallop.

They traveled in silence. Outside the walls of Dragon Forge they'd encountered the worst of the aftermath of the battle; week-old decaying corpses of sun-dragons, the stench of rot thick even though the cold snap of recent days had frozen the bodies. Lizard had clung to her tightly as they'd passed through the killing fields, trembling, from the cold or from fear she couldn't guess.

She'd half expected to find the town of Mullton razed by the retreating dragon armies. Thousands of earth-dragons and dozens of sun-dragons had fled in the aftermath of defeat. Burke had said there would be reprisals, earth-dragons attacking undefended human villages for revenge or banditry now that law and order had broken down. Yet, as they crested the top of the hill, she was relieved to see the village a few hundred yards away. Little stone cottages were interspersed with log cabins in a model of rustic serenity.

She felt a tension she hadn't been fully aware of until now pass from her body. She breathed a little easier to find this vision of peace so close to Dragon Forge. Except, as she took that easy, deep breath, she couldn't help but taste rotting meat in the air, the same battlefield stench she thought they'd left behind. She noticed that there wasn't a single light in the village. No candle, lantern, torch, or fireplace burned anywhere that she could spot. As they rode past the silent farm houses, no dogs barked as they caught the scent of strangers passing by.

Anza quickened the pace of her horse and caught up to Jandra. She held the reins in one hand, in her other she held a drawn sword.

Jandra asked, "Do you think—?"

Anza brought her fingers to her lips and guided her horse into the lead. She sat tensely in the saddle, her head turning back and forth as she watched the shadows. They rode toward the center of town, toward a stone well. Behind the well was some sort of monument, like a small pyramid of piled round stones. As they drew closer, Jandra realized they weren't stones.

One by one the four riders drew up in a line, halting before the well. All eyes were fixed on what lay beyond—a neatly stacked pyramid of heads, mostly human, a few dogs. The eyes were all hollow—the ground was littered with the black feathers of buzzards.

Vance was the first to speak. "I've been to Mullton once or twice. My village used to trade with them." He paused, swallowing hard. "It's... it's only half a day's ride from here."

Jandra noted that the heads were mostly women and children. All the adult men, no doubt, had been pressed into service by Ragnar for the invasion of Dragon Forge. His army had roamed the countryside, raiding villages, offering all men a choice: join or die.

"There was a girl here named Eula," Vance said, softly. "She smiled at my brother Vinton last spring and he spent all summer thinking about her. I kept telling him he should ride up here and court her if he was that crazy about her."

"Guess he missed his chance," said Shay.

Jandra thought this was a particularly callous sentiment, but Vance didn't seem to take offense. "Vinton died the night we took Dragon Forge. In the end, I guess it don't matter if he'd talked to her or not." He shook his head. "Looking at this, it's hard to know. Did we do the right thing? Was taking Dragon Forge worth this price?"

Shay said, "I was taken from my family when I was four. Chapelion selected me because he thought the color of my hair went well with the décor. I've been whipped a hundred times, for little things, like getting ink smudges on a sheet of parchment. I can't pull my shoulders all the way straight because of the scars."

He looked at Vance. "I'm one of the men your brother died to free. If I ever have children, they'll be free because of him. I promise every one of them will understand the price that was paid."

Vance responded with a brave, thin smile.

Anza raised her hand toward her cheek, as if to wipe away a tear, but turned her face away before Jandra could focus on it.

Jandra looked back at the mound of skulls. She felt the pressure of all their empty stares, accusing. Bitterwood had tried to tell her that peace with dragons wasn't possible. Even Pet, before he died, had preached that war was the only answer. Burke, the smartest man she'd ever met, didn't believe that dragons and men could ever share the earth.

So why was she cradling a dragon as if it were her own blood? Why, with the world so obviously split by this enormous rift between men and dragons, was she still straddling the chasm?

The world was broken. This pyramid of death bore plain testament to that. And yet, some tiny, small voice inside whispered that if she could only get her powers back, it wasn't too late to fix the world, to patch back together all the broken pieces and spare both man and dragon from the dark days coming.

"Let's ride on," said Jandra. "I'm not tired at all."

* * *

BURKE WOKE TO feverish heat and darkness. He felt as if his brain had swollen to three times its normal size and was threatening to split his skull. He was awash in sweat. Invisible ants were crawling over his whole body, from scalp to toes.

Toes.

Since Charkon had broken his right leg, he'd not felt the toes of that foot, or anything much below his hip. Now, his leg felt restored—not good, for it was subject to the same fevered agony that plagued the rest of his body—but at least it felt like part of his body once more, not simply dead meat hanging from his hip.

Why hadn't Biscuit performed the amputation? He ran his hands beneath the heavy woolen blankets down his right hip. The steel splint he'd fashioned was gone. His fingers traveled further, and found bandages.

His leg ended only six inches below his hip.

While his mind felt ghostly toes wiggling, his fingers revealed the truth. Biscuit had done what needed to be done. Burke let out a long, slow, shuddering breath. He felt a pang of loss as sharp and clear as if he were at his own funeral. He swallowed hard, feeling tears rising. He hadn't cried since he was six. His brothers had long ago pummeled this weakness out of him. He sniffed and clenched his jaw, fighting the urge to surrender to the grief. He closed his eyes tightly, grateful that he was alone in his bedroom. He was certain that if anyone had been here with him, he would have burst into tears. This feeling turned out to be wrong.

"It's been a long time, Kanati," a raspy voice said by his bedside.

Burke sucked in a sharp gasp of air; his heart jumped around in his chest like a startled rabbit. He sat straight up, his eyes wide, searching the darkness for his mysterious visitor. By his bed sat a figure in a dark cloak, his face hidden by a hood. Burke was a rational man; until this moment he'd had no fear of some anthropomorphic manifestation of death coming to carry him away. His throat, wet with unshed tears only seconds before, went as dry as the parched fields around Conyers in the decade of drought.

"Who are you?" he tried to say. His lips moved, but only the barest sound came out.

The figure pulled back his hood, revealing an old man, his hair thin and gray, his skin wrinkled and leathery. "Have I changed so much?"

Burke stared at the visitor. There was something familiar about his eyes. "Bant?" he asked, his voice cracking. He swallowed and tried again. "Bant Bitterwood?"

"I always wondered if you'd made it out of Conyers in one piece."

Burke stared at the flat spot on the blanket where his leg should have been. "Defeat left me with a few scars. It's taken a victory to rip me in two."

"Not a bad victory," said Bitterwood. "The fields around here are full of dead dragons. The stench for miles is unbelievable. I was walking by buzzards too fat to flap away. You did good, Kanati."

"I did what I had to," said Burke. "Ragnar had no plan; he had passion and an army, but I knew that wasn't enough. If I'd let him take this fort, then allowed the dragons to crush him, the dragon's grip on this world would only be stronger. This wasn't a battle I chose. Still, I admit, watching those dragons rain from the sky made it worth it." He looked down at his missing limb. "It was worth even this."

Bitterwood's face went slack. It looked as if Burke's words had triggered some distant memory. Burke thought he might be about to speak, but when he didn't, Burke chose to break the silence.

"You've been busy yourself. Jandra tells me you killed practically the entire royal family, including

Blasphet. And, you took down Jasmine Robertson, the so-called goddess. She was the real threat to humanity, even more than the dragons."

Bitterwood scratched the raspy stubble under his chin. "You know me," he said. "I've never been good at nothing but killing. Killing the goddess wasn't a big deal. Once I saw past her tricks, she was only a woman." His shoulders sagged. His voice was softer as he said, "If you'd told me twenty years ago I'd one day kill a woman, I'd have said you were wrong. I thought there were some lines even I wouldn't cross." He wasn't looking directly at Burke as he spoke. As he finished, he slowly shook his head.

"Don't beat yourself up over killing that monster," said Burke.

Bitterwood looked him in the eyes. Something hardened in his expression. "I did what I had to. I don't regret it. I'd do it again."

"I'm sure you would," said Burke. "I didn't mean to imply that you wouldn't."

"Blasphet claimed he was the god of murder. He believed it, I think. He thought he was a god."

"I never met him," said Burke, uncertain where this change of subject was heading. "I always did admire the body count he racked up among dragons, though. You too, by the way. You put the fear of God into every dragon in this kingdom, Bant."

"No," said Bitterwood. "That wasn't who they feared. There is no god, Kanati, to dispense vengeance upon the wicked. I had to do the job myself. I am the Death of All Dragons. I am the Ghost Who Kills."

Burke studied the lines of Bitterwood's face. There was a haunted look to the man's eyes. Something about dragon-hatred eventually broke the minds of almost anyone it seized.

"What brings you here, Bant?" asked Burke.

"A girl who talks to ghosts."

Burke furrowed his brow. "What do you mean?"

"I'm not traveling alone," said Bitterwood. "I'm the guardian of a girl named Zeeky, and her brother, Jeremiah, once I find him. Their family was killed by the goddess. The ghosts of everyone from their village are trapped in a crystal ball. Zeeky can hear them whispering to her. They've told Zeeky we need to save Jandra."

"You're here because you're guided by ghosts?" Burke asked. Saying it out loud didn't help it make more sense. "I'm afraid the ghosts have led you astray. Jandra was here, but she left at sunset. What time is it?"

"Almost dawn," said Bitterwood.

"She's miles away by now."

Bitterwood sighed. "In fairness to Zeeky, the ghosts didn't say Jandra was here. We followed her first to the Nest. We learned that she'd come to Dragon Forge. I should have come straight to the gates yesterday. Instead I wanted to investigate the area. It wasn't a waste of time. I killed a few slavecatchers."

"Did the ghosts say what you're saving Jandra from?"

"No," Bitterwood said. "I can't hear them myself. Only Zeeky can. She says they're tough to figure out. They all talk at once."

"I don't place any faith in the words of ghosts, but if you want to chase after Jandra, she's heading up the Forge Road. My own daughter, Anza, is with her."

"You have a family now?" Bitterwood asked.

"Only Anza. Biologically, she's my niece, but I've raised her as my own. She's definitely my child in spirit."

"How so?"

"Do you remember what they called me at Conyers?"

"Kanati the Machinist."

"Now I'm Burke the Machinist. My name I wear lightly; the Machinist is my true identity. I've always been comfortable working with cogs and clockwork and springs, far more than I have with my fellow men."

"What's this have to do with your daughter?"

Burke lowered himself back down onto the bed, his weight resting on his elbows. Perhaps it was the pain in his head that weakened him. Perhaps it was the presence of the man who'd shared in his darkest defeat, long ago. Whatever the source of the weakness, there was something he had to confess: "From the day Anza was old enough to pick up a dagger I've been… programming her. When she was five, I captured a young earth-dragon and had her kill it."

Bitterwood didn't look shocked by this confession. Somehow, this caused Burke's guilt to well up even faster. "I've raised her with a single-minded focus on combat. I've taught her to think of her body as a weapon, precise and tireless. She fights like nothing you've ever seen, Bant. She's my ultimate weapon. But there are times when I look into her eyes, and there's something cold and mechanical staring back at me. Fate gave me a daughter. I turned her into a machine."

Bitterwood winced as Burke's words triggered memories. "I had daughters once," he said, softly.

"I remember your story. Albekizan killed your wife and children and burned your village. It was the spark that brought flame to that time of drought."

"I was wrong," said Bitterwood.

"About what?"

"My family hadn't been killed. They were taken captive and sold as slaves. They lived another twenty years, beyond the day I believed they'd died."

"Oh," said Burke.

"They were executed the day after I killed Bodiel, Albekizan's beloved son. The king ordered all the palace slaves slain in retribution."

"Oh," Burke said again. What else was there to say?

"It'll be light soon. I should leave."

"I hope you find Jandra," said Burke. "Do you... do you need anything before you go? I've made a new type of bow that's going to be far superior to whatever you're using."

Bitterwood grinned. It was an unsettling expression. "I doubt that."

"How about fresh horses?" asked Burke. "We don't have many to spare, but I..." He let his voice trail off. Bitterwood was still grinning.

"What's so funny?" he asked.

"I was thinking of what you would say if you saw my ride. I won't be needing a horse."

Burke lay back on his pillow. The movement made his brains slosh. He closed his eyes, fighting back a wave of nausea. A cold draft washed over him. He welcomed its cool touch. "If you don't need anything from me, I guess you should be on your way."

Bitterwood didn't answer. Burke opened his eyes. He was alone in the room. For a moment he wondered if he'd dreamed the whole encounter, a phantom companion to match his phantom toes. But he could still smell Bitterwood's distinctive smell, a mixture of sweat and dried blood. Not for the first time in his life, Burke wondered if he'd done the right thing. He hadn't known Jandra long, but he liked her, and judged her to be competent and sane. Had he done her any favors by putting this strange ghost onto her trail?

CHAPTER FIVE

SLAVERY AS AN EVOLUTIONARY STRATEGY

THE CHILL OF night yielded as the winter sun climbed in a flawless blue sky. Shay unbuttoned the collar of his coat as they stopped by a stream to allow the horses to rest. The cool fresh air felt good against his throat. The tiny puncture wounds from Zernex's claws were scabbed up and puffy beneath his fingers. He wished he had a mirror. The grooves on the underside of a sky-dragon's claws collected a foul-smelling goop that harbored disease. Shay hoped he hadn't survived the encounter with the slavecatchers only to perish of some horrible illness.

Shay was exhausted but didn't complain when the others voted to keep going. As the day wore on they passed through three villages, all destroyed, the severed heads gathered into mounds. The tracks of earth-dragons were everywhere. They all rode in silence. Anza looked especially withdrawn, her face an emotionless mask. She had to be wondering if her home had also suffered this fate.

Shay was also worried about the town. Had Burke's hidden library been destroyed? He felt guilty that the fate of the books weighed so heavily on his mind, when Anza no doubt faced the loss of friends and family. He could still feel the empty hole that had opened in his gut when he saw *The Origin of Species* crumble to ash. How could he have been so wrong about Ragnar? The prophet had been delivering firebrand sermons calling for human rebellion for years. His words traveled throughout the kingdom as hushed whispers from slave to slave. Burke may have been the strategist who supplied the rebels with a worthy arsenal, but it was Ragnar's vision that the rebels followed. How could such a great leader despise books?

It was late in the evening when the dragon tracks they followed suddenly veered south, leaving the Forge Road. Ruts from a convoy of supply wagons led up the sloping hill of a field gone fallow. Shay looked toward the top of the ridge, wondering if an army was on the other side.

"Where do you think they've gone?" Vance asked, pulling his horse beside Shay.

Anza snapped her fingers and traced a wavy line in the air. Shay was puzzled by what she was attempting to convey. Anza looked frustrated, and repeated the motion.

"A river?" Jandra asked.

Anza nodded.

"I'd noticed we hadn't passed any good drinking water in several miles. They must have gone to the river to camp. How far south is the water?"

Anza held up two fingers.

"Two miles?" asked Jandra.

Anza nodded.

They all stared at the hill. The trampled ground was reasonably fresh, but whether the army had turned south an hour ago or a day ago was beyond Shay's guess.

Lizard stood up on Jandra's shoulder, his head held high. He sniffed, then crouched down and assumed a brown shade that matched Jandra's hair.

"Bad bosses," he whispered.

"If they're close enough for Lizard to smell, we should get going," said Shay.

"Or we should spy on them," said Vance. "Find out how many there are. See if they're settled in for a long stay, or just resting for a night."

"No," said Jandra. "We should press on to Burke's Tavern. Warn any towns along the way that the dragon armies are on the march and they should run."

"Run where?" asked Vance. "If they head toward Dragon Forge, they might run into the army."

"Then east," said Jandra. "Toward Richmond. Shandrazel may be dead, but Androkom, the High Biologian, will maintain law and order around the palace. The High Biologian can command the aerial guard in the event of the king's absence. He'll keep the peace in his immediate vicinity, at least."

"You have a lot of faith in Androkom," said Shay. "He was somewhat infamous at the College of Spires. He was a prominent abolitionist, and made a lot of enemies among the biologians. I'm not certain the other sky-dragons will obey him."

"I didn't like him either," said Jandra. "He had a snooty air that made it clear he didn't think anyone else in the world was as smart as he was. Still, while I have every reason to hate dragons"—Lizard whined; Jandra stroked his arm—"I trust Androkom. If anyone is smart enough to keep the kingdom from spinning into chaos, it's him."

"Don't we want the kingdom to be spinning into chaos?" asked Vance. "Order and peace haven't been all that great for humans. That's the whole reason I joined up with the rebellion. If peace means that dragons are in charge, count me as friend of war."

Before they could debate this any further, Anza gave a silent sigh, rolled her eyes, and turned her horse in the direction of Burke's Tavern. She dug her heels into the flanks of her steed and trotted off.

"I guess we're following her," said Jandra, shaking the reins of her mount.

"For someone who can't talk, Anza always manages to win arguments," said Vance.

IT WAS LONG past dark when they reached Burke's Tavern. Jandra was exhausted. She'd almost forgotten what it was like to be truly weary. When she'd worn her genie, the device had constantly monitored her physical state, negating the fatigue poisons that built up her blood. She resolved not to complain about her discomfort. She knew she was experiencing nothing worse than the others.

Burke's Tavern, the town, wasn't much more than a cluttered spot on the Forge Road, a few dozen houses clumped together. In the center of all this was a two-story building with a large porch and a painted wooden sign that read, "Burke's Tavern." The town was silent and still, but it was the quietness of sleep, not death. There were no signs of violence; the retreating dragon armies hadn't reached this far. It was quite possible no one here knew anything about the events from further down the road. The size of a dragon's world and a man's world were quite different. Sky-dragon messengers could cover two hundred miles a day, spreading news quickly. Humans lived much more insular lives—it could take many days for information to spread a hundred miles among humans. For a winged dragon, a town ninety miles distant was part of the neighborhood. For a human, a town ninety miles distant was out of sight and out of mind. Vendevorex had told her that most men never traveled more than fifty miles from their birthplace, though Jandra wondered if this was true or merely a myth believed by dragons. Many of the men she knew, like Bitterwood and Burke, had traveled through more of the world than she could imagine.

Lizard was asleep, his limbs draped over the horse's neck like it was a tree branch. The swaying motion didn't disturb him. In sleep, his coloration had taken on a drab, dark shade of green—a shade she remembered well. It had been the color of the earth-dragon that had slit her throat during the battle of Chakthalla's castle. Though that had happened only a few months before, it felt like some impossibly distant past. So much had unfolded in her life in the intervening weeks, she felt as if her adventures could fill a book, perhaps an entire trilogy of books, one that any biologian worth his salt would salivate over.

It was difficult to accept that this tiny dragon-child would one day grow up to be a fierce warrior. All the earth-dragons she'd ever known had led violent lives as soldiers and guards. Was this the result of their biology or their upbringing? Earth-dragon children were treated with abuse and neglected their whole lives until they became big enough and strong enough to be the abusers. Yet, Lizard responded to her affection. Could raising an earth-dragon with compassion, teaching it reason instead of rage, result in a new kind of dragon? Or only a weaker one, fated to never fit in with his peers? Would her act of kindness leave Lizard as much an outcast as she was?

Anza dismounted on the steps of Burke's Tavern. She walked onto the broad porch, stood next to a chessboard atop a large barrel. A sculpted monkey

sat on the far side of the board, a grinning beast crafted from tin and copper, with large glass eyes. Though
immobile, its hand was held in such a way that it
looked ready to reach out and grab a chess piece, had
there been any on the board. Vance and Shay got off
their horses, stretching their backs.

"I need brandy," said Shay.

"What's brandy?" asked Vance.

Shay looked puzzled by the question. "It's a
liqueur. You drink it. It warms you."

"Like moonshine?" asked Vance.

"I think brandy is only going to be found in the
dens of sky-dragons," said Jandra, getting off her
horse to join the others on the porch. Lizard
remained sound asleep, breathing peacefully. "I'm
not sure human palettes are refined enough to distin-
guish between the various liqueurs."

As she said the words "human palettes" she realized she was still thinking like the daughter of a
dragon. The others didn't react to her words—were
they avoiding her gaze because they recognized how
alien she was? A voice within her thought, "*Not
alien. Superior.*"

A chill ran down her spine. It wasn't her own voice
in her head—it was the voice of Jasmine Robertson.
Before Jazz had died, she'd "gifted" Jandra with a
thousand years' worth of her memories. Jazz had told
Jandra she'd done this as a time-saving device to help
Jandra understand why Jazz had aided in the fall of
mankind and the rise of dragons. Jazz was dead now,
but her memories lived on inside Jandra. This is why
Hex had stolen the genie. He'd been worried that
Jazz was still alive inside Jandra, since what was a
person but the sum of their memories? Jandra knew
she was still in control of her own personality, but
these stray thoughts and recollections worried her.

Ironically, Hex had robbed her of the very tool she needed to fix her brain—she was certain she could have commanded the genie to erase the alien memories.

"I can't think of the last time I was this tired," said Vance, addressing Anza. "Can we get some sleep before we find the person your father wants you to see? What's his name? Thorny?"

Anza nodded, though since Vance had asked three different questions, Jandra wasn't certain which one she was answering.

Shay looked even more exhausted than Vance, but he said, "Before we go to sleep can I see the library? The thought of it will keep me awake all night if I don't see it."

Anza motioned with her head for the others to follow. She pressed a board beside the door to the tavern. The panel of wood looked like any of the countless shingles that covered the place, but there was a click from inside the wall. Anza pushed the door open and slipped into the dark room beyond.

The others followed into the large room that was the heart of Burke's Tavern. There was a huge stone fireplace, with a faint orange flame still flickering over a mound of red coals. The room was warm, and the air was rich with the sweet aroma of ale. Jandra held her breath when she realized they weren't alone. An old man sat beside the fireplace in a wooden rocking chair, his head tilted back, softly snoring. His open mouth sported the most snaggled collection of teeth Jandra had ever seen—it was as if the old man had lost every other tooth in his mouth. His face was framed by an ill-groomed salt-and-pepper beard. The old man's hair jutted out from his head in all directions, composed of a hundred shades of gray, in every hue from charcoal black to cotton white.

Anza walked up to the sleeping man. She carefully reached out and touched his shoulder.

His head slowly lifted as his eyes opened.

"Anza?" he whispered. He rubbed his eyes. Jandra noted that his fingers were horribly knotted and twisted by arthritis. He lowered his hands and stared at Anza with bloodshot eyes. His breath was absolutely rotten, a stench that carried all the way to Jandra, nearly fifteen feet away, as he said, "It *is* you."

The old man rocked forward, looking at Jandra, Vance, and Shay. "Where's Burke?" he asked. Anza held out the folded letter. He grasped the paper awkwardly in his bony fingers.

"You must be Thorny," said Shay.

"That's what my friends call me," the old man acknowledged. His speech was slightly slurred. "Thor Nightingale is my birth name." He sounded quite proud of this fact. He looked around the empty tavern as he unfolded the letter, slowly, awkwardly, wincing as he moved his fingers in delicate motions for which they were ill formed. "I guess I fell asleep again." He grinned sheepishly. "Drank a few too many celebrating a birthday."

"Whose birthday?" asked Shay.

"It's always someone's birthday," said Thorny. He rose, swaying, his unbuttoned, threadbare coat hanging loosely on his frame.

Anza went to the fireplace to stir the ashes. The light brightened as the flames leapt back to life. A large clock beside the fireplace ticked rhythmically as she worked. Suddenly, the ticking was overpowered by the sound of gears within the wooden framework of the clock. A door opened near the floor and a brass frog hopped out. It released a series of croaks, a loud, metallic sound somewhere between a washboard's rasp and a bell's chime. The frog hopped in a circle back into the clock. The gears sounded again as the door closed.

"That was odd," said Vance.

"You get used to it," said Thorny, looking down at the unfolded letter. "Just another of Burke's gizmos, like the chess monkey. Burke's always tinkering on something." He squinted as his eyes flickered over the letter. "Looks like he's got more than tinkering in mind. I gather he's taken control of the foundries?"

"Yes," said Jandra. "But there've been unanticipated ramifications. The defeated dragon armies are taking revenge on human villages in the area, killing everyone."

Thorny shook his head. "That's not unanticipated, girl. Burke knew. He's spent the last twenty years plotting to overthrow the dragons, but he was like a chess player thinking ten moves ahead. He could imagine a hundred gambits that would produce quick and satisfying victories against the dragons. But any victory he imagined was followed by chaos and slaughter throughout the kingdom. He could have launched a war at any time, a war he thought he could win, but he didn't because he didn't want the blood of innocents on his hands. He would have lived out the rest of his life here in peace if Ragnar hadn't forced him to war."

Anza frowned as Thorny spoke. She glared at him and made a few rapid hand signals. Thorny looked embarrassed.

"You're right," he said. "Ragnar couldn't have forced Burke to do something that wasn't already in his heart. I was here when Ragnar confronted Burke. Burke could have killed the prophet where he stood. We both know that. But, no matter what Burke's gut feelings were toward dragons, I think his head was in charge of his emotions. Ragnar is nothing but emotions—he's like Burke's hidden anger given human form. Ragnar needed Burke, but maybe Burke needed Ragnar as well."

Jandra was surprised by Thorny's analysis. On the surface, he looked like nothing more than an old farmer, and a drunken one at that. But his words hinted at a level of education and thoughtfulness she didn't often encounter in her fellow humans.

Anza gave a few more hand signals. Thorny nodded. "You're right," he said, heading for the bar. "Let's get packing. We might not have much time." He led them through a door behind the bar into a kitchen, then through a second door that opened onto a set of stairs heading down. The stairs descended at least thirty feet, until they reached a third door that opened into darkness. Anza bounded ahead, moving confidently in the gloom. There was a series of clicks and suddenly a score of lanterns leapt to life, illuminating a large cellar with a high ceiling. The walls were made of red brick and the floor was crafted from huge flagstones. The rafters were full of gears and rods and wires, including a grid of long metal shafts that looked as if they were holding up the floor of the bar above. Jandra couldn't even begin to guess at their purpose. Chains draped around the room in all directions, like the web of some unseen iron spider.

Tall shelves lined the room, full of wooden boxes holding an impressive collection of springs, levers, rods, pins, screws, and cogs. Other shelves held hundreds of thick books bound in leather. A large iron stove sat on the far side of the room with a bin of coal beside it. A bellows affixed to the side was powered by a clockwork mechanism. The room stank of rust, must, and dust.

Thorny said, "Anza was only a baby when Burke arrived. He needed an assistant to build all this. I showed up a few months after he did. I was a former slave with no place to call home. I'd been trained to read and write, so Burke hired me to assist him in making this workshop. It's sort of a combination of foundry, library, and apothecary all rolled into one."

"You were a slave?" Shay asked.

"Long ago," said Thorny. "I used to serve as a living quill to the biologian Bazanel before he changed his position on slavery and freed me. Still, my ruined hands bear testimony to my service to him. I was made to write until every bone in my hands ached, and would face whippings if I failed to keep pace with Bazanel's nearly endless speeches and lectures. I take it, judging from your garb, that you were once a slave at the College of Spires?"

"I served Chapelion himself."

"Ah. You must have escaped. Chapelion would never willingly free a slave."

Shay nodded. "Chapelion's convinced that slavery is of benefit to mankind. He believes that people wouldn't long survive in the world in direct competition with dragons—only by serving dragons can humans endure. I know the argument well. I was the living quill that recorded every word of his five volume history of human bondage, *Slavery as an Evolutionary Strategy*."

"Isn't it risky to trust his words defending human slavery to be recorded accurately by a slave?" asked Jandra.

"Chapelion doesn't see it this way. Dogs are carnivores, with the instinct to hunt, yet they're trained by men to protect sheep and cattle. They're even trusted as companions for human children, though in the wild a wolf would no doubt regard the same child as a meal. Chapelion trusted me with his words the way men trust dogs with their families."

"You're lucky you escaped before you were used up," Thorny said. "These days, I can't even button my own clothes."

During this discussion, Anza had her arms crossed. She looked impatient. Thorny, apparently sensing this, said, "I should get a wagon from the barn to load Burke's inventory. Since we're abandoning the place, the rest of you can look around and see if there's anything you want to take. If you don't grab it, the dragons will. I'll wake some of the other men to help; it looks like you all could use some rest."

He and Anza moved toward twin wooden doors on the southern wall. She pulled them open to reveal a long tunnel leading up. Unlike the steep stairs, the tunnel had a gentle slope. Anza grabbed a lantern and stayed at Thorny's side as they walked toward the far end of the brick-lined tunnel. Vance trailed after them. Shay remained in the workshop, taking books from the shelves and reverently looking at their title pages. Jandra decided to stay behind as well. She'd witnessed Burke's handiwork at Dragon Forge, and was intrigued by the unfamiliar tools that lay around the room.

Fresh air swirled into the room as Anza and the others reached the end of the tunnel and opened the broad doors. Jandra looked up the long shaft, seeing starlight.

Shay let out a gasp. Jandra looked at him. He was in front of the bookshelf.

"By the bones!" said Shay. "He has all seven!"

"All seven what?"

"The Potter biographies! The College of Spires only had five of the volumes... four now, since I stole one."

"What's so special about these books?" She picked up one of the fat tomes and flipped it open.

"Potter was a member of a race of wizards who lived in the last days of the human age," said Shay.

Jandra frowned as she flipped through the pages. "Are you certain this isn't fiction?" she asked.

"The books are presented as fiction," said Shay. "However, there are other artifacts that reveal the actual reality. I wouldn't expect you to know about photographs, but—"

"I know what a photograph is," she said. In truth, the goddess knew what a photograph was, and Jandra was only borrowing the memory.

"Photographs recorded the physical world, and a handful of photographs of this famous wizard still survive. Some show him in flight on his..." His voice trailed off. He turned toward Jandra, studying her face carefully. She knew what he was about to ask.

"Is it true you know magic? That you and your master Vendevorex command supernatural forces? Are you one of the secret race?" His voice was quiet as he asked this, his tone almost reverential.

Jandra twisted a strand of hair around her finger as she contemplated her answer. When she still had her genie and could turn invisible, or disintegrate solid matter, or heal almost any wound, she'd always been quick to deny that she possessed supernatural powers. She'd shunned the label *witch*. Now, stripped of these powers, it might be dangerous to deny them. Having people believe you commanded supernatural forces was a kind of power in its own right.

She decided to answer his question with a question. "How did Potter control his magic?"

"With a wand and words. Is this how you use your magic?"

Jandra was intrigued. Her genie could take on any shape she desired. Why not the form of a wand? Of course, she'd never needed any magic words—the genie responded to her thoughts. Still… could this Potter have been a nanotechnician? Perhaps one of the Atlanteans Vendevorex had warned her about?

She knew little about Atlantis, but perhaps Shay knew more. "Have you ever heard of Atlantis?"

"Certainly," said Shay. "It's referenced in…"

His voice trialed off. He cocked his head toward the tunnel.

Jandra tilted her head as well. What was that noise? Was someone screaming?

Now, there could be no doubt. It was Thorny's voice they heard as he ran toward the tunnel doors. He stumbled as he reached the slope, falling on his chest, the air forced out of him. He rose to his knees, sucking in breath. The entire workshop echoed as he shouted, in a high, panicked voice, "Dragons!"

CHAPTER SIX

A VICTORY,
MORE OR LESS

JANDRA RAN UP the tunnel, shotgun at the ready. She stopped in front of Thorny, who was still sprawled on the ground. She glanced over her shoulder at Shay, whose face was pale as he trailed behind her.

"You ever been in a fight?" she asked.

"Once," Shay said.

"You win?"

"I survived," said Shay. "Because of Bitterwood."

"Bitterwood?" Jandra took Thorny's twisted fingers into her hand as she helped him back to his feet. "You've met him?"

"'Met' really isn't the right word," said Shay. "I watched as three slavecatchers were brought down by an archer I never saw. The slavecatchers thought it was him, though."

"Sounds like him." She nodded toward the gun in Shay's hands. "Burke's placing a lot of faith in you. You think you're up to this?"

Shay clenched his jaw. "Let's do it."

Jandra gave Thorny a gentle shove back down the tunnel. "Lock the doors behind you," she said.

"I'd be out there if I could still hold a sword," Thorny said mournfully as he loped down the slope.

In the distance, Jandra heard a woman screaming. She turned toward the sound and ran out into the starry night. A half moon cast stark shadows over the town. The bare branches of a nearby apple tree swayed in a rising wind. She spun around, trying to get her bearings. The Forge Road was almost a hundred yards behind her. She ran, staying in the shadows of Burke's tavern. Dozens of earth-dragons swarmed on the road, their steel armor glinting in the moonlight. Beyond the tavern lay a simple stone cottage. She watched as a trio of brawny earth-dragons kicked in the door and charged inside. A dog barked savagely at the invasion, then yelped and fell silent. Somewhere in the distance, a baby was crying.

Jandra pressed her back against the tavern wall, mere feet from the road. The earth-dragons hadn't spotted her yet. There were too many to count, a hundred at least, maybe twice that number. Even though this town hadn't been stripped of its men by Ragnar's recruiting, the villagers were still hopelessly outnumbered.

Jandra fingered the silver bracelet on her wrist. Should she turn invisible? The shotgun was a powerful weapon. Burke assured her it would punch through a dragon's armor. But it took so long to reload. After one or two shots, she'd be swarmed. From an invisible fighting stance, perhaps she'd have a chance. On the other hand, invisibility wasn't the greatest tool against earth-dragons. As a race, they were notoriously near-sighted. They compensated with sharp hearing and a sense of smell far superior to humans. The shotgun was loud and the smoke stank. It wouldn't take them long to find her.

She looked over her shoulder to see if Shay was behind her. He was nowhere to be seen. In the distance, there was a clap like thunder. He'd apparently found a place to make his stand. Many dragons in the street paused at the sound, turning their heads toward a nearby barn.

The brief moment of inactivity quickly gave way to resumed violence. One of the earth-dragons glanced in her direction. He cocked his head as he untangled the shadows that concealed her, and then narrowed his eyes. He lifted his battle axe in meaty paws and stalked toward her. Jandra raised her gun.

She never got the chance to fire. The dragon toppled as a silver tomahawk dug into the back of its neck. As the dragon fell, Anza was revealed, standing in the middle of the street, a second tomahawk in her left hand, her right hand going for one of the throwing knives strapped to her leg. Anza spun on her toes and whipped out her arms. Two more dragons toppled as she released her weapons. A score of dragons all looked her way. As one, they raised their axes and charged.

Anza drew the longsword from the scabbard slung over her back. In her left hand, she produced a smaller, curved blade. A dragon neared. Before it reached her, an arrow flew down from above and punched through the dragon's breast plate with a loud *thunk*. The dragon dropped to his knees as a *ZING* rang out and a second dragon that neared Anza suddenly had an arrow in its belly.

Bitterwood? thought Jandra.

There was another *ZING* and Jandra realized where she'd heard the sound before. It was a sky-wall bow. Vance was on the roof of Burke's Tavern, slaying dragons with every shot. The kid really was as good as Burke claimed.

Anza also proved worthy of her reputation. Even as Vance slew a half dozen dragons in under a minute, there was a crowd of the scaly soldiers mere yards from Anza, with more approaching. Anza faced them calmly, her face utterly devoid of emotion.

Anza's arms were close to her chest. She crouched down, looking small against the backdrop of the brutish earth-dragons. She was taller than Jandra, but still had the slim, willowy build of a girl in her late teens. Any one of the dragons surrounding her outweighed her three to one. All were armored in heavy plate, while she wore only buckskin.

Jandra raised her shotgun, wondering how close she could aim to Anza without risking hitting her.

Before she could pull the trigger, Anza unfolded, a motion that reminded Jandra of a flower blossoming, but at the speed of an arrow leaving a bow. Anza's blades flashed in the moonlight, and suddenly the turtle-like head of one earth-dragon was freed from the shoulders that held it. The axe-hand of a second dropped to the ground, leaving its owner staring wide-eyed at a blood-spurting stump.

As Vance continued to rain arrows down upon the dragons, Anza whirled like a dervish. Dragons dropped around her in a neat circle. Their bloodied bodies formed a small wall that the other dragons would have to step over. She stopped spinning, as the remaining dragons hesitated, their jaws agape as they looked down at their slain brethren.

In the distance, there was a second *BOOM*. Jandra grimaced. If Shay was killing more dragons than she was, she wasn't pulling her weight. She darted onto the porch. The horses were gone. Perhaps they'd fled when the invasion began—she hoped that Lizard was okay.

She paused at the door to the tavern and smacked the shingle Anza had pressed earlier. She charged into the open door and turned, looking out into the street. She raised her shotgun and fired into the crowd of dragons. She slammed the door shut without waiting to see the result of her shot, running to the stairs that led to the second story. At the top, there was an open trapdoor to the roof. A ladder was leaned against the opening. She climbed the ladder and found Vance. He startled as he heard her step onto the flat roof and spun around, an arrow drawn. She flinched, knowing that this was a stupid way to die. She relaxed as Vance lowered the bow.

"Whew!" he said. "Good thing I'm running out of arrows. A minute ago I'd have shot first and figured out what I hit later."

"How many arrows are left?" Jandra asked, running to the edge of the roof.

"Three," said Vance.

"Burke needs to build bigger quivers," said Jandra, looking down into the street below. There had to be at least fifty dragons circled around Anza. Who knew how many were unseen, in the houses of villagers, bringing havoc?

Yet, Anza wasn't completely alone. There was another blast, much closer, as Shay fired again. Some dragons behind Anza dropped. Jandra didn't know where Shay was, but apparently he was holding his own. Further down the road, she saw a half-dozen humans banded together. They were middle-aged men with longswords similar to the one Anza used. While they were dressed in nightgowns, they did at least have helmets and shields. They charged a small band of dragons near the barn and joined battle.

The pile of dragons around Anza had grown. There were at least thirty corpses. Jandra felt an acute sense of her own inadequacy. Two weeks ago, she could have rained Vengeance of the Ancestors, a disintegrating flame, down upon these dragons with the speed of thought. She reloaded her shotgun, counting the long seconds. Vance perched on the edge of the roof, his arrow drawn, but held his fire.

"What are you waiting for?" Jandra asked.

"Anza's amazing, but she ain't got eyes in the back of her head," said Vance. "I gotta put my last three shots into dragons attacking where she can't see them."

Jandra nodded. "Good strategy. I'm going to be messier."

She brought the shotgun to her shoulder and took a bead on the thickest cluster of dragons she could find. With a flash and a thunderclap, the gun rained down a shower of deadly missiles. Four dragons were staggered by the blast, one falling over, the other three clutching at the wounds that suddenly peppered their shoulders. They looked toward the rooftop, squinting. A dragon pointed toward Jandra and barked, "Up there!" A dozen dragons broke from the crowd and thundered onto the porch. The whole building shuddered as they kicked at the door. Burke's engineering held better than most of the other doors in town, but she could still hear woodwork splintering with each kick.

"Vance," said Jandra as she pushed another gunpowder charge down the barrel with her ramrod, "Why don't you go pull up the ladder?"

"Good idea." He ran back across the flat roof to the trap door. He crouched over the ladder and grabbed it, as another voice yelled, "Hold on!"

"Shay?" asked Vance.

"I saw you on the roof," said Shay, panting as he bolted up the ladder. "Thought I'd join you. Things were getting hot in the stables. That's not a joke. The stables are on fire."

Jandra could see the flickers of flame from a building several doors down. The odor of burning hay and dung flavored the night air. She squeezed the trigger again and every odor but the sharp kick of gunpowder vanished. As the smoke cleared, she saw three more dragons had fallen. Perhaps hoping Anza would be distracted by the blast, a pair of dragons lunged, swinging axes. With a flurry of silver blades, the barrier of corpses surrounding Anza grew by two. Shay fired his shotgun, and another dragon fell. By now, the band of armed villagers had proven victorious in their initial skirmish and were shouting for blood as they charged toward the tavern.

The earth-dragons below looked frightened and confused. Anza circled slowly within her knee-high fortress of armored corpses. Vance's sky-wall bow sang out as a dragon behind Anza lifted its axe, preparing for a charge. The dragon fell, and the dragon next to him spun on his heels and ran, his thick tail jutting straight out behind him.

Jandra finished loading her gun and fired. By chance, Shay fired at precisely the same instant. The twin blast was deafening. Amidst the smoke, Jandra couldn't tell how many they'd hit, but when the air cleared, full blown panic had seized most of the remaining soldiers. Only a handful nearest to Anza weren't running, either braver than their brethren, or dumber. Jandra reloaded. Vance targeted a dragon with one of his two remaining arrows. *ZING!*

Shay reveled in the apparent victory, standing right at the edge of the roof. "Ha!" he shouted, holding his gun over his head. "Run you green-scaled bastards! Run from the light of a new human dawn!"

The moonlight grew dim as a shadow fell over the roof.

"How poetic," a voice said, as blue talons shot down from the sky and snatched the shotgun from Shay's grasp. Spreading its wings wide, a sky-dragon dropped to the roof behind them.

"Vulpine!" Shay shouted as he twisted around, his voice changing from triumph to despair.

Vance swung around with his final arrow, drawing a bead on the new arrival, but before he could complete the movement a second blue form shot down toward the roof. The sky-blue crocodilian jaws of a second sky-dragon clamped onto Vance's face. The momentum of the impact jerked Vance from the roof. The sky-dragon released the young archer and Vance dropped twenty feet onto the hard-packed earth below. He landed on his head with a sickening crunch. His arms fell limply to his sides as he stared up with unfocused eyes, his face bleeding from twin rows of puncture wounds.

Anza leapt to attack the remaining dragons that surrounded her, but Jandra didn't have time to watch. The sky-dragon who'd attacked Vance was wheeling back around toward the roof, its jaws wide, a satisfied look in its eyes as it targeted Jandra. Jandra pulled the ramrod from her shotgun, having just finished tamping down the shot. She raised her gun. The dragon's open jaws were only yards away when she pulled the trigger. The gap closed as the fuse sputtered.

Half a second later, there was a tremendous amount of smoke and noise. Jandra was knocked from her feet as the dragon's now headless corpse crashed into her. The wind gushed from her lungs as the wet, twitching body pressed her down into the tarred boards of the roof. As she kicked and rolled to get free, Vulpine chuckled softly. Shay made a pained squeak, a noise like a kitten getting stepped on. At last, she crawled free of the corpse. Still on her knees, she wiped hot blood from her eyes as she tried to make sense of what was happening.

Shay was pressed flat on the roof, face down, with Vulpine's hind-talon pinning the back of his neck. Vulpine was searching Shay, his long serpentine neck swaying back and forth. He held Shay's shotgun in one of his fore-talons. He'd pulled free the belt that contained the bags of powder and shot. The sky-dragon sniffed the flash pan of the gun, his nostrils suddenly contracting, as if he found the smell unpleasant.

"An interesting toy, Shay," said Vulpine. "But not the grand prize. Where are the books?"

"I'll... never... tell," Shay said, straining to breathe.

Smoke was starting to rise from the trapdoor that opened onto the roof. Had the earth-dragons who'd charged in earlier set the place on fire? Jandra had to admit it was a rather straightforward approach to dealing with snipers on the roof.

Vulpine eyed Jandra as she tried to stand.

"Girl, if you move another inch, I'll kill you."

Jandra glanced down at the silver bracelet on her wrist. She still had one chance...

There was a creaking noise behind Vulpine. Two sets of human fingertips grasped the edges of the open trapdoor to the roof. The hands were small, tanned, and female. Anza's head appeared above the edge as she pulled herself up.

Jandra felt a tremendous sense of relief. Short of Bitterwood, Anza was the person she most wanted on the roof beside her.

Vulpine calmly pulled Shay's head backward and slammed it down, hard. Shay went limp as Vulpine leapt toward the trap door. He kicked out with his hind-talons, aiming for Anza's face. Anza ducked, letting her body drop back down into the room below, but maintaining her grasp on the edges of the hole. Vulpine grabbed the wooden door, which was held up by a wooden pole, knocked the pole free, and then slammed it down. Anza let go a fraction of a second before the wood could crush her fingers.

Sparks swirled up from the sudden rush of air. The roof was growing hot. Thick smoke poured from the sides of the building. The fire beneath them roared as the winter wind whipped through shattered windows.

Jandra didn't waste the handful of seconds Vulpine was distracted by Anza. She shoved in the wad containing the gunpowder. She was ramming down the shot when Vulpine turned toward her.

"I told you not to move," he snarled. "I saw how your toy worked," he said, pointing the shotgun toward her with his fore-talon. He flinched slightly as he pulled the trigger, no doubt anticipating the explosion. However, the flintlock shot its sparks into an empty chamber. Shay had never reloaded. Vulpine looked baffled as Jandra pulled the ramrod free. She pressed the gun into her shoulder as she snarled, "This is how it works!"

Before her finger could twitch on the trigger, Vulpine spun. His long, whip-like tail struck the barrel of her gun as she fired. When the smoke cleared, Vulpine was still standing, looking amused. He leapt toward her, his jaws open wide. Jandra swung the iron barrel of her shotgun up, grasping the metal with both hands. The just-fired gun burned her fingers as she jammed it sideways into Vulpine's mouth, blocking his bite. The slavecatcher knocked her backwards, pushing her closer to the edge of the roof. Though his teeth were blocked, the sky-dragon still bristled with natural weaponry. He kicked his hind-talon into Jandra's gut and raked... snapping the tips of his claws. Jandra was grateful that Burke had insisted she wear the chain-mail vest beneath her coat.

"No eat!" a small voice cried. The slavecatcher hissed and staggered backwards as Lizard leapt from his hiding place near the chimney and landed on Vulpine's back, claws digging in, his turtle-beak clamping onto Vulpine's shoulder blade.

Vulpine snarled, whipping his tail up, knocking Lizard free. "Enough of this madness." Vulpine leapt for the sky, the downbeat of his twenty-foot wingspan fanning the smoke. A dozen small fires erupted across the wooden roof.

Jandra tried to reload, but it was hopeless. Vulpine lifted further into the sky with each second. By the time she was ready to fire again, he was hundreds of yards away. Still, they'd chased off the most notorious slavecatcher in the kingdom. She would count this as a victory, more or less.

Lizard leapt onto Jandra's shoulders. "Bad hot," he said, looking at the flames.

"It's okay," said Jandra, going over to Shay. She wasn't certain if it was her imagination, but the roof felt shakier than it had earlier. The earth-dragons couldn't have set the fire more than five minutes ago. Even with the wind, should there be this much structural damage already? Almost in answer, something beneath her groaned, then crashed. She wondered if Anza had made it out.

"Shay!" she cried, kneeling beside him. She shook his shoulders.

He groaned as he opened his eyes. There was a large gash across his chin. He coughed violently as he sat up in the ever-worsening smoke. He looked disoriented. "Where's Vulpine?" he asked.

"Gone," said Jandra. "I think he was rattled that my gun worked and his didn't. Lizard pounced on him like a bob-cat and Vulpine turned tail."

"Wait. His gun?"

"He took yours. Your ammo too. I hope he's not clever enough to figure out how to use it." Shay looked like this was a dumb thing for Jandra to say. "I'll cling to any hope I can get at the moment, false or not. You may have noticed we're on top of a burning building. And, unlike that wizard you mentioned earlier, I've never been able to fly."

"Good thing Vance dragged up the ladder then," said Shay, rising. "We can get down to the porch roof with this, then down to the ground."

Jandra nodded. It was a sound plan. Shay lowered the ladder to the roof and held it as he motioned for her to go first. It was an unexpected gesture. The two human men she was most familiar with, Bitterwood and Pet, would have escaped down the ladder first and left her to fend for herself.

"Hurry," he said.

Jandra descended the ladder. Anza was in the street again, crouched over Vance. There was no sign of any living dragons in either direction down the Forge Road. Human families were now rushing into the street, running from house to house to check on the wounded and count the dead.

Shay came down the ladder to the porch roof. The heat from the open windows made it hard to breathe. They lowered the ladder to the street and climbed down, then ran to Vance's side.

"Is he okay?" Jandra asked Anza. Anza looked up, frowning. She shook her head.

Vance's eyes were wide open, fully dilated, focused on nothing. He was bleeding from a gash on his scalp. "Why is it so dark?" he whispered. "Why is it so dark?"

Jandra turned away, utterly powerless. With her genie, she could have looked inside Vance to discover the nature of his injury. She could have repaired whatever damage she discovered from the cellular level up. She looked back toward the tavern as the roof collapsed, sending a whirlwind of flames heavenward. "Thorny!" she said. "He's still in the basement!"

She tossed her shotgun to Shay. "This will only slow me down." She took off running, darting down the alley that led behind the tavern. She looked up as a shadow flickered overhead—Vulpine?—but it was only the smoke blotting out the moon. She tripped as she reached the back of the ally, landing hard, skidding in the dirt. Lizard's weight on her shoulder vanished as he flew off. A darker shadow fell over her. The hairs on the back of her neck rose at the metallic clank to her right. From the corner of her eye, she saw the thick, scaly foot of an adult earth-dragon.

She rolled as the earth-dragon grunted. A battle-axe bit into the earth where she'd been an instant before. The earth-dragon was dressed in full battle gear, breast plate, helmet, and shield.

"Bad boss!" shrieked Lizard, sounding terrified.

The earth-dragon growled as it pulled the axe free of the cold ground, brandishing it above its head to strike again. Jandra kept her eyes fixed on her attacker. As it swung, she rolled again, to the side of the blow. Earth-dragons were strong, but not especially fast, definitely not under a full load of armor. Jandra braced her back against the ground and kicked up with both feet, targeting the dragon's elbow. Her feet connected with a satisfying crunch and the dragon hissed as its talon released the axe handle. The beast staggered back, pain flashing in its eyes. Just as quickly, the pain turned to rage. The dragon dropped its shield and lunged, his free talon aimed at Jandra's face. Jandra again rolled away, using her momentum to spring to her feet as the earth-dragon landed with a clatter on the spot where she'd been.

She leapt over his body before he could rise, grabbing the axe buried in the ground. The weapon was impractically heavy, probably fifty pounds. Before the genie tuned her body, there was no way she could have swung it. She spun around, letting momentum add to the strength of her swing. The dragon was raising his head as she sunk the axe into the back of his neck, just below the helmet. The force of the blow tore the weapon from her hand. She looked down, wincing at the large black splinter buried in her palm.

The dragon collapsed, lifeless. Lizard skittered forward and poked the half-decapitated earth-dragon on the beak.

"Not move?" he asked.

"Not move," she said.

She turned as she heard footsteps behind her. It was Shay. He looked at the dead dragon, wide-eyed. "Are you all right? I heard a fight."

"I have a splinter," she said, holding up her palm. Her words were drowned out by a loud crash from inside the tavern. Sparks shot from every window. The fire roared as the wind whipped it into an ever-growing fury. Jandra scooped up Lizard and cradled him against her breast as she ran toward the tunnel. Shay followed at her heels. Her eyes searched the shadows for any further sign of dragon-stragglers.

"Thorny!" Shay shouted as she reached the tunnel doors. There was a small pile of clutter next to the tunnel, boxes full of tools, several round dials, their faces covered with numbers, plus stacks of notebooks, and vials of unrecognizable fluids. "Thorny!" Shay shouted, using his hands as a megaphone. No one answered.

"Come on," said Jandra, running down the tunnel. The doors at the end were closed, but reddish-orange light danced through the gaps. The air was distinctly smoky. Before they could approach the doors burst open, sending forth a blast of heat and a cloud of smoke. A tall, black-haired girl in buckskins with an old man slung over her shoulders marched out of the cloud.

"Anza?" Shay asked. Anza gave a slight smirk, as if to ask who else he might have been expecting. Thorny coughed violently. Anza marched up the slope, breathing evenly. Her buckskins were splattered shoulder to ankle in blood, but as near as Jandra could determine, Anza didn't have a scratch on her.

"But… you were just in the street," Shay said, following Anza. "How did…?"

Behind them, there was another crash, and another wave of smoke gushed up the tunnel, hiding everything from view. Jandra found the tunnel wall and held her breath as she groped her way back toward fresh air. Behind her in Burke's workshops, things began to pop and sizzle in small explosions. Over this noise came a series of powerful *twangs* as springs began to burst free of the braces that held them.

Jandra made it outside and took a deep breath of the relatively clean air. She looked toward the tavern. Red hot iron rods six feet long were shooting up into the air, rising a hundred feet before they fell back toward the burning building, already losing their glow. The heat of the flames could be felt even here. The human villagers gathered around to gawk as the building began to tremble. Something deep within the guts of the building exploded with a deep bass rumble and the entire structure fell in upon itself. Jandra stepped away from the tunnel entrance as a jet of sparks shot out into the night air.

"Good light!" Lizard said, excited. The sparks swirled up into the winter sky like some sort of reverse snow. Jandra did have to admit that, stripped of all the horrors of the night, the sparks possessed a sort of primal beauty.

Shay stared down the tunnel, his face forlorn. "All those books," he whispered. "Have I been cursed? Why does every book I touch lately go up in flames?"

"It's just bad luck," said Jandra.

"It's more than bad luck," said Shay. "It's the end of my dreams. I had no plan but to escape to Dragon Forge. Now that I'm not welcome there, I don't know where I'll go. I had thought perhaps, with a few books, I could find some village that would want my services as a teacher. Without books, what do I have to offer?"

"You could come with me the rest of the way to the palace," said Jandra. "If I get my tiara back, we can move freely through the place since I'll have full control over my invisibility again. You can take all the books you can carry."

"So… you admit you're a wizard?"

"No," said Jandra. "I'm a nanotechnician."

"I don't know what that word means," said Shay.

"It means I command unimaginably tiny machines," said Jandra. "At least, I used to."

Shay looked at her skeptically, as if judging whether she was putting him on. He held the shotgun he carried out toward her. Jandra shook her head and loosened her gun belt, offering it to him.

"You keep it. You have a talent for it."

Anza had laid Thorny on the grass after she'd carried him from the tunnel, but now the old man was back on his feet, his cheeks tarnished with soot. "Damn," he said. "I didn't get a tenth of the stuff on his list. If I were younger, or my hands a little stronger…"

Anza flashed him a few rapid hand gestures.

"You're right," he said. "I'm alive. That's what counts."

"You understand Anza a lot better than I do," said Jandra.

"She grew up in my company," said Thorny. "I'm like an uncle to her. By the time she was seven or eight, I never even thought much about the fact she didn't speak. Once you know how to read her, she gets her thoughts across just fine with her eyes and her hands."

"She's never talked?" Shay asked.

"She made some noises as a baby, but stopped when she was about a year old. After that, she didn't even make sounds when she'd cry. Some of the townsfolk whispered that she might be an imbecile, but anyone who knew her could see that she was smarter than other kids her age. Burke used to tell anyone who asked about her that it's better to be silent and be thought a fool than to open your mouth and remove all doubt."

Anza crossed her arms, looking uncomfortable with this discussion.

"I guess I should go talk to the rest of the townsfolk," Thorny said. "Tell 'em what I know, have them get ready to head to Dragon Forge. Get Burke his notebooks and those gauges. The note said the rest of you were heading on to the dragon palace. We can probably find somewhere in the village where you can rest up for what's left of the night. Get you washed up, too. Anza, you look a fright."

Anza shrugged and brushed back a loose lock of her hair from her cheek, leaving a streak of dark blood like war paint.

CHAPTER SEVEN

SUCH
IMAGINATION

IT WAS DAWN when Vulpine arrived at the Dragon
Palace. The ancient structure loomed like a small
mountain near the banks of a broad river that
gleamed like silver in the morning mist. The human
city of Richmond lay nearby, the docks already
bustling with laborers. The rebellion at Dragon Forge
must seem very distant to these men, thought
Vulpine. Richmond was a bustling center of trade, a
gateway between the flat coastal plains to the east
and the hills and mountains to the west. Thirty thousand humans dwelled in Richmond, by far the largest
city in the kingdom.

Even though Richmond lay in the shadow of the
Dragon Palace, it had escaped Albekizan's genocidal
schemes unscathed. Albekizan had drawn upon the
labor of the humans here when he built the Free City
not ten miles distant. The Free City had been
designed by Albekizan's wicked brother Blasphet to
serve as a trap for humanity, a promise of paradise

that was actually intended to bring about the final solution to the human problem. Yet, in the end, the trap did more damage to dragons than men. The first wave of humans brought to the city had fought back when Albekizan ordered their slaughter, led by the legendary dragon-hunter Bitterwood, aided by the treacherous wizard Vendevorex. During all this turmoil, the men of Richmond had simply carried on with business, keeping the canals open, buying and selling goods. Every scrap of lumber, every nail and hammer used to build the Free City had passed through these docks.

Vulpine had considered Albekizan's plan to wipe out humanity sheer madness. As a slavecatcher, he was keenly aware that dragon society was built upon the labor of humans. None of the three dragon races could ever replace them.

Earth-dragons were fit only for lives as soldiers; blacksmiths were the closest thing to artisans that their race had ever produced. There was no earth-dragon sculpture or literature, and earth-dragon music was barely distinguishable from noise. Earth-dragon cuisine was even more abominable—all pickled sausages and salted meat, spiced to eye-watering heat. Earth-dragons could never replace the skills of human farmers, carpenters, and craftsmen.

Of course, his own species was a poor substitute for human labor as well. Most sky-dragon males were averse to actual work. The majority devoted their lives to scholarship. Over the centuries they had produced poems, statues, operas, and lengthy treatises on every topic under the sun. They'd filled libraries and museums with their creations; but every one of those libraries had been built by the labors of men. The diet of sky-dragons was more sophisticated than earth-dragons—fish, fresh fruit, crusty bread, and vegetables in a rainbow of colors—and all of this was grown by human farmers and cooked by human slaves.

Vulpine had become a slavecatcher because it was one of the few professions available to his race that truly mattered. Slavecatchers were the invisible glue that held the world together. They were greatly feared among men. Their reputation for brutality was well-deserved, but it did not spring from any innate cruelty. The poets, artists, and musicians of the world would starve if not for the work of slavecatchers. Men benefited from the system as well, as strict discipline allowed the war-prone humans to live in relative peace. Without the valiant efforts of slavecatchers, the world would spin into anarchy.

Who else kept order? The sun-dragons? Albekizan and his incompetent heir Shandrazel had done the world far more harm than good. Albekizan had triggered the human uprising with his inept attempt at genocide. Shandrazel had allowed the problem to explode by showing weakness, allowing a ragtag band of humans to defeat his army at Dragon Forge. Albekizan had lit a fire; Shandrazel had poured oil upon it. It was left to Vulpine to squelch the flames.

Fortunately, he would not be without allies. Aside from the slavecatchers, there was one more small subset of sky-dragon males willing to dirty their talons: the aerial guard, a hundred or so sky-dragons who served as protectors of the Dragon Palace.

It was these guards who now rose into the sky. A dozen of them quickly assumed an arrow formation and shot in his direction, ready to defend the palace. The living wall of sky-dragon guards that closed quickly in on Vulpine made his heart glad. It was such a waste that his brethren devoted themselves to studies and art—a martial sky-dragon was a glorious thing, a hundred pounds of muscle, bones, and scale that commanded the air like no other creature on earth. The members of the aerial guard were especially impressive. Red and yellow ribbons trailed from the mane of blue scales that ran down their necks and backs, coloration that matched the banners of Albekizan that still adorned the palace. In their hind-talons, the aerial guard carried long-spears, their razor-sharp tips dazzling in the morning sun.

The eyes of the aerial guard were hard as they neared. One by one, their gazes softened as they recognized Vulpine. Seventy years old, Vulpine was well known to all sky-dragons. He'd been Slavecatcher General for nearly thirty years, and he'd been present for the initiation of every last one of these dragons. All carried a two-inch long, talon-shaped scar below their right eye—a scar made by a branding iron that Vulpine himself had wielded, marking them forever as warriors.

"Greetings, warrior," Vulpine called out to Sagen, the lead guard. Sagen was a fine specimen, his muscles moving beneath his azure scales like precisely-tuned machinery. Sagen was the product of one of the most respected bloodlines of the sky-dragons—Vulpine's own. Breeding was strictly controlled among the sky-dragons, with all pairings guided by the Matriarch to capture the most worthy traits of the sky-dragon race. The upbringing of sky-dragons was strictly communitarian; they didn't form family units like humans or sun-dragons. While most sky-dragons knew their lineage, their loyalty was to their race, not their relatives. Still, Vulpine had always had an interest in each of his many offspring, and Sagen had made him especially proud when he'd embraced the warrior's path and begun his meteoric rise in the ranks of the aerial guard.

Vulpine and Sagen began to gyre in a tight orbit, looking across a circle little wider than their combined wingspans as the other guards spread out into a wider circle.

"Sir," said Sagen, with a respectful nod of his head. "What is the purpose of this visit?"

"I've come to see the High Biologian," Vulpine said.

"Androkom is... unavailable at the moment," said Sagen.

"You can speak the truth," said Vulpine. "I know that Androkom is either dead or in a dungeon. Chapelion should have arrived days ago with a squadron of valkyries from the Nest to overthrow him. The Matriarch opposed the appointment of Androkom as High Biologian due to his flawed bloodline. Chapelion was her choice; I assume you now serve him, though I understand that he may not yet be ready to announce this news."

Sagen looked thoughtful as he continued to fly in his counter orbit, contemplating his answer. Vulpine assumed his son was under orders not to admit that Chapelion had accomplished his coup. At last, Sagen said, "I cannot confirm your speculations, sir. I can acknowledge that Chapelion is currently a guest of the palace. I can personally provide you with safe escort to see him."

"Of course," said Vulpine, and the two broke from their gyre. Sagen barked out orders to his fellow guards and flew ahead, leading them toward the great open amphitheatre that served as the throne room of the sun-dragon king.

Vulpine opened his wings and tilted backward to slow himself, skidding ungracefully as he landed on the polished marble floor. He was tired from his flight through the night; the weapon he'd taken from

Shay was slung over his shoulder and its weight threw him off balance. The amphitheatre was a half dome open to the west, which meant its interior was still in shadows in early morning. Torches lined the walls, flickering in the breeze stirred up by their landing.

At the head of the hall, seated atop a mound of golden cushions large enough for a sun-dragon, was a familiar blue form: Chapelion, master of the College of Spires. He was flanked on each side by a score of valkyries, female sky-dragons dedicated to the military arts.

Chapelion was younger than Vulpine by seven years, though a casual observer might not have guessed this. Vulpine had spent much of his life outdoors. Fresh air and exercise had left Vulpine stronger than many sky-dragons half his age, and a life on the hunt had left him with his senses sharpened. Chapelion, having lived a more sedentary life indoors, was pot-bellied with spindly limbs. His hide sagged on his frame. A lifetime of reading by lantern light had dulled Chapelion's eyes. He compensated with a pair of specially designed spectacles that sat atop his broad snout.

Chapelion's head was lowered as he scanned across several large rolls of parchment laid out on the floor before him. A trio of younger sky-dragons surrounded the elder biologian, quills in hand, jotting notes as he mumbled. Vulpine was so used to seeing tall, red-headed Shay in this role that his absence felt odd.

"Chapelion!" Vulpine shouted out in greeting. His voice echoed in the vast room; Chapelion was becoming hard of hearing in his old age, so Vulpine was used to adjusting his tone.

The dragon looked up, peering over the rim of his spectacles. He lifted his neck, looking more alert as he recognized Vulpine. "Old friend," said Chapelion. "I'm happy to see you! I assume you've recovered my books?"

"No," Vulpine said, drawing closer to the throne. He could see now that the pages spread before Chapelion were copies of maps, the ink still fresh. "Unfortunately, I bring you neither books, nor slaves. Hemming and Terpin are dead. Shay survives; I encountered him last night, but made the tactical decision to retreat."

"What?" Chapelion said. At first, Vulpine thought he hadn't spoken loudly enough; then he realized that Chapelion didn't believe what he'd heard. "You fled from Shay? You let my books remain with him? In all the years I've known you, this is the first time you've ever reported such failure."

Vulpine grimaced. "I said that I retreated, not that I fled. In truth, my encounter with Shay was pure accident. He didn't have the books with him; if he had, I'd have secured them. However, I feel confident we shall catch him soon. He was in the company of Jandra."

A deep furrow appeared in Chapelion's brow. "Jandra? Should I know this name?"

"You should," said Vulpine. "Jandra was the human child that Vendevorex raised from infancy. I've heard she isn't his equal as a wizard, but she's still in command of formidable forces. I was traveling with Balikan and he was killed by Jandra. I had defeated Shay and was about to slay Jandra when a third combatant ambushed me from behind. I knocked him away but never saw him; he must have been invisible, a power attributed to the wizard."

"Yes," said Chapelion. "I've seen Vendevorex turn invisible." He paused, raising his fore-talon to stroke beneath his chin. "That sentence doesn't sound accurate," he said, softly, speaking to himself. "I watched him turn invisible? Does that sound better?" Chapelion's voice trailed off as he mulled over the question in his head.

Vulpine waited patiently. Conversations with Chapelion were like this; a lifetime of dictating manuscripts had left him constantly editing his thoughts, especially if he was tired or distracted. Catch Chapelion in the wrong state of mind, and a conversation that should take but a moment could turn into an hour-long ordeal.

"I understand your meaning," Vulpine said, hoping to regain control of the conversation. "It's early; you'll find the correct word after breakfast."

"Is it early?" asked Chapelion. He looked beyond Vulpine, his eyes taking on a dreamy cast as he saw the brightening sky. "Once more we've worked through the night, it seems. Events continue to build faster than we can respond to them."

"Events?"

"Word of the massacre of Shandrazel's armies at Dragon Forge has now reached all the sun-dragons." Chapelion motioned toward the maps. "In the absence of a king, all sun-dragons who control the various provinces are renouncing the shared defense treaties that had been signed during Albekizan's reign. The kingdom is now full of sun-dragons who imagine they alone are worthy to sit upon the Dragon Throne. Full civil war awaits, I fear, unless we preemptively place a sun-dragon on the throne who is strong enough to dissuade challenges. Unfortunately, no worthy candidate has emerged. Albekizan's eldest son, Hexilizan, made a brief return to the palace several weeks past, but hasn't been seen since. If we could locate him, perhaps he would accept the crown."

"Why bother?" asked Vulpine. "We both know that the High Biologian is the true power behind the throne—though Metron in his dotage certainly lost control of Albekizan, and Androkom was a disaster with Shandrazel. I assume your presence on the throne indicates Androkom has been dealt with?"

"Yes. Androkom is currently... hmm... shall we say, on sabbatical? Yes, that sounds acceptably diplomatic. In his absence, the Matriarch has appointed me acting High Biologian. In addition to the support of the valkyries, I have the loyalty of the aerial guard and the remaining earth-dragon contingents here in the palace."

"Why bother appointing a puppet? Declare yourself king and be done with it."

Chapelion shook his head. "We sky-dragons operate best as the power *behind* the throne. Sun-dragons aren't to be trifled with. Whatever their intellectual deficiencies, they're still the largest winged predator the earth has ever seen, and they..." Again his voice trailed off. He seemed to be looking inside himself, as if searching for the right word, but when he spoke again, it was to correct something he'd already said. "Perhaps the phrase 'intellectual deficiencies' reveals my own prejudice. In truth, by any objective standards, sun-dragons may be our intellectual superiors. Their brains are much larger, after all. It's an overly comforting fiction that we sky-dragons embrace to think that sun-dragons aren't our equals. It's led to our underestimating them in the past."

"I'll take your word for it," said Vulpine. "You've educated the sons of many prominent sun-dragons; I'm certain in the university they show promise. But I deal with sun-dragons in the real world; they call on me when they've failed to keep their slaves under control. Most strike me as self-centered and slothful."

"Many are self-centered," agreed Chapelion. "But slothful? One sun-dragon alone disproved that notion. Did you know that, when I was but a young lecturer, one of my students was Blasphet himself?"

"The Murder God?" said Vulpine.

"The same. Though, back then, he hadn't yet turned to his murderous path. I remember him well. Blasphet possessed a genius that surpassed any dragon I've since met, of any species. He could read the thickest of tomes in the span of a few hours and recall the minutest details. What's more, he was quick to make connections between the things he learned; as a student he possessed an understanding of anatomy and chemistry that was unrivaled. The world lost a great mind when he was killed."

Vulpine swayed backwards on his hind-talons. Praise for the hated Murder God was like a slap across his snout. "Blasphet died invading the Nest! He was attempting genocide against our race! How can you proclaim him a great mind?"

"By choosing my words carefully," said Chapelion. "I didn't claim that Blasphet had a kind heart. I'm aware, in retrospect, that his intellectual pursuits were driven by his darker urges. He became an expert botanist to identify the various poisons produced by plants; he excelled in chemistry because it gave him the tools to extract and refine these poisons. He understood the detailed workings of the anatomy of dragons and humans primarily because it gave him insight into the most effective tortures. Most impressively, he was a keen student of the mind—his insights into psychology allowed him to manipulate humans to such a degree that they worshipped him as the Murder God. Yes, in his passing, the world was rid of a monster. Still, I mourn the loss of the knowledge he possessed. If he'd ever wearied himself of murder and turned his attention to writing down all that he knew, he could have advanced many disciplines by decades."

"Hmph," said Vulpine. "I'll leave you to ponder timelines that involve 'if' and 'could'. I'm more focused on here and now." He glanced down at the map. He unslung the metal tube he'd captured from Jandra, and thrust the end of it to a piece of parchment on which a small city by a river was circled in thick red lines. "Dragon Forge is the most urgent threat we face, Chapelion. I'll leave you to deal with politics. You can send diplomats to the abodes of the various sun-dragons and flatter, bribe, or deceive them into obeying you. But if the human rebellion spreads beyond Dragon Forge in any meaningful way, the entire fabric of the kingdom will be rent."

"Agreed," said Chapelion. "This adds urgency to my desire to select a new king. A strong army can…"

"Respectfully, sir," interrupted Vulpine, "you make a grave mistake if you wait for a new king to deal with this problem."

Chapelion shook his head. "You overestimate the threat these rebels pose. They only command one city; it is far from the abode of any sun-dragons. They can't spread their power far."

"It's not power I fear they will spread, but chaos," said Vulpine. "As I journeyed here, I saw many human towns abandoned. I see that the Free City is occupied, I assume by human refugees. If this unrest lasts into the spring, it will threaten the food supplies of the dragons. If no planting is done by humans, famine will spread through the land."

"What would you have me do? The rebels at Dragon Forge are said to possess a new type of bow that repelled an army of sun-dragons and earth-dragons."

"Give me command of half the aerial guard and a contingent of valkyries. Allow me to access the king's treasuries and buy back the loyalties of the earth-dragon soldiers that currently roam the kingdom as bandits. We need to establish a complete blockade of Dragon Forge."

Chapelion nodded thoughtfully. "You've always possessed a better strategic mind than I have, Vulpine. I've been so occupied with politics I've paid little attention to the human uprising."

"Right now humans around the kingdom are learning of mankind's little victory. Instead of allowing this news to spread hope of rebellion among the humans, it's important that men shiver with horror when they hear the words Dragon Forge. Humans are creatures of habit; they fear change. As long as they are kept relatively content, we control them because they have a difficult time imagining life any other way. Let Dragon Forge remain in human hands for long, however, and soon every last man in this kingdom will be embracing the romantic notion that he's a heroic rebel. It's a vision that infected Shay, after all, and you were certain he'd never betray you."

Chapelion sighed as he stared down at the map. He nudged his glasses further up his long face. His brow wrinkled as his eyes focused on the iron rod in Vulpine's fore-talon.

"What is this device you carry?"

"That's an excellent question," said Vulpine, lifting the instrument. "I took this from Shay. Jandra killed Balikan with an identical weapon. The device produced a loud, focused explosion that propelled lead pellets at an unimaginable speed. Balikan's head simply vanished. You are more the historian than I am, but I suspect this may be something that hasn't existed in this world for centuries: a gun."

"By the bones," Chapelion said reverently, reaching out to take the weapon. "The secret of manufacturing gunpowder vanished ages ago."

Vulpine held up the belt he'd taken. "This contains cotton pouches filled with black powder. I can identify some of the components by smell; I imagine Bazanel at the College of Spires can make short work of the recipe."

Chapelion turned the gun over and over in his claws, studying the firing mechanism, sniffing at the barrel. "The scale pattern in the steel is curious. Could it be evidence that it was manufactured by a dragon?"

Vulpine shook his head. "Since the steel is of recent origin, and since Shay's trail took him to Dragon Forge, I can only deduce the rebels at the foundry produced these."

"This is horrible," said Chapelion. "It was reported that they possessed a new type of bow. I didn't expect that they'd manufactured something like this."

"And they didn't expect us to capture one so quickly," said Vulpine. "If Bazanel can reproduce the chemistry of the powder, I'm certain that valkyrie engineers can duplicate the mechanics, or even improve them. We can negate their advantage in short order. If there's anyone left to kill at Dragon Forge when we've armed ourselves, I suspect we'll have the advantage."

Chapelion looked up from the gun. "What do you mean, 'if there's anyone left to kill?'"

"As Slavecatcher General, I receive reports on the conditions of slaves throughout the kingdom. There's always some new outbreak of disease: malaria, leprosy, yellow-mouth, or cholera. I have the authority to impose quarantines on slave trading with infected abodes until these outbreaks run their course. I propose that we harness one of these diseases as a weapon. We need something with a high mortality rate, something easily spread, and something that doesn't immediately produce symptoms. Our carrier will need to be healthy enough to get inside Dragon Forge, after all. There is currently an outbreak of yellow-mouth in the abode of Rorg. It doesn't have quite the mortality rate I'd like... more than half its victims survive. But it's active now, and spreads easily. A single infected human within the walls of Dragon Forge will cripple the place."

"You've given this some thought," said Chapelion.

"It's the nature of my job," said Vulpine. "I've spent years imagining responses to mass uprisings such as the one we face."

"Such imagination! Turning plague into a weapon of war," Chapelion said, shaking his head. "Not even Blasphet ever latched upon such a plan."

"Do you object to it?"

"No. I'll dispatch a messenger to the valkyries at once. Sagen here can serve as head of a squadron you select from among the aerial guard. The full treasury is at your disposal as well. Your plan is sound. Make it happen."

Vulpine lowered his head respectfully. "I'm honored by your trust."

"I recognize a great mind when I see one," said Chapelion.

CHAPTER EIGHT

CONSORT Of
DEMONS

JANDRA HELD THE silver bracelet in her fist as she
knelt on the cobblestone road. She gave the metal
ring a powerful *whack* against a stone. Anza
raised an eyebrow as a shower of sparks erupted
from the metal. She swiveled her head, as if trying to
pinpoint some distant sound.

Shay couldn't hear anything out of the ordinary.
They were well beyond the bustling activity of Richmond now, no more than a mile from the palace.
They'd left the fresh horses from Burke's Tavern in a
stable in town to make a stealthier approach.

It was still a few hours before dawn; Shay's breath
was coming out in great clouds. The world was perfectly still, quiet enough that the rustle of Shay's coat
as moved sounded loud.

The sparks from Jandra's magic bracelet swirled
around them. The air began to smell as if a storm had
recently passed through the area.

"We're invisible now," said Jandra.

"No we're not," said Shay, staring down at his hands.

"The mirrors have a radius of about fifteen feet. Anyone inside can see clearly. If you're outside the circle, the mirrors edit the scene and show only a background image."

Shay looked around. "I don't see any mirrors."

"These aren't the sort of mirrors you shave with. Magnetically Integrated Rapidly Rotating Optical Reversers are no bigger than a fleck of dust, all kept dancing on magnetic waves generated by the bracelet." She slid the bracelet back onto her arm.

Shay nodded, understanding at least part of her sentence. "You've made us invisible with magic dust?"

Jandra rolled her eyes. "Shay, you're going to have to trust me. I don't have time to explain everything I…" Her face paled as she gazed off into the distance. Anza drew her sword and turned to follow Jandra's gaze.

"What?" whispered Shay, clicking the safety off his shotgun.

"Put down your weapons," Jandra said. "I didn't mean to scare you."

"Why did you fall silent? Did you see something?" Shay asked, looking toward Anza. He wasn't going to put the safety back on until she relaxed. Anza stared into the dark, crouched as if ready to strike. Finally, she stood, the tension flowing from her body, and she silently slipped the sword back into its sheath.

Jandra ran her fingers through her hair. "It… it's hard to explain."

"Try us," said Shay.

Jandra didn't look directly at his face as she spoke. "Fine. I stopped talking because I suddenly had the urge to rewire your brain."

"I don't understand."

"When I said I didn't have time to explain everything, I found myself with the urge to reach out and physically rewire your brain. I wanted to give you some of my knowledge, until you were someone I could carry on a less frustrating conversation with."

Shay frowned. "I wasn't aware I was such a difficult person to talk to."

"You're not," said Jandra. She brought her fingers to her lips and started to bite her fingernails. Lizard watched her hands carefully. She caught herself and lowered her hands to her sides. "The urge to alter your brain came from the goddess. She manipulated my memories so that I'd be a better companion for her. Now I'm thinking the same way she did. Maybe Hex was right. Maybe Jazz has tainted me so badly I can't be trusted with power anymore."

As Jandra spoke, Anza wandered further up the road, about twenty feet away. She turned around and broke into a grin. She gave a thumbs-up sign.

"That one I understand," said Shay. "Apparently, we really are invisible. What I don't understand is why you won't admit to being a wizard. You use magic dust. You once possessed a genie. Why be coy about what's so plainly the truth?"

Jandra gave him a stern, serious look. "Jazz had the same powers I once had. It corrupted her. She allowed people to worship her, to think she was something more than human. I don't want anyone's worship. I think honesty is my best hope of avoiding corruption when I get my powers back."

"If you're afraid of getting your powers back, why have we come all this way?" asked Shay.

"I don't see any other option. So much in this world is broken, and I need my powers back if I want to fix it. I could heal Burke's leg, and restore Vance's sight." They'd left Vance in Thorny's care; his sight had never returned after his fall from the roof. "I might even figure out why Anza can't talk."

Anza tapped her foot on the cobblestones and looked toward the night sky.

"Let's move on," said Jandra. "But not too fast. The magnetic field of the bracelet isn't all that powerful. If we took off running, or encountered a strong wind, it would disrupt the pattern and we'd be visible again. It's a good thing it's a calm night."

Anza watched as the others walked toward her. Shay could tell the moment when they became visible to Anza by the way her eyes shifted their focus. He found himself increasingly comfortable with staring at Anza's face. There was a lot she could communicate with only subtle motions of her eyes and mouth. Anza didn't seem to mind being stared at. She projected a calm confidence when people were watching her. When Shay thought someone was watching him, he became self-conscious and awkward.

While he was comfortable staring at Anza, he still felt uncomfortable if Jandra caught him looking at her. Anza was beautiful, feminine in her grace and balance, yet somehow the multitude of weapons she boasted removed all temptation to think of her in a romantic fashion. Jandra was different. At first, he'd been put off by the idea that she was a dragon's pet. He'd assumed she'd be snooty and shallow, like other pets he'd encountered. Despite Jandra's impatience with his questions, he found her to be anything but snooty. She seemed, instead, to be driven by a need to help and protect others. Perhaps it was arrogant of her to assume that she could fix the world's problems, but Shay didn't judge her harshly for this. He found himself attracted to her nobility. Of course, he also found himself attracted to her in other ways.

Even dressed in her ill-fitting, borrowed clothes, Jandra had a simple beauty about her that he found enticing.

The Dragon Palace loomed before them like a mountain. The night felt colder in its shadow. Jandra pointed toward a tower. "I used to live there. See those high windows? My bed was just underneath them."

"It's dark," said Shay. "Do you think it's empty?"

"I'm keeping my fingers crossed," she said. "I'm hoping Blasphet's reputation kept visitors away."

Anza turned her head at the mention of the name.

"Blasphet?" asked Shay. "The Murder God?"

Jandra nodded. "He took over the tower after we fled. He's dead now. I left my old genie by my bed; if someone has taken it, this mission is going to have a disappointing end."

"Is the genie in a lamp?" Shay asked.

"No," said Jandra. "Whoever named the device had a sense of humor. A genie is a Global Encephalous Nanite Interaction Engine. It was the source of my powers, not magic."

Shay thought that this was splitting hairs but decided not to argue, as by now they were less than a hundred yards from the palace gate. Four earth-dragon guards stood at attention. Unlike the rugged, battle-scarred warriors they'd faced in Burke's Tavern, these guards were dressed in bright crimson uniforms.

"We can't sneak past them the way they're spaced," Jandra whispered.

"Should we find another entrance?" asked Shay. "If we fight, the noise will bring other guards."

Anza looked at him and smirked. She unsheathed her sword silently as she pressed her fingers to her lips. She crouched, slipping off toward some decorative bushes near the road side. She quickly vanished from view.

"I don't think we're going to have to worry about noise," whispered Jandra, as she waited for Anza to work her own brand of magic.

As THEY SLIPPED through the gates into the palace, Jandra felt a sense of disorientation. Having spent her recent weeks living among men, she'd gotten used to moving through landscapes built on a human scale. Stepping back into the home of sun-dragons made her feel tiny once more. Sun-dragons stood more than twice as tall as any human, even in a relaxed state. From snout to tail, adult sun-dragons averaged forty feet. Burke's loft at the central foundry would barely serve as a closet in the palace. The glazed ceramic bowls that sun-dragons used as drinking dishes could serve as a wash basin for her.

Anza had hidden the bodies of the four guards she'd slain, but it was only a matter of time before the breach in security was noticed and an alarm went out. Their invisibility would lose its strategic value if ox-dogs were brought in to search for intruders.

Perhaps sensing her worries, Lizard grew still. He was perched on her shoulder, one arm wrapped around her neck for balance. He had his head pressed against her cheek. Lizard's breath was somewhat worse than dog-breath—his diet consisted mainly of bugs, worms, and small rodents he caught himself. She lifted her hand and stroked the side of his head to soothe him, and also to gently nudge his beak a little further from her nose. His scales were dry and warm.

Jandra led Anza and Shay through a maze of hallways, arriving at last at the stone stairs that led up into the tower she'd once called home. A lone earth-dragon stood guard, but the stairway was broad enough that they could slip past him unseen. The earth-dragon cocked his head slightly as they neared. Shay's coat made a noise as he walked, a faint *swish swish*. Jandra's heavy boots also proved a poor choice of footwear for a stealth mission.

They slowed their pace to a crawl. The guard turned his head away, looking incurious. They tip-toed past, holding their breath. Anza, in her leather moccasins, never made even the faintest sound no matter how swiftly she moved.

They reached the top of the tower without any difficulty. Jandra had imagined a variety of worst case scenarios on their journey but so far their path through the palace was easier than she could have hoped. If her genie was still in the room, leaving the palace unseen would be no problem at all.

She pushed the heavy oak door of her former home open. The room was much as she'd left it only a month ago. The chamber was the shape of a vast star, with high windows overhead through which moonlight filtered, painting the flagstone floor with patches of pale white. Blasphet had emptied the chamber of Vendevorex's possessions. The room had once been filled with shelves stocked with books and curiosities. Jars of preserved snails and serpents, and skeletons of rabbits and turtles had all been learning aids in her study of anatomy. From a tender age she'd been led through dissections of sundry creatures, from the simplest slugs to the elaborate architecture of a bat's wing. Looking at the bare walls she was astonished that an absence of pickled worms could make her feel lonely.

After Shandrazel took the throne, the few meager items that Jandra could call her own had been brought back into the room. Her possessions were few: a small iron bed, its mattress stuffed with goose-feathers; a full length mirror in an oval wooden frame; a dresser upon which sat a collection of combs; a tall wardrobe; and a large oak trunk at the foot of her bed.

Her spirits lifted when she saw the lid of the trunk open, and various books and papers scattered randomly around it. This was how she'd left it after she'd searched through the trunk for Vendevorex's skullcap. She'd removed her tiara, donned his skullcap, and instantly discovered that his genie was more powerful than her own. Unfortunately, she'd donned the helmet on the same night that the Sisters of the Serpent had gone on a murderous rampage through the palace. This had launched Jandra into an adventure that had kept her from returning to the room. Her old tiara had been left sitting unprotected on her dresser.

In the moonlight, it was impossible to see from across the room if the tiara still sat on the dresser. She held her breath as she led the way toward it. A low, ragged groan escaped her as she neared. The tiara was gone.

"I'm so sorry," she said, shaking her head. "I've put you both in danger for nothing."

"It's not here?" asked Shay. "Who could have taken it?"

Jandra bit her nails as she thought. She said, "Hex was the only one who knew about the tiara's power. Maybe some palace guard took it. It looked like silver. It could have been sold easily enough."

"You've mentioned Hex a time or two," said Shay. "Why would he take this genie if he already had your other one?"

"Hex would want to destroy both genies. He had an innate distrust of power."

"That's an odd quality for a sun-dragon," said Shay. "They're the most powerful creatures of all."

"Hex didn't believe that might made right. In fact, he thought that might always eventually turned into wrong. He thought that all kings were inherently immoral."

"In other words," said Shay, "he was an anarchist."

"To the bone," said Jandra. "Fortunately, this made him the perfect companion to stand by my side and face up to the goddess. She was the embodiment of a power that had corrupted absolutely." She glanced into the mirror by the dresser, and then quickly looked away. With her baggy second-hand clothes and unwashed, tangled hair, she found herself frightening to look at. She sat down on the edge of her bed. Lizard hopped down from her shoulder. She stared down at the floor. "Until Hex betrayed me, I thought he was my best friend. I'm such an idiot."

Anza sat on the edge of the bed beside Jandra. Her eyes widened at how soft it was. She grinned and fell backwards onto the bed, her arms spread as she sunk into the silk-covered down.

Shay picked up one of the bone combs on the dresser, turning it over in his hands. Vendevorex had carved it from the femur of a bull, using the nanites at his command to carve Jandra's name in the surface of the comb hundreds of times in tiny decorative letters. Vendevorex had possessed the power to give her anything he could have imagined, but his gifts over the years had tended to be simple ones—objects of bone and stone and wood rather than gold or ivory. He hadn't wanted her to become enamored with wealth.

After a long, silent moment, Shay asked the question ringing loudly in Jandra's mind. "So, now what?"

Anza rolled over to her side, her head propped on her fist as she stared at Jandra. She obviously wanted to hear the answer to this as well.

Lizard didn't care about the question at all, assuming he even understood it. Instead, he hopped down to the floor and stared into the mirror. The row of bristly scales along his neck stood up as he spotted the small earth-dragon on the other side of the glass. He stretched out his claw, then snatched it back as the other dragon reached to touch him at the same time.

Jandra got up and paced as she thought. If a guard had taken the tiara, it might be in the palace barracks, or it could be in Richmond at some pawn shop. Where could she begin the search for it? And what if it wasn't a guard who took it, but Hex? The genies were too advanced to be destroyed outright, but Hex could hide them, maybe dropping them into the sea, or burying them like they'd buried the goddess's genie.

Jandra snapped her fingers. Lizard startled at the sound, jumping away from the mirror and leaping back onto Jandra's shoulder.

"We need to go to the mountains," she said. "We'll probably never find my old genie. But I know the location of a third one. It's my best hope at regaining my powers."

Even as she said the words, she questioned their wisdom. They'd buried the goddess's heart—her genie—to ensure that no unseen remnant of her could somehow be revived. Was she really so hungry for power that she was willing to go back and risk the return of the goddess? Was this her idea, or the idea of the unwelcome second passenger in her brain? For an instant, she started to tell the others it was a dumb idea, that they should just return to Dragon Forge and help Burke build guns. But thinking of Burke's broken leg let her remember all the good she could do if she had her powers once more. She had to take the chance. What was there to fear? The goddess was dead. Her body had been burned. Genies responded to a person's thoughts, and thoughts were the product of a brain, and Jazz's brain had been reduced to cinders that had blown off in the breeze. The chances of recovering from that were somewhat remote, thought Jandra.

Anza got up from the bed. She looked toward the door, cocking her head as she held up her hand, motioning the others to stop talking.

"What is—?" Shay began to ask.

Anza gave him a dirty look and drew a finger across her throat. Jandra heard noises in the hall, the sound of armor-clad guards climbing up stone stairs.

"Hurry," she whispered. "The invisibility circle is still active. Get to the center of the room. The more open space we keep around us, the easier it will be to evade them."

A hushed voice murmured beyond the door: "It's as you said. The door's open."

A louder voice replied: "Vulpine's understanding of human motivations is unsurpassed. It's... perhaps motivations isn't the correct word. It implies a higher order of thought for which there is only the faintest evidence in humans. Urges? Desires?"

"Oh no," said Shay, grabbing Jandra's arm, speaking as softly as he could. "It's Chapelion!"

"He's not very good at stealth," whispered Jandra.

"He's half deaf. He probably thinks he's whispering."

An earth-dragon poked his head into the open doorway, his dull eyes scanning the darkness. Jandra recognized this dragon—it was Ledax. She'd saved his life during the attack of the Sisters of the Serpent, neutralizing a poison in his blood. Of course, he'd been unconscious and she hadn't stuck around to take credit. She couldn't count on his gratitude. Lizard's hind claws sank more firmly into her shoulders as he stared at the adult earth-dragon.

Anza silently drew her sword from its scabbard. With her left hand, she freed a tomahawk from her belt. Jandra reached out and touched her shoulder; Anza looked back. Jandra shook her head. They were still invisible. It wasn't yet time for violence.

"Nobody's here, boss," said Ledax, looking back into the hallway.

Chapelion said, "Make certain."

Ledax entered the room, a battle axe clutched in both hands. Behind him, Jandra heard the shuffling of other guards. It sounded as if a small army was waiting on the steps. Anza crouched lower, ready to spring. Ledax didn't approach the center of the room. Instead he followed the wall, eyeing a slender rope that lead high up into the darkness. It was one of the ropes that held the unlit lanterns. Only, when Jandra looked up into the gloom, she couldn't see any of the lanterns. Instead she saw... what? It was like some sort of grid laid out on the ceiling, millions of small squares covering the entire space.

Suddenly, she knew what she was looking at. Throwing away all hope of stealth, she cried out, "Stop him!"

It was too late. Ledax swung his axe toward the rope. Sparks flew as it bit into the stone wall, severing the hemp. The frayed end shot upward. Anza leapt as Shay brought his shotgun to his shoulder. Jandra grabbed Lizard and held him to her breast as she curled down to absorb the impact on her back.

The net hit. It was heavy, woven from ropes a half inch thick, in a mesh of three inch squares. The impact caught Anza in mid-leap, and knocked the shotgun from Shay's hands as he pulled the trigger. The gun barked out, spitting fire, sending chips of granite flying as the shot tore into the flagstones.

Jandra calmly stood up, pulling out the knife Burke had given her. The air was full of silver dust. The rush of wind that had accompanied the falling net had disrupted their invisibility, not that it mattered much now. She grabbed the mesh before her as earth-dragons marched into the room, encircling their prisoners. There were at least fifty guards plus another ten sky-dragons. She noted with some surprise that the sky-dragon group was of mixed sex—there were four males from the aerial guard, and five valkyries from the Nest. The sexes rarely mingled among sky-dragons. Stepping in front of all these was an older sky-dragon, a familiar face from many of the formal events at the palace, though she'd never personally met him.

"Chapelion!" Shay cried out, now down on his knees, growing more entangled in the net as he struggled. "How could you know I'd be here? How?"

"Don't be so egotistical, Shay," Chapelion said. "We didn't lay this trap for you. Jandra is the true prize."

Anza was perfectly still beneath her section of the net. Jandra wondered if the impact had knocked her out. Then, with a barely perceptible motion, Anza carefully cut another of the ropes that entwined her with a knife no longer than her thumb. Frayed ends lay down the entire mid-section of her body.

Jandra decided to make sure the dragons were focused on her instead of Anza.

"You know I'm Jandra, daughter of Vendevorex," she said, mimicking the deep, theatrical voice that her master used to summon. "I command the same mystical forces he possessed. Leave if you value your life! This net cannot hold me."

"Your claims would be more convincing if you weren't still in the net," said Chapelion. Sky-dragons couldn't smile, but there was a gleam in his eyes that indicated he was pleased with himself. "If you do possess mystical powers, I invite you to demonstrate them. The slaves whisper that you gain your powers from consorting with demons. I have other, more rational theories. Vulpine delivered a device he took from you, a weapon that an uneducated observer might think of as a magic wand. I know it was only a trick of chemistry and metalwork—I've sent it to Bazanel at the College of Spires for analysis. I do not fear your so-called magic."

Chapelion glanced toward the guards. "Place manacles on Jandra and Shay. The girl in the buckskins is unimportant. Dispose of her."

Before the guards could move, Anza leapt to her feet, the sliced ropes falling away from her body. She spun in a graceful circle, her sword extended full length, at throat-level for the earth-dragons. She made a noise, the first Jandra had ever heard from Anza's mouth, as she rapidly clicked her tongue against her teeth while sucking in air, *"tk-tk-tk-tk!"* The noise was as a chilling as a rattlesnake's warning.

Jandra took inspiration from Anza's dark skin and pitch black hair and the icy menace of her gaze.

"You should have listened to your slaves, Chapelion. I do consort with demons. This one sloughed off your net as if it were water. She can kill your guards before you can blink. Leave this place at once."

Chapelion stared through his spectacles at Anza. His eyes narrowed as he analyzed the situation. Anza met his stare with an unblinking gaze.

"I see moisture upon her neck," he said. "Would a demon sweat?"

"How would you know?" asked Jandra.

Chapelion furrowed his brow, contemplating the matter.

Before he could speak, Jandra heard distant shouts from below. Jandra wasn't certain, but it sounded like someone was shouting, "Fire!"

Chapelion's eyes flickered toward the door, as if he, too, heard the cries.

From outside the tower, there was a strange skittering sound. The noise resembled nothing so much as the scratching of a thousand large squirrels climbing the stone walls. A shadow passed across the high windows as something long and serpentine slithered across one, then another, then another, spreading darkness.

Jandra could sense the panic building among the earth-dragons. With no idea whatsoever what was climbing the walls outside, she decided to bluff: "Anza isn't the only demon I've summoned tonight."

Almost as if her words had made it happen, one of the high windows exploded inward, shards of glass flying through the room. Cold night air swirled into the chamber as a human figure appeared in the window. He was mostly in shadow, his body contours partially concealed by a cape. One thing that was easily visible, however, was the bow he held, and the arrow pointed straight at Chapelion's heart.

With a voice as cold as the winter wind, the new arrival said, "I've set your library on fire, dragon."

Chapelion chuckled and looked to Jandra. "I can't help but notice that all your demons look human. This is a rather quaint bluff. I'm more entertained than intimidated, however. Hmm. 'Entertained' isn't quite what I mean. Amused, I should say."

The man in the high window released an arrow. It landed not in Chapelion, however, but in the valkyrie who stood beside him. She fell to her back, the green-fletched bolt jutting from the round disk of her right ear.

Before any of the dragons could react, loud voices echoed up the staircase leading to the tower. "Find Chapelion! He must know!" Chapelion turned his head upon hearing his name.

"Your love of books is legendary, Chapelion. I could place an arrow in your brain, but that would rob me of the satisfaction of imagining you standing in the remnants of the Grand Library with all its millions of books nothing more than ash and smoke."

Chapelion shuddered as his eyes grew wide. An earth-dragon ran up the stairs, stumbling to a halt in the doorway. "The Grand Library!" he shouted. "*Fire!*"

Chapelion silenced him by raising his fore-talon.

"Take your guards," said the archer. "Leave this place. Perhaps a book or two may still be saved. Jandra and the others will remain. They're mine now."

"Who are you?" Chapelion growled.

"You know who I am."

Jandra knew as well: Bant Bitterwood, dragon-hunter, god-slayer, psychopath. His sense of timing, as always, was impeccable.

Chapelion looked as if he were in physical pain as he motioned to his guards. "We can waste no more time. Leave the humans. Go to the library."

"Hurry," said Bitterwood. "Old paper burns so quickly."

Chapelion looked up as the dragons filed past him. "You'll never escape this castle!" he snarled, before turning and marching from the room, leaving the humans alone. The door to the tower slammed shut.

"Seal it!" Chapelion barked from the stairs. "Have every member of the aerial guard surround the tower! They must not escape!"

Anza danced across the net. Jandra flinched as Anza's sword slashed out at her, again and again. Seconds later, the net fell away. Anza turned to free Shay.

Bitterwood dropped from the high window into the room. He looked at Jandra as Lizard climbed back onto her shoulder. "Is that an earth-dragon child? He can't come with us."

"He can and he will," said Jandra.

Bitterwood opened his mouth, but Jandra cut him off. "You always lose these arguments, so let's skip over the banter and get out of here."

Bitterwood glowered at her and nodded.

Shay shook free of the cut ropes that draped him as Anza stepped back. His voice was trembling as he walked toward the man who'd just saved them. "Did... did you... did you really set fire to the Grand Library?"

"Of course," Bitterwood answered in a matter-of-fact tone, as if Shay had asked something trivial.

"Monster!" Shay swung out his lanky right arm in a furious arc, planting his balled-up fist directly into the teeth of the dragon-slayer.

Bitterwood's head snapped sideways, but he wasn't knocked off balance. He calmly wiped his lips with the back of his hand as he stared at Shay. Shay was trembling with rage, his fists clenched, raising his arms to strike again.

Bitterwood kneed Shay in the groin. Shay doubled over and Bitterwood brought both of his fists down onto the back of Shay's skull. The former slave slammed down onto the net, completely still.

Bitterwood looked down and spat. His saliva was pink with blood as it splashed onto Shay's neck. "He looks familiar," he said. "Did I save his life some-where?"

"You can ask him after he wakes up," said Jandra, rushing over to her wardrobe and swinging its doors open. "Since you knocked him out, you'll be carrying him."

"Like hell I will," said Bitterwood. Jandra gave him a stern glance. Bitterwood shook his head in disgust as he leaned down and grabbed Shay's collar.

CHAPTER NINE

A TORCH TO VANQUISH

SHAY COUGHED HIMSELF awake; smoke scoured his lungs. At least, he felt like he was awake, though the evidence of his eyes argued that he was trapped within a nightmare. He was a hundred feet in the air on the exterior of a stone tower, slung over a white saddle on the back of a fifty-foot long, copper-colored serpent. He should be falling—the beast he rode was moving along the vertical wall of the tower, racing across it as easily as if it were flat ground, gripping the walls with dozens of sharp-clawed legs. Fortunately, the saddle felt as if it were coated with glue—his stomach was held firmly against it in defiance of gravity.

Craning his neck and squinting to see through the haze of smoke, he found that the copper serpent was studded with riders both familiar and strange. Jandra sat on the saddle in front of him with Lizard standing on her shoulder, hissing loudly as he shook his small fist at the flock of sky-dragons wheeling toward them. Behind him Anza crouched upon a white saddle, her fingers bristling with throwing knives. He felt a sense of vertigo… given the angle at which she was perched, she should be falling. Behind her, near the tail of the beast, a black and white pig wore a silver visor that hid his eyes. It sat upon the saddle serenely, oblivious to the swaying, lurching gait of the serpent as it undulated across the tower. Beyond the pig sat a little blonde girl, perhaps ten years old, thin even by Shay's scarecrowish standard. She, too, wore a metal visor that hid her eyes.

At the beast's head Bitterwood stood in his saddle, his bow drawn, firing arrow after arrow into the swarm of dragons that dove toward them. Shay stared at the legendary dragon-slayer. He was a good deal shorter than Shay, and not particularly heroic in his stance or gestures. He looked like one of the field slaves at middle age, weathered, wizened, and worn out. The deep wrinkles around his eyes twitched as they flickered from target to target. His hands moved with inhuman speed back and forth from quiver to bow. The bowstring sang with a musical rhythm, humming for a few seconds until an arrow was placed against it once more, *zuum, zuum, zuum, zuum*. The arrows, he noted, had the same bright green leaves fletching them as the arrows that had killed the slavecatchers by the river.

Shay tried to rise, if "rise" had any true meaning in this strange sideways world he'd woke in. As he moved, his center of gravity began to spin. He felt the ground below calling to him. He grabbed at the beast's scales, overlapping thin disks, metallic in their chill. He found himself slipping.

"Don't struggle," the blonde girl called out. "The saddle will hold you if you let it."

Shay struggled. His legs were now dangling straight down.

He was looking toward Anza, who rolled her eyes. She hurled her throwing knives heavenward and a sky-dragon suddenly tilted and fell, its wings limp. Anza pulled her long sword from the scabbard over her back. She raised it over her head, and swung the flat of the blade at Shay.

Thunder cracked somewhere near the base of his skull and the world went dark once more.

SHAY WOKE TO the slightly sweet stink of manure and hay. He was flat on his back on a large bale of straw, his head pounding with each heartbeat. He raised his hand to discover a knot the size of walnut on the back of his scalp. He sat up, trying to remember where and why he'd gotten the injury. He was in a barn, with horses in stalls staring at him lazily. It was distantly familiar; he knew he'd been here before. This barn was attached to an inn on the edge of Richmond. It was where they had left their horses before going to the Dragon Palace.

He rose on trembling legs. There were voices outside, familiar ones. He stumbled toward the barn door. It hurt to walk. He remembered Bitterwood's ungentlemanly assault. Kicking someone in the balls wasn't behavior he would have expected from a legendary champion of humanity.

Shay pushed the barn door open and his eyes were instantly drawn toward the horizon. Flames shot into the air in a huge inferno that reached to the stars themselves. The Grand Library, housing a thousand years of history and literature, was now the world's largest bonfire. He dropped to his knees in the barnyard muck, feeling ill. Not more than ten feet away, sitting on the edge of a rain barrel, Jandra watched the flames as well. Squatting on the ground before her was the old man, Bitterwood.

Jandra was now wearing a calf-length coat that fit as if it had been tailored for her. The fabric was pale blue, the same color as a sky-dragon's wings. Shay had gotten used to seeing Jandra in the shapeless, drab, earth-dragon coat. She looked smaller now, yet at the same time more powerful, more like a sorceress than a refugee. She shook her head as she watched the flames. "Bant, it's not that I don't appreciate the rescue, but this was a pretty horrible thing to do."

"It got you out of the palace with minimal danger," said Bitterwood.

"Since when do you worry about danger? I'm amazed you let Chapelion live. You're normally not so merciful."

"Mercy had nothing to do with it," said Bitterwood. "I came here to save you, not kill Chapelion."

"You had him in your sights," she said.

"He wasn't the biggest threat. You were trapped by a net, surrounded by armed earth-dragons. As good as I am, I'm not positive I could have kept you alive if a battle had broken out."

"The one thing I'm not clear on is how, exactly, you knew I needed saving?"

"You understand it better than I, no doubt. Zeeky still hears whispers from the crystal ball the goddess gave her. The ghosts inside can see the future. They told Zeeky to save you. I wasn't in favor of dropping everything to chase you across the countryside, but I don't fare any better arguing with her than I do with you."

"Hmm," said Jandra. "Jazz said that if you were trapped in underspace, you could see the past and future with equal clarity. I know Zeeky's crystal ball contains a tiny sliver of underspace. Jazz said she kept her best secrets to herself... Underspace was one of those secrets. I have only a rough understanding of the science behind it. Apparently there are more dimensions to the world than the three we normally perceive. Alas, the practical science of traveling through these extra dimensions wasn't shared with me." In the distance, there was a horrible rumble. Sparks shot into the air like fireworks as a huge section of the upper tower crumbled and collapsed inward. "Shay's going to have a fit when he hears about this," Jandra said.

Shay realized they didn't know he was there. He pulled himself up from the muck, his fists clenched. "Y-you..." he growled as he stalked toward Bitterwood. "You... you... *you!*"

"Unclench your fists, boy," said Bitterwood, his eyes narrowing into slits. "I let you off easy. Swing at me and you'll never eat solid food again."

Shay couldn't open his fists if he wanted to. He couldn't move at all—rage paralyzed him. His voice came out in a low, hissing whisper: *"How could you?"*

Bitterwood shrugged. "I'm good at hitting things. If I can knock the teeth out of a sun-dragon, I reckon I can do the same to a skinny house-slave."

Jandra smirked. "I think he meant how could you set the library on fire."

"Oh," said the dragon-slayer. "That was nothing. I just broke a lantern."

"RRRaaah!" Shay snarled as he threw his arms up in the air in his frustration, shaking his fists at the stars. He hopped up and down, releasing guttural growls, his anger stripping him of all coherent thought. Within the barns, a horse whinnied.

"Calm down, Shay," said Jandra. "You're spooking the horses."

Shay stopped moving. He concentrated on the breath flowing in ragged gushes across his lips. He opened and closed his trembling hands as he tried to gain control of his rage. He whispered, "Th-there... there were over a m-million books in that Library. Do you have any idea what an *evil* thing you have done?"

"Books have never done the world any good, boy," said Bitterwood. "At least, no good for humans. Dragons have spent a thousand years writing books that justify why they rule the world. Good riddance, I say."

Shay was certain that he was going to vomit in his anger. He dropped to his hands and knees, shuddering, feeling as if his heart was going to burst. "I'm cursed," he moaned. "It's the only explanation. Every book I'm near bursts into flame. I've nothing left to live for."

Bitterwood shook his head in disgust. Jandra hopped off the barrel and crouched next to Shay. She put her hand on his shoulder. "There's no such thing as a curse," she said. "We've just had a run of bad luck. It's a time of war. Things get burnt."

"But—"

"Listen," she said. "Burke was right. Books are more than paper and ink. The information inside them is essentially immortal. Not all the books in the library are lost. I have images of thousands of them inside my head, complete editions. If I can get my genie back, I can recreate them molecule by molecule, the paper, the ink, everything."

"I don't understand," Shay said.

"I'm not following you either," Bitterwood said.

"I mean when I had my genie, I possessed total recall. Any book I'd ever read was still stored in my brain. They're still there, I just don't know how to access them."

"No," said Bitterwood. "I mean, you said you needed to get your genie back. I know you had changed it so that it no longer looked like a helmet, and were wearing it beneath your clothes. Are you saying you've lost it?"

"I guess quite a bit's happened since we last saw each other. Hex and I went from the Nest to Dragon Forge to learn more about the rebellion and see if there was anything we could do to help."

"But… Hex was a sun-dragon," said Shay. "Why would he help the rebels?"

Jandra stood up and turned away. She had her back to them as she said, "I mean we came to help Shandrazel put down the rebellion." She tensed as she said this, as if expecting Bitterwood to pounce on her. Bitterwood didn't appear to be surprised by this revelation, however.

"Why would you side with the dragons?" asked Shay.

"I was raised by a dragon. I'm afraid my loyalties have always been divided. I don't think that humans have gotten a fair shake in this world, but I also know from personal experience that most dragons are good, reasonable beings."

"Dragons hold slaves and hunt men for sport. We have different definitions of what comprises good and reasonable," said Shay.

Jandra's shoulders sagged at these words.

"I'm surprised Hex would side with his brother," said Bitterwood. "His philosophies leaned toward anarchy."

"I'm afraid you're a better judge of his character than I was," said Jandra. "I visited Dragon Forge as Shandrazel's ambassador. Pet accompanied me back to see Shandrazel, saying he was the one human who had a chance of peacefully negotiating a settlement between the warring sides. Unfortunately, he had a poisoned dagger hidden in his cloak. He murdered Shandrazel. Before I could neutralize the poison, Hex pounced on me and ripped my genie away, robbing me of my powers. I was left to watch both Shandrazel and Pet die, while Hex flew off with the most powerful weapon in the world."

"Hex is only alive because you made me promise not to kill him."

"I know," said Jandra.

"Hex is the only blood kin left of Albekizan," said Bitterwood.

"I know," Jandra said, biting her nails once more.

"Will you free me from my vow?"

Jandra wrung her hands. "Do what you have to do," she said. "But he may not have the genie. He's probably hidden it somewhere. If you find him... it... it's possible that..."

"I know how to bleed a dragon of his secrets," said Bitterwood.

"I... I don't think Hex is evil," she said, her voice trembling. "He... he thinks he's doing the right thing. He thinks he's making the world a better place."

Bitterwood looked toward the burning tower. "You'll sleep better after you give up that hope."

Shay rose up onto his knees. "Jandra, if you have books inside you, I will do everything in my power to bring you back your genie."

"You have no power, boy," said Bitterwood. "Hex would eat you for supper."

Shay wished his shotgun were nearby. It hadn't been by his side when he woke up. He would gladly demonstrate this power for Bitterwood.

"I think we should go back to Jazz's underground kingdom," said Jandra.

"Why?" asked Bitterwood.

"Hex and I left in a hurry, since we wanted to get back to the Nest to help in the aftermath of Blasphet's atrocities. We didn't search her island. I might find another genie there."

"You wouldn't survive the journey," said Bitterwood. "That kingdom was held together by her will. Now that the goddess is dead, many of the beasts she cared for will be hungry."

"I can't believe they'd still be alive," said Jandra. "That whole ecosystem had to collapse once the artificial sunlight went out."

"I won't go with you," said Bitterwood. "I rescued you as a favor for Zeeky; I don't plan to make a career of it."

"So what will you do?"

Bitterwood pulled an arrow from his quiver. "The goddess gave me this bow and quiver. The quiver constantly refreshes itself, growing new arrows. The arrows are living things, twigs straight and true, with leaves for fletching and a thorn for a head. This bow, which is strung with a braid of the goddess's own hair, is the most perfectly balanced weapon I've ever used. It, too, constantly renews itself. When the bowstring frays in the heat of usage, it reweaves moments later. I've scuffed the bark of the bow and watched it heal itself. I don't know how long this magic will last, now that she's dead."

"It could last a long time," said Jandra. "Bio-nano is resilient stuff. As long as your quiver gets sunlight, it should function for years."

"How do plants grow with no water?" Shay asked. "Or no soil, for that matter."

"Orchids and other epiphytes don't need soil," said Jandra, "Bitterwood is probably supplying the quiver with all that it needs. The human body sheds moisture and nutrients, like dead skin cells. The quiver grabs those for fuel, I'm guessing. After you work for a while on the nano-scale, you get used to thinking of dust as a resource."

"Perhaps," said Bitterwood. "But I'm used to thinking of dust as the fate of all men. My days on this earth are numbered. Watching this endlessly renewing quiver has brought many things to mind. I think I died in that cave above Big Lick. You brought me back, Jandra."

"Oh," she said. "That. Your heart was only stopped for a minute or two. You were in a state of cardiac arrest, but you still had brain activity."

"If I were in a similar state now, you couldn't save me," said Bitterwood.

"Not without my powers, no," said Jandra.

"You asked me why I didn't kill Chapelion. Why I didn't simply leap into the fray and take on fifty dragons at once. The truth is, despite the fact that you've restored me to full health, I'm growing old, Jandra. Zeeky has no relatives, save for her missing brother, Jeremiah. If I die, who will care for her?"

"What are you saying, Bant?" asked Jandra.

"I'm saying that I'm giving up my life as a dragon hunter." Bitterwood looked up toward the sky, at the few stray stars visible through the smoke that veiled the night. "If I stumble across Hex, I'll kill him, but I'm not hunting him. I'm going back to the mountains to search for Jeremiah. Once I've found him, I want to return to the life I once lived as a farmer. I'd like to raise Zeeky and the boy in an environment as close to peace and stability as an old fool like myself can provide."

Jandra's jaw slackened. "You're retiring?"

"I've killed more dragons than I can count. I've rid the world of Albekizan's family, save for Hex. There are no sun-dragons who legitimately claim the bloodline of the ancient kings. The sun-dragons are fracturing polit-ically. They can fight among themselves for a while. Let Kanati and his rebels at Dragon Forge deal with the survivors."

Shay felt his anger rise again. "I can't believe you won't go to help the rebels. You're famous through-out the kingdom as the greatest hope of humanity. Why turn your back on us now?"

Bitterwood walked toward Shay, who was still on his knees. Shay turned his face as Bitterwood bowed down to his level. The old man's hot breath washed over him as he whispered, "Hope has never caused a single arrow to fly from my bow-string. Hate is the only cause I've fought for. Hate is like a fire in a man's belly, feeding him when all the food in the world cannot abate his hunger. I've lived with this hate for twenty years, boy. If a man's soul burns long enough, eventually nothing is left but ash. The fire fades once all the fuel is spent."

Bitterwood had two voices. There were times when he was relaxed and spoke like any other man. But other times, in more poetic language, he spoke with a low tone cold as a winter wind. If the damned in hell could speak, they must surely possess voices like this.

Shay blurted out, against his better judgment, "I don't know who these children are that you speak of raising, but I have pity for them."

Bitterwood chuckled. "I'm not a fit father for a normal child," he admitted, sounding human once more. "Luckily, Zeeky doesn't require a father so much as a taller person to get things for her off shelves. She really doesn't even need that now that she has the long-wyrm."

"Long-wyrm?" asked Shay. "I had a dream after you knocked me out. We were on the side of a tower, riding on a copper-colored serpent with a hundred limbs as sky-dragons darted all around."

"That wasn't a dream," said Jandra. "Long-wyrms only have twenty-eight legs, by the way. It just looks like more."

"There weren't that many sky-dragons either," said Bitterwood. "I think my reputation may have kept the full aerial guard from turning out... or perhaps they were busy with the fire. I couldn't have shot more than twenty-three before the sky was empty."

"But... were we sideways on the tower? Why didn't we fall?"

"Hyperfriction," said Jandra.

"What?"

"Gravity isn't that hard a force to overcome. The Atlanteans know how to craft material with exotic properties, and the saddles are made of a type of plastic that exhibits something called hyperfriction. You could sit upside down on one and not fall off unless you struggled. It doesn't take much energy to break the hyperfriction's grip, but it's more than strong enough to resist gravity."

"I don't understand anything you just said to me," said Shay.

Jandra shrugged. "Sorry. Working with nanites, I'm used to dealing with surface tension and static. A sticky saddle is useful for a mount that can cling to a ceiling. I can see why Jazz invented it."

"Then... if I didn't dream the long-wyrm, where is it? And where's Anza? And Lizard, for that matter?"

"Skitter spooks the horses," said Bitterwood, "Zeeky took him down to the river. Anza went with her, and so did Lizard."

Shay was surprised. "Lizard never lets himself get more than a few yards away from Jandra."

"Zeeky has a way of winning over the loyalties of beasts," said Bitterwood.

"Lizard isn't a beast," said Jandra. "He's a child. A dragon child, perhaps, but he's not an animal. Young dragons aren't that much different than young people."

"You know nothing about earth-dragons," said Bitterwood. "They're far more animalistic than men. They're instinctually tuned to both respect and fear older, bigger dragons. They respond to being bossed around. Once they get bigger than the dragons who boss them, however, they're quick to test their position in the pecking order. You see a lot of earth-dragons with scars, missing claws, or tails bitten off at the end. They aren't earning these injuries in battle with humans. They inflict these wounds on each other in their constant need to test their position in the hierarchy. Once Lizard puts on another fifty pounds, don't be surprised if he tries to test his strength against you, probably when you least expect it. Even little, his beak is sharp enough to take off a finger if you're careless. Give him a year, and it might be your hand that winds up missing."

"It doesn't have to be that way," said Jandra. "Lizard has a sweet nature. He's responding to my nurturing."

"Believe what you want," said Bitterwood.

Shay agreed with Bitterwood, but there was no way he was going to admit it. He leaned back against the barn wall and looked off toward the distant fire. Another large section of the tower crumbled. Long tongues of flame leapt up and licked the smoke above. Sparks swirled until they vanished in the darkness. In truth, there was something mystically beautiful about the sight. When Shay talked with other humans, he'd never been able to fully explain the magic of books, the sheer illumination and heat that came from crisp, lyrical prose revealing some hidden aspect of the world. Now, at last, here it was, revealed for all to see: the hidden energy of books released, a torch to vanquish the night.

CHAPTER TEN

SCARECROWS

ZEEKY SAT ON a boulder on the river bank as Anza slipped out of her buckskins. Anza's breath hung before her in clouds as she contemplated the deep, slow-moving water before her. Skitter had already slipped into those waters and was slithering about unseen beneath the surface, no doubt feasting on fat and drowsy catfish in the predawn stillness. Skitter was always a little nervous; the smell of smoke from the burning library, combined with the attack of the aerial guard, had left him especially high strung. A swim in the dark, ice-cold water was just the thing to calm him, Zeeky knew. No doubt, Anza had similar motivations. But where Skitter had slid right into the river without hesitation, Anza stood with her arms crossed over her breasts, looking as if she might be on the verge of changing her mind.

"It's best just to jump right in," said Zeeky. "It won't be so bad once you've taken the plunge."

Anza cocked her head and looked at her with challenging eyes, as if she was daring Zeeky to prove her assertion.

"I'm not the one who wanted to swim," said Zeeky. "And I'm not the one who's standing here buck naked. Go on and get in the water before you corrupt my pig."

Anza and Zeeky both looked at Poocher. Poocher was staring at Anza with something akin to a leer. Poocher was almost six months old, on the verge of pig puberty. His front teeth had recently begun to push from his mouth as tusks, giving him a somewhat threatening appearance even when he was perfectly content. Poocher was also starting to get really big; the sweet little runt that Zeeky could cradle in her arms was long gone. As a piglet, Poocher had been sweet, completely open to Zeeky's mothering. Now, Poocher was more standoffish. He was pushy and grabby with food, and could become sulky and sullen if denied something he wanted. Poocher had become more assertive around the time that he'd helped kill the goddess, charging her from behind and knocking her from her feet at a pivotal moment of the battle. Something had changed in the pig's self-image. He was no longer Zeeky's cuddly friend. He was now a young warrior boar with an attitude.

Anza stepped to the edge of the flat stone and started to stick a toe in the water. She stopped, balanced above the dark surface. Her face hardened as if some voice in her head had suddenly won an internal argument. She crouched and sprang, shooting out over the water, her long black hair trailing behind her in a perfect arc. With her hands held like an arrow before her, she sliced into the river with barely a splash.

For a moment, there was only the faint outline of her body moving beneath the surface. Her head burst back into the air as she sucked in a deep gasp. She bobbed in the water as her teeth chattered.

"I'm curious," said Zeeky. "Why don't you ever talk?"

Anza raised an eyebrow, as if she found this to be an absurd question.

"When the goddess kidnapped me, she said she'd changed my brain before I was born. She said I was the harbinger of a new kind of human, able to communicate with almost all animals. Most people aren't aware of all the things around them that are talking. Dogs talk, pigs talk, birds talk. And people especially talk even when they aren't using words, even when they don't know they're talking."

Anza sank lower in the water, hiding her lips beneath the surface. "I know more things than I tell Bitterwood," said Zeeky. "I'm the only one who can hear the whispers that come from my magic ball. The villagers inside tell me things; they don't always make sense. And half the time, they get stuff wrong. But knowing the future half the time ain't bad."

Anza continued to stare. Beneath the surface, her arms traced serpentine paths as she gracefully held her balance.

Zeeky looked around the riverbank, making certain they were alone. She reached into her bag and pulled out the heavy cotton towel she'd taken from the goddess's abode. She unwrapped it, revealing a sphere of flawless crystal, about the size of a large orange, with a faint rainbow flickering in its center. Gazing into its surface here in the darkness, she once again caught a glimpse of the tiny tornadoes that bubbled into existence around the rainbow then just as quickly vanished. Wormholes, Gabriel had called them. They were shaped like trumpets, tinier than gnats. The angel had explained it was through these trumpets that her relatives trapped in underspace could speak to her. She listened closely, tilting her head as she tried to pull words out of the constant ghostly murmuring.

There was a soft splashing sound as Anza rose from the river and walked up the rocky shore. Zeeky tossed her a white cotton towel. Anza's skin had looked almost snowy beneath the water, but against the white of the towel it was brown as a pecan shell. Her lips were tinted blue as she drew closer to Zeeky. She stooped to study the crystal ball while she used the towel to dry her hair.

"Listen," said Zeeky. "Do you hear them?"

Anza leaned closer, holding her breath. A long moment passed before she let the air slide between her lips. She looked disappointed.

"I thought you might hear them," said Zeeky. "Even though the goddess didn't change your brain, you've changed your brain yourself."

Anza cast a quizzical gaze at Zeeky.

"The villagers told me I would meet a girl with a stone in her throat. You can't make the same sounds most people can; you can whistle, make tongue clicks, and some other sounds, right? If you'd want-ed to communicate by sound, you could."

Anza pursed her lips, as if she wasn't ready to reveal her secrets.

"You also found out at an early age that by not talking, you were better at listening. You hear and see things other people don't; you can smell and taste and feel things better too. I'm right, aren't I?"

A hint of a smile flickered across Anza's lips. She lifted a finger and made a shushing motion.

"Your secret's safe with me," said Zeeky. "But I was told something by the villagers before we left the cave. The stone is going to be taken out of your throat. You'll be able to talk normally if you want. Would you like that?"

Anza narrowed her eyes and curled her lips downward, a look somewhere between disgust and skepticism.

"'We shall all be healed,' they whispered," said Zeeky.

Anza tilted her head.

"I don't know exactly what it means either," said Zeeky. "I wanted to tell you before you leave us tonight."

Anza's eyebrows rose again.

"How did I know? According to my crystal ball, you're going to leave us to go recover the shotgun Vulpine stole."

Anza nodded, looking impressed.

"I wish I could tell you more," said Zeeky. "But the villagers say that talking about the future runs the risk of changing it."

Before they could discuss the matter further, there was a rustling sound in the nearby forest. Anza leapt like a doe back to her clothes on the rock, the white towel fluttering in the air where she'd released it mid-leap. She had her buckskins up over her shoulders in the span of seconds, though they gaped in the front, unlaced all the way down to below her belly button. She grabbed her sword and spun to face the rustling leaves.

Lizard scampered out from the woods. He skipped toward Zeeky, his fists full of fat white grubs. More grubs—or at least grub parts—spilled from his turtle-like beak as he chewed on his newly discovered treat.

He squatted before Zeeky and held out his treasure. "Good eat, wise boss," he said.

Zeeky shook her head and pointed toward Poocher. "I'm vegetarian. Fat boss would enjoy them, though."

Poocher grunted happily at the offering. He gave a snort as he rose and waddled over. Lizard looked at Poocher with an expression that conveyed awe—and also hunger. As Poocher's skillful lips and tongue snatched the grubs one by one, Lizard chewed his own grubs more slowly. Zeeky knew what Lizard was thinking. It was almost cute that the little green turtle-monkey was seriously weighing his odds of making a meal out of Poocher. Almost.

"Don't even think about it," said Zeeky. "Poocher knocked a goddess onto her butt in the last fight he was in. You wouldn't stand a chance."

Poocher sneered at the little dragon.

"And don't you go getting too cocky, Poocher," said Zeeky. "Bitterwood says we're retiring after we find Jeremiah. Your fighting days are almost over."

Poocher narrowed his eyes and snorted.

"Yeah, you're scary," said Zeeky, scratching the pig's bristly neck.

THEY FLEW THROUGH the night. Vulpine led the way, with Sagen and a squadron of fifty aerial guards at his back. Vulpine kept a pace that no doubt tested many of the guards, though most were a third his age. He wished he could fly even faster. A blockade should have been in place within hours after the rebels took the fort. Come the dawn, this strategic error would be rectified.

They were roughly forty miles from Dragon Forge. They'd veered south slightly to follow the river that flowed past the town. Sagen increased his speed and drew beside Vulpine. Vulpine admired Sagen's power as his son's finely chiseled muscles pumped in his breasts and shoulders to overtake him. Truly, the Matriarch had chosen well in pairing him with a valkyrie a quarter-century earlier. Sagen was a fine specimen; if his intelligence was equal to his physique, the future success of the sky-dragon race was assured.

"I wonder what those fires are," Sagen asked.

Vulpine scanned the horizon in the general direction of Sagen's gaze. Multiple fires flickered in the distance. Vulpine was mildly disturbed he hadn't spotted them on his own. Perhaps his eyes weren't what they once were.

"Let's find out." Vulpine veered toward the lights. Perhaps these were campfires of humans journeying toward the forge. If so, it would be a satisfying warm-up to have the aerial guard deal with them. After they'd flown another mile, however, his eyes began to untangle the glowing riddle. It was the remains of a human farm. What had once been a large farmhouse, a barn, and various outbuildings were now little more than mounds of cinders where the occasional fire still burned.

Beyond the house was a five-acre field full of humanoid figures. He squinted. No, earth-dragons. They were too broad and squat to be humans, plus they had tails. They were not the only figures in the field.

"Your keen eyes may have earned us valuable allies," Vulpine said to Sagen.

Vulpine soared over the burning buildings, the smoke stinging his eyes. He tilted his wings to slow his flight, drifting downward. Their descent was nearly silent as they landed a few dozen yards behind the mob of earth-dragons and were almost instantly spotted. A flurry of shouts ran among the assemblage as they all turned to face the sky-dragons.

"Greetings," he called out. "I'm Vulpine, Slave-catcher General. I've been given authority to take command of Albekizan's troops to establish a blockade of Dragon Forge. Who's in charge here?"

Ninety-nine earth-dragon heads instantly swiveled to stare at a single beast. Beast was exactly the right term; this was the largest earth-dragon Vulpine had ever seen, over six feet tall and almost that broad across the shoulders. Unlike many soldiers, this earth-dragon wore no armor, and was naked save for a necklace of human teeth that draped round and round his shoulders. He carried a weapon in both hands that looked like a fence post topped with an anvil. His most arresting feature, aside from his overall mass, was his beak. Unlike the normal smooth lines resembling a turtle's beak, this dragon's bony jaws had been carved and chiseled into ragged, jagged edges that reminded Vulpine of the blade of a saw.

The beast stomped forward, drawing ever closer, as if his intent wasn't to march to Vulpine, but to march over him. The squadron of aerial guards readied their weapons. Vulpine raised a fore-claw, motioning for them to remain still.

The beast stopped inches from Vulpine.

"I'm Sawface!" he yelled, at a volume appropriate only if Vulpine had been standing on the other side of the field. "These are my Wasters! I'm the boss here!" His breath smelled heavily of goom, the booze of choice among earth-dragons, fermented from cabbages and hot chilies.

Vulpine nodded respectfully, looking over Sawface's shoulder. "I admire your artistry," he said.

Beyond Sawface, fourteen human bodies were lashed to upright poles, like scarecrows in the field. They ranged in age from an elderly man to an infant. Not all were dead. Several were missing limbs. Two were missing heads. As frightening a scene as this presented, Vulpine was certain they would fail as scarecrows. No doubt by the following evening, crows would be devouring the eyes.

Sawface shouted, forcefully enough that Vulpine's feather scales were stirred by the wind of his voice. "We are the death of mankind! Look upon our work and tremble!"

"Yes," said Vulpine. "Quite. However, if you rid the world of humans, who will grow the cabbages and chilies to make goom? Is a world without goom a world worth living in?"

Sawface opened his jaws to shout a response, but then some dim light flickered in his eyes.

Vulpine said, "I would like to engage your services in establishing a blockade around Dragon Forge. I can pay more gold than you can imagine. More importantly, I can supply you with all the goom you can possibly drink. I have full command of the kitchen barracks at the Dragon Palace. Join me, and I'll have fifty wagons of the stuff rolling toward us before sunset."

Sawface ground his lower jaw against his upper one, a grating noise like un-oiled, rusty gears grinding together inside the beast's head. Finally, Sawface held up his weapon. "I want a chest of gold that weighs more than the head of my hammer!"

"Done," said Vulpine. "I will double it, in fact, once you've performed a service for me."

"Name it," said Sawface.

"I want the four main roads leading to Dragon Forge decorated with these scarecrows of yours," he said. "Two miles on each road should suffice. I understand it may take you some time to find enough bodies—"

"Do they need to be fresh?" asked Sawface, rubbing the underside of his jagged beak with his blood-encrusted hammer. His voice was quieter now. He almost sounded like he was thinking.

"I can't see why."

"Have your gold ready in a week," said Sawface, gruffly, before turning and stomping back to the rest of his mob.

Vulpine looked back at Sagen. "That went well."

"Shall I send one of the guards back to requisition the goom?"

"Of course not," said Vulpine. "I gave the order for the wagons to roll before we left. I anticipated we would find remnants of Shandrazel's army. In fact, it's time we divide our forces. There are four main roads leading into Dragon Forge. Send ten guards to each to establish the blockades. Have your remaining guards spread throughout the area seeking out earth-dragons. Make them similar offers of gold and goom."

Sagen nodded. "At once, sir. On which road will you be establishing your command post?"

"I won't be establishing the command post. You will. Pick whichever road you think is most vital. I have other business I must attend to."

"Other business, sir?"

"I need to pay a visit to the sun-dragon Rorg," Vulpine said. He grimaced. "A most unpleasant task. Rorg tends to divide all of life's problems into two categories: those he can solve by killing something, and those he can ignore. Dealing with him is always tedious."

"How many guards will you need as an escort?"

"None," said Vulpine. "I said he was tedious, not dangerous. The day I can no longer handle negotiations with a sun-dragon is the day you may build my funeral pyre." He looked toward the east. The scarecrows were black silhouettes against a brightening sky. "A new day approaches," he said. "The humans have had their moment of glory. Today begins their time of terror. When we're done, they'll be begging for our merciful guidance once more."

* * *

GETTING TO THE top of the city wall was more challenging than Burke anticipated, especially with his
crutch in his left hand and the case that held the spy-
owl strapped to his back. The spy-owl weighed close
to fifty pounds, which had the effect of pressing his
belly up against the ladder, preventing him from seeing his remaining foot as it searched for the rungs.
His aching arms supported most of his weight as he
slowly worked his way up, one frustrating rung at a
time.

Of course, he could have called out and any of the
sky-wall bowmen would have run to his aid. But
after all that time feeling helpless in his wheeled chair
as his right leg died, he was eager to return to independent mobility. Getting around on his crutch felt
like sprinting after his confinement to the chair.

He reached the top of the ladder and tossed his
crutch onto the walkway that ran along the battlements. He grunted as he tried to slip the straps that
held the spy-owl off his shoulder. Unfortunately, this
threw off his center of gravity as he leaned backward.
The ladder swayed slowly back from the wall.

A large brown boot, filthy with muck, slammed
down onto the rung by his fingers, stopping the
motion of the ladder. Stonewall stood above him,
frowning as he looked down. Stonewall muttered
something Burke didn't quite catch, then leaned
down and grabbed Burke's wrist. Before Burke could
protest, the giant lifted him, moving him through the
air with no more effort than lifting a house cat.

Stonewall brought Burke even with his eyes.
Despite his great size, Stonewall possessed youthful, even boyish features. His cheeks and chin were
smooth, with no hint of beard, and the skin
around his eyes was free of wrinkles or blemishes.
His eyes were a piercing gray, the color of freshly

cooled pig iron. His ebony hair framed his face in curly locks.

"You should be more careful," Stonewall said, his voice deep as a sun-dragons, yet also gentle.

Burke nodded. "You can put me down now." Stonewall sat Burke down. Burke hopped over to the wall and balanced against it while Stonewall handed him his crutch.

"Should you be up yet?" asked Stonewall. "You've only had a few days to recover from your surgery."

"I can't rest anymore," said Burke, wrestling the spy-owl case from his shoulder. "There's too much to be done. I'm tired of running this fort from a bed."

Stonewall crossed his massive arms. His chainmail shirt rattled as he moved. "I was unaware you were running anything," he said. "Ragnar commands this fort by God's grace. You merely advise him."

Burke didn't want to argue with this oversized farm boy. He'd known the moment he'd signed up for this revolution that he'd do all the work and Ragnar would get all the glory. To be honest, he wanted things this way. He'd been one of the leaders of the Southern Rebellion twenty years ago, and in his dreams he still heard the screams of the men he'd led as the sun-dragon army tore them to shreds. This new rebellion may have been following his plans, but Ragnar's fire and brimstone speeches were what motivated the men. Burke was blameless if these men chose to die for Ragnar's glory.

Ignoring Stonewall, Burke flipped the brass clasps of the heavy case. Three legs dropped down, creating a tripod that the case balanced on. The panels of the case folded away revealing a brass statue of an owl almost two feet high. The owl's glass eyes reflected his image in the soft morning light. He leaned, as if wiping away a smudge from the eye-lenses, but in reality it was some faint trace of vanity that drew his eye. He'd bathed this morning for the first time in weeks. His hair was clean and shining, with three crimson feather-scales woven into the braid that draped over his shoulder. His spare spectacles made his brown eyes look oddly small, but for the first time in weeks the whites of his eyes were truly white, untainted by illness. Three parallel scars ran down his right cheek, testament to his first encounter with Charkon twenty years prior. Yet despite the scars and wrinkles, despite the gray that streaked his hair, he looked pretty good for a man who'd been at the gates of death only a few days before. He straightened up and spun the spy owl around to face the western road. It was two hours after sunrise. Normally a stream of refugees, volunteers, and traders would gather around the city walls during the night. This morning, they were absent.

He leaned down and looked into the window in the back of the spy-owl's head. An elaborate set of mirrors and lenses caught the light from two miles down the road and brought it crisply to his eyes.

It didn't take him long to understand what he was looking at. A platoon of earth-dragons were lashing human corpses to poles set along the roadside. From the look of things, these weren't fresh bodies. A trio of sky-dragons stood nearby, supervising things. From their armor, Burke recognized them as members of the aerial guard.

"It took them long enough," he said.

"It took who long enough for what?" asked Stonewall.

"A blockade. Earth-dragons and sky-dragons. We've had an easy couple of weeks since Shandrazel's army collapsed. With two kings dying back to back, the second with no heir, there's been no one to seize control of the earth-dragons and guide them into the rather obvious strategy of a blockade. They've been randomly running around the countryside killing people in an unfocused rage. They've made life miserable for people directly in their path, but as a strategy for retaking Dragon Forge, it has obvious shortcomings."

"You shouldn't speak so lightly of the people who've died due to the dragons' rampage," said Stonewall. "I've spoken to many of the refugees. They've seen horrible things."

"I know," said Burke, rising up from the spy-owl. "I told Ragnar what he was unleashing before we took this fort."

"Can I look?" asked Stonewall, pointing to the owl.

"Be my guest," said Burke, hopping backwards to make room, keeping his balance with a hand on the battlements.

Stonewall dropped down on one knee and brought his eyes tentatively to the window on the back of the owl's head.

"You may need to adjust the focus," said Burke. "There's a dial—"

Before he finished speaking, Stonewall raised his beefy fingers to the dial on the back of the bird's head and began to fiddle with it.

"Amazing," he said softly. "It's like I'm standing right next to them. I can count the fringes on the back of that sky-dragon's head." He turned and looked at Burke with something approaching awe. "You designed this?"

"Yes," said Burke.

"How did you grind the lenses so precisely?"

Burke lifted an eyebrow. "I'm glad you know it's done with lenses," he said. "Ragnar thought it was magic."

"I'm originally from the Drifting Islands," said Stonewall. "Many of the sailors use spyglasses."

"Back at the tavern, I had special instruments that would let me shape glass to almost any specification."

Stonewall stood up. "You're a man of many talents, Machinist." He sounded almost respectful. "I should go tell Ragnar. He'll know what to do to break this siege."

"Respectfully, he won't," said Burke. "For the moment, we don't need it broken." Stonewall frowned. "We've had three weeks to load in coal and supplies. We've got more pig iron stacked in the foundries than I can use in a year. We have a good, deep well, and, if my orders have been carried out in regards to upgrading the sewers, our sanitation practices have beaten back the threat of disease. We're in no immediate danger. If someone has taken control of the renegade earth-dragons, then things should calm down in the countryside. The fact the sky-dragons are involved is a good sign. They're smart fighters. They'll take as long as they need to build up their forces and establish order."

"We should strike before they can consolidate power," said Stonewall.

"No. I've not had enough time to explore the possibilities of gunpowder. You've seen the shotguns. I've got mortars and cannons coming out of the forge this week. We have a technological advantage they don't know about. They're building their blockade out of the range of the sky-wall bows. They have no idea of the hell we're going to unleash if I have time to build half of the inventions that are in my mind."

Stonewall looked out toward the western road, at the tiny figures in the distance. From here, it was almost impossible to tell these were dragons.

Stonewall said, without looking directly at Burke, "They say you don't believe in God."

Burke shrugged. "I've never been a man of faith."

Stonewall straightened his back, adding inches to his towering frame. "Yet you ask us to have faith in you. You keep these inventions in your head, keeping your master plans secret while workmen labor on the individual parts. You won't even share the secret of the gunpowder you ask us all to trust our lives to. Have you no faith in your fellow men, Burke?"

Burke was surprised by the bluntness of the question. He was more surprised by the bluntness of his answer. "No." He sighed. "I... as bad as I've seen dragons treat humans, I've seen men do worse to each other."

"Do you feel no sense of responsibility at all?" asked Stonewall. "Whether or not you believe that Ragnar's war is a holy cause, if you have the knowledge that can lead to human victory, shouldn't you share it with as many people as possible? If you were to die—"

"I've made plans," said Burke. "I write down everything. It's coded, but Anza can read it, and so can... so can another person here. If I die, the technology isn't going to die with me. But as long as I'm alive, I'm going to retain control as long as I can. I don't want to see my weapons used against humans."

"Anza's not here, Machinist. You ask us to place our faith in an unknown confidant?"

Burke looked out over the rolling hillsides, at the scattered mounds of refuse that had once housed the gleaners, fellow humans loyal to the dragons of the forge, who had been the first to die at rebel hands. He'd killed more men than dragons that night. Anza had not shown a shred of remorse as she'd moved among the shadows, killing everyone she met. He closed his eyes, blocking out the memories. "For now, I'm the only one I trust," he said.

"I hope your pride isn't the death of us all, Machinist." Stonewall turned and walked away without glancing back.

CHAPTER ELEVEN

BONE AGAINST STONE

VULPINE SOARED OVER the seemingly endless valley with its patchwork quilt of farms and villages. It was midday, though thick clouds muted the light and gave the land a gray pall. Snow covered the nearby mountain peaks, and the clouds hinted at more to come. Despite the ominous weather—or perhaps because of it—the dirt roads below were bustling with humans moving between villages, riding atop donkey carts packed with various goods. This valley was famous for being the breadbox of Albekizan's kingdom. The human uprising at Dragon forge felt like a distant nightmare. Looking down, Vulpine couldn't imagine how any human could truly despise the authority of dragons. Humans farmed, dug mines, engaged in commerce. Dragons guided them in these efforts, moving humans back and forth as the needs of the kingdom dictated. Dragons maintained order. It was a beneficial arrangement for both humans and dragons. A few malcontents couldn't be allowed to ruin the Pax Draco.

The valley stretched for over two hundred miles. Due to its size, it was divided into two abodes, each ruled by sun-dragons who couldn't have been further apart in their philosophies and manners. The southern end had been ruled by Chakthalla, Albekizan's sister-in-law, a refined sun-dragon with courtly tastes. She'd lived in a palace respected for its elegant architecture, a dwelling that contained nearly as much stained glass as stone. She'd dressed her earth-dragon guards in elaborate, lacey uniforms, drilled them endlessly, and never used them for war. In truth, Vulpine had always liked Chakthalla. She'd appreciated poetry and drama, and was a fine patron of sky-dragon scholars and artists. She'd also treated her human slaves well, which meant she hadn't created much work for Vulpine. Humans could be rendered passive through either fear or fairness, and she'd definitely taken the gentler path. She'd been one of the few sun-dragons to oppose Albekizan's plan of genocide. Of course, she was now dead because of this, assassinated by the Black Silence. Her castle lay gutted and looted, a stark example of the fate of those who defied Albekizan.

In contrast to the high-mannered Chakthalla, a brutish bull sun-dragon named Rorg ruled the northern reaches of the valley. At birth he'd been named Zanatharorg, but Rorg had shed most of his syllables, along with many other things, fifty years ago when he'd adopted the philosophy of beastialism. Beastialists were dragons who shunned the trappings of civilization. They lived in caves rather than castles. They wore no jewelry, kept no paintings or sculptures, and disdained the weapons and armor that other dragons had adopted centuries ago. The oldest known poem written by a dragon, *The Ballad of Belpantheron*, told the stories of how dragons had once lived like beasts while the world had been ruled by angels, smaller, weaker beings who nonetheless kept power through their use of weapons. Sun-dragons were blessed with formidable natural weaponry, but a sword and a spear were longer, sharper, and harder than any tooth or claw. The dragons had won their long struggle against the angels when they, too, had learned to forge steel and create their own weapons of war.

Beastialists, however, believed that the dragons of ancient times simply hadn't tried hard enough. They regarded the adoption of weapons as a shameful admission that angel culture was superior to dragon culture, and felt that any unhappiness in dragon society could be traced to the fact that dragons were trying to be something they weren't. They weren't angels, visiting this earth from some higher realm. They were the apex of evolution, the most finely honed predators the earth had produced. Embracing their natural role was the key to true happiness.

Of course, one aspect of civilization they hadn't rejected was the use of human slaves. Vulpine had paid many a visit to Rorg's abode, due to the high rate of runaways. Unlike the pristine, well-groomed villages of the southern valley, the villages in Rorg's domain were squalid and bleak, often festering with disease. This, of course, was the reason for Vulpine's visit. The latest outbreak of yellow-mouth was well timed. Yellow-mouth only affected humans, most often humans exposed to sun-dragon dung. Once infected, humans could pass the disease to other humans via exposure to nearly any bodily fluid. The disease manifested first as mild fevers and weakness; a modest sickness little more bothersome than a cold.

The only hint that it might be something more serious was that the inside of the victim's mouth would slowly change from pink to yellow. The early stage could last as little as a week, or as long as a month. Finally, the afflicted human would experience a twenty-four hour period best described as an eruption. He would cough, sneeze, vomit, shit, and piss uncontrollably, sweating until blood seeped from his pores. The disease killed nearly half its victims. The most sinister aspect of the disease was that it could spread not just in the final, violent stage, but in the earlier phases as well. A mother placing her hand on the forehead of her child to feel for a fever could contract the disease, and then spread it to her husband with a simple kiss on the cheek. Even handling the clothes or blankets of one of the victims could spread yellow-mouth.

The disease was now rare through most of the kingdom. Most sun-dragons lived in palaces with good plumbing, meaning that their human slaves didn't deal with vast quantities of dung. Beastialists, however, let their droppings fall anywhere the urge struck. Since dwelling in a cave full of your own excrement was unpleasant even for beastialists, human slaves had the ongoing task of mucking out the cave.

Vulpine at last saw the bone field that marked the entrance to Rorg's lair. For half a mile in every direction, white bones gleamed against the gray winter ground: cattle, deer, humans, pigs, and earth-dragons. Smoke rose from the ground in tendrils at a hundred scattered spots extending well beyond the bone field. Beastialists had clung to one technology, at least. Since they couldn't see in the dark they still used fire to light their homes, though they eschewed metal and glass lamps in favor of torches and fire pits.

Vulpine swooped down into the black pit that was the entrance to an expansive underground kingdom, a network of caverns with ceilings hundreds of feet tall. Some individual chambers were several acres in size. It was dangerous to fly in a cavern. All sense of perspective was thrown askew by the absence of sky. However, Vulpine had grown familiar with the contours of the place over his many visits. He flitted like an oversized bat above the heads of human slaves carting out buckets of muck. A few fat and napping sun-dragons peeked up through half-open lids as the wind of Vulpine's passage stirred their feathers. Beastialists kept their large families close at hand. At least thirty adult sun-dragons shared this cavern.

Vulpine wound his way to the central chamber. He was startled to hear music as he approached. Not singing, but notes from an actual musical instrument. The tones had a bell-like quality to them, but Vulpine sensed they weren't bells. What was making this haunting sound?

Arriving at the central chamber, he found his answer. This room covered several acres, and around the edges of it humans stood on ladders, striking the stalactites that hung from the ceiling with large thighbones. The blows caused the long, slender columns of stone to vibrate, emitting musical tones. The men followed an unseen conductor, timing their strikes to create a slow, mournful melody of low, long notes that called back and forth across the chamber.

In the center of the room an enormous fire pit glowed brightly. The sharp creosote stink of the pine smoke provided a welcome mask to the pervasive odor of raw sewage that hung in the dank air.

A dozen dragons lay around the fire pit. Due to their slightly smaller size and the finer mesh of their ruby scales, Vulpine judged them to be female. Rorg's harem, no doubt. They all stared at Vulpine with sullen, bored eyes as he landed near the fire pit.

Just beyond the fire pit, on an enormous pillow of stone, slouched Rorg himself. The old bull dragon was hideously fat. No doubt it had been many years since he'd been able to get airborne. He was currently picking his teeth with his long, black, hook-like claws. The bloodied remnants of an ox lay before him.

"Greetings, Rorg," Vulpine said, raising his voice over the music of the stalactites.

Rorg turned his eyes, large as saucers, toward the new arrival. They glowed green in the dim light. Even the folds of skin around his eyes looked fat and heavy. "Slavecatcher. What brings you to my abode?"

The music suddenly grew louder. Vulpine didn't know the tune, but apparently the song was reaching some sort of dramatic climax. Vulpine had to shout as he said, "I've heard you had an outbreak of—" suddenly, the music stopped, the last few notes of the song drifting off gently as Vulpine screamed, "—yellow-mouth!"

Rorg narrowed his eyes. "I don't find your tone respectful, slavecatcher. Have a care. Do you know that, with the death of Albekizan, I am the most senior ruler of any abode? Forty years I've ruled this valley. Forty years, the labor of my slaves has fed the rest of the world. Remember who you speak to, little dragon."

Vulpine bowed his head. "My apologies. I was merely trying to be heard over your music. It was quite loud; though also quite lovely. It has an unearthly quality that I find—"

"Unearthly?" Rorg grumbled. "It is the precise opposite of unearthly. These are the tones of the earth itself! I had long noted that some of the stalactites in my cavern possessed a musical tone when struck. Last winter, during the coldest, most dreary part of the year, I began to hear music in my head. It occurred to me that if I positioned my slaves correctly and trained them to strike notes at the proper time, I could make the music in my head a reality."

"How innovative," said Vulpine. "You are not so uncivilized as you would like to pretend, Rorg."

"Nor are you sky-dragons as civilized as you imagine," Rorg said. "Your books, your paintings, your plays and poems and choirs... you've stolen all your so-called culture from the angels. I may be the first true artist the dragon races have ever produced. This is natural music, Vulpine, bone against stone, the product of a true dragon heart."

Vulpine bowed his head once more. He knew from experience it was simplest just to flatter the old swine into doing what he wanted, then leave as quickly as possible. "I meant no offense. I am, in fact, awed by your invention. It is, no doubt, the harbinger of a greater dragon civilization to come. However, we can debate the artistic future of dragons another day. Today, I've come because I need one of your slaves."

"No," said Rorg.

"No?" asked Vulpine, bewildered. He hadn't known he'd asked a question.

The sun-dragons he'd flown over in the entry chambers were now lumbering into the room. These were males, younger than Rorg, no doubt his many sons. There were at least ten in the room now. One of them, a strong young bull, approached Rorg's stone pillar. This dragon had the bulk of a fully grown male, but still possessed the tight, balanced musculature of a younger dragon. He was a formidable specimen, a dragon in his prime. His red scales were so vibrant in their sheen they looked like wet rubies as the firelight danced across them.

"I may live in a cave, slavecatcher, but I'm not ignorant of the world outside," Rorg said. "I know that Albekizan is dead, and his successor, Shandrazel, was killed by the human rebels at Dragon Forge. I know, further, that Chapelion currently sits on the dragon throne, intending to be king in practice if not in title. You sky-dragons believe yourselves clever. Your biologians train the sons of other sun-dragons. You serve as their advisors in adulthood. You believe yourselves to be the true power in this world. In my abode, I have no libraries or colleges. I have no biologians to whisper lies in my ear and call it wise counsel."

"Your independence is admirable," said Vulpine. "I do not see how my request for a slave threatens it."

"You slavecatchers tout your importance to maintaining order among the human rabble. Yet, we now see the failings of your methods. Humans have seized the most shameful and decadent icon of your so-called civilization, Dragon Forge, the foundries that supplied the kings' armies with swords and spears and armor."

Vulpine ground his teeth. It was grating to hear Shandrazel's failures blamed on the slavecatchers, but perhaps there was some tiny grain of truth to it.

"Rorg, I concede all that you say. Events unfolded more rapidly than I anticipated after Albekizan's death. In retrospect, stationing reinforcements at Dragon Forge would have been an obvious precaution. Despite his heritage, Shandrazel wasn't well trained in the art of war. I should have personally advised him on security precautions. I didn't. Now, however, I will rectify my error by taking charge of reclaiming the foundries. I know that you've had an outbreak of yellow-mouth. I need a freshly infected slave, one who can survive long enough to travel to Dragon Forge and have his disease progress to the final stages soon after his arrival. The human rebels sleep packed into tight barracks and dine elbow to elbow in communal halls. Currently, they enjoy the benefits of a well-built sewer system, but a dam will end this advantage. A single infected individual should spread the disease quickly. Within a month, the place will be a ghost town."

"A sound plan," said Rorg. "One I anticipated. This is why I deny your request. The shameful age when dragons used tools draws to a close. The future belongs to my kind. Look at my son, Thak." Rorg gestured to the young bull-dragon who stood beside him. Thak stood on his hind-talons, his neck held high, towering above Vulpine. "He is the pinnacle of my bloodline. He and his brothers will journey to Albekizan's palace and throw Chapelion from the throne. He will burn the angel-tainted contents of the grand library and knock down its walls. The tapestries will be shredded, the sculptures crushed to gravel. Once Thak has firmly established his claim to the throne, the dragon armies will spread throughout the kingdom and bring mankind to its knees."

"This is rather short-sighted on your part, Rorg," said Vulpine. "The present human rebellion—"

"There is no hint of rebellion among my slaves! I maintain them in a state of perpetual hunger and weakness, allowing them only the most meager scraps of their labors. Despite the hunger, they work harder than any ten slaves in any other abode in the kingdom. Do you know why, Vulpine?"

"The bone field at your door no doubt has certain motivational powers."

"Indeed," said Rorg. "I've built that bone field with my teeth and my claws. Thak will not reclaim Dragon Forge, Vulpine. He will raze it. No wall of the foundry will be left standing."

Vulpine looked Thak over. Thak returned his gaze with an expression that suggested hunger, as if he were sizing up Vulpine as a snack. Turning back to Rorg, he said, "I admire a dragon of vision. Chapelion seeks a new sun-dragon to serve as king. Thak looks the part. If he wants the throne, we'll give it to him—with the understanding that he will respect the counsel of the High Biologian. Consider my offer carefully. You'll be the father of a new dragon dynasty."

"You seek to give us what we can take with our superior power?" Rorg asked.

"Have a care, Rorg," said Vulpine. "If you attempt to take the throne by force, the aerial guard will crush you."

"Thak," said Rorg in a low voice, "kill this fool."

Thak's jaws opened and his head shot toward Vulpine like a viper striking. Vulpine sighed as he flapped his wings and flew straight up. Thak's teeth snapped onto empty air inches beneath him. Vulpine kicked down. The young sun-dragon's jaws smacked into the stone floor, sliding in the gritty muck-film coating it.

The kick propelled Vulpine upward. The ceiling here was at least a hundred feet high, studded with countless stalactites that hung down like stone icicles. He swung his hind-talons up and grabbed one that looked especially sturdy, his claws biting into it so that he wound up in a perpendicular crouch. The other sun-dragons stared up at him, but none looked like they were going to interfere. Rorg had given his order specifically to Thak. Both Thak and

Rorg would lose face if they called on the others to help.

Looking up, Vulpine's snout was only inches away from a second stalagmite. As Thak rose up on all-fours, shaking the muck from his snout, Vulpine reached out with his fore-talon, flicking his claw against the tip of the stone. It chimed like a bell, though the note was much softer than the ones the slaves had sounded, and this particular rock was out of tune. It pealed with something that was almost, but not quite, an E-flat. He winced at the off-key note.

Thak rose up to his hind-talons and roared up at the ceiling. It was an impressive noise, one that set the whole chamber ringing. The cavern as a whole was tuned to an almost perfect C. He had to admire Rorg's inventiveness in creating such a wonderful instrument. It made it all the more puzzling that Thak was so blind to the obvious advantages of other inventions. What did it matter if a sword was the invention of angel, man, or dragon? It was, Vulpine felt, time to demonstrate why tool-users would retain control of the earth.

Below him, Thak leapt, his mighty wings beating a powerful downbeat that sent embers from the fire pit dancing around the room. He raced toward Vulpine, his jaws open once more, as Vulpine pulled his whip from his belt. He flicked the weapon in his fore-talon, aiming the leather through the forest of stalactites to a slender one ten feet distant that caught his eye. The leather wrapped around the tip of the stone. Vulpine gave a sharp tug. With a *crack* the stone snapped free about five feet up the shaft. He flicked his wrist again to free his whip as the stone spear began to plummet, right into the path of Thak's approach. The stone tore through Thak's outstretched left wing near his armpit.

Thak's jaws clamped shut and he sucked in air through flared nostrils. His injured wing spasmed uncontrollably. His good wing vainly tried to keep him airborne, but it was of no use. He landed on his back in the middle of the fire pit, extinguishing most of the flames. He howled as he rolled from the pit, sending sparks and smoke in all directions. A new stink fouled the atmosphere, the stench of burning feather-scales.

Rorg dropped from his perch amid a cacophony of shouts. Shadows danced around the chamber as humans ran for safety, carrying torches. The air was thick with black smoke.

When the chaos cleared, Thak was flat on his back, his wings stretched to the side, his head pressed firmly against the stone floor. Standing on his throat, right at the junction of Thak's jaw and neck, was Vulpine. He'd drawn his sword and buried it in the underside of Thak's jaw, where he held it with both fore-talons as blood gushed from the intersection of flesh and steel with each heartbeat. Vulpine stared at Rorg calmly.

"This blade is three feet long," he said, his voice dispassionate, as if he were merely explaining the attributes of the object. "You will notice that two feet of the weapon is still exposed. The tip of the sword is presently resting on the base of Thak's skull. The bone there is relatively thin. With only modest pressure, I can drive this into Thak's brain."

"You won't leave here alive," growled Rorg. Vulpine heard the fear beneath the great beast's anger.

"Regardless of the outcome of our encounter, I'd encourage you to reflect on the validity of your philosophy. I've bested the mightiest warrior among you with little more than braided leather and a pointy rock. Do you honestly think you stand a chance going up against the aerial guard at the palace, with all their weapons and war-machines?"

"No one can stand against our teeth and claws!" Rorg bellowed, then grew still as his eyes fixed on the juncture of the sword and Thak's throat. Thak was breathing in shallow, rapid breaths. Beneath Vulpine's hind-talons, the blood in the sun-dragon's jugular vein raced in strong, panicked pulses.

"I will repeat my request for a single slave," said Vulpine. "And some blankets."

"One slave is hardly worth this rudeness on your part. I don't understand why you chose to provoke this fight. We purchased new slaves a few days ago to replace those lost to yellow-mouth. You can have your pick of the lot. There are fresh corpses piled above, with the blankets they died beneath still wrapped about them. Take as many as you wish."

"Thank you, Rorg," Vulpine said, pulling his sword free and stepping down from Thak's throat. "This is most generous of you."

Vulpine started to sheath his sword, then looked up at Rorg once more. "So we're clear, none of your relatives are going anywhere near Chapelion now."

"What use have we for a palace?" grumbled Rorg. "A cave surrounded by bones is the natural abode of the dragon."

Vulpine nodded with a new appreciation of Rorg's old-fashioned wisdom. "So where are these new slaves?"

"Most are already out in the villages," said Rorg. "We'll use them in the fields come spring. But over in the corner is one of the new arrivals. He's small, so we put him to work mucking out the tighter crevices."

Rorg pointed toward a blond youth cowering in a narrow alcove. If Rorg hadn't used the pronoun "he," Vulpine wouldn't have instantly recognized the human as male. His hair was shoulder length and his limbs were slender. Still, he looked old enough to be useful, perhaps twelve or thirteen. It was an age at which one might plausibly run off to join a rebellion. "He'll do. What's his name?"

"They have names?" Rorg asked.

Vulpine walked over to the trembling youth. "What are you called?" The boy looked away, as if praying that Vulpine was talking to someone else.

"I asked you a question," said Vulpine, uncoiling his whip. He allowed the tip to rest on the cavern floor at a spot where the boy couldn't help but see it.

"J-j-j-juh… Jeremiah," the child whispered.

"Are you cold boy? This dank cave air too much for those rags you're wearing?" Jeremiah looked up and nodded. "Let's get you back into some fresh air. We'll get you a blanket you can wrap up in. Maybe two. Would you like that?"

The boy looked confused by this offer. He didn't shake his head yes or no. The wheels of his mind were locked with fear. Vulpine grew impatient. "Follow me, or I'll thrash the skin off you," he snapped and turned away, walking through the phalanx of sun-dragons who glared at him with a mixture of hate and awe. He didn't look back. Behind him, he heard the patter of the boy's feet as he scrambled to keep up, slipping on the slimy stone.

CHAPTER TWELVE

THE IMPORTANCE OF CLEAN WATER

THE LAST TIME Bitterwood had passed through Winding Rock it had been a ghost town. Its citizens had been among the first taken to the Free City, and the empty town had quickly been stripped of anything of value by the few humans who remained in the area. As Skitter carried them into Winding Rock, he saw that it was inhabited once more. Timid faces peeked out from behind torn curtains. Doors that had been kicked from their hinges were patched and repaired, once more keeping out the winter chill. Smoke drifted from the chimneys of at least half the homes. It was nearly dinnertime and the air was flavored by pans of cornbread baking in wood-fired stoves, atop which simmered pots of potatoes and beans, if Bitterwood's nose could be trusted.

At the center of the town was a stone well with a shingled roof. A brick walkway surrounded the well bordered by muched flower beds no doubt sheltering daffodil and iris bulbs. Bitterwood had helped build a well similar to this one, years ago, in Christdale. He and the other men had dug the well during the second year of drought; there's nothing quite like three months without rain to drive home the importance of clean water. When he'd dug that well he'd assumed he'd be drinking from it for the rest of his life. He could have grown soft and content in Christdale, tending his crops and raising his family. He could have spent his winter evenings by a fireplace, with a mug of hot cider to warm him. Instead, dragons had destroyed Christdale. He'd spent the last twenty years avenging this act.

What had it gained him? A legend. Dragons trembled at his name. Men spoke of him as a hero. He would gladly trade this fame—or infamy—for an anonymous life as farmer and father.

Skitter carried them up the well. He poked his snout down it and sniffed.

"I guess he's thirsty," said Shay. The young man sat on the saddle directly behind him and turned his face away. He never made eye contact with Bitterwood now, either due to fear, or, more likely, the grudge he carried over the burnt books. Behind Shay sat Jandra, looking worn and ragged. Once, Jandra had used her magic to keep her appearance immaculate; with the loss of her powers, she'd decayed somewhat. Her hair draped in oily tangles around her shoulders. Her blue coat, fresh only two days ago was covered in burrs; mud speckled her boots and pants. She sagged in her saddle. There were dark circles under her eyes.

Sitting on her shoulder, Lizard had changed color to match Jandra's brown hair, save for his feet and tail, which were blue to match her coat. Bitterwood scowled at the little dragon. The beast turned its gaze, and slipped down behind Jandra's back.

Behind Jandra sat Poocher. The pig was definitely going through a growth spurt. He looked bigger than he had even yesterday. Poocher's barely sprouted tusks gave him a permanent sneer. Unlike Lizard, Poocher didn't turn his gaze away. The pig's eyes were hidden by his silver visor, but Bitterwood could sense his judgmental stare. He'd never really gotten along with Poocher.

On the final saddle sat the reason Bitterwood hadn't turned Poocher into bacon. Zeeky sat with her legs crossed atop the saddle, staring at the crystal ball that sat in her lap. She wasn't dressed warmly enough, thought Bitterwood. She had only a thin blanket for a cloak, over a shirt and trousers that were little more than rags. Yet, she had a look approaching serenity as she stared into the glass orb. Whatever she was seeing or hearing within, it seemed to make her happy.

Zeeky didn't look up as she said, "Get Skitter some water, please." The long-wyrm was staring at the well with a look that was as close to desire as a reptile was ever likely to convey.

"We just crossed a stream. Why didn't he drink then?"

"Because a lot of the outhouses around here empty into that creek. The well is drawing pure water. He'll probably be able to drink a bucketful, maybe two."

Bitterwood peeled himself off his saddle. The surface held onto his tan buckskin britches like glue, though once he started pulling himself free there was no residue. He picked up the heavy oak bucket on the edge of the well. The rope that held it was thicker than his thumb, woven from hemp. Poocher hopped down from Skitter and trotted up to Bitterwood. He snorted in a demanding tone.

"You'll get your turn, Poocher," said Zeeky.

"Do we get to drink before the pig?" Shay asked Jandra quietly. He was adapting to the idea that the rules of

Zeeky's world were somewhat different. Poocher squealed and shook his head in response.

"Stop being rude," said Zeeky. "Skitter will go first. He's had to do all the hard work carrying us. Then Jandra, because she's a lady, and Lizard, since he's still little. Then Shay, because if you're going to be mean, Poocher, you'll have to go last." Poocher made a noise that was part grunt, part grumble, and trotted away, back toward the stream. Apparently, he wasn't going to wait around for the well water.

"He's been so bratty lately," said Zeeky, shaking her head.

Bitterwood heard the bucket splash. He began to turn the wooden wheel to raise it back to the surface. He noticed he'd been left off Zeeky's list of who would get a turn drinking. He also noticed that no one beside Poocher had challenged her list.

As he lugged the heavy bucket up over the rim and sat it down on the cobblestones for the long-wyrm to drink, he heard a noise behind him. The door of a nearby cottage had opened a crack. Hushed voices whispered back and forth within. The cottage was larger than most in the village; a few weeks ago, it had been stripped of its slate shingles. Now, the shingles had been replaced. Whoever resided there must be someone important among the locals.

A pot-bellied older man stepped out of the door. He was followed by four guards, wearing stolen earth-dragon chainmail and helmets and armed with spears. The armor might have fit a large man reasonably well, but it was laughable on these four—as near as he could tell, they were all teenagers, younger than Jandra. In fact, unless the dimming light was playing tricks on him, they were all girls, which made sense. Most able-bodied men who'd been at the Free City had run off to join Ragnar's rebellion. Only women, children, and elderly men would have returned to Winding Rock.

"Strangers," said the pot-bellied man, looking nervously at the long-wyrm. "You didn't ask permission to use our well. I must inform you that there's... there's a user fee."

"For water?" Bitterwood scoffed.

"Hello, Barnstack," said Zeeky.

"You know him?" Jandra asked.

"Sure. Barnstack's the mayor of Winding Rock."

Barnstack eyed Zeeky astride the long-wyrm. He looked mildly befuddled, as if he didn't know why she knew him.

"I'm Zeeky. From Big Lick." Big Lick had been a collection of miner's shacks not five miles from here. It wasn't quite large enough or organized enough to truly be called a village.

Barnstack nodded slowly upon hearing the name. "You're Jeremiah's sister."

"You know Jeremiah?" Bitterwood asked.

"No," said Barnstack, shaking his head solemnly.

"No?" Bitterwood asked.

"Oh," said Barnstack. "Um. I mean, yes, obviously, I knew him. I knew his name, didn't I? Alas, he's dead now. All of Big Lick was burned to the ground. There were no survivors."

"Actually, everyone survived," said Zeeky. "Sort of. It's complicated. But, for Jeremiah, it's simple. He ran away and escaped."

"Have you seen him?" asked Bitterwood.

"Now listen here," said Barnstack, trying to sound angry, but not quite achieving it. "You're changing the subject. Our town has been through hard times. We were taken to the Free City, and when we returned, everything of value was gone. That's why there's a fee to drink from our well. But I'm a fair man. You didn't know about the fee. So that first bucket is free. If you want to keep drinking, you'll need to pay up."

"What's the matter, Barnstack?" asked Zeeky. "Have you already spent Albekizan's gold?"

Barnstack turned pale. His lips twisted into an expression that bore little resemblance to a casual smile. "I don't know what you're talking about."

"I was hiding in your kitchen when you took a bribe from an earth-dragon and agreed to tell the rest of your village to go to the Free City without fighting."

Barnstack's right eye twitched. He chuckled softly at Bitterwood. "Children have such imaginations."

Skitter had finished drinking the water in the pail. The long-wyrm looked toward Barnstack with a lazy eye. Bitterwood assumed that Zeeky wasn't angry with Barnstack; if she had been, Skitter would be showing signs of hostility. Bitterwood dropped the bucket back down the well.

"Go back inside, old man," he said. "We'll drink our fill and move on."

"Actually, we won't be moving on," said Zeeky. "Jeremiah didn't have that many places to run. He might turn up here. Right, Barnstack?"

"There's no place for you to stay here," said Barnstack.

Jandra interrupted. "We're only a few miles from Dead Skunk Hole. That's the entrance to the realm of the goddess. Perhaps we can return here after we go there?"

"You and Shay are going to have to go without us," said Zeeky. "We're not going to Dead Skunk Hole."

Jandra looked surprised by these words. "You won't take us the rest of the way?"

Zeeky shook her head. "Bitterwood and I don't have much time to save Jeremiah."

"Save him from what? How do you know he's in danger?" Zeeky gave an inscrutable half smile. "Fine," said Jandra, sliding down from the long-wyrm. Shay dismounted as well.

Zeeky reached into her saddle bag and pulled out a pair of silver visors like the ones she and Poocher wore. She tossed them to Jandra. "We took these from the guards Bitterwood killed in Dead Skunk Mine. They let you see in the dark."

"What about Lizard?" she asked.

"He won't need one," said Zeeky. "He can see in the dark just fine."

By now, Bitterwood had drawn up another bucket of water. Since the others were focused on Zeeky and Jandra, he paused to take a sip of the cold water.

Barnstack made a choked noise, looking back at his quartet of guards. The girls looked sheepish, as if they were aware of their failings as intimidating muscle. Barnstack opened his mouth, looking as if he were about to yell, then snapped it shut again. He turned and stomped back into his cottage. The girls followed, slamming the door.

"What a pleasant man," said Shay.

Bitterwood nodded. "I look forward to talking to him further."

As SHAY AND Jandra walked away from the well, Lizard waved in a fashion that Shay found unnerving. It was slightly too human a gesture from a scaly green beast that currently had its foot long tail wrapped around Jandra's neck. Shay wondered about the wisdom of choosing to follow Jandra on her quest into the underground kingdom. There were certainly less dangerous paths available to him to gather books.

Yet, he didn't have to dig deep into his own thoughts to discover that he liked Jandra. It wasn't simply that she was smart and driven; he found himself admiring her for her compassion toward Lizard. Despite her own history of mistreatment at the hands of dragons, she didn't display the faintest sliver of hatred. This was a rare quality; it was difficult not to appreciate Jandra for it. Not that this changed his mind about Lizard. With luck, perhaps the little beast would run off as it got bigger and never bother them again.

They followed a well-trod path that wound near the creek up toward Big Lick. It was quite dark now, especially here in the shadow of the mountains. The sky above was gray with clouds.

"Once we get a little higher, there are caves everywhere. We can take shelter in one of them," said Jandra.

Shay stumbled on a tree root in the dark and nearly lost his grip on the shotgun as he reached out and grabbed a tree trunk for balance. Visions of bright red horse bone jutting from a hide flashed into his mind. "I wouldn't mind sleeping on the ground," he said.

"Take this. It should make travel at night much easier." She held out a circlet of silver metal identical to the ones Zeeky and Poocher wore. The visor was surprisingly light. For something that looked like solid metal, it weighed no more than a sheet of parchment. Curiously, despite the chill of the evening, the metal was warm to the touch.

Jandra slipped her visor over her own brow, letting it rest on her nose. The eyeless band looked more like a blindfold than an aid to sight. He slipped the band over his eyes. Instantly, the surrounding landscape was as bright as if it were noon. "Now this is magic!"

Jandra put her hands on her hips. "You can't go around calling everything you don't understand magic," she said sternly.

"Why can't I?" Shay asked. "Why should you care how I organize my experiences?"

Jandra sighed and shook her head. Lizard shook his head slowly, as if he, too, were in the presence of a frustrating child. The little beast rolled his eyes, a gesture he'd seen Jandra perform; perhaps her visor spared him this outlet of her judgment, at least.

"It's not fair arguing with you," Shay said. "Lizard sits on your shoulder like he's your second head. I feel outnumbered when I'm talking to you."

"I'm sorry," she said. "I know I must come across as short-tempered and intolerant. I don't think I used to be like this." She sounded sad now, as she gazed up the rugged mountain pathway. "I don't know if it's stress that's making me so mean to you, or if Jazz's personality is bleeding into my own more and more. She wasn't the most patient person. I'll try not to bite your head off from now on."

"You really haven't been all that mean to me." Shay felt bad that she felt bad. "I was a slave. I'm used to being lashed when I displease others. It really isn't an unbearable burden to have you scold me from time to time."

"The world has enough conflict without me adding to the total. If you want to think the visors are magic, I don't see why that should bother me. It's not your fault you don't have the training to understand the science behind them."

Her apology slipped in the realm of insult. Was she dismissing his ability to learn?

Jandra tapped her visor. "These things are more than just fancy glasses," she said, sounding happy to change the conversation. "The long-wyrm riders could communicate with them over long distances. I wonder if I can figure out how to use them for that?"

"Actually," said an unseen voice, "you're already on an open channel. I can hear you fine."

Jandra startled, looking around for the source of the ghostly voice. Shay spun in a circle, trying to spot the speaker, his shotgun at the ready.

"Adam?" Jandra asked.

"Who's Adam?" whispered Shay.

"Adam Bitterwood. He's Bant's son. He was captain of the long-wyrm riders."

"Yes, it's Adam," said the disembodied voice. "Is this Jandra? Who's with you?"

"This is Lizard," she said, raising a hand to stroke the earth-dragon's paw. "Oh, do you mean the other voice you heard? That's my new friend Shay. Where are you?"

"I'm in the temple in Winding Rock. Look to your left."

Half a mile distant on the edge of Winding Rock sat a temple of the goddess. These places of worship were stone platforms ringed by trees planted closely together to form living walls.

Jandra motioned for Shay to follow. As they neared the temple, a tall, long-haired man appeared on the stone steps. He was dressed in a long robe woven from green thread. A braided honeysuckle vine sat upon his brow like a crown; even though it was midwinter, the vine was fresh and green, studded with soft yellow flowers. *Magic.*

Shay caught himself. He needed to think critically about the wonders he encountered. The biologians at the College of Spires maintained greenhouses. It didn't require magic to keep a plant green in winter.

"Adam," said Jandra. "I wondered what had happened to you."

Adam walked down the steps, holding his arms wide open. "It's good to see you," he said, embracing her. The hug lasted several seconds. Shay wondered if there was something more to Jandra's and Adam's relationship than he was aware of. Or was this hug only a greeting? And why should it matter to him?

Adam released Jandra. "Welcome, brother," he said, and wrapped his arms around Shay. "You're an honored guest here."

The hug lasted for a few seconds longer than Shay felt it needed to. Within the temple, he could see a life-sized statue of a nude woman carved from mahogany. The goddess, he supposed. Chapelion had never educated him much in the various human faiths, but he'd picked up some knowledge from his fellow slaves.

Adam finally released Shay from his embrace. "What brings you back to these mountains?"

"I'm returning to Jazz's kingdom," said Jandra.

Adam frowned. "For what purpose?"

Jandra started to speak, then stopped. She finally said, "I think Hex might be going back underground to find the goddess heart. I have to stop him. I could use your help."

Shay wondered why Jandra was lying. This wasn't her true motivation. She was going because she wanted to reclaim her magic.

"I won't go back into the underworld," said Adam. "My days as a warrior are behind me. After seeing the scars my father bore upon his soul after a lifetime of fighting, I've taken a vow of non-violence. I intend to serve the goddess in more benign ways. It is a path, I pray, that will spare me my father's fate."

"The goddess is dead," Jandra said. "You watched us bury what little remained of her. How can you serve a dead goddess?"

Adam waved toward the town of Winding Rock and the valley beyond. "Winter has gripped this valley. The fields are brown and barren. Yet is the earth dead? Spring will awaken the sleeping land. So, too, shall the goddess wake from her slumber."

"Bitterwood stabbed her in the heart with Gabriel's flaming sword," said Jandra. "She was burned to ash. I don't think she's waking up, Adam."

"My father slew only an aspect of the goddess. You'll see. She'll rise again."

"Speaking of your father, he's down in Winding Rock. Do you want me to let him know you're here?"

"No," said Adam. "My father and I have said all we need to say to one another. In the years we were apart, I dreamed of reuniting with him. I imagined him as a hero, and imbued his dream with all the best qualities of humanity. The man I met was a cruel monster who was only happy when he was fighting. Perhaps I'm to blame as well. No doubt our reunion was poisoned by my own idealism. No flesh and blood man could have ever lived up to my vision."

"I understand," said Jandra. "I always wanted to find my human family. I longed for relatives more than anything else in the world. Now, I've finally met my brother. His name is Ragnar. He's a wild-eyed, naked, long-haired prophet of the Lord who wants to burn me at the stake. It's really made me miss Vendevorex. I wish I'd understood how important he was to me while he was still alive."

"The kindest thing my father ever did for me was spare my life after he'd slaughtered my companions and my mount," Adam said. "Contrast this with the compassion of the goddess in taking me in as an orphan and giving me a life filled with wonders. It's not mere blood that defines a family."

Jandra's hand dipped into her coat pocket and pulled out a square of folded paper and a pencil. She circled something on the paper.

"What are you writing?" Shay asked.

"This is something I've started doing to organize my thoughts," said Jandra. "I'm keeping lists of all the things I need to do. To be honest, I think this was one of Jazz's habits—she called these 'to do lists'. All this talk about Vendevorex reminded me that I still have to find his stolen body."

She unfolded the paper. There were at least two dozen items on her list. "Find Ven's body" was now circled. Two slots above it, "Get back genie!" was underlined several times. Near the bottom of the page was written "Find Atlantis." This had three question marks off to the side. Lizard leaned down to study the paper. Of course, earth-dragons couldn't read. Could they?

"The evening is growing cold," said Adam.

"It looks like snow," Shay said, glancing toward the clouds.

"It won't snow," said Adam, with a curious certainty. "Still, I have a small cabin not far from here. You can spend the night there. Tomorrow I'll send you on your journey with fresh provisions and my best wishes."

"Thank you," said Jandra. "I appreciate your hospitality." She smiled. "You really didn't turn out a thing like your father."

"That means a lot to me," said Adam.

As DAWN CAME to the village of Winding Rock, Zeeky waited patiently on the edge of the well. Skitter was curled around the stone structure. He snored as he slumbered, a sound like gravel pouring from a wheelbarrow. The poor thing needed his rest.

They'd really put him through his paces over the last few days. Poocher was already awake. He was snuffling around in the flower beds, pushing away the mulch and dirt, digging up the bulbs he found and wolfing them down. He didn't offer any to Zeeky.

"I don't know why you've been acting so bratty lately," she said. Poocher looked up. It was harder to read his expressions while he wore his visor. She couldn't see his eyes. Still, his overall posture conveyed offense at being called a brat.

"You used to be sweet," she said.

He snuffed, then thrust his face back into the dirt, declaring the conversation over.

She turned her gaze toward the cottage. The curtains in the window moved slightly for the tenth time since daybreak. The smoke rising from the chimney carried the scent of baking biscuits. Her stomach grumbled. Those would really taste good.

She waited patiently as the sun rose higher into the sky. Poocher finished digging up the last flower bed. Looking content, he climbed up onto his saddle. He did so with gentle, sure-footed movements. Even though he was now quite portly, Poocher still possessed a certain gracefulness. Skitter didn't even stir.

Long after the smell of biscuits had faded, the curtains pushed aside for one more peek. When they fell, she heard muffled voices from inside.

Here and there around the village, there were signs of life as the other houses woke. A few heads poked from doorways from time to time to stare at the well and the snoring long-wyrm. From the backs of the houses, Zeeky could hear doors opening. She caught glimpses of old men and young children as they tiptoed to reach the outhouses by the creek. The doors were swiftly pulled shut behind them.

At last, the rear door to Barnstack's cottage creaked open. From where she sat, she could see Barnstack's outhouse if she leaned a bit to the left. She saw the old man skulking toward it. He glanced back over his shoulder. Seeing that she could see him, he broke into a jog. He yanked open the privy door.

A man's arm reached out from the darkness of the outhouse and grabbed Barnstack by his collar, yanking him from his feet. The door slammed shut and Barnstack shrieked. His high-pitched cries lasted for several minutes. Around the village, dogs began to bay. Skitter lifted his head at the sound of the dogs. He let loose a low growl and bared his teeth. Instantly, all the village dogs fell silent.

Barnstack's screams faded. They were followed by incoherent sobbing as a gruff voice shouted out questions. The occasional brief, sharp, shriek of pain caused Skitter to jerk nervously. He uncoiled from the well and looked at Zeeky with anxious eyes.

Poocher stood up in his saddle. The bristles on the back of his neck stood on end. He glanced at Zeeky with a look that said, "Say the word. I'm ready for action."

"Patience," she counseled.

Several long minutes passed where no sounds at all came from the outhouse. Finally, the door swung open and Bitterwood stepped out. He marched to the cottage, disappearing from sight. Skitter flinched as a loud *wham* erupted from behind the house.

"It's okay," said Zeeky, stroking his neck. "He just kicked in the door."

Ten minutes went by without a sound coming from the cottage. At last, Bitterwood stepped out, raising his hand to shield his eyes from the morning sun. His knuckles were bloody. He carried a wicker basket with a bright yellow towel draped over it.

"Got some biscuits and boiled eggs," he said. "Took a crock of jam and some flour. A block of salt. Couple of onions. Some dried beans we can fix up later. A big slab of salt pork, though I guess you and Poocher won't want any of that."

"Toss me one of them biscuits."

Bitterwood pulled back the towel and tossed her a hard, brown, lumpy disk of bread. Zeeky snatched it from the air. It felt heavy as a rock. She bit into it; it was almost as hard as a rock as well. It sucked all moisture from her mouth as she chewed. After her first swallow, she took a long drink from the well bucket. "I'm going to need some of that jam," she said.

"Eat as we ride," Bitterwood said, tossing her the basket and hopping up onto his saddle. Skitter swayed to compensate for the sudden weight. Unlike Poocher, Bitterwood didn't mount the long-wyrm with any hint of gentleness.

Zeeky climbed onto her own saddle. "Which way?"

"North," said Bitterwood. "You were right. Jeremiah did come here. Barnstack found him hiding in one of the empty houses and sold him to a slave-trader nine days ago."

Zeeky clenched her jaw. No wonder the voices in the crystal ball had hidden this from her. "Did you break any of his bones?" she asked.

"Probably," Bitterwood said. "Four, maybe, not counting fingers." The number brought her grim satisfaction.

"The slave-trader is a tatterwing called Nub-tail. He works the whole valley. Prices are high for healthy slaves at the moment. The south is half-empty due to Albekizan's carting off folks to the Free City, and apparently there's a big yellow-mouth outbreak up north. I've a hunch we'll find Jeremiah in Rorg's cavern. Beastialists go through a lot of slaves. Jeremiah is too small for field labor, and too skinny to be purchased as food. He'll probably wind up as a mucker. Let's get going."

Zeeky gently nudged Skitter with her heels. The giant beast slithered forward on its many claws. As they crossed the stream, Zeeky looked toward Barnstack's outhouse. The water beneath it was pink, and dark red drops plinked down from the wooden floor. It wasn't something she wanted to think about any more, so she wouldn't. She instead lifted up the yellow towel and found the crock of jam.

In the saddle bag by her left leg, from inside the clear orb, she could hear the distant murmurs coming from a place that was not a place. She couldn't make out the words, but the mood of the voices struck her as angry. This too, she didn't want to think about. She uncapped the crock of jam, filling the air with the scent of blackberries.

CHAPTER THIRTEEN

DRAGONSEED

S WEAT POURED OFF Burke's face as he shoveled coal through the iron door beneath the boiler. The glow of flames painted the confined space hellish red. Burke closed the furnace, darkening the interior, but he still felt like he was sitting in an oven. He was working in the belly of a low, squat wagon, with iron walls and an iron roof. He'd salvaged the wagon's oak platform, the boiler, and the steel treads on which the whole device rolled from Big Chief, the war machine that had helped repel Shandrazel's army. Big Chief had served its purpose, but had obvious shortcomings as a practical engine of war. It had been too tall to be armored properly and still roll without toppling. The consequence of skimping on armor came back to him as he reached down to scratch the itch on his right knee and found his fingers touching air.

Burke was a rational man; he'd never believed in ghosts. So what was the source of this phantom that haunted him? What was he to make of the fact that he could feel his absent toes? If he could still feel a missing leg, would the same be true if he lost his arm? Or even his head? How much of him could be cut away before he'd stop feeling everything? Or, was it true after all? If you destroyed a man's body, was there still some spirit that lingered, invisible, intangible, yet still capable of feeling the world, just as his missing leg was now feeling the heat?

Could Ragnar be right? Did he, in fact, have a soul that would one day be judged by an unseen God?

Burke shook his head and reached for the greasy towel he used to clean his tools. He found the cleanest swatch on it and mopped up the sweat stinging his eyes. He scooted across the oak platform on his butt, opening the gun slits to let in air, then slid onto the squat wooden stool that served as Big Chief's new driver's seat. Of course, Big Chief was no longer an apt name. The war machine was no longer humanoid in shape. The wagon was now twenty feet long from end to end, and five feet tall at its highest point. It looked more like a turtle than a man now. In fact, given that it was more oval shaped than round if seen from above, and was solid cast iron black, it looked more like a beetle than a turtle. An angry beetle, bristling with spikes to discourage any dragons from trying to land atop it, assuming they made it past the twin cannons, or the alcohol-based flame-thrower, or the small guns that could be aimed out gun slits.

The Angry Beetle. Burke smiled. After he worked on a machine long enough, it would eventually tell him its name.

Feeling confident, Burke released the clutch to engage the low forward gear. He let it out carefully—he only had thirty feet to roll without crashing into the door of the warehouse he'd commandeered for the Angry Beetle's construction. Alas, thirty inches would have been enough space. Burke winced as metal ground against metal. The machine lurched barely a foot before something in the underbelly popped. The steel walls of the structure rang as if they'd been struck with a hammer.

"Wonderful." Clenching his teeth, he stepped back onto the clutch and pulled the lever to shift power to the reverse gears. He laughed, amazed, as the machine lurched again and rolled backward. He quickly knocked the machine back out of gear.

"If the dragons attack from behind, I'm golden." The machine's weight brought it to a halt after a few inches. Setting the brake, he flipped the release switch to vent the steam. He slid over to the hatch and pushed it open. The cooler air of the warehouse washed over him. He sat at the edge of the hatch, stretching both his good leg and his phantom one, and looked around the warehouse. Once, the earth-dragons of the foundry had filled this place with swords and shields and other armaments. He'd ordered them all melted down, turned into sky-wall bows, shotguns, and cannons. Now teams of men were already at work building components for a fleet of Angry Beetles, even though no one but himself had any idea what the final project was.

Was Stonewall right? Was his distrust of Ragnar leading him to levels of secrecy that would damage the chances of not only holding onto Dragon Forge, but of projecting force outward, letting humanity win the ultimate war against the dragons?

He was confident the Angry Beetle was worth his time and energy. These mobile platforms of war wouldn't roll far given the restraints on fuel storage, and they wouldn't move fast given their weight, but they'd still cut down earth-dragon armies like a scythe through wheat. As a mobile platform for cannons, they'd also remove the aerial advantage of the dragons. The cannons could hurl steel balls over a mile nearly straight up; he was confident he'd soon solve the problem of how to make those balls explode at their apex, filling the sky with shrapnel that would devastate the winged beasts.

Yet, with Anza gone, was this too much of a project for him to tackle alone? He wasn't daring to make eye contact with Biscuit now, let alone consult with him. After admitting to Stonewall that he'd taught someone else to read his coded notes, he didn't want to give Ragnar any reason to suspect Biscuit was his confidant.

He grabbed the steel crutch that leaned up against the armored vehicle and winced as he placed it beneath his raw and blistered armpit. His armpit was proving ill-designed to provide support for half his body weight. Once the wound of his amputated leg finally healed, he looked forward to fitting himself with a prosthesis. He already had in mind a design that would incorporate a leaf spring to serve as his new foot, and a self-adjusting gear and ratchet that would make a passable knee.

Burke limped around to the rear of the Angry Beetle, to the big sliding doors that closed off the warehouse. He slid one open a crack and raised a hand to shield his eyes. He'd come to work while it was still dark outside. He guessed it must be noon by the way the shadows hugged the buildings. As his eyes adjusted he saw a crowd gathering further down the avenue, in the big central square.

Three of Ragnar's Mighty Men loped past the warehouse with Frost at their side. Frost cast a menacing glare toward Burke, but said nothing. As they passed, Stonewall stepped from a nearby doorway, raising a hand to greet Frost and the others.

Burke lingered in the shadows of the barn, straining to hear the conversation.

"What's going on?" Stonewall asked.

"It's Shanna," Frost answered. "She's back. And she's... different."

Stonewall looked confused. Burke wasn't sure what Frost meant either. Shanna was one of Ragnar's spies. She'd had the dangerous task of infiltrating the Sisters of the Serpent and stealing Blasphet's secrets. Burke liked her for her daring and her intelligence, even if she was fiercely loyal to Ragnar. They owed their possession of Dragon Forge to the poisons Shanna had stolen perhaps even more than to the sky-wall bows. Shanna had left Dragon Forge shortly after the dragon armies fled to try to reconnect with the remnants of Blasphet's cult. Blasphet was dead, slain by Bitterwood, but the worshippers of the Murder God still possessed knowledge of vast stocks of poisons that would be useful in the coming war. Burke leaned onto his crutch and swung out into the street, following the crowd.

Soon he could see the central square. A woman draped in a heavy white cloak stood on the thick stone rim of the town well. Burke assumed this was Shanna, though the sun reflecting off her pure white cloak made it difficult to look at her. Her face was hidden by a deep hood.

Hundreds of men gathered in the square. Who was watching the foundry if everyone was out here? He looked around and saw that the bowmen standing watch on the walls were facing inward, curious about the commotion, paying no attention to potential sneak attacks by dragons. What was Shanna doing making such a splashy entrance? She was a spy, after all. She should appreciate the value of subtlety.

"Stand aside." The crowd parted as he hopped along on his crutch. Even half-crippled, he was still a respected figure in Dragon Forge. He'd proven his value with the sky-wall bows; dozens of these men had trained with the shotguns, or witnessed the blasts of the first cannons off the line. Still, perhaps it was his imagination, but he felt a sense of unease when the crowd looked at him. *"They say you don't believe in God,"* Stonewall had said. It wasn't a healthy rumor to have whispered in the midst of a holy war.

As he reached the well, the crowd on the far side parted. Ragnar, prophet of the lord, strode forth. Burke had been avoiding Ragnar since their confrontation over Jandra. The hairy prophet narrowed his eyes as he spotted Burke. By now, he'd seen the cannons in action. Burke felt confident that he was still too valuable for Ragnar to spare. After glowering at him for a moment, Ragnar's expression changed to a smile.

The well was a yard high. Shanna, standing upon it, was a good deal taller than Ragnar, or even Stonewall, who loomed behind him.

"Shanna," Ragnar said, his voice unexpectedly soft. "I'm pleased you've returned safely. I'm eager to learn how you slipped through the blockade. Let's return to my house so that we can discuss what you've learned in private."

Shanna pulled her hood back. Burke squinted as he pushed his spectacles back up his nose. Was this Shanna? The face was right, the same lips and eyes, the same overall structure of the face. But Shanna had possessed a stark black tattoo, a serpent that coiled along her neck and shoulders, and she'd kept her head shaved. Now jet black hair hung down past her shoulders. A wig, perhaps? All traces of the serpent tattoo were absent from her snow-white neck.

"I want everyone to hear my message," Shanna said. "There's no more need for war! Not long ago, I pretended to serve the Murder God. I tattooed and scarred my body to prove my loyalty. You all can see my tattoos are gone. My scars are gone as well, both physical and spiritual."

She rolled up her sleeve and showed off her forearm. Ragnar furrowed his brow. Burke hadn't known Shanna well enough to know if she should have a scar there, but judging from the confusion in Ragnar's eyes, apparently, she used to.

"What witchcraft is this?" Ragnar grumbled.

Shanna ignored him, speaking to the crowd over Ragnar's head. "I've met a healer. He intends to cure this world of all diseases, all hunger, all hate. Throw down your arms and follow me. I will lead you to the Free City."

At the mention of the Free City, the mob began to whoop loudly. *"Remember the Free City,"* was a common rallying cry for the rebels, many of whom had been present when Albekizan had ordered the slaughter there. That battle had been mankind's first victory against dragons in centuries. Just hearing the words "Free City" was enough to stir men to shouting. But had they listened to what Shanna was actually saying?

"Shanna, have a care," Ragnar growled. "Healing is a gift of God alone."

"The healer says he is not a god," said Shanna. "But I've watched him work miracles! A man with no eyes was given the gift of sight once more. The lame cast off their crutches and walk. The healer is here to cure the pains of all men. Follow me to the Free City, and there will be no more hunger, no more fear, no more pain, and no more war."

The crowd again began to whoop at the words "Free City," though most of the cries came from the back, where they probably had difficulty following what she was saying. People closer to the well mumbled in confusion. Ragnar glared back over his shoulder, scowling. The crowd quickly fell silent.

Burke limped forward. "Shanna," he said. "Did the Sisters of the Serpent give you anything odd to eat? We know that Blasphet had poisons that would enslave the minds of dragons. Is it possible you've been given some drug that is altering your perceptions?"

"Yes," said Shanna. She knelt down on the edge of the well and extended her hand. She turned her palm up and revealed what looked like a handful of large, flat, black ticks. She said, "These are the dragonseed. They are plucked from the healer's own body. Take them. Eat them. Your eyes will be opened to his truth, and you shall be restored. You will walk to the Free City on two legs."

Burke's curiosity compelled him to take one of the strange objects. Once he picked it up, he saw it was more like an oversized watermelon seed than a tick. It was jet black and warm. It smelled vaguely like cloves. Despite his curiosity, he had no intention of putting the seed in his mouth. He thought of Ragnar's earlier cryptic smile. Was this some elaborate attempt to poison him? Or some unfathomable power play, a gambit to make him look foolish in front of the crowd?

If it was a ploy by Ragnar, it only made the prophet's next move all the more shocking.

"Blasphemer!" Ragnar shouted, grabbing Shanna by the wrist. The seeds spilled from her hand and littered the packed red clay around the well. Ragnar yanked her down from the wall. She landed on her knees before him, a cry of pain escaping her lips. "Who has corrupted you? What evil force drives you to utter such foul lies?"

He raised his hand as if to strike her. Shanna looked up, her face somehow serene despite the violence being perpetrated upon her. "It's never corruption to speak the truth," she said.

Ragnar slammed his fist down, a blow that should have knocked all the teeth from Shanna's mouth. Only, the blow never struck Shanna. Burke tossed aside his crutch and reached out, catching Ragnar's hand. The force of the halted blow threw Burke off balance. Ragnar snarled and shoved Burke away. Burke landed in the dirt, flat on his back. He rolled to his belly, ready to push up on both hands.

Stonewall stepped forward and placed his foot into the small of his back, pinning him. Behind him, Shanna let out a gasp of pain. Burke turned his head and saw Ragnar lifting her to her feet by her long hair. So much for the assumption she was wearing a wig.

Ragnar apparently was confounded by Shanna's tresses as well. "What witchcraft has restored your hair, woman?" he demanded.

"My shaved scalp was a symbol of the Murder God," she said, crying out the words through her pain. "My new hair is a gift of the healer! It's a symbol of his grace! Everyone who looks upon me knows the truth. The time of war is passed! The time of healing has begun!"

Ragnar let out a horrible, guttural scream of wordless rage. He slammed Shanna's head down onto the lip of the well with a sickening crack.

"You bastard!" Burke screamed, struggling to free himself. "What are you—"

Before he could complete the thought, Ragnar held out an open hand. Frost stepped up and placed a long knife into his palm. Shanna's arms hung limp at her sides. Ragnar still held her by her hair. Her once white robes were now streaked with red. Her eyes were half open, but she looked stunned by Ragnar's blow.

"Death is the fate of all blasphemers!" Ragnar shouted. "Let no man be led astray by the lies of a witch! These are not the days of healing! These are the days of wrath! We shall not rest until we've driven the last dragon into the sea! Remember the Free City!"

The crowd cheered at this battle cry.

"War!" Ragnar cried.

"War!" the crowd echoed.

"War!" he cried again.

"WAAAARR!" the crowd howled, their voices causing the earth beneath Burke to tremble.

Ragnar looked at the bloodied, half conscious woman dangling in his grasp, wrinkling his nose in disgust, as if he'd just discovered a dead skunk in his hand. With a grunt, he jerked her backward and up, until she sat atop the well. He sank the knife deep into her left breast. He yanked the knife free and released her. She toppled backward, her legs flipping into the air, and disappeared down the stone shaft.

The crowd continued to cheer. Burke pushed up with all his might, but Stonewall only pressed down harder.

Ragnar leaned down, staring into Burke's face. He looked calm as he said, "If I discover you were behind this, you'll join Shanna in her watery grave."

Burke wanted to grab the prophet by his beard and yank the flesh off his skull. Alas, Ragnar crouched several inches beyond his reach. Despite his anger, there was a cool, mechanical voice inside him, counseling him on practical matters. "A corpse in the well will poison our water, idiot," he hissed.

Ragnar's calm expression changed to a frown. He turned and addressed Stonewall in a tone of voice that bordered on sanity. "Let him go," he said. "Have your men fish Shanna's body out at once."

"Of course, sir," said Stonewall, though he didn't move his foot. Indeed, he shifted even more of his weight onto it. Burke felt certain his spine would snap.

Ragnar walked away. Only once he was gone did Stonewall release Burke. Burke rolled over and found the giant bodyguard gazing down at him.

"Burke, I understand your actions," said Stonewall. "No man enjoys seeing a woman struck. However, I cannot allow you to hurt Ragnar."

"Why didn't you stop him?" Burke grumbled as he sat up. "Instead of standing on my back, you could have saved her life."

"Ragnar is a holy man," said Stonewall. "You heard the crowd cheer his words. The Lord has chosen him to lead us to war. It's not our role to judge him. It's our role to obey him."

"Those may well be the most brainless words I've ever heard spoken," said Burke.

"Ragnar won the battle of the Free City. He took Dragon Forge from the dragons, and repelled the immense army gathered to take it back. It's hardly brainless to trust his judgment, or conclude that the hand of God guides his actions. If you would only accept this, and trust him with your secrets, think of the good he could do."

"You have a body to fish out of our water," said Burke. He leaned back against the well and looked down at the black seed still in his palm. Botany wasn't his strong suit, but he was certain the seed was some sort of hallucinogen, whatever it came from. It was the simplest explanation for Shanna's insanity. The missing tattoo was odd, but women were good with make-up, and he hadn't gotten a really good look at her neck. He personally had never noticed a scar on her arm, no matter Ragnar's reaction. As for the hair... a wig and glue? What else made sense?

"Maybe she had a twin?" he mumbled it out loud to test the words for plausibility. They instantly failed the test.

"Ragnar's lucky Anza wasn't here to see this," said a well-known voice. "It wouldn't be that woman's body at the bottom of the well right now." Burke looked up to find a grizzled old man before him. A familiar figure stood behind him, his hand on the older man's shoulder. Despite the horrors of the last five minutes, Burke smiled broadly.

"Thorny!" he said. "You made it. And Vance! You're back! How did you get through the blockade? Are the others with you?"

Vance shook his head. There was something disturbing about the way he wasn't looking directly at Burke. Did he come bearing bad news?

"We thought we weren't going to make it," Thorny said. "The dragons have every road into town blocked off. Worse, they've lined the roads with corpses. Even if the roads weren't guarded, I don't think many people would be coming here. They took all the refugees from Burke's Tavern captive. All the healthy people they've gathered into a holding pen, to be sold as slaves. The sickest of us, they let through the blockade. There was me, Vance, and old Dealon. Unfortunately, Dealon was weakened from the journey and worn down by the terror of walking past all those corpses. He's dead, Burke. Fell to the ground not a half mile from the gate."

Burke lowered his head. When Ragnar had started his little rebellion, Burke had refused to let anyone else from his village join his army, hoping to shield them from the worst of what was to come. Dealon had been the first man to welcome him to Burke's tavern. He'd been outgoing, kind, and didn't have an enemy in the world. He didn't deserve a death like this.

"I guess it makes a sort of cold strategic logic to let the old and infirm through the blockade. But Vance, you're young and healthy. How'd you slip through?"

Vance shook his head. "I'm blind," he said. "I took a bad blow to my head. The world's been dark since. I'm useless now."

"Don't think that," said Burke. "You're a brave kid with a good head on his shoulders. I'll find useful work for you." He looked back to Thorny. "As for you, the dragons obviously don't know what a treasure they've given us by letting a man with your know-how slip through."

"I don't hold a candle to you, Burke," said Thorny. "And it's not like I can handle a wrench anymore."

"You know how to read a plan, though. More importantly, you know how to spot a flaw in a plan. I can't wait for you to see the Angry Beetle."

Vance sagged at these words. Burke bit his lip, realizing the word "see" might have been a poor choice. "I'm going to need some help standing up," Burke said, lifting his hand.

Thorny placed his useless claws onto Vance's wrist and guided the young man's healthy hand to Burke's outstretched fingers. "It looks like war has taken a bite out of you as well," said Thorny.

"It was just a leg," said Burke. "Not even my favorite one."

As Vance helped him stand, he asked, "What happened to the girl? The one talking about how we'd all be healed? Did Ragnar kill her?"

Burke nodded. Then, catching himself, he said, "Yes."

Vance shook his head slowly. "When I heard about Ragnar, me and Vinton left Stony Ford to join him, thinking he was a hero. Now I'm thinking he's a monster."

Burke looked around. Some of the Mighty Men were nearby, talking about who was going into the well. If they'd heard Vance's words, they didn't react.

"Sometimes, to fight monsters, you need an ally who's a monster," said Burke. "For better or worse, there are men in this fort who are willing to die for Ragnar. I don't like him and I don't trust him. I know he feels the same about me. But we both know that we need each other if we're going to reach our goals. Ragnar needs me to build weapons. I need him to build armies that will put those weapons to good use. As long as we have the dragons to fight, we'll muddle through. It's what happens after we defeat the dragons that's going to be messy."

Vance nodded. "Did I hear the girl offering you something to eat? 'Cause I'm starving."

"You don't want what she was offering. Come on back to the shop," he said, hopping around, his hand on the well for balance. He crouched down on his one leg to reach his crutch. "I've got some grub there. Nothing fancy, but you'll sleep with full bellies tonight."

"What was she offering?" asked Vance.

"A lot of nonsense, mostly," said Burke. "Blasphet possessed an unparalleled knowledge of poisons. She must have ingested something that drove her crazy."

"But what was she talking about? The dragon-seed?"

He couldn't fault the boy for his curiosity. Burke took the seed Shanna had given him and placed it in Vance's palm for the boy to examine. "They're like big watermelon seeds. I can't even guess what plant they come from. But I'm not so desperate that I'm going to put something strange in my mouth because an obviously insane woman promises it will heal me."

Vance rolled the large black seed between his fingers. "Yeah," he said. "Only a fool would fall for something like that."

CHAPTER FOURTEEN

MACHINE HEART

BAZANEL, THE MOST acclaimed chemist among the sky-dragons, stood before the black slate wall in the Golden Tower of the College of Spires, writing out the recipe for gunpowder. He turned and faced his guest, nervously rolling the small rod of bone-white chalk in his left fore-talon. Suddenly self-conscious of his fidgeting, he put the chalk down. With the single remaining claw on his mangled right fore-talon, he scratched at the scaleless mass of scar-tissue where his ear used to be and cleared his throat.

"The key component is saltpeter... potassium nitrate. This contains three oxygen molecules, bound to one molecule of potassium and one of nitrogen. When mixed with the other compounds it's stable until energy is introduced. The oxygen unbinds, then rebinds, producing explosive combustion."

The sky-dragon seated upon a leather cushion looked at the board with a blank stare. Unlike the students he normally lectured, this guest probably had little training in chemistry. She was a valkyrie, a female sky-dragon, one of the warriors who guarded the Nest.

Ordinarily, sky-dragons lived with the complete segregation of the sexes. The extraordinary events of recent weeks had produced the current cooperation. The aerial guard had always been a small force, and it had suffered losses in the battle of the Free City. The valkyries had lost hundreds during Blasphet's assault on the Nest. Only a combination of forces could now have a hope of restoring order to the fractured land.

Bazanel could count on his claws the number of times he'd been in the presence of a female of his species—even though he had fewer claws than most. Breeding was strictly controlled by the matriarch, the leader of the Nest who guided the genetic destiny of the sky-dragons. Male sky-dragons who excelled in scholarship were rewarded with the opportunity to breed so that their desirable traits might remain in the species.

At the age of fifty-four, Bazanel had never been invited to the Nest, though he was widely acclaimed as the most knowledgeable chemist the biologians had ever produced. No doubt his physical appearance had some bearing in this decision. He'd long had a special interest in the study of unstable chemicals. A side-effect of this interest meant that more than half of his body was marred by scar tissue. He was completely deaf in his right ear and plagued by incessant ringing in the left. Holes riddled both wings, rendering him flightless. His once fine tail was now only a stub. And yet, against all odds, his reproductive organs remained intact. Genetically, he was a whole being. The matriarch had to know this. Why was he snubbed?

The valkyrie's name was Rachale; she had several burn wounds along her neck, still red and puffy. During the attack on the Nest, some of Blasphet's forces had used a crude flame-thrower—no doubt she was a veteran of this battle.

She asked, "You're certain saltpeter can be found in bat guano?"

"Oh yes," said Bazanel. "Most abundantly. It's in any number of other sources as well—almost any urine will have the necessary components. Caves merely provide a convenient, stable environment for the crystals to grow."

"Given your knowledge of the ingredients, how much gunpowder do you think the rebels could have made in this short period?"

"Perhaps quite a bit," said Bazanel. "Some of the ancient waterworks in that area have been the undisturbed home of bats for centuries."

Rachale nodded slowly. "We're placing a great deal of faith that you've gotten this right."

"This requires no faith," said Bazanel. "This is chemistry. If you follow the formulas I've provided you, you will manufacture gunpowder by the barrelful. I stake my reputation as a scholar upon it."

"It isn't your reputation as a scholar that causes our concern," said Rachale. "It's your reputation for carelessness."

"I see," said Bazanel. Her use of the word "our" was of interest to him. Was this an opinion of the matriarch?

"Over the course of the last three decades, you've gutted four towers, caused structural damage to six others, killed two students, seventeen human slaves, and injured countless more. You're lucky to be alive. Luckier still, I think, that Chapelion has allowed you to retain your position. At the Nest, such carelessness would not be tolerated."

Bazanel drew his shoulders back and tilted his chin upward. Rachale's words displayed such staggering ignorance that, if all females were this limited in their intellect, he was grateful he'd never been invited to breed.

"Chapelion understands that mine is the work of a pioneer. I've expanded the frontiers of knowledge. My scars are badges of honor, not marks of shame. I believe this meeting is over. Return to Chapelion with my report. He will have the intellect to appreciate the treasure I am giving him."

Without waiting for her reply, he turned and limped toward the staircase that spiraled down the outer rim of the tower. Rachale's accusation festered in his mind. Carelessness? *Carelessness?* In his indignity, a previously unthinkable course of action formed in his mind.

The action he contemplated violated the most fundamental moral code of the sky-dragons, but they had pushed him to this. It was time for him to draft the most scathing letter any dragon had ever crafted, a letter that would make the matriarch weep with shame when confronted with the tremendous injustice she'd perpetrated.

His rage was still burning by the time he limped his way into his laboratory in the cellar. The cool, musty air calmed him somewhat. The familiar smell of his lab soothed him further. He did note, however, that the atmosphere smelled heavily of lamp-oil.

When he pushed open the door, he found his laboratory in complete darkness. Why had Festidian allowed the lanterns to burn out? The young biologian was normally much more diligent.

"Festidian?" he asked. No one answered.

Bazanel stepped into the room slowly, groping his way forward until he bumped into his lab table. He carefully swept his scarred claws across it until he found the beaker he was looking for. He had a nugget of phosphorous within, stored under a two-inch layer of oil to keep it from contact with the air. He found a glass dish and poured the contents of the beaker onto it. In the shallow dish, the phosphorous, now exposed to air, took on a faint green glow. Seconds later it began to spit sparks, setting the oil in the dish on fire. The nugget now blazed like a shard of the sun. Stark shadows were cast on the wall. The phosphorous hissed as it burned. The smell brought to mind toasted garlic.

"Festidian?" he called out, more forcefully. No answer.

Bazanel shrugged. Perhaps, Festidian had slipped back to his chambers to catch a nap. He'd worked the young dragon to the point of exhaustion. Ever since the shotgun and the ammo belt had been brought to the College of Spires, Bazanel had heard the ticking of a clock in the back of his mind. He instantly recognized the importance of the compound and knew it was vital to the survival of all dragons to match the humans' sudden advantage in power.

He walked to one of the wall lanterns to light it, so that he might have a softer, steadier light than the overly energetic phosphorous and the flickering oil. He slipped as he neared the wall. A sharp pain sliced into his left hind-talon.

Oil covered the floor. A shard of glass jutted from the outer pad of his talon. The lantern was broken— a polished steel tomahawk was buried into the tin well that held the oil. The glass globe was gone. The stark, flickering shadows had hid the damage from him until he was right on top of it.

"Oh no," he whispered, understanding the full implications of what he saw.

He spun around, slipping again in the oil, reaching out to the table edge to steady himself.

"Festidian?" he whispered again, though now he knew there would be no answer.

He looked across the table, toward the locked cabinet where he kept the rarer substances he studied, including the recently delivered shotgun. The lock was gone, the wood where it had once hung was splintered.

His eyes searched the dancing shadows. "Sh-show yourself," he said. "I know who you are." His pounding heart drowned out the sizzle of the phosphorus.

"Y-your name is Andzanuto," he said, addressing his unseen visitor. "It's the Cherokee word for heart. Thor Nightingale tells me your father calls you Anza. He... your father... he's now called Burke. Twenty years ago, he was better known as Kanati the Machinist. He was once my friend."

Again, his words were met with silence. He edged his way around the table, his fore-talon gripping the thick oak to maintain his balance. Where was she?

"There's no point in hiding," he said. "Kanati wouldn't have sent you to only recover the gun. The weapon was unmistakably of his design. Who else would have bothered with the decorative scale pattern? No doubt, he wants you to destroy all records of my research. You're too late. I've given a scroll with the formula to a valkyrie who even now carries it back to Chapelion. The secret cannot be contained."

He reached the cabinet. The padlock lay in the floor, still intact. She'd simply torn the metal braces that held it from the wood. That security flaw would have to be remedied, obviously. He opened the cabinet and peered inside. The shotgun was gone.

Bazanel took a deep breath. His heart rate slowed. She could have killed him by now. Did she know of his relationship with her father?

"Years ago, while I was still a student—five years before the failed rebellion at Conyers—I heard the legend of the Anudahdeesdee. I wasn't blind to the fact that dragons thrived among the ruins of a once dominant human culture. It was said that your people were dedicated to preserving secrets from the Human Age. I traveled through the southern foothills to find them—only to be almost killed when I did so. I fled, grievously wounded, taking refuge in the City of Skeletons. Your father found me there. He nursed my wounds. He said he'd long wanted to talk to a biologian. Much of the knowledge his people preserved had been corrupted or lost. Kanati knew that biologians were dedicated to scholarship, and thought that by sharing our research, we might improve the knowledge of both species. We began a long correspondence. Of course, the rebellion at Conyers put an end to this."

Bazanel sighed, shaking his head. "Such a waste. Humans accomplished so much in their time as the only intelligent species. With the rise of dragons, species equal, if not superior, to human intellects, the mind power available to solve the world's problems doubled. The world should have entered a golden age. Instead, wars and plagues and hatred have reduced both men and dragons to shadows of their possible greatness."

He shut the cabinet and leaned against it, weary. He hadn't slept in two days.

"After the fall of Conyers, I learned of a clever inventor named Burke. There was no mistaking that this was, in truth, Kanati. I sent Thorny to find him. Over the years, he's served as my spy, sending me news of Burke's inventions. I've paid him well for his efforts, though from what I've heard, he gives all his money to your father in exchange for alcohol."

Bazanel paused, listening for a response. Still nothing. Was it possible he was talking only to his imagination?

"Thorny told me about you, Anza. He says you're an unsurpassed warrior. You are your father's ultimate invention... a killing machine, crafted from muscle and bone instead of cogs and springs."

This time, when there was no reply, the last of the fear drained from Bazanel. She must have taken the shotgun and fled, thinking her mission was over. He was reminded of Kanati's clockwork-driven beasts. They could give the impression of intelligence in a limited series of tasks, such as moving a chess piece, or playing an instrument. But beyond this narrow range of abilities they had no awareness at all, no capacity for independent thought. Perhaps this was true of Anza as well. In raising her with a single-minded focus on killing, no doubt other aspects of her intelligence had been allowed to wither.

Now that he no longer feared for his life, the pain in his talon took dominance in his mind. He snaked his long neck down to better examine the sliver of glass. As his head lowered below the lip of the table, he discovered most of Festidian's corpse beneath, his wings neatly folded. "Oh dear," he said, rising.

Anza stood on the other side of the table. The tomahawk was gone from the ruined lantern behind her left shoulder. Sheaths filled with blades of various sizes ran along her arms and legs. Her hands hung down by her side, hidden by the edge of the table.

Bazanel whispered, in a dry, trembling voice: "What did you do with his head?"

Anza lifted up her grisly trophy, a scaly blue head with a pale gray tongue hanging loosely from the jaws. Festidian's eyes were open slightly, gleaming like polished amber in the phosphor luminance.

Anza tossed the head toward Bazanel. Reflexively, he caught it. He looked down at the severed head, at the high crown of Festidian's fine skull. Such a magnificent specimen. He hoped that the matriarch wouldn't hold a prejudice against Festidian's mating simply because of his association with Bazanel.

Not that it mattered, he realized.

When he looked back to Anza, she held a long, razor-edged sword. He instantly recognized the work as Kanati's.

"Before you kill me, there's one last thing I'd like to point out," he said.

She cocked her head.

"You're the one standing in lamp oil." He hurled his former assistant's head at the oil-filled plate sitting in the center of the table. The flaming oil splashed toward Anza. Rather than leaping away, however, she leapt up, springing onto the table as the flaming oil splattered across her torso. She paid no heed to a fist-sized gob of fire that flickered at the top of her left breast as she somersaulted to land on the table before Bazanel.

With a motion smooth and certain as clockwork, she ran the blade across his throat in a precision that brought pressure but no pain. Bazanel raised his fore-talons and found blood gushing from his neck. He tried to speak, but all that came out was a bubbling wheeze. He fell to the floor, fighting to breathe.

Above him, Anza sucked in air as the gob of flaming oil burned through her buckskin. She placed her gloved fingers over the flame to squelch it.

On the far side of the table, the oil in the floor erupted. Anza strode toward it. Seconds later, a stack of Bazanel's notes fell into the center of the flames. Spots danced before his eyes as Anza tore a second lantern from the wall and poured its oil over the fire, trailing away to lead the flames to bookcases and shelves full of chemicals.

She ended near the bench where he'd been testing the gunpowder he'd already made. He could no longer keep his eyes open. He drifted into darkness as his blood pumped away. He heard the soft pad of Anza's moccasins walk through the blood that pooled before him.

Bazanel's greatest regret was that he wasn't going to be alive a moment from now. He was going to miss the grandest explosion ever to come from his laboratory.

ANZA WAS WELL into the woods when the third explosion shook the earth. Ahead in the darkness, her horse whinnied loudly. The Golden Tower was simply gone, with only a cloud of reddish smoke billowing into the evening sky to give evidence that it had ever been there. Seconds later, chunks of gravel began to rain down. She took shelter behind the trunk of a large pine.

She looked down at the red and blistered skin a few inches below her left collarbone. The oil had burned through her buckskin in an almost perfect circle, though the edges of the buckskin were curled up like little teeth.

The teeth and the circle combined in the dim light to look like one of the toothy wheels in her father's clockwork animals. The burn would leave a scar in the shape of a cog right above her heart.

Her machine heart.

Were Bazanel's words true? Had her father raised her only as a machine for killing? Growing up in the tavern, listening to the ceaseless, mindless chatter of the patrons, she'd realized that their heads must be full of words. While she understood words, she didn't often think with them. Instead, her thoughts were formed by movements. She lived in a world of ceaseless motion, and understood intimately her relationship to that motion. She was swift and sure enough to pluck an arrow from the air. Other people moved as if their bodies were puppets being pulled by the strings of their graceless thoughts. Her body and mind functioned as a single mechanism.

As the rain of gravel ceased, she headed deeper into the woods. She wanted to return to Dragon Forge, to warn her father that Thorny was a spy. However, it sounded as if the secret of gunpowder was carried by a lone messenger. A single scroll carried the formula. Perhaps there was still hope of protecting the secret. Her next destination would be the Dragon Palace. She grimaced as she thought of the hard ride before her, back to the very place she'd just left. Her butt was already sore enough.

She smiled. No machine would ever complain of the work before it. There was a human heart within her after all.

JEREMIAH WAS TOO terrified to scream as the wind buffeted his body. He was wrapped up tightly inside a scratchy blanket that smelled like stale pee, tied securely with ropes. The sky-dragon who carried him, Vulpine, grunted from time to time as they flew. It sounded as if he were straining to remain in the air with Jeremiah's weight. With his face covered by the blanket, Jeremiah had no way of knowing how high they were. Having been raised in the mountains, he was used to high places, and had no fear of standing at the edge of a cliff to stare out over a valley. This was something far different, though. He imagined they must be high enough to touch the moon.

All his life, Jeremiah had heard that winged dragons could snatch up children. He used to have nightmares about it. Now, his nightmare was coming true. The dragon's long wings beat the air, carrying them ever higher. Despite being completely enwrapped, the cold air stabbed through the thin blanket, turning his skin to ice.

He had no way of measuring time, save for a slight brightening and darkening of the threadbare fabric before him as day passed into night, then brightened into day again. Three times, Vulpine stopped to rest for what felt like hours, but never once offered Jeremiah any food or water. Jeremiah remained as still as a corpse the entire time, afraid that any movement might cause the dragon to attack him.

The fourth time they landed, something was different. Jeremiah was dropped to the ground roughly, but he paid little attention to the impact. He could hear voices. There was a delicious smell heavy in the air, like fish being cooked over coals.

"Sir," someone said. "Welcome back. How was your journey?"

"As delightful as I thought it would be, Sagen." Vulpine chuckled, a low sound that made Jeremiah shiver. "Rorg, as ever, is a font of invigorating conversation."

"Did he give you what you wanted?"

The blanket that held him was lifted by the ropes around his shoulders. He was set to his feet. Vulpine's claw snagged the rope for a second. With a grunt he jerked his claw free. The rope suddenly felt slack.

"He doesn't look like much," said Sagen.

"We'll fatten him up," said Vulpine. "He'll make a fine meal."

Jeremiah bit his lower lip to keep from crying out. Why would they want to eat *him*? He was nothing but bones!

Vulpine said, "Throw him in my tent for now. We'll clean him up later and put him in the meat pens."

Jeremiah thought he might faint.

"Sir?" said Sagen, sounding skeptical. "Your tent isn't terribly secure. What if he slipped free of his ropes? He might crawl out the back."

"*Bah*," Vulpine said dismissively. "Those ropes have held so far. He won't be going anywhere."

"I hope not, sir. Dragon Forge is only a few miles away. It's the stronghold of the human rebellion. If he reached it, we'd never get him back."

Jeremiah caught his breath. What human rebellion? If he could wriggle free... but, almost the instant he felt hope flickering, it was squashed again by Vulpine's voice.

"Even if this future meal did escape, how could he find the fortress? He doesn't even know where he is."

Jeremiah sagged as he contemplated this reality.

"But, sir," protested Sagen. "At night the foundries glow like a beacon. And by day, anyone could follow the smoke from the smokestacks."

Vulpine laughed. "You act like this is a dragon we're talking about. This is a muck-slave, not clever enough to slip out of his ropes, crawl under the tent flaps in the back, then search the sky for clues as to which direction he should run. You worry too much."

"Of course, sir," said the other dragon.

Jeremiah was lifted up by the rope around his hips. He was carried a few dozen yards, then tossed unceremoniously into a place where the sounds of voices and the smell of cooking were more muted. The ropes around his shoulder snapped completely as he hit the ground. He wriggled, freeing his head. He was inside a tent. It was dark, with only a few faint rays of light seeping through the flap that covered the door. He wriggled more. He was suddenly grateful he was skinny. He started kicking, and was free of the blanket in no time.

He looked around. The place was sparsely furnished; only a few cushions piled in the corner to serve as a bed. A small crate sat next to the cushions, and atop it sat a long knife in a sheath. He grabbed it and pulled the weapon out. He stood quietly and listened to the dragons just outside the tent. He crouched as they passed, and grabbed the blanket. It was so cold he could see his breath in front of him; despite the stench, he draped the blanket over his shoulders like a cloak.

He dropped to his knees beside the back wall of the tent and peeked under a gap he found there. He could see no dragons in this direction, only bushes. Off in the distance, beyond some low hills, there was a red smear of smoke and clouds in the sky.

Clutching the knife tightly, he rolled beneath the tent flap and scurried for the bushes.

VULPINE WATCHED AS the small, shadowy figure crept up the hill. Sagen shook his head in amazement.

"I can't believe he fell for that," said Sagen.

Vulpine chuckled. "I'm a bit surprised myself. You lack talent as an actor, I fear. Could you possibly have been any more wooden in the delivery of your lines?"

"I'm a soldier, not an actor," said Sagen.

Vulpine placed his fore-talon on Sagen's shoulder. "I cannot possibly express how happy I am this is so."

Sagen looked away, embarrassed by the praise. He watched as the boy vanished over the hill. "You're sure he's infected?"

"He'd better be. I'd hate to think I carried him wrapped in that reeking corpse blanket all this way for nothing. But if we waited for him to develop symptoms, it would be too late. We need him to get inside while he still looks healthy. How goes the blockade?"

"It's… solid," said Sagen.

"I sense some doubt in your voice."

Sagen shook his head. "There's no need for concern. The blockade is perfect. We're penning up the healthy humans we find on the road as you ordered. Whatever their lives once were, they'll be sent to the slave markets. I did, however, deviate slightly from your orders."

"Oh?"

"I've allowed some of the more pathetic refugees to pass through. Men who are too blind, lame, or old to be of any use. My calculation is that this gives the humans more mouths to feed without giving them any more warriors to stand against us."

Vulpine nodded slowly, appreciating his son's cleverness.

Sagen still seemed tense, however. "There is… one more thing."

"Yes?"

"Some of the guard have gone missing."

"Some?"

"Four."

"Do you suspect humans killed them?"

Sagen clamped his jaw shut. He looked as if he were choosing his next words carefully. "I must also report that four valkyries have gone missing."

"Ah," said Vulpine. "I see why the math concerns you."

"The members of my guard are unaccustomed to working so closely with females, sir. I've noticed... unprofessional behavior. I've established the highest standards of discipline possible, but... bluntly, sir, I don't trust the valkyries. Their commander for this blockade is named Arifiel. She's too young for her duties. I fear she can't keep her soldiers under control."

"I've never heard of her, I admit. Still, her youth is unsurprising. The Nest lost over eight hundred valkyries to the Murder God. I imagine this created gaps in their ranks that required many premature promotions. That said, the matriarch is committed to this cause and wouldn't have chosen Arifiel lightly. I'll talk to her."

Sagen nodded, apparently satisfied that Vulpine would solve the problem. Vulpine wasn't as confident. There was a reason the sexes had been separated for centuries. Military discipline was a powerful force; hormones and instinct, however, were just as powerful, and sometimes more so.

"Shall I continue the policy of allowing the more pathetic refugees access to the fort? Arifiel disagreed with the policy. She said that, should the rebels eventually turn to cannibalism to deal with food shortages, we're simply helping stock their larder."

"If it reaches that stage," said Vulpine, staring at the blood-tinted clouds that hung over the fort like an omen of doom, "I think we can chalk this up as a victory."

CHAPTER FIFTEEN

VIOLENCE AS AN ACCEPTABLE ARGUMENT

SKITTER RACED DOWN the winding hillside path at a speed that would have put the fastest horse to shame. The winter wind stung Bitterwood's eyes. Whenever he blinked, dozens of yards had passed. At the bottom of the hill was a broad rocky stream crossed by a covered bridge. Skitter shot into the darkness of the bridge without hesitation. His claws raced through the wooden structure like a drum roll. A second later they were back in daylight, and Bitterwood squinted as the sun glinted on Skitter's coppery scales.

When Bitterwood first laid eyes on a long-wyrm he hadn't put any thought into whether or not he should kill it. It was big, it had scales, it would die. He had dispatched that first long-wyrm in a matter of seconds, despite being armed with nothing more than a fireplace poker. Twenty years of constant war with dragons had honed his reflexes to a razor's edge, and his pure and total hatred of all dragons was quick to draw that edge across any serpentine throat.

So Bitterwood was more than a little disturbed that he was starting to like Skitter. Over the course of his personal war on dragons, he'd traveled many thousand miles on horseback. He was, among his almost endless list of sins, a horse-thief many times over. He'd developed good judgment in sizing up any horse he met. Skitter surpassed them all. The big lizard could gallop along at twice the speed of the swiftest horse. His stamina was phenomenal as well. No horse could cover a hundred miles before resting the way Skitter could. And when Bitterwood had ridden horses at a full gallop for even a few miles, his body paid for it. Riding a horse at full speed was demanding work. Riding Skitter was like riding the wind. He moved with such smoothness it was easy to believe the beast was flying.

If it had only been Skitter's advantages as a steed that Bitterwood admired, he wouldn't have been uncomfortable. He was also starting to appreciate the aesthetics of the beast. The copper-colored scales caught the sun the way that goldfish had flashed in the fountains at Chakthalla's palace. The sheen also reminded him of the metallic wings of the angel Gabriel. Bitterwood had slain Gabriel without remorse. When Zeeky had found Skitter on the shores of the goddess's island, Bitterwood had assumed he'd eventually kill the beast. Now, he couldn't imagine hurting Skitter. Riding the long-wyrm stirred unfamiliar emotions within him. As they crested the next hill and zoomed down into another gray-green valley he felt something he suspected might be joy. For two decades, he'd seldom felt a moment of peace, let alone happiness.

Something was changing within him. Instead of planning his next kill, his thoughts these days were more like dreams. He would rescue Jeremiah, then take the boy and Zeeky, Skitter and, yes, even Poocher, and ride far away from here, beyond the Cursed Mountains, to a land where there were no men or dragons. He'd build a small cabin, and hunt deer rather than winged serpents. He could once again have a family, or something not unlike a family.

The idea made him... hopeful? Could this actually be hope? He frowned, remembering his advice to Jandra in the shadow of the Free City.

Life is easier without hope.

NIGHT HAD FALLEN when they finally reached the caverns. The bones scattered around the big hole were stark white in the pale moonlight. Red light glowed deep inside the cavern, and smoke rose from dozens of holes around the forests. The ground beneath them vibrated and an unearthly howl rose from the mouth of the cave. It was the sound of dozens of dragons singing in unison.

Bitterwood watched from a grove of trees at the edge of the bone-field as a trio of sun-dragons spiraled down from the sky and crawled into the hole, summoned by the otherworldly song.

Bitterwood grunted at the new arrivals. "Beastialists," he said.

"Beastialists?" asked Zeeky.

"You noticed none of them carried spears? Beastialists think it's a show of weakness. They believe the only weapons a dragon needs are his teeth, his only armor his hide."

"Their hide looks pretty tough to me," she said, as yet another big bull dragon drifted down to land in the bone-field. It paused, sniffing the air. Bitterwood tensed. Could it smell Skitter? Finally, the dragon turned and skulked into the cavern.

"Trust me," said Bitterwood. "Sun-dragon hide is tough enough. Hit a dragon on his breast scales with the edge of a sword and you'll be lucky to scratch him. But I can put an arrow through two inches of oak—a dragon's hide isn't as tough as that. Once an arrow has punched through the hide, the veins of a dragon bleed as freely as any other animal."

"You really know a lot about dragons," said Zeeky. She was finally accepting the fact that Bitterwood was, in fact, Bitterwood. When they'd first met, she thought he was lying.

"I've taken enough apart to know how they're put together. The breast scales are tough, but there are plenty of spots on a dragon where the hide is no thicker than your skin, some with big arteries right beneath them. I can kill a dragon without damaging the meat if I need to. I'd make a good butcher."

Zeeky furrowed her brow. "You wouldn't eat a dragon, would you?" She had strong opinions on what should and should not be food.

"Fighting dragons is hard work," he said, apologetically. "I get hungry."

He looked at Poocher, who he could swear was grinning. The pig appeared to be taking pleasure at Bitterwood's discomfort. "I told you I was a dragon-slayer when I met you," he said. "If I'm willing to kill them, I should be willing to eat them. It would be wasteful otherwise."

"You killed Jazz also," Zeeky said. "And all those long-wyrm riders. Would you have eaten them?"

"I'm not a cannibal."

"Dragons talk," Zeeky said. "Even you can understand them. I talk with dogs and owls and horses. I talk with long-wyrms and ravens and pigs. They're all smart creatures who don't deserve to be eaten."

Poocher snorted, as if saying, "Amen!" Bitterwood didn't plan on giving up bacon, but right now wasn't the time to debate it.

"I don't want you eating dragons any more," she said.

"Do you mind if I go in now? I should warn you I might kill a dragon or two trying to save your brother."

"There's a difference between killing to eat and killing to save a life," she said patiently.

Bitterwood grabbed a fist-sized chunk of half-inch rope from the saddle bags. The rope was lightweight; it was also a vibrant shade of pink that glowed faintly in the gloom. They'd found this fragment of rope in the kingdom of the goddess. It was, as near as he could determine, unbreakable. It was also sensitive to his thoughts, just as Gabriel's sword had been. It would grow as long as he wanted it to grow and never get any heavier. With a thought, the rope would shrink back to this convenient size. He had no idea why it worked, but, like his new bow and arrow, he found it hard to remember how he'd ever gotten along without it.

"I scouted this area five years ago," he said. "I wiggled down some of the chimney holes into the main cavern. I came here to kill Rorg, but had to abandon the mission. Since he was always surrounded by his family, it was too risky a fight."

"The way you throw yourself into a fight, I didn't know you were worried about risk," said Zeeky.

"I spent a lot of years tracking down dragons responsible for the atrocities at Conyers," he said. "Albekizan, was, of course, the big target. Rorg was there too. He was a few hundred pounds lighter, and a good deal less insane. By the time I tracked him down, he'd gotten too heavy to fly. His beastialist philosophy made him more of a joke than a threat. I decided to focus my efforts on other targets. I always knew I'd be back."

"If this dragon's a joke, saving Jeremiah shouldn't be so hard."

"It's not Rorg I'm worried about," Bitterwood said as he tied one end of the rope to a tree. "It's the few dozen other bulls who are part of the clan. Until now, I didn't really have a good way of carrying in enough arrows to make sure the job got done." He reached back and fingered one of the arrows in his quiver. "I'll try to do this quietly. If you start hearing screams, don't be alarmed."

He walked to one of the smoke vents and dropped the rope down. "Stay in the shadows," he said. "You've got six hours until daylight. If I'm not back, ride up the mountain and find a safe place to wait out the day. Meet me back here at sunset."

Bitterwood slung the bow over his shoulder and backed into the hole, the smoke tickling his nose. He climbed down the twisting, natural chimney, his hands growing increasingly black with soot. He reached a junction where the shaft opened into another shaft. The hole was barely two feet across. He shoved his bow through, then his quiver, balancing them on narrow ledges. He shed his cloak and wiggled through, then reached back and grabbed the cloak. He willed the rope to lengthen, letting it dangle down the shaft to the next level spot fifty feet below. From there, he would have to crawl through a shaft only three feet tall for almost a quarter mile, until he reached the side cave where Rorg's slaves slept.

He doubted that they would be sleeping much tonight. The deep bass rumble of the singing sun-dragons shook the stone. A haunting melody accompanied it, played on an instrument Bitterwood couldn't identify. It sounded something like bells, only not as metallic in tone. He could make out various bits of the lyrics. *Dragons are mighty, humans are weak,* and other such puffery. As long as they were singing, their attention would be focused on Rorg.

He wriggled through the last narrow gap of the long tunnel and found himself in a cavity of a rock wall thirty feet up in a large, round chamber. Several small fires were scattered around the cave. Perhaps a hundred humans sat around the fires, staring sullenly into the flames. The singing from the nearby dragon rally echoed within the room.

"With our claws we rend their flesh!" the dragons sang. *"With our jaws we crush them! Their blood slakes our thirst!"* Beastialist lyrics weren't famed for their subtlety.

Bitterwood dropped the rope into the room. Instantly, every eye turned toward the motion. Frightened humans tended to be hyper-alert. Fortunately, no one screamed.

Bitterwood held his fingers to his lips, signaling for silence, then rappelled down to the floor. The walls were slimy. Due to the condensation of breath, the whole cavern glistened as if it were coated with a fine layer of spit. Urine and shit fouled the air. The humans were boiling turnips in carved stone bowls sitting in the fire pits.

Everyone rose as he reached the ground. These humans were a wretched lot. They were clothed in thread-bare rags. Both men and women had their hair cropped close to the scalp in uneven clumps, no doubt to make it easier to pick off fleas and lice. All stood with slumped shoulders. They stared with sunken eyes set in faces that were little more than skulls covered with paper-thin, boil-covered skin.

"I'm looking for a new arrival," said Bitterwood. "A blond boy, no older than twelve. His name is Jeremiah." Not a voice was raised as the crowd watched him with unblinking gazes. "He would have arrived about a week ago." He waited. Did they understand him?

"Our wings block the sun!" the dragons sang. *"The earth trembles as we land!"*

A woman took a tentative step forward. She was covered in brown smudges, thin as a sapling, and perhaps seven months pregnant. She cradled a small bundle wrapped in rags. The bundle wasn't moving; if it was a baby, Bitterwood hoped it was asleep. She cast her gaze toward the floor as she spoke, in a voice so soft and hesitant he barely understood it: "He's gone."

"Gone?" Bitterwood asked. "Dead?"

The woman shook her head. "Vulpine took him."

"Took him where?"

"Dragon Forge?" the woman said. She didn't sound certain of this.

Bitterwood furrowed his brow. Why would the Slavecatcher General want Jeremiah? And why would he take him to Dragon Forge? His heart froze in his chest.

"Was the boy well?"

The woman shrugged.

"No sign of yellow-mouth?"

The woman raised her head when he mentioned the disease.

"We've lost hundreds to yellow-mouth since winter came. Most of us who're left have survived it and are immune. The boy said he'd never been exposed."

Nor, for that matter, had Bitterwood. The foul atmosphere suddenly felt especially heavy in his lungs.

"Who are you?" the woman asked.

"I'm nobody." He turned away, taking the rope in hand. If Jeremiah was gone, there was no reason to linger.

"Your cloak... your bow... are you the hope of the slave? Are you Bitterwood?"

Bitterwood flinched at these words. He didn't mind that his legend was widespread among dragons. The more dragons who feared him, the better. But he regretted that so many humans knew his name. To dragons he was death incarnate, a soulless, faceless force of nature stalking them in every shadow. There was a dark thing inside him that shivered with delight knowing he caused so much fear. This same darkness had no desire to be anyone's hope.

He looked back at the sad, hungry, skeletal crowd. Any one of them, even the pregnant woman, could have climbed through the dragon-free tunnels he'd navigated. True, they didn't have the advantage of a magical rope, but he'd explored these tunnels five years ago without one.

"Why do you stay here?" he asked, his voice low. "There's an open path between this cavern and freedom. It's a risky climb, but certainly better than remaining here."

"Anyone who runs winds up as part of the bonefield," the woman said.

The darkness inside Bitterwood rose up in a great angry wave. "You fear death more than you value your freedom," he said. "Humans outnumber dragons. All that keeps the dragons in power is the cowardice of mankind."

The crowd flinched at his words. Grown men fell to their knees, as if he'd kicked their feet out from under them. Tears welled in the pregnant woman's eyes.

"You have no right to scold us," she said, swallowing a sob. "Who are you to judge us?"

Bitterwood turned back to the rope. The dark thing that had once been his soul now clawed at his skull from the inside, shouting curses. In truth, as much as Bitterwood hated dragons, he held a special contempt for other humans. He'd once been this soft. He'd once been a slave to fear and doubt. Hatred had burned away these weaknesses. Why did other humans not share this hate?

"You're just going to leave us?" the woman asked as he took the rope into his hand and began to climb the wall.

"What if your own wife or child was a slave?" she asked.

Bitterwood stopped climbing. Recanna and Ruth and Eve, his now dead wife and daughters, had been sold into slavery after the fall of Christdale. He'd thought them dead, when in truth they'd lived as the king's property for almost twenty years. Did he hate them for not escaping? If they had been among this rabble, would he have held them in the same scorn?

The dark thing inside suddenly grew quiet. Bitterwood dropped back to the floor. In the chamber beyond, the dragons stopped singing.

"Anyone who has the courage can climb this rope," he said, facing the crowd. "Follow it and you'll be outside. From there, you can go wherever you wish."

"What if Rorg's sons catch us?" the woman asked in a trembling voice.

Bitterwood drew an arrow and placed it against his bowstring.

"No dragon will follow you."

Without waiting to see what they would choose to do, he sprinted toward the tunnel that led to the main chamber. A faint glow lit the tunnel, the light from the fire pit that Rorg's clan gathered around. He sprinted along, hugging the walls. With his soot-darkened cloak and skin, he would be almost invisible among the deep shadows thrown off by the bonfire.

As he reached the central chamber, he dropped to a crouch.

Rorg, pot-bellied and elephant-limbed, stood before the crowd of sun-dragons. There were too many for Bitterwood to count. This was a welcome development in the confined space. Only one or two at a time would be able to squeeze into the tunnel he was currently in. His main worry was that he would block the tunnel with corpses too quickly. His eyes searched about the room, the forest of stalactites and stalagmites, the countless nooks and alcoves and tunnels, looking for the best spot to make his stand. He had the luxury of picking the proper moment to strike. The dragons remained focused on Rorg.

"Treachery!" Rorg shouted. "The foul villain Vulpine nearly crippled Thak with his unholy weapons, taking advantage of our honor and fairness. He challenged my son to single combat, then resorted to the trickery of a blade! Can this injustice be allowed to stand?"

"No!" the beastialists roared. Bitterwood's teeth rattled in the wave of sound.

"Sons! Brothers! Honored friends! Join me in my cause of vengeance! We will march upon the Dragon Palace! We shall throw the interloper Chapelion from the throne! We will end the moral plague that has sickened our fellow dragons! The time has come to rule as nature intended. From shore to mountain, we must make this land one endless bone-field! We are predators! All others are prey! That is the only law!"

The dragons erupted into a frenzy of roaring and shouting, hungry for blood. Bitterwood pursed his lips in grim satisfaction. He no longer cared what Zeeky thought. He was having a dragon steak for breakfast.

He drew his arrow. Unfortunately, Rorg, who had been standing on his hind legs, dropped back to all fours. Bitterwood no longer had a good shot at the big beast. Killing Rorg with a single arrow through his ear-disk would have sent panic through the room. He scanned the remaining targets, trying to decide whose death would have the most dramatic impact.

As the seconds unfolded, the bloodthirsty roar of the crowd fell off, replaced with a confused murmur. Long, serpentine necks began to sway as heads turned toward the back of the chamber. Bitterwood lowered his bow. What was going on?

"Rorg," said a deep voice from behind the assembly, obviously that of another sun-dragon. "I hear you plan to make yourself king."

With all eyes focused on the new arrival at the back of the room, Bitterwood scrambled for a ledge he saw on the western wall. It was about twenty feet up, with a good view of the whole room. Beyond was a hole deep enough that he could safely retreat from the jaws of anyone who tried to reach him. It was also high enough that the piling corpses wouldn't keep him from seeing new targets.

As he scrambled up the slimy rock, the crowd of dragons grew deathly quiet. There was a clanking, clanging sound that reminded Bitterwood of the movements of the now-dead sun-dragon Kanst—the former commander of the king's army had always covered himself in thick plates of iron armor. Bitterwood reached the ledge and turned around. The new arrival was indeed a sun-dragon wearing armor—it looked like it might actually be Kanst's armor, given the high level of craftsmanship. A heavy helmet concealed the dragon's face; chain mail covered his throat. His breast and back were protected by overlapping plates of steel. Even his tail was covered with bands of armor, ending at the tip with a heavy-looking ball studded with blades—a new accessory if this was, in fact, Kanst's armor. A large square shield was slung over his back. Only the great sheets of the dragon's wings were unprotected, but that was of little help. In the air, shooting a dragon in the wing could be fatal with a little assistance from gravity. On the ground, punching holes in a dragon's wings would do little more than annoy him.

The armored dragon lugged what looked like a bulging cow's stomach. Bitterwood thought this was an odd thing to be carrying; from the way the pale blue-white sack roiled with the dragon's motion, it was obviously filled with something liquid. In the dragon's other fore-talon he carried a formidable looking steel-handled axe. Bitterwood's heart skipped a beat when he recognized the weapon—it was the axe of the prophet Hezekiah, an axe that had almost taken his life not long ago. Who was this?

"You have no business here, stranger," Rorg said, eyeing the iron-clad dragon.

The new dragon came to a clanging halt a few feet from the fire-pit. "I'm no stranger, Rorg," said the visitor. "My father knew you well. While he never adopted your foolish beastialism, he always admired your brutality. He thought that, of all the abodes in his kingdom, you had the best approach to handling the humans who lived on his land."

"*His* kingdom?" asked Rorg. "The only king I've ever served is Albekizan. He's dead, and has no sons."

Bitterwood knew that Rorg's statement wasn't quite true. There was one surviving son.

"My name is Hexilizan," said Hex, using his formal name. He drew up to his full height. The light from the fire pit gleamed on his polished breast plate. "You know me, Rorg."

A light slowly flickered in the fat dragon's dull eyes. "Ah," he said. "The disgraced son. Castrated, shamed, sent to live as little more than a slave. Now you come here wrapped in your armor, showing you fear the natural weaponry of the true dragons! Bow before me, Hexilizan, and I may let you leave this cavern with your life."

Hex shook his head, the chain mail on his neck jingling. "Your recitation of my history is correct. I've lived much of my life as another dragon's servant. I found the experience distasteful. The age of kings has reached its end, Rorg, as has the age of slaves."

"You sound like your spineless brother, Shandrazel." Rorg pushed the name from his mouth as if it were a turd he'd found upon his tongue.

"My brother foolishly believed in the equality of all beings," Hex said. "My belief is different: I stand for nothing more or less than freedom. I'm grateful you've called this gathering, Rorg. It makes it convenient for me to address you all. You must all free your slaves. This should be compatible with your philosophy, after all. You call yourselves beasts. Where in nature has slavery ever been found outside of dragonkind? No other creature on this world has ever adopted the practice of slavery."

"Humans are useful parasites," said Rorg. "Without them, who will muck our caves?"

"Even earth-dragons have embraced plumbing," Hex said. "It's time for you to evolve."

"Who are you to come here issuing commands? You are no king!"

"No," said Hex. "I'm not a king. I collect no tax; no patch of the earth is my property. I'm merely a philosopher who sees the myriad injustices of this world. Unlike my pacifist brother, I'm also a warrior. I regard violence as an acceptable argument for convincing others to see things my way."

Bitterwood had seen Hex in action. Bitterwood liked him better as a warrior than a philosopher. Not that he liked him overly much as either.

"You're outnumbered sixty to one!" Rorg snarled as he rose once more to his hind legs. "You're in no position to threaten violence!"

Rorg's fellow beastialists formed a tight circle around the fire pit. Hex was surrounded.

Bitterwood took aim at Rorg. From here, he had a clear shot at the sun-dragon's throat. It would be a simple matter to sever the main artery supplying his brain. The beastialist would be dead within seconds.

His eyes drifted from Rorg to Hex. In his armor, the only vulnerable spots were the narrow eye-slits in the helmet. It would be a more challenging shot. Given the angle of attack, there was also the risk he would merely blind Hex without a clean kill.

Bitterwood contemplated the matter for half a second. He'd been waiting to put an arrow into Hex since the moment he'd met him.

His breath crossed his lips in a slow, calm stream as he let his arrow fly.

CHAPTER SIXTEEN

BLOOD-HUNGRY AVENGER

THE LIVING ARROW flew from Bitterwood's bow-string with a loud *zzzmmm*. The note sang musically in the narrow stone alcove. Hex turned his head barely an inch in reaction to the noise. It saved his life. The arrow hit the edge of his helmet's eye slit and bounced off. The ricocheting arrow sliced across the face of a sun-dragon beyond. That dragon howled in outrage as Bitterwood drew another arrow. The other dragons began to snarl. The awareness that they were under attack spread through the assembly like a wave. Yet, an arrow was a tiny thing, nearly invisible in the firelight. None of Rorg's brethren turned their eyes toward Bitterwood. Instead, they focused upon Hex as their muscles coiled, ready to pounce.

Bitterwood suspected if he did nothing but sit and watch, Hex would be dead inside a minute, given the odds he faced. Still, the opportunity to put an arrow into the brain of Albekizan's only surviving son was something he couldn't pass up. Bitterwood placed the fresh arrow on his bowstring and searched for an opening.

Hex didn't provide the opening. Instead, he tossed the cow stomach into the air above the fire and hacked at it with his steel axe. The bulging sack burst, spraying oil over the fire pit. Bitterwood felt the heat on his cheeks as the oil ignited in a violent conflagration. He turned his face, closing his eyes to protect them from the sudden burst of light.

When Bitterwood opened his eyes, he saw three of the beastialists pounce upon Hex. Bitterwood watched with grudging admiration as Hex made short work of them. The sun-dragon buried the axe into the breast of his first foe, a blow that was almost certainly fatal. With the blade affixed to his tail, Hex sliced across the throat of the attacker at his rear. From the spray of blood, Bitterwood concluded the attack had hit an artery. He wondered if it was only luck, or if Hex was a better fighter than he'd given him credit for. The final attacker was a young, aggressive sun-dragon who charged forward with no hint of caution. Hex opened his jaws wide and caught his foe's smaller head between his teeth. There was a sickening crunch as the dragon's skull split under the force of Hex's crushing bite.

A thick blue smoke rose from the fire. Through the haze, Bitterwood saw a shot as Hex spat the young dragon's head away. Despite his armor, Hex's open mouth was a vulnerable spot. An arrow straight down his gullet would bury itself in the sun-dragon's brain-stem. He let the arrow fly.

Hex snapped his jaw shut as the arrow reached his mouth, tilting his head so that the arrow was deflected by his armored snout. Bitterwood cursed the dragon's luck. Or was it luck? Hex turned his gaze toward the ledge where Bitterwood stood. The other dragons might not be aware of him, but Hex plainly was.

Before Bitterwood could fire again, Thak, Rorg's eldest son, plunged into battle. He blindsided Hex, knocking the armored dragon from his hind-talons. The two crashed against the stone floor. Hex's armor clanged like an alarm meant to wake the gods. The two dragons rolled, necks and tails entwining, as Thak used his powerful claws to peel back part of the armored plate covering Hex's belly.

Traces of the blue-tinged smoke reached Bitterwood. His nose twitched at the stench of burning peanuts. He recognized the odor, having smelled it when Blasphet attacked the Nest. The smoke was a paralyzing poison that affected all manner of dragons.

Around the cavern, sun-dragons were starting to sway drunkenly. They stared at random shadows, glassy-eyed, oblivious to Thak and Hex's furious tussle. The two rolling dragons toppled the nearest beastialists as if they were huge, red bowling pins. A few tried to stagger from the cavern but none made it to the exit, as their eyes rolled back into their heads and they collapsed.

Bitterwood remained focused on Hex's armored form. The excitement of combat was sparing Thak the soporific effects of the smoke so far, so the motions of the two dragons as they wrestled prevented Bitterwood from finding a good opening.

It was increasingly difficult to ignore the fact that there were nearly three score sun-dragons lying immobile, stupefied by the poison smoke. Here was an opportunity to rid the world of an entire clan of sun-dragons. His hatred of all dragons burned in his throat like thirst and he could no longer resist spilling blood. His bow sang out in the alcove in a steady rhythm as he targeted the immobile forms of dragon after dragon. He emptied his quiver faster than his living arrows could grow back. He studied his hand-iwork as his heart pounded in his ears. The floor was red and glistening. He'd killed more sun-dragons in a moment than he'd managed to kill in most years. It wasn't enough.

It could never be enough.

Impatient with waiting for his quiver to replenish, he leapt from the alcove, skidding along the slimy stone, drawing his sword as he raced toward an old sun-dragon who was feebly crawling away, his breath ragged and labored. He turned toward Bitterwood's footsteps. His left eye was murky with cataracts as he lifted his head.

Bitterwood buried his sword between the beast's eyes, pausing for a moment of dark pleasure as death twitched all the way to the tail-tip of the once mighty beast. He pulled the blade free. A shiver ran along his spine as he watched dark red fluid running down the blood-grooves of his blade.

Nearby, a dragon rolled to his back, clutching at the arrow buried deep in his breast. Blood bubbled in the creature's mouth. His remaining life could be measured in moments.

The dark thing that drove Bitterwood would not grant those moments. He hacked and hacked and hacked at the beast's neck, as the ghosts of the uncountable, nameless, faceless men who'd suffered a thousand years of cruelties beneath the talons of dragons whispered for vengeance.

As the beast's head came free from its body, Bitterwood straightened, scanning the room. He no longer felt like a creature of muscle and bone. He was crafted from lightning and stone. He wiped his red hands across his lips. Salty blood burned on his tongue like distilled fire.

He spun toward the sound of a dragon crying out in agony. It was Thak, flat on his back, with Hex crouched above him. Hex had his snout buried deep into Thak's belly. He jerked his head from side to side, producing a slurping sound as he tore away strips of bloodied hide.

Bitterwood was beyond all caution or strategy. He raced toward Hex, screaming, more beast than man, his sword brandished above his head with both arms. Hex drew back, his emerald eyes widening, as Bitterwood leapt over the bodies of fallen dragons.

Hex swung his tail around, in the tripping attack hardwired into the nerves of all sun-dragons. Bitterwood instinctively leapt over the tail-blade. A shout of "DIE!" tore from his mouth. Using the full weight of his body and the pure power of the righteous rage of all humanity, Bitterwood drove the tip of his sword against Hex's breast plate, right at the point where it would pierce his heart.

The armor dented.

The blade shattered.

Bitterwood's attack ended abruptly as he slammed face-first into the iron wall that was the sun-dragon's torso. He staggered backward, blood streaming from his nose, his lower lip split open. He was only barely aware of Hex's tail swinging back. He jumped, but he was too slow. The armored tail caught him at the hip and threw him across the room like he was little more than a doll. He crashed into a stalagmite.

Sliding down the column, he stared up at the countless stone icicles above. The world spun in a sickening twirl. Some distant sliver of awareness waited for Hex's jaws to snap onto his torso.

Instead, back near the fire pit, there was a cavern-shaking roar. Bitterwood turned his head toward the noise. The ground trembled as Rorg thumped down from his pedestal and charged Hex, two tons of reptilian fury. Hex spun to meet him, burying his mighty axe deep into the dragon's fat neck. The sheer momentum and mass of the patriarch sun-dragon ripped the weapon from Hex's grasp. Hex tumbled backwards and Rorg trampled over him. Rorg's neck swayed; he was obviously drunk from the poison that had paralyzed the others. Just as a large man can hold his liquor better than a thin one, the corpulent beastialist proved more resistant to the airborne toxin.

Rorg whipped his head back as Hex tried to rise. His jaws clamped down on the chain mail draping Hex's neck. Hex's eyes bulged as he let out an almost airless squeak. Even though Rorg's teeth failed to pierce the mail, the power of his jaws was like a vise upon Hex's windpipe.

Bitterwood rolled to his hands and knees, shaking his head. The bloodlust that had driven him began to ebb. He'd long been torn by the forces within him. There was the blood-hungry avenger who craved the death of dragons regardless of consequences, and there was the cool, rational hunter who carefully planned each move, following well-practiced strategies to kill prey without endangering himself. The latter Bitterwood was back in control. Rising, he reached over his shoulder and found half a dozen fresh new arrows ripening in his quiver. He calmly walked to where his bow had landed. He lifted it and turned to the two dragons. Rorg's back was to him. Hex, his neck still firmly clamped in Rorg's jaws, was staring at Bitterwood. His eyes pleaded for mercy.

If Hex wanted to be put out of his misery, Bitterwood was happy to oblige. He drew a careful bead on Hex's left eye. He'd never have a cleaner shot.

As the arrow flew, Hex jerked his head sharply, dragging Rorg with him. The arrow lodged several inches deep into the top of Rorg's skull. With a groan, the beastialist's jaws loosened. He sank to the ground before Hex. His head came to rest upon the bloodied belly of Thak, as if he'd chosen this for a pillow.

Bitterwood reached for another arrow. Hex opened his jaws wide, drawing in a gasp of air as deep as a bellows.

Bitterwood placed the arrow against his bowstring.

Hex lunged toward Bitterwood, jaws open wide, his neck coiling out like a whip.

Bitterwood aimed his arrow straight down Hex's throat. He let the bowstring slide from his fingers. The arrow flashed straight toward its target.

Yet Hex once more anticipated Bitterwood's attack. He snaked his head to the right as the arrow left the string. The arrow punched through the back of his cheek, the shaft jutting from the outer edge of his jaw rather than lodging in the base of his skull. Hex carried through with his strike. Bitterwood leapt backward, trying to get out of Hex's path, but the sun-dragon compensated for that as well. His head shot toward the point in space where Bitterwood landed. His jaws closed in on Bitterwood's bow hand.

Bitterwood released his bow and jerked his fingers away. The living wood of the bow splintered as Hex's jaws crushed it. Bitterwood danced backwards, only to slip on the blood of a dead dragon behind him. His feet caught on the edge of the dragon's wing and he fell, landing in the middle of the great sheet of feather-scales. An instant later, Hex's hind-talon landed on his torso. The sun-dragon's enormous weight bore down upon him, enough to pin him, but not crush him. Hex lowered his jaws to within inches of Bitterwood's face. His hot breath carried a fine mist of gore. Beneath the scent of blood, the dragon's breath carried the sweet aroma of flowers. The arrow hanging from his cheek looked like the world's ugliest piece of jewelry.

Bitterwood grabbed the hind-talon that pinned him and pushed with all his strength. Hex didn't budge.

Hex finally spoke, his words coming between gasps for air. "I ... take it ... you've spoken ... to Jandra?"

Bitterwood gave up on trying to free himself. He grabbed the dangling arrow, pushing it back deep into Hex's mouth, and twisted. Hex pulled back, air hissing through his teeth as he sucked in a pained breath.

With the sun-dragon's weight shifted, Bitterwood pushed the talon away and rolled free. His eyes fixed on Hezekiah's axe. He scrambled for it on his hands and knees. Hex's armored tail whipped down inches before his eyes, the steel striking sparks as it chipped the stone floor. The weapon was still a full yard from his grasp.

"Would you shtop trying to kill me!" Hex shouted.

Bitterwood leapt to his feet. Hex kept his gaze locked on him.

Bitterwood suddenly deduced why Hex seemed so fast.

He said, "You're wearing Jandra's genie."

"No," said Hex.

"If you're not wearing it, where is it?"

"Now you ashk questions," said Hex. He was lisping from the injury to his mouth. "What would you have done if you'd killed me?"

"I don't care whether Jandra recovers her toy or not. But, I know that she was faster when she wore it. Now, you're faster."

"I'm not fashter. I'm prepared. We've fought shide by shide. I've shtudied you. You're more predictable than you might realize." Hex reached up and grabbed the arrow in his jaw. He tore it out with a yank that caused him to wince without fully closing his eyes. He was watching Bitterwood with an almost unblinking gaze. "You're waiting for me to let my guard down to go for the axe. It won't happen."

"Then we're at a stalemate," said Bitterwood.

"Are we?" Hex asked. "I'm pretty sure I won this fight. I could have killed you if I'd wanted."

Bitterwood grimaced.

"Where's Jandra?" Hex asked. "Did she remain at Dragon Forge?"

"She's returned to the kingdom of the goddess to search for a new genie."

"And you let her?"

"I have no say where she goes," said Bitterwood.

Hex spat out a gob of blood. "Don't you think it's possible she's going back because the goddess is driving her? I detected subtle changes in Jandra after Jazz gave her new memories. What if the goddess isn't truly dead? What if she lives on inside Jandra?"

Bitterwood frowned. He hadn't considered this possibility.

"We have to go after her," said Hex. "We've stood together before against common foes. We can do so again."

"Blasphet was one of those common foes," said Bitterwood. "Yet you've come here wielding one of his weapons. I recognize the poison smoke, smoke that Blasphet himself was immune to. I find it suspicious you aren't affected."

"After I left Jandra near Dragon Forge, I returned to the Nest to see if any further progress had been made in locating Blasphet's body. The valkyries had been interrogating some of the captured Sisters of the Serpent. They'd discovered three locations for his hidden temples. I worked with the valkyries to search these locations. Two proved to be false leads. At the final location we found barrels of the smoke-oil. We also discovered notes revealing that chewing the stems of the ephedra plant in advance negates the poison. There were pots of these flowers at the temple."

"Ah," said Bitterwood. "That's the sweet scent I smelled on your breath."

"It smells better than it tastes, I assure you."

"Where did you get Kanst's armor? And Hezekiah's axe?"

"Hmm," said Hex. "I didn't know the axe's previous owner. These items were among the treasures at the temple. It appears the Sisters of the Serpent did a fair amount of looting in the aftermath of the battle of the Free City."

Bitterwood looked around the cavern. "Many of these dragons are still alive. I promised the slaves that no one would pursue them. Can I use the axe to keep my promise?"

"No," said Hex. "When the beastialists who've survived your butchery awaken, they'll be more inclined to see things my way. Killing sleeping foes is dishonorable."

"I've never given a moment's thought to honor," said Bitterwood.

"I've given many decades of thought to honor," said Hex.

"Was it honorable to strike Jandra when she least expected it? To betray a friend and steal her most valued possession?"

"I did what I judged necessary. I've answered your questions. Answer mine. Will you help me find Jandra?"

"No," said Bitterwood. "I'm going back to Dragon Forge. My priority is to find Jeremiah."

"Zeeky's brother? What's he doing there?"

"I think Vulpine is using him to spread yellowmouth among the rebels."

Hex looked stunned. He shook his head. For a second, he wasn't focused on Bitterwood. Bitterwood glanced at the axe. He was certain he could reach it before Hex knew what was happening. Yet, he didn't move. Perhaps Hex was more useful alive, for the moment.

"That's simply monstrous. I've never liked Vulpine. Very well. I can't deny the importance of your mission. You can find Jeremiah while I deal with Jandra."

"I'm glad I have your approval," Bitterwood said. "You never did tell me what you've done with Jandra's genie. Or her old tiara from Vendevorex's tower, which I assume you stole?"

Hex's eyes widened. "By the bones. I'd forgotten that! She did say she had a second genie. In the rush of events, I never even thought to look for it. If she reclaims it—"

"It's gone," said Bitterwood. "Someone else stole it."

"Let us hope this someone doesn't know its true power."

"And the genie you stole?"

Hex sighed. "You've asked me three times. Since I changed the subject twice before, you might deduce I have no intention of answering. Suffice it to say that I've hidden it in the last place any human would want to look."

Bitterwood nodded. Had Hex purposefully told him the location of the genie? Or was it a careless slip?

"I'll take my bow and be on my way," said Bitterwood.

Hex glanced at the shattered remains. "If you wish. I doubt it will be of much use to you."

"It's a good bowstring, at least," said Bitterwood, crouching down to gather up the pieces. The splintered ends were green, dripping sap.

"I'm not your enemy, Bitterwood," said Hex. "In a better world, I'd like to think we would be friends after the adventures we've shared. There aren't many warriors who've stood shoulder to shoulder against gods. We make a good team."

"In a better world, I'd have aimed my first arrow an inch to the left," said Bitterwood. "But my world isn't a better world. It's…" He paused, looking for the word that described the reality he lived in.

"A bitter world?" said Hex.

Bitterwood grimaced. He'd forgotten Hex's penchant for word play. The big lizard confused this for humor. But then, how would Bitterwood know a genuine sense of humor if he ever encountered it? Whatever part of a normal man's soul that possessed the capacity for mirth had long since withered to dust inside him. Pun or not, the sun-dragon was right. The flavor of his world was undeniably bitter.

SHORTLY AFTER BITTERWOOD had vanished down the chimney, Zeeky guided Skitter back toward the road. Bitterwood's mission would take hours, she knew, and there was someone she needed to meet. She rode toward a human village they'd passed earlier. This village made Winding Rock look wealthy. The houses were nothing but shacks built from sticks and straw. The shallow ditch that ran through the center of town stank of human waste. Mounds of trash littered the landscape.

Zeeky waited at the edge of the village, her eyes fixed at the point where the road vanished over the rise of a hill. Poocher snorted softly.

"Whatever," she said. "When *don't* you think it's a good time for a snack?"

Poocher hopped down and trotted toward a trash mound.

Zeeky normally trusted his instincts as to what should and should not be considered food. She'd eaten many a strange root or berry he'd brought to her. She hoped he wouldn't be bringing her any gifts from the trash mound.

As he thrust his snout into the garbage, a small dark shadow peeled off and dashed away, charging right toward Skitter at first, then turning at a sharp angle. Everything happened so fast that Zeeky barely had time to recognize the shadow as a mangy gray cat. A half-second later, the cat vanished, as Skitter's toothy jaws closed around it with a wet *snap*. The long-wyrm swallowed before Zeeky could react.

She waited in the cold dark night, alone with her thoughts. She was always alone with her thoughts. Even though she could understand any animal or person and communicate with them in their own fashion, she knew that no one could truly understand her. She'd been born different from other people; Gabriel had said the goddess had changed her in the womb. When Jazz had captured her, she'd told Zeeky things that made her understand how different she truly was. Gabriel had been correct in calling her a harbinger. She'd been created for a purpose. Jazz had told Zeeky that she wasn't alone—there were other children who the goddess had also changed. She wondered if she would ever meet them.

From her saddle bag, the faint murmur of voices caught her attention. It was time.

A brown horse rose over the edge of the hill. Astride it was a woman in a long white cloak. She looked ghostly in the darkness. Her horse froze as it saw Skitter. The woman stroked its mane.

Zeeky called out, "Skitter won't hurt you. My name is Zeeky. I need to talk to you."

The woman nodded. She shook the reins of the horse and it nervously inched forward.

"I'm Filia," the woman said. "I've come with a message of hope."

Now that she was closer, Zeeky saw that Filia was only a few years older. She was thin, and her hair hung around her face in soft blonde curls.

"You've come to tell everyone about the healer," said Zeeky.

"You've heard?"

"Bits and pieces. I know you're telling people to go to the Free City. I know you want to help people. What I don't know is if your healer is as nice as he pretends to be."

The woman smiled. "He's given us no reason to doubt him. He's done nothing but good since he returned to us. He has broken the shackles of death and now brings the promise of life."

Zeeky shrugged. "I'll know the truth once I see him, which won't be much longer. For now, it doesn't matter. I'm going to have to trust him, and you. I need your help."

"How?" asked Filia.

"Follow me back to the bone-field surrounding Rorg's cavern. In a few minutes, slaves will be climbing up from the chimneys. They're going to be frightened and hungry, and they'll have no place to go. Take them to the Free City."

Filia nodded. "How many?"

"A hundred or so," said Zeeky.

Filia opened her saddle bag. She pulled out a white cloth and unwrapped it, revealing a crusty loaf of bread. The end was torn off.

"I can feed them," she said.

"I know," said Zeeky.

Poocher apparently knew as well. He materialized from the darkness to sit in front of Filia's horse. He looked up expectantly.

"Don't beg," said Zeeky.

"It's okay," said Filia. "The healer has touched this loaf." She tore off a palm-sized chunk and tossed it to the pig. "It will never go stale. No matter how many pieces I tear from it, I've yet to exhaust it."

"You'll have a chance to test its limits, I think," said Zeeky. "Follow me."

Zeeky shifted in her saddle and Skitter understood her intention. The long-wyrm turned and moved back toward the bone field, pacing itself so that the horse and Poocher could keep up. Zeeky could have had Skitter stop to let Poocher back onto his saddle, but she thought her friend could use a little exercise. Burning off a bit of his restless energy could only do the pig some good.

CHAPTER SEVENTEEN

UH-OH

BURKE SLID OPEN the warehouse door and lifted his lantern overhead, revealing the Angry Beetle. Lamplight glinted on its spiky shell; dust swirled in the winter draft. He ushered Thorny and Vance inside and pulled the door shut. The air inside was cool despite the cast iron stove near the entrance.

Thorny let out a whistle of appreciation as he looked over the new war machine. "You've outdone yourself," he said.

"What?" Vance asked. His hand was on Burke's shoulder for guidance. "What is it?"

"Remember Big Chief?" Burke asked.

"Of course," said Vance. "All them earth-dragons turned tail and ran the second Big Chief rolled into the square."

"Not all of them," said Burke, limping forward on his crutch. "I've got proof of that every morning when I pull on my boot. The Angry Beetle is Big

Chief's successor. One day it's going to be the most powerful war machine I've ever built."

"One day?" asked Thorny, walking around the massive machine. "It looks ready for action now."

"Appearances can be deceiving," said Burke. He leaned down before the pot-bellied stove and opened the door. He shoveled in more coal. He touched the pot of chili he'd left cooking on the stove. He'd forgotten all about it during the commotion at the well. The pot still felt warm. The meal could probably be salvaged. "The Angry Beetle has some glitches that need to be worked out."

"Glitches?"

"Outright failures," Burke sighed. "The extra weight of the armor has made a joke of my gears. Currently, it can only roll backwards. I've also got space problems. I can't carry enough coal on board to keep the boiler powered up for more than a couple of hours."

"That's not so bad," said Thorny. "You could roll out a wall of these things a mile or so at a time. Wipe out anything in your way. Wagons could roll along afterward to refuel."

"Maybe," said Burke. "It's not an elegant solution, but we need some way of pushing our force outward. Long term, the dragons can beat us with this blockade if we can't develop a way to take the battle to them. They can treat our rebellion like a brush fire— clear the area around it, deny it fuel, and eventually it will burn itself out. That's our fate, unless I can think of something clever and think of it fast."

"I saw the shotgun in action," said Thorny. "That's pretty impressive."

"It's only a toy compared to the cannons. I've got small cannons on the Beetle that can hurl a lead ball a mile or two. I've got big cannons rolling off the lines that shoot even further. I've spent decades imagining what I could do to dragons if I could learn how to make gunpowder." Burke reached out and placed a hand on the barrel of the rear-facing cannon of the Angry Beetle. He shook his head. "Now I'm wondering if my dream isn't going to become a nightmare."

"How so?"

"You saw what Ragnar did to Shanna. When he built this army, he marched from town to town shouting, 'join or die!' I've heard what happened to some of the men who refused to cooperate. Right now, I'm able to temper his brute force approach by constantly dangling the promise of more powerful weapons in front of him. But there's going to be a point where he thinks he's got enough. I'm not so much worried about what he'll do to the dragons as by what he'll do to the men who don't blindly obey him."

Vance was moving around the perimeter of the Angry Beetle, feeling his way from spike to spike. Burke started to warn the boy to be careful but held his tongue. It was important to let Vance feel independent despite his blindness. For someone who said he couldn't see anything, Vance certainly was moving around the edge of the machine quickly enough.

"What's that weird smell?" said Vance from the other side of the Angry Beetle.

"It was supposed to be my dinner." Burke lifted the lid of the iron pot on the stove and stirred the contents. The air filled with a pungent, spicy aroma, along with the scent of charred meat. The contents were sticking to the bottom of the pot.

"Oh lord," said Thorny. "Not your chili!"

"Chili sounds good," said Vance.

"Burke's cooking isn't for the faint of heart. His chili has killed more people than his guns ever will."

Burke chuckled as he used a ladle to scoop out a large glop of stringy meat into a wooden bowl. He handed it to Vance, who reached out and took it in a confident manner that made Burke wonder again if perhaps the boy could see more than he let on. "Don't listen to Thorny. I still say most of those deaths were just coincidence. Besides, this is a new recipe. I'm currently limited by the items in the earth-dragons' larders. They had some hot sausages I've chopped up and added to this."

The wooden spoon stopped inches from Vance's lips. He said, "I've, um, heard there were human bodies in the larder. You didn't... um..."

"Any human remains were turned over to Ragnar for proper burial. The man has his faults, but he's not a cannibal. I hope."

Vance started to put the spoon in his mouth, then pulled it away again. "I also heard there were jars of pickled earth-dragon babies."

"Yeah. Some folks have been sampling them. I've not been that hungry yet."

Vance looked relieved and popped the spoon in his mouth.

"Especially not with so much fresh meat from the adults lying around," Burke continued. "We had to cremate most of the bodies as a hedge against disease. But, we cut off the tails and have been curing them in the smoke house. Earth-dragon tails taste like gator. We used to eat those all the time down south."

Vance chewed slowly, looking as if he might spit the chili out. Suddenly, his eyes bulged. He swallowed quickly.

"Oh my gosh!" he said, waving his fingers in front of his mouth. "My mouth is on fire!"

Burke reached down beside the stove and picked up a clay jug. "Take a swig of this."

Vance lifted the jug, swallowed, and then quickly pulled it away from his lips. His face was all puckered for about half a minute before he could speak again.

"Have I done something to make you angry?" Vance asked weakly.

"Nope. That's goom," said Burke. "We've got about nine hundred gallons of it. The earth-dragons distill it from cabbage and chilies. Fortunately, it's so alcoholic that a few swigs numbs your mouth. Can you still feel your tongue?"

Vance's tongue flickered across his lips. "Nothing. Guess it works."

"Don't burp around any open flames," Burke said. "Goom ignites easily. It's the fuel for the Angry Beetle's flamethrower."

Vance took another bite of chili. Sweat beaded his brow as he chewed the stringy meat.

"If you survive this meal, you'll have a good story for your grandkids," said Thorny with a chuckle. Thorny then turned his attention back to the Angry Beetle.

"How many people does it take to run this thing?" he asked.

"A perfect crew would be four," said Burke, lifting the hatch. "But, it's a tight fit with two people, and three people need to be real friendly. If there were more women around, I'd recruit them for crew."

Thorny peeked inside the open hatch. "They'd need to be skinny."

Burke shrugged. "At least I don't need to worry about Ragnar's Mighty Men commandeering this. I don't think Stonewall could squeeze through the hatch."

As he said this, a chill winter wind swept across the room. The sliding door to the warehouse shuddered on its tracks. Burke looked up and found Stonewall standing in the doorway, glaring at him. To his left stood Ragnar, with his twin scimitars held loosely in his hands; a half dozen armored Mighty Men lurked behind him. To Stonewall's right stood Frost, grinning like it was his birthday.

"Burke," said Ragnar, in a voice that was oddly calm and controlled. "We should discuss what happened at the well."

Burke crossed his arms as he leaned back against the Angry Beetle.

"I agree," said Burke. "That was quite a show. I'm still trying to make up my mind as to precisely what it was that happened. How did Shanna get through the blockade? How did she get to the well if your men didn't let her in? Shanna's been a spy for years. She's a good actor. And, the more I think about it, if you faked her death, tossing her into the well was a good way of keeping anyone from seeing her get up and walk away once the performance was done. What I haven't figured out yet is, what are you up to? What are you trying to prove?"

"You have lived a life of lies so long you cannot see the truth," said Ragnar. "I would never deceive my followers with base theatrics."

"If it wasn't staged, that's even worse. Shanna helped us win Dragon Forge. You killed her like she was a dog."

"A mad dog," said Ragnar, still calm. "It was clear from her words that she'd been corrupted by the worship of a false god."

"Or hallucinating from those dragonseeds, whatever they are. You should have jailed her and let her sober up. We'll never know what really happened to her now."

"You're quick to criticize my decisions," said Ragnar. "Your open defiance in front of the crowd was intolerable."

"You'll have to tolerate my criticism a bit longer," said Burke. "You need me if you're ever going to break the blockade and spread this rebellion further."

"Do I?" asked Ragnar. "The Lord has given me an army. We now have the sky-wall bows. We have shotguns and cannons. I believe your usefulness draws to an end."

"Without gunpowder, all you have are a bunch of iron tubes," said Burke, crossing his arms. "I'm the only one who knows the formula."

Ragnar smiled, an expression that made Burke's blood turn cold.

Frost said, "I noticed that Biscuit was capable of mixing up gunpowder while you were recovering from your surgery."

Burke's jaw tightened. "Biscuit's a good man, but he's no chemist," he said, carefully controlling his tone.

Frost held up a scrap of paper that Burke instantly recognized. It was the formula for gunpowder. "I spoke to Biscuit earlier today. He found my arguments... persuasive. He has reaffirmed his loyalty to the cause."

Burke clenched his jaw. He looked away from Ragnar and his Mighty Men, shoved his iron crutch back into his armpit, and hobbled to the stove. "So what now?"

"Now we assemble the men at dawn," said Frost. "You repent your sins and swear your obedience to the Lord and his prophet. Or we behead you in front of the crowd as a reminder that no single man is greater than the cause."

Stonewall furrowed his brow at the mention of the beheading.

Frost grinned like this was the happiest moment of his life.

Burke picked up a tin cup sitting at the edge of the stove. He poured himself a cup of goom.

Ragnar and his Mighty Men were ten feet away. The Angry Beetle was close enough to touch. He contemplated his choices. He could avoid violence just by standing in front of the crowd, saying a few words he didn't believe, and then going back to work.

He shook his head. "If you're planning to kill me, I'd rather not wait for dawn."

It was Stonewall, not Frost, who stepped forward. His big beefy hands reached for Burke's shoulders, as he said, "Sir, if you'll come with us, I promise to—"

Burke flung the goom into Stonewall's face.

The tall man staggered backwards, hissing in pain. Goom in the mouth was bad enough; Goom in the eyes was crippling. Frost tried to get out of the way of the stumbling giant, but crashed into the Mighty Man behind him. Stonewall tripped over Frost, and as he fell he toppled the rest of Ragnar's thugs.

Ragnar, however, had been spared from the flailing of his henchmen. Burke was getting tired of the seemingly divine hand that spared the prophet from misfortune. Ragnar brandished his scimitars and leapt toward Burke with a growl, apparently agreeing that dawn was too long to wait for Burke's beheading.

Burke grabbed the iron handle of the chili pot and swung it with a grunt. The cast iron connected solidly with the side of the prophet's shaggy head. The force of the blow knocked the scimitars from Ragnar's grasp. Hot, thick chili splashed down Ragnar's bare body, matting his chest hair. The prophet's eyes grew large. A very unholy word formed on his lips.

Burke didn't wait to hear it. With the heavy pot still in his hands, he swung upward, catching the big man under his hairy chin, knocking him from his feet.

"Get in the Beetle!" Burke screamed.

Thorny was already two steps ahead of him. His scrawny legs disappeared into the shadowy interior of the war machine. Burke turned to grab Vance by the wrist, but Vance, too, was already moving, diving into the interior. For a third time since they'd come to the warehouse, Burke suspected the boy could see more than he let on. But, why would Vance lie about such a thing?

Burke threw his crutch in and rolled into the Beetle, hitting the catch that held the metal hatch open. He pulled his leg in as the hatch slammed shut. Seconds later, loud bangs shook the Beetle as the Mighty Men who'd regained their footing began to hack the war machine with their swords.

Burke sat up, grabbing Vance by the wrist. "You're going to have to shovel coal," he said. "Let me put your hand on the—"

"I can see," said Vance.

"What?"

"I can see! My sight's not fully back yet, but it's getting there. I only see blurry colors out past a few yards, but up close I see pretty good."

"So… you've been faking it?" Burke asked.

"No! My sight's just started coming back in the last little bit."

Thorny scratched his scraggly beard. "I've heard of men going blind after they drink goom. Maybe it works the other way around, too."

"I'm pretty sure it's because of the dragonseed," said Vance.

"What?" asked Burke.

"I swallowed it five minutes after you gave it to me. What did I have to lose?"

"Your life, if it had been poison. Your mind, if it had been a hallucinogen." Burke frowned. "How do you know you can really see? Maybe you're just imagining it."

Vance reached out and put his finger on the tip of Burke's nose.

"The dragonseed worked. My sight's been getting a little better since I took it. First I could just detect light from dark, then shapes started coming back, then colors."

Burke grimaced. He lived in a world that followed certain rules. Magic seeds were the stuff of fairy tales. They didn't belong in a world of gears and guns. Vance had lost his sight due to a head injury. Sometimes these things got better on their own. The timing must be a coincidence.

The hull shuddered violently.

"I'm guessing they found the sledgehammer," said Burke as the ringing in his ears abated. "Here's the ten-second guide to running this thing. This is the boiler." He opened the iron door next to Vance. A small red flame still flickered inside. "Shovel coal. There's a foot-operated bellows. Pump as if your life depends on it. We need a lot of heat to build up steam."

Burke checked the gauges. There was still a little pressure left over from this morning, but nothing like what they'd need to escape.

The hull rang out again from another blow of a sledgehammer. He wondered how long it would be before one of the Mighty Men was clever enough to wheel a big cannon out of the foundry and use the Angry Beetle for target practice.

"Thorny, the Beetle can only roll backwards. I designed all the controls to sit up front. You need to look out that little hatch in the back and tell me what you see."

"Got it," said Thorny.

"Don't open the hatch until we're moving," said Burke. "The Mighty Men might be smart enough to poke a shotgun inside."

Burke looked around at the mention of a shotgun. He had one shotgun inside, which he'd been using to test the visual span of the various gun slots. He had plenty of shot, and two barrels of gunpowder. The Beetle also had fixed cannons at the front and back, and there was the goom-powered flamethrower, with maybe thirty gallons in the reserve. He also had a sky-wall bow and a quiver of arrows. He'd wanted to test if there was enough space to actually use a bow at one of the slots. There wasn't.

Burke wiggled his way past Vance to reach the driver's seat. Burke calculated the odds of escaping and frowned. Sometimes it was a curse to be good at math. He was certain he hadn't killed Ragnar. Stonewall probably wasn't permanently blinded. Was it too late to find some reasonable way out of this? Or was he going to have to kill a lot of people?

All this time, he'd been worried about what Ragnar might do to his fellow men once he had guns and cannons. Now he was in a situation where he was going to be turning his weapons against humans, and for what? So that they might die a mile away instead of here in the warehouse?

He realized that nothing had hit the hull for at least a minute. He cracked open the sighting hatch at the forward cannon. He was facing the open doors leading to the street. The Mighty Men were now milling about outside. Ragnar and Stonewall were nowhere to be seen. Burke watched through a slit only an inch high and six inches long. It was hard to say what he might be missing. Why had they stopped trying to get in? The Mighty Men stood back as a new group came onto the scene, straining as they pushed one of the newly forged wheeled cannons into place and turned it toward the warehouse.

Burke looked at the pressure gauge. They needed more time.

People were going to have to die.

"I'm going to fire the cannon," he said, reaching into one of the many pouches on his leather tool belt. He pulled out a clump of cotton wads and leaned back in his seat, stretching out to Vance and Thorny.

"Stuff these in your ears and cover your ears with your hands. Keep them covered until I've taken my shot."

"With cotton in our ears, how will we know?" asked Thorny, as Vance helped him jam cotton into his ears.

Burke smirked. "You'll know."

He stuffed cotton into his own ears as he looked back out into the street. They were still ramming gunpowder down the shaft of the cannon. A five pound keg of black powder sat on the street. He couldn't have asked for a better target.

Burke spun the sighting wheels for the forward gun. The Angry Beetle's cannons weren't as big as the one in the street, but it would get the job done. Unlike the Mighty Men, he'd loaded his cannon in advance.

"Hands over your ears!" Burke shouted, as he pulled the flint trigger.

He squeezed his hands over his ears and closed his eyes, his jaw clenched as tightly as possible. The seconds passed with unbearable slowness.

The noise hit him in the chest like a hammer. The Angry Beetle lurched as the five-pound charge in the street exploded.

Burke pulled his hands away, yanking out the cotton. His teeth felt loose.

"Everyone all right?" he asked. There was no answer. He could barely hear his own voice over the ringing. He tried again, shouting, "Vance? Thorny?"

"You're right that we'd know," said Thorny.

"I should've used more cotton," said Vance.

"Keep pumping the bellows," Burke said. "The pressure is almost in the zone."

He slid the sighting hatch open once more. The front wall of the warehouse was gone. There was a crater where the cannon had been a moment before. Unidentifiable lumps of meat were scattered in all directions. He slid the hatch shut before he had a chance to identify any of the chunks.

"Gentlemen," he said. "It's safe to say we've worn out our welcome. I'm sorry you got swept up in this."

"You apologize too much," said Thorny. "Let's roll."

"What's it look like behind us?"

Thorny pushed the rear sighting hatch open with the back of his twisted hands. He shook his head. "The doors are closed."

"I don't think that's going to matter," said Burke as he let out the clutch and engaged the gear. The Angry Beetle shuddered as it crept backward. It took a surprising length of time to cover the short distance to the rear door. Fortunately, when it finally reached the barrier, the war-machine pushed through the wood as if it were a paper curtain.

"Since we can only move in one direction, it's important we don't hit anything the Angry Beetle can't push over. I'm going to follow the southern boulevard to the city gate. Let me know if I'm getting close to any buildings."

Burke leaned over to watch out the sighting hatch as they rolled away from the warehouse. He knew the layout of Dragon Forge as well as anyone. He just might pull this off.

"We're getting close to a big building on the left," said Thorny.

Burke turned the wheel.

"No!" said Thorny. "My left!"

Burke hastily steered the other way.

"We should be coming up on a big broad avenue now," he said. "See it?"

"Yeah," said Thorny. "People are moving fast to get out of our way. A lot faster than they need to, honestly. Pokey Turtle might be a better name for this contraption."

"Duly noted," said Burke. "Keep shoveling, Vance. We need to build up more pressure if we want to get up any kind of speed."

"We're at the avenue," said Thorny.

Burke turned the wheel sharply. The treads churned beneath the Angry Beetle with a satisfying rumble. The steering mechanism worked like a dream. If he had any real power getting to the treads, this might turn into an interesting ride. He disengaged the clutch.

"We're slowing down," said Thorny.

Burke was surprised that they were still rolling at all. But, the southern avenue did slope down slightly. He'd take whatever help from gravity he could get.

"We took off before the pressure was in the zone," Burke said. "Let's give the boiler another minute. I'm worried about the southern gate. You see it?"

"Yeah," said Thorny. "We're maybe two hundred feet away."

"Can you see down the shaft of the rear cannon? Does it look like we'd hit the gate if we fired on it?"

Thorny was quiet for a moment. "I guess," he said.

Vance said, "Burke, we worked hard to get that gate closed. Forget Ragnar. Do you really want to open that gate to the dragons?"

"It's not the gate keeping the dragons out," said Burke. "It's the sky-wall bows. No winged dragon wants to fly within a mile of the walls. Thorny, I know you don't have much grip, but triggering the flintlock fuse only takes a nudge. Think you can do it?"

"I'll try," said Thorny.

"Okay then. Cotton in ears, everyone. Thorny, on the count of ten, do it."

Burke shoved cotton in his ears. Thorny's count-down went by in silence.

The Angry Beetle trembled as the cannon fired. Burke's brain felt like goom sloshing around in a jug.

He pulled the cotton from his ears. Thorny's distant voice sounded panicked. "The gate's still there!"

"Did we miss it?" Burke asked, incredulous.

"No. We punched a hole in it. The left half looks tilted back a little."

"That's the part we'll ram, then."

Burke looked back out his own sighting window. The street was mostly empty. It was good this was happening at night. Here and there, faces peeked around the corners of buildings to watch the progress of the Angry Beetle as it rolled at its leisurely pace toward the gate.

What now? The cannons could be loaded from the inside, but it was a pain. Thorny definitely couldn't manage with his hands. He looked at the barrel of gunpowder beside him. He had a small spool of gunpowder-infused cotton to cut fuses from. Getting out of the Beetle to hop up to the gate and fashion a quick bomb didn't seem wise, however.

Did the Beetle have the speed and mass necessary to push open the gate?

He peered at the gauge. The needle hovered at the bottom edge of the green zone.

"We only live once, gentlemen," he said, and engaged the clutch.

The Angry Beetle's treads rumbled beneath the floor. On the incline, they quickly reached a speed that surprised even Burke. They might well be rolling at almost fifteen miles per hour. With a horrible crunch, they crashed into the gate. The Beetle felt as if it were going to tip over as the damaged gate fell from its hinges and one tread rode up onto it while the other stayed on the ground. Seconds later, the Angry Beetle shook violently as it dropped back to level and rolled on. Stunned guards looked down from the walls as the Angry Beetle roared away from the fort. The road sloped sharply downward toward the river. Burke disengaged the gears, allowing gravity alone to propel them so that they could build up enough pressure to climb the hill on the other side of the river.

"There's a bridge ahead," said Thorny.

"I know," said Burke. "It's going to be like threading a needle to cross it."

"Can the bridge even hold us?" Vance asked nervously.

"It's stone," said Burke. "The earth-dragons moved wagons loaded with armor and weapons across it. It'll hold."

He peeked back out the rear sighting hatch. His heart sank. There were a dozen men walking along behind the Angry Beetle, all bearing shotguns. They were spread out so that the rear cannon would never hit all of them. If they followed the war machine long enough, they'd be able to peel it open once it ran out of steam.

"Uh-oh," said Thorny.

These were quite likely the worst two syllables anyone could have uttered, given the circumstance. "What?" Burke asked.

"Earth-dragons," said Thorny. "They're climbing up from under the bridge. I guess they've heard the racket we're making. There might be fifty of them."

Burke barely had time to contemplate this news before a shotgun blast rang out. Then another, then another. No balls clanged off the Angry Beetle's armor. How could they possibly miss?

"That's about five fewer earth-dragons," said Thorny.

As the angry war-cries of earth-dragons at full charge filled the air, a faint hope suddenly sparked within Burke's chest. Sometimes, two problems were better than one. In the best case scenario, the men and the dragons would fight one another and ignore the Angry Beetle.

In the worst case scenario, the dragons would kill the men, capture their guns and the Beetle, and suddenly have over a dozen shotguns, two cannons, and a barrel of gunpowder for the biologians to reverse engineer.

The Angry Beetle lurched as Burke contemplated their situation.

"We just ran over a fallen dragon," said Thorny.

Shotgun blasts continued to ring out.

"The humans have to win this battle," said Burke, grabbing the shotgun. "Even if Ragnar's men kill us, we can't let the dragons get their hands on the gunpowder."

"Burke," said Thorny. "You might want to concentrate on steering. We're only fifty feet from that bridge."

Burke handed the gun to Vance. "Open the rear gun slit. Fire at will."

"I don't know if my eyes are good enough for me to target anything," said Vance.

"Let's find out," said Burke.

Vance nodded. He moved swiftly to slide the small hatches open. Burke craned his head over his shoulder, trying to see as much as possible through the tiny holes. He could see the edges of the bridge. It looked like he was on track. There were a half-dozen earth-dragons on the bridge. Vance fired the shotgun.

When the smoke cleared, most of the earth-dragons were running. There was now a huge shadow on the bridge. What was it? Burke squinted, trying to make sense. It was moving...

With a start, he realized that the biggest earth-dragon he'd ever seen was charging straight toward the Angry Beetle. He brandished a war-hammer that no human could ever lift. His jagged beak was open in a war cry louder than the rumbling treads on the stonework of the bridge.

With a horrifying grunt, the huge dragon swung his hammer. Burke's end of the Angry Beetle suddenly shot into the air. Shrill whistles rang out as jets of steam shot from the seams of the boiler. With a gut-wrenching chewing sound, Burke heard the left tread seize up.

"Reload," Burke shouted.

The Angry Beetle jumped as the war-hammer once more slammed into its leading edge. One of the exterior spikes suddenly punched down into the belly of the war machine, missing the back of Thorny's head by a fraction of an inch. Vance was thrown against the boiler.

"Aaaah!" he cried out, pulling back. The chamber suddenly smelled like burning hair. Vance's wispy beard was gone from the left side of his face, now a bright beet red.

The rear gun slot Burke had been looking through was crushed completely shut. He could barely see out one of the remaining holes. A wall of reptilian flesh rippled as the dragon lifted the hammer for another blow.

There was a rumble beneath the Angry Beetle. The dragon attacking them jumped backward. Dust shot into the air.

"Uh-oh," Thorny said again.

In a symphony of pops and cracks and groans, the bridge beneath them crumbled and they dropped twenty feet, landing sideways. The entry hatch snapped open, showing the river water rushing past only inches below. The Angry Beetle was precariously perched on the rubble of the bridge. The air was hot with steam.

Vance had his hands pressed against the roof, straining to keep from falling against the boiler again. "Y'all okay?" he asked.

"I think so," said Burke.

Thorny's voice was feeble. "I don't suppose you brought that jug of goom, did you? I could drink a gallon right about now."

"There's thirty gallons on board," said Burke, looking down at the water. He glanced over at the spool of fuse. "We're not drinking it though. It's going to be part of the explosion."

"Have we moved on to some part of the plan I was unaware of?" Thorny asked.

"There was a plan?" asked Vance.

"Get into the water," said Burke. "We can't let the dragons capture the Angry Beetle. I'm going to blow it up. Between the gunpowder and the goom, we might destroy the cannons."

Vance nodded. "Works for me." He let go of his handhold, grabbed the sky-wall bow and quiver, and dropped into the water. The boy really was fast with his hands. He popped back to the surface a second later. The water was up to his neck. He reached up. "Let me help you, Thorny."

Thorny did his best to navigate the cramped space without hitting the boiler. He didn't succeed. His face scrunched up in pain when his shin hit the hot metal, but he never made a sound of complaint. He slipped down into Vance's hands and fell into the water.

"Take my crutch," Burke said, handing it down to Vance. He pulled several feet of chord off the spool and shoved it into the top of the nearest barrel. "We'll have less than a minute to get out of here. I don't move fast these days, so I might not make it."

Thorny's head popped back into the hatch. He was shivering violently.

"T-that's why y-you should get a head start. I'll light the f-fuse."

"I got us into this," said Burke. "Both of you go on."

"Burke," said Thorny, sounding grave. "For the last f-fifteen years, I've been s-spying on you for Bazanel. If I die, I d-deserve it."

"I knew," said Burke. "It was too big a coincidence that you'd been the slave of the only dragon I'd ever thought of as a kindred spirit."

"I'll light the fuse," said Vance.

"But…"

"I'm faster than both of you. I can hold my breath underwater a long time. Now get out of there and let me blow this thing up."

Burke grabbed the fallen shotgun and slipped down into the icy water. He lost his footing almost instantly. He reached out and grabbed Thorny's arm to steady himself.

"What's h-he going to l-light it with?" Thorny asked through chattering teeth.

"There's still fire under the boiler," Vance grumbled. "Get out of here!"

It was the closest thing to anger Burke had ever heard in Vance's voice. Grabbing his crutch, he took a deep breath and dropped beneath the water. The current pulled him away. He popped back to the surface several yards downstream. The water was unbelievably cold. Each winter his father used to throw him into the river and make him swim a mile. Supposedly, it was meant to make him tougher. In practice, it left him hating swimming. It was one aspect of his childhood training he'd never had the heart to inflict on Anza. He was suddenly grateful for it.

On the bank above him he saw a flash and heard thunder. A bloodied dragon toppled down the bank, limp and lifeless.

Thorny popped to the surface beside him. His lips were dark blue.

"Keep moving," Burke said, grabbing his friend by the collar.

"If y-you knew," Thorny asked, "why d-didn't you k-kill me?"

"You were the only halfway decent chess player in town."

"Anza's b-better," said Thorny.

"Anza beats me," said Burke.

They hopped, floated, and scrambled downstream a hundred yards, seldom bringing anything more than their heads above water. In the darkness, the fallen bridge and the upended war machine were nothing but shadows. On the far bank, Burke saw movement. Vance?

The shadow he saw was too large and had a tail. The shadow brandished a large hammer and shouted incompressible words of rage at the fallen bridge. So much for the hope the brute had been crushed in the collapse.

"It's been too long," said Burke. "The fuse should have—"

The night went white. The shockwave knocked them beneath the water. Hot shards of metal rained down, sizzling as they punched into the river. Burke lost all sense of up and down as the water roughed him up. Finally, he surfaced. Thorny popped up too, gasping. Burke spun around, trying to get his bearings, until he spotted the pillar of bluish flame on the water where the Angry Beetle had once been. The burning goom, no doubt. Black smoke hung heavy in the air. All around, little *plips* sounded in the water as shrapnel continued to fall.

Burke wanted to call out Vance's name, but didn't dare. He didn't know how many men or dragons had survived. No matter who was still up on the banks, it wouldn't be long before sky-dragons swarmed the area. Their only chance was to stay quiet, stay low, and keep moving.

"Do you th-think he…?" whispered Thorny.

"Shh," said Burke. "Keep moving. He'll find us."

As the minutes dragged on, Vance didn't find them. Burke helped Thorny crawl from the water after a mile had passed. They were both freezing, drenched to the bone. Their only hope was to keep moving. They raced not only against the sky-dragons who no doubt searched the area, but against hypothermia and frost-bite as well.

They limped along with Burke's arm wrapped around Thorny's shoulder for balance. Burke had the shotgun and his crutch pressed against his chest with his free arm. Any time Thorny slowed, Burke pushed him on, ever eastward. Stopping even a minute to catch their breath would be fatal.

They'd traveled a few miles when Burke smelled smoke. At first, he thought it might be his imagination, until Thorny whispered hoarsely, "S-smells like a f-fire."

They limped on, rounding a bend in the river. Like some dream, a windowless log cabin sat high up on the bank, with smoke curling from the stone chimney. Burke hobbled toward it, not caring who might be inside. The cabin was tiny, barely ten feet by five. He let his crutch drop from his numb hands as he fell against the door.

The door opened. Vance looked down on them. His hair was sopping wet. He was wrapped in a thick wool blanket. The redness of his burned cheek had faded. Behind him, a fire roared.

"This place used to belong to my uncle Jig," Vance said. "He's back at Dragon Forge. He won't mind us passing the night."

"How did you…"

Vance shrugged. "I must have passed y'all in the darkness. Get inside before you let the heat out. We need to put out the fire before dawn. Don't want the dragons seeing the smoke."

Thorny stumbled into the cabin. He fell before the fireplace, rolling toward it, until he was practically in it. Steam rose from his clothes.

"Don't cook yourself," said Burke, dropping to the floor next to him.

Vance closed the door.

Burke closed his eyes and instantly plunged into sleep.

CHAPTER EIGHTEEN

WE SHALL ALL BE HEALED

ANZA PRESSED HER back against a stone dragon atop the roof of the palace. The night sky was full of aerial guard and valkyries. Within the palace a dozen ox-dogs bayed. They were all searching for her. She'd spent most of the day skulking around the palace, trying to establish who'd seen the scroll containing the secret of gunpowder. Tonight, she'd acted. Two dozen sky-dragons were dead in her wake. The only important target she'd missed was Chapelion himself. She hoped he hadn't committed the formula to memory. She'd recovered Bazanel's original scroll and two copies and burned them.

Unfortunately, it had proven impossible to execute her plan in complete secrecy. The first bodies had been discovered long before she was finished with her targets. She'd been increasingly on the defensive as news spread through the palace that an assassin was present. With the ox-dogs now on her trail, she'd spent the last hour retreating to ever higher ground.

She pressed her cheek against the cold marble scales of the carved sun-dragon she hid beside. The wind whipped around the peaks of the palace. She looked toward the southwest. Somewhere in that direction lay Dragon Forge. She imagined how her father would stand when he heard the news of her death. She could feel the sag of his shoulders.

The wound on her chest throbbed with each heartbeat. It felt as hot now as the night the fire had actually touched it. Not a quarter mile distant was the river where she'd swum with Skitter little more than a week ago. It would feel good to dip back into that water.

The door to the rooftop terrace burst open and an ox-dog emerged, dragging an earth-dragon handler behind it, followed by a squad of nine earth-dragons and a second dog. Anza could handle the guards. The ox-dogs were another matter. Standing six feet tall at the shoulder, ox-dogs had a bite that even sun-dragons envied. Pound for pound, there were few creatures on the planet that matched them for sheer muscle. Like all dogs, they were fiercely protective of their pack, and would fight to the death once combat began. Worst of all, their sense of hearing and smell made them nearly impossible to elude.

If there was ever a moment in her life when it would have been useful to sprout wings, it was now. Given the improbability of that development, she improvised.

She pursed her lips and let out a long, loud whistle. As all heads turned toward her, she scrambled onto the stone dragon, climbed its long neck, and stood on its head. The statue looked out over the edge of the roof. Below her was a five-hundred-foot drop into darkness. To her right, in the distance, she could see the lights of Richmond, gleaming. If she could make it there, she could disappear among the crowds. To her left, there were other lights. She cocked her head, trying to make sense of what she saw. It looked like a second city, but her study of maps of the area hadn't revealed a city there before. Was this the Free City? She'd heard that was abandoned.

The earth-dragons and ox-dogs surrounded the base of the statue. The ox-dogs were too bulky to climb up the statue's neck to reach her. One of the bolder earth-dragons looked ready to make the attempt. She loosed a throwing knife. It shot like an arrow to the exact spot on the stone that the dragon's thick claw was about to grasp, throwing up bright sparks. The earth-dragon pulled back and cast a wary eye toward her.

Anza looked up. Her true target wasn't the earth-dragons or the ox-dogs. A sky-dragon dove at her, a valkyrie judging from the armor. In her hind-talons she carried a spear nearly twenty feet long, with the point on a path that would stab right into Anza's heart.

Anza counted the seconds, her legs tensing until the last possible instant.

She leapt up, slapping the tip of the spear down and to the side. The shaft painlessly slid along her rib cage and hips. At the apex of her leap, she closed her fingers, clamping onto the sky-dragon's leg.

Her feet jerked from the statue. The sudden weight sent the valkyrie into a spin. Anza held on with all her might as the world whirled around her. The dragon fell at a sharp angle, beating her wings furiously to regain control. Anza tucked her legs up as they dashed past the tips of the trees that lined the river. The dragon carried her out over the dark water and she let go. She tumbled through the air and smacked into the water with the full surface of her back, her arms and legs outstretched. It was the most painful landing possible, but it wasn't fatal. She sank beneath the icy water, breathless from the impact.

She kicked, driving herself further downriver, struggling to stay below the surface. Her lungs were burning. White stars danced before her eyes. At last, she could take no more. She rose to the surface, turning to her back, floating gently upward so that only the tip of her face broke the water. She drew in a long silent breath as she scanned the sky. Dragons were everywhere. She plunged below the surface again, kicking hard to get as close to the bottom as possible. She wanted to leave no ripples that they might follow.

The current was strong, lending her speed, but she was swimming blind. She had no way of knowing how far she'd come. She swam until she couldn't help herself. She had to surface again. This time, she rose with much less grace and control. She'd pressed too far. Her heart felt full of needles. She splashed to the surface, gasping loudly. She fumbled to free a knife from her belt, but it fell from her trembling fingers. She tried to catch it but the sudden motion plunged her face underwater.

She inhaled a chilling lungful of icy liquid. She grew still, trying to calm herself, letting the buoyancy of her body carry her upward. She lay immobile at the surface, drifting, her nose barely above water. She wanted to swim for shore, but anytime she tried to turn her head she sank back beneath the river.

She closed her eyes, feeling numb. Water washed into her throat. She coughed violently, her limbs flailing uselessly in an attempt to find something solid to grab.

She forgot where she was or why she was so cold and closed her eyes again.

A HAND WRAPPED around her wrist. Her eyes fluttered open as she was dragged through shallow water across smooth river rocks. Her rescuer was a woman about her own age, dressed in a long white robe that was wet from the knees down. Anza coughed again, so violently that she pulled her arm free of her rescuer. She rolled over onto her belly on the stony bank and coughed up water. Her coughing triggered something deeper inside her and she started to vomit, bringing up teaspoons of clear, pale, bitter fluid. In the aftermath, she lay on the uneven stones, completely empty. All her life her father had trained her to treat her body as a machine. She knew how to push it to the limits of its engineering. Her muscles and bones composed a finely-tuned master clockwork. Now her gears were stripped. She couldn't even lift a finger.

"Poor thing," the girl who had pulled her from the river said as she squatted next to her. She placed a hand under Anza's shoulder and rolled her to her back. "We have to get you back on your feet. If you don't keep moving, you'll freeze. You'll go to sleep and never wake up."

Anza found this thought acceptable. Her eyes closed. It would feel good to drift off peacefully, never to—

SLAP!

For a half-second, Anza wondered about the source of the sound. Her ice-cold skin was numb. She dimly felt the pressure of the blow on her cheek but no actual pain. Slowly, a tingling set in, as if her cheek were being stung by a thousand bees.

She lifted her hand to her cheek, rubbing it.

This small motion wore her out. She noticed fingers lingering near her face. The fingertips were pale white and puckered. Were they hers? She dropped her arm back to her side, and released a long, shuddering breath as her eyes closed once more.

SMACK!

Anza's eyes snapped open. The girl had her hand raised, preparing to strike a third blow. Instinctively, Anza caught the girl's hand as it raced toward her face.

She sat up, giving the girl a stern glower.

"Sorry," the girl said. "Can you stay awake now? Do you think you can stand?"

Anza shook her head. She was surprised she was even sitting. The white-robed woman moved behind her and wrapped her arms around her torso, lifting her. Anza found her footing and was soon standing on wobbling legs. The girl draped Anza's arm across her shoulders to support her.

"My goodness," her rescuer said, looking down at Anza's buckskin clad body. "You certainly have a lot of knives."

Anza shrugged.

"I'm Colobi," the girl said. Anza looked more closely at her rescuer. She was shorter than Anza and a bit heavier, with large breasts and plump shoulders. Her hair hung loosely around her face, so blonde it was almost white. Colobi's face was flawless as porcelain, without a scar or blemish. Her eyes were a bright, crisp blue.

"Let's try walking," said Colobi, taking a step forward.

Anza strained to move her feet. She had to look down to see if they moved. She really couldn't feel much save for the two burning suns in her cheek where Colobi had slapped her.

"What's your name?" Colobi asked.

Anza made no effort to answer. She focused on putting one leg in front of the other as they slowly walked away from the dark river.

ANZA REGAINED CONTROL of her legs by the time they reached the Free City. The town was surrounded by a palisade of logs. Hundreds, perhaps thousands, of tents had been erected by the road leading to the gates. Anza sniffed the air. There were earth-dragons nearby, a lot of them, as well as humans. She tried to remember everything she knew about the Free City, but her head still felt stuffed with snow. She did remember, however, that the place had been abandoned in the aftermath of the attempted genocide within its walls. So who were all these people?

A tent flap lifted and a sky-dragon stepped out. The sky-dragon looked straight toward them and raised a fore-talon in a gesture of greeting. "Good evening, sister," the sky-dragon said. "I see you've found an injured soul."

"I pulled her from the river, brother," said Colobi. "I think she's the one the aerial guards were hunting."

Anza pulled free of Colobi, stunned by this betrayal. She raised her hand to the scabbard on her back. Her fingers were still too numb to grasp the sword.

She shoved her fingers beneath her armpits to try to warm them.

"There's no need for alarm," the sky-dragon said, shifting half his body back into the tent. "No one will betray you. Everyone is welcome here, human or dragon, no matter your past. I was once a tatterwing, surviving as a bandit, until the healer found me. He repaired my body and then charged me with the duty to repair my soul." The dragon pulled back from the tent carrying a heavy quilt. He approached Anza and draped it over her shoulders.

Anza frowned, her body tensing. Was this some trick? Through sheer will, she commanded her fingers to move again, opening and closing as blood flowed back into them. The bones of her fingers ached.

"I can see you're skeptical," said the sky-dragon. "You'll see the truth once you meet the healer."

"We shall all be healed, brother," Colobi said.

"We shall all be healed, sister," said the sky-dragon. He gave a respectful nod, then spread his wings and jumped into the sky, journeying toward whatever his original destination had been.

Anza lowered her hands from her armpits to the steel tomahawks on her belt. The handles had been machined to fit perfectly in her grasp. She felt a little stronger as she held them. Colobi looked toward her with a gentle smile.

"There's no need for weapons here," she said. Anza looked down. The quilt wasn't fully closed around her. The tomahawk in her left hand was plainly visible. "The Free City is the safest place on earth. The healer sees to all our needs. He restores our bodies so that we may work on the more difficult task of restoring our hearts and minds."

Anza ground her teeth. She didn't have the energy to deal with crazy people. On the other hand, she also didn't have the energy to flee. She was dead on her feet. And right now, following Colobi offered the greatest probability of survival. Anza hooked the tomahawks back onto her belt.

"Are you able to talk yet?" Colobi asked.

Anza shook her head.

"Once the healer feeds you, you'll feel better," said Colobi. "I imagine you have an interesting story given the commotion at the palace."

Anza shrugged, attempting to convey the impression that she didn't have a clue what Colobi was talking about.

"There's nothing to be ashamed of," said Colobi. "I once lived the most violent life imaginable. I was a Sister of the Serpent, a sworn devotee of the Murder God. I fell victim to his dark seductions due to painful events in my past. I grew up believing the only law was to kill or be killed. Until the healer opened my eyes, I was blind to the magic of simply being alive. You, too, will be freed from all your pains. Are you ready to be healed?"

Anza wasn't sure how to respond. The Sisters of the Serpent were deranged. They killed because they thought it was an act of holiness. Anza had never taken a life in the name of a higher power, nor had she ever struck a blow in hatred, anger, or fear. Her father had taught her that it was only ethical to use violence when it was guided by the rational mind. Colobi was obviously not a rational mind.

Still, Anza was cold, her legs felt like rubber, and she couldn't remember when she'd last eaten. Dawn brightened the eastern horizon. Off in the distance a cock crowed, joined quickly by another, and another. Within the Free City, she could see the smoke rising from hundreds of chimneys and could smell oats boiling as people rose to greet the day.

The most rational path was to stay near Colobi, at least until she could knock the chill from her bones and get some food in her stomach.

"Are you ready?" Colobi asked again.

Anza nodded.

Colobi smiled. "The healer may not be awake yet, but he will be soon. He'll be happy to receive you."

Colobi held out her open hand. Anza tentatively placed her palm against Colobi's. The white-robed woman led Anza through the wide-open gate of the Free City, humming softly beneath her breath.

The most disturbing thing about the streets was their unnatural cleanliness. At Dragon Forge, grime fell constantly from the sky. Even Anza's home town of Burke's Tavern had shown the wear and tear of daily life, with cracked paint on the houses, fallen slats on fences, and windows forever dimmed with lamp soot. In contrast, the Free City looked as if it had been built only yesterday. Every wall was bright with fresh paint. Granite cobblestones paved the streets, speckled with crystals that glittered in the morning light. Every shingle on the houses that lined the boulevard was precisely parallel to its neighbor.

There was no hint of the savage battle that had covered these streets with blood. Anza wondered if reports of the Battle of the Free City had been exaggerated. Or perhaps the people who now lived here were simply working overtime to erase all traces of the unpleasant history.

They turned onto a boulevard where the houses were still half-finished. A crew of five human workmen stood near a stack of freshly cut lumber, mumbling words and laughing as they drank hot broth from tin cups. Their white canvas overalls looked newly tailored. There were no rips, patches, or stains. The men, all middle-aged adults, had a curiously pristine appearance as well. Anza couldn't recall the last time she'd ever seen five men together where at least three of them didn't show some obvious facial scar. Nor were these men sunburned or wind-chapped. Odd.

The hair on the Anza's neck rose as a trio of green, scaly heads approached the workmen. Earth-dragons. The humans raised their hands and offered greetings as the dragons sauntered up to them.

Additional cups of the broth were poured from a ceramic kettle and offered to the dragons, who took them gently in their massive claws.

Colobi must have noticed that Anza was staring.

"Here, there is no hatred between humans and dragons," she said. "For centuries, we've struggled to distribute the resources of the land between four intelligent species with uneven talents and abilities. Now, the days of hunger and bitterness are at an end. We've reached the time of plenty. Dragons and men shall be part of a greater family. We've been sickened by poisonous philosophies. We shall all be healed."

As if to prove her words, a pair of sky-dragons descended to the construction site to be greeted with open hands by the humans and the earth-dragons. The sky-dragons unrolled a large parchment sheet atop the boards and everyone gathered around to look at the plans.

Colobi walked on, heading toward a large red barn. As Anza followed, Colobi said, "You may be surprised to find that the healer resides in such humble surroundings. There are those among us who would prefer to build a temple for his comfort; he insists, however, that we use our labor for the good of the many rather than the good of the one. Priority must be given to building homes for the refugees."

As they approached the broad double doors of the barn, faces peeked out through small windows. The doors opened slowly as they neared.

Within the barn, it was as warm as springtime. The room was full of candles that lined the walls and sat along the rafters. They flickered from the breeze of the opening door.

Near the rear of the barn there was a large pedestal built of bales of hay covered with a bleached canvas that might have once served as the sail of a ship. The only people in the room were a score of young women Colobi's age. All wore white robes and knelt around the canvas platform, their heads bowed, as if praying to some unseen deity.

Colobi came to a halt before the platform. She grasped Anza's right hand and looked into her eyes.

"You haven't said a word since I pulled you out of the river," she said. "I know this is overwhelming. You'll soon understand. You'll be one of us."

As Colobi spoke, the hairs on the back of Anza's neck began to rise. She detected a hint of ozone in the air, the same odor that she'd smelled when Jandra had struck her bracelet against the stone to turn them invisible. Fixing her gaze upon the canvas platform, she couldn't help but sense that there was some giant entity before her, despite the testimony of her own eyes that she was looking at empty air. Her pulse quickened and her fingers fell to the steel tomahawks at her hips.

"You're nervous," said Colobi, placing her fingers on her arm. "There's no need for fear. Everything will be made apparent when the healer arrives."

In response to these words, the air on the platform began to shimmer. Suddenly, a huge dome of sparks covered the canvas, a million small flares bursting into existence before fading almost instantly. In their wake, a sun-dragon was revealed sitting upon the platform.

Unlike most sun-dragons, this one possessed scales of pure black, as smooth and dark as the surface of a lake on a moonless, windless night. His eyes were green as jade as he peered at Anza. A silver halo hovered a few inches above his forehead, glowing faintly.

The sun-dragon looked toward Colobi and said, "Faithful one, you need not wait for my arrival. In truth, I am with you always."

As one, the kneeling women held up their arms, with outstretched palms, and said in a single voice, "Welcome, oh merciful healer!"

Anza let the quilt that warmed her slip to the ground, revealing the tomahawks in her grasp. She only knew of one sun-dragon with a black hide. But... he was dead. Jandra said Bitterwood had killed him. This couldn't possibly be the Murder God, could it?

As if in answer, the chorus of women spoke again. "Hail, oh beloved Blasphet!"

CHAPTER NINETEEN

BRAIN-DAMAGED FREAK WITH A VIOLENT STREAK

Three heartbeats.

Beat one: Anza inhaled deeply as she pushed all distractions from her mind. The ice in her bones, the weakness of her legs, and the pain of the burn mark on her breast were blocked out as she twirled the twin steel tomahawks around her fingers.

Beat two: Her eyes narrowed, turning the world into a tunnel. At the end of that tunnel was Blasphet's throat. His trachea slid beneath the smooth onyx scales of his neck. His jugular vein, thick as a man's thumb, would run directly beside this.

Beat three: Anza danced forward, swinging both tomahawks around in a graceful arc. Using the full momentum of her body, she released the left tomahawk, holding the right in reserve in case she needed a second shot. She wouldn't. The small, finely balanced hatchet spun almost lazily through the air in her hyper-aware state. The axe edge hit Blasphet's hide and sank into it.

His serpentine neck jerked as blood gushed from the wound.

Anza knew she'd just killed Blasphet. Unfortunately, it might take the giant beast a moment before he'd lost enough blood to realize it.

She stood before him, blinking off her tunnel vision, cataloging the gauntlet of potential dangers around her. The Sisters of the Serpent were numerous, but none were armed, and they looked stunned by Anza's action.

Behind Blasphet, there was a sky-dragon who glowered at her. This dragon, too, was unarmed but that didn't mean he wasn't a threat. The dragon spread its wings, revealing diamond studs within the folds of skin there. As he moved, silvery dust fell from his fore-talons. Anza blinked. In the span of that blink, the sky-dragon vanished.

She'd spared as much time as she could surveying the room. She was ready to make her retreat, once she dodged Blasphet's counter attack. She focused on the Murder God, anticipating that his huge jaws would be shooting toward her any second.

Instead, Blasphet reared up, his head nearly brushing the high rafters of the barn. He didn't look angry or frightened. Instead, he gazed at her with eyes filled with pity. His fore-talon moved to his throat and pulled the tomahawk free, letting it drop. Splashes of red dappled the canvas he stood upon.

Whatever the cause of the delay, Anza decided to exploit it. She spun, bolting for the door. She didn't make it even a yard before Colobi jumped on her back. She hit the ground hard as Colobi fell on top of her. The white-robed woman straddled Anza's hips, pinning her.

"Defiler!" Colobi shrieked as she closed her hands around Anza's windpipe. "This is how you repay our kindness?" She squeezed with all her might.

The battle gears in Anza's mind clicked forward a notch. Colobi's choking attack was a reasonable one for unarmed combat. Under the present battle conditions, however, it possessed a rather serious flaw. Anza swung her remaining tomahawk, driving the blade several inches into Colobi's forehead. The young woman's eyes rolled upward until only white showed, and she fell.

Anza pushed the corpse aside, freeing her tomahawk with a *slurp*. She rolled to her hands and knees and looked up.

If not for her ordeal in the river, she might have stood a chance. The remaining Sisters of the Serpent fell upon her like a wave. Anza swung her hatchet, but it was too late. A trio of women caught her arm, pressing it down, tearing the tomahawk loose. Another woman wrapped her arms around Anza's waist and pushed her once more to the ground. A dozen hands grabbed her legs. More hands grasped her right arm, pinning that limb to the straw-covered floor.

Anza arched her back, wriggling, trying to kick free, but for every hand she knocked loose, four more seized her. In seconds she was pinned, immobile, spread-eagle on the ground as the dark form of Blasphet loomed above her.

Blasphet had his fore-talon pressed against his throat. When he pulled his gore-wet claws away, blood no longer squirted from the wound. The blood on his claws and neck faded, absorbed into his dark hide. The wound was no longer visible.

The black beast stared at Anza, his brow furrowed.

He ran his claws along his chest. The scales of his breast were malformed, no doubt due to the poisons that ran within his blood. The scales were bunched up, looking more like fat ticks than the smooth overlapping plates of a serpent. He plucked one of the scale polyps free and handed it to the woman who sat on Anza's chest.

"Feed this to her," he said.

Anza clenched her jaws. One sister pinched her nose shut. Another clawed at Anza's lips, sinking her nails into the gums beneath. Anza fought the pressure until she trembled, but it was of no use. Slowly, her jaws were pried open. One of her own knives was placed between her teeth to keep them from closing. A woman's fingers flickered against her tongue, pushing the seed-like scale toward the back of her throat.

A jug carried by one of the women was held over her head. A stream of water poured into her open mouth. Suddenly the knife was pulled free and her jaws were forced shut. She closed her eyes, fighting to the urge to breathe. Against her will, Anza swallowed.

The women released her mouth. When she opened her eyes, Blasphet no longer loomed above her. The black dragon leaned over Colobi's fallen form, ignoring Anza for the moment.

"Ah, my faithful one," he said, his voice mournful as he lifted her limp body. "You've known nothing but violence all your life." He brushed the bloody hair away from her forehead. He placed his scaly talon over her face. "I know you acted out of love, but there's no need for fighting."

He pulled his talon away. Colobi's forehead was intact; there was no sign of the tomahawk wound, not even a scar. Colobi's eyes opened, glistening with tears. She whispered, "I've defiled your holy presence with my anger. I'm not deserving of your mercy."

"You are wrong, my child," said Blasphet. The skin around his eyes creased. Dragons couldn't smile, but his eyes signaled affection. "All are worthy of wholeness and mercy. You understand what you did wrong; you won't transgress again. You've paid for your sins. When I picked you up, you had no heartbeat. The woman who acted in anger is dead. You are a reborn creature now, free from the sins of your past."

Blasphet set Colobi down. She stood on unsteady legs; tears ran down her cheeks. Driven by emotions that Anza couldn't fathom, Colobi spun and ran from the barn, weeping.

Blasphet turned toward Anza. His great, long face, bigger than a horse's head, snaked down toward her. He exhaled as he studied her. His breath was pleasant, smelling of mint. It was nothing like the carrion breath of most dragons.

He took a long, deep breath inches from her face. A fine silver dust rose from Anza's flesh. It reminded her of the residue that had been left behind by Jandra's bracelet.

Blasphet's eyes stayed focused upon her as she searched his face for any possible weak points. If she could get her hands free, she still possessed a chance. The silver halo that hung above Blasphet's scalp reflected candlelight, meaning it was solid. It was plain, and didn't look strong, but it did have a small triangle near the front that rose up into a decorative peak. A sun-dragon's ears were large, flat disks on the side of their head, almost like the surface of a drum. If she could grab the circlet, then drive the point into Blasphet's ear, the pain would immobilize him. Then, if she could reach her throwing knives…

Blasphet observed, "You're still calculating how best to kill me. This is one reason I hold such affection for mankind. The best of you cling to hope long after a more rational being would succumb to despair. Tell me my child, what is your name?"

Anza glared at him.

"There is no need to fear me. I will not harm you."

Anza stared silently as Blasphet cocked his head, waiting for her answer. In the candlelight, she saw more of the silvery dust riding in and out of Blasphet's nostrils. Blasphet turned his head to the right, then to the left, his eyes running up and down the length of her body.

"You've not lead an easy life," said Blasphet, touching the festering burn wound on her chest. She sucked in air as a jangle of pain ran through her. "You possess far more scars than a typical woman your age. You've broken several bones over the years. Yet, you've received better medical attention than most humans. Your cuts have been expertly stitched and your bones have been reset by a confident hand."

Blasphet turned his attention to her face. He stroked her cheek. "A typical female your age would already be a mother. Yet I see you retain your virginity. It's obvious from your rather formidable skills that someone has trained you as a warrior, not a wife. What a curious life you've led. Won't you tell me your story?"

Anza ground her teeth together and strained against the hands that held her. Though she was still fully clothed, she felt as if Blasphet was somehow undressing her. She'd never felt so vulnerable.

"Whoever trained you... he was never able to teach you to speak, was he?" asked Blasphet. He didn't wait for Anza to answer. His eyes were fixed on her throat. "He couldn't have. I see a small tumor on your recurrent laryngeal nerve. It looks quite old; perhaps you've had it since infancy. It's become calcified. It's a tiny stone in your throat that blocks nerve impulses to your vocal chords. The muscles in your larynx have atrophied, producing your present aphonia."

Blasphet's talons fell upon Anza's throat. He lightly rubbed her skin. Anza shuddered, then tipped her head back as searing pain ripped through her neck. It felt as if Blasphet were attempting to decapitate her from the inside out. She couldn't breathe—it felt as if a dozen thick worms were squirming and coiling in her windpipe.

She opened her mouth and tears welled in her eyes. She'd lived her life as a tool of death, like a sword or a bow. She'd known that the day would come when she would break and be discarded, as was the fate of all tools. She'd never told a soul that she was afraid of this day. Who was she to tell? It was her shameful secret that she sometimes woke up in the dead of night, from dreamless sleep, shivering at the thought of nothingness, of non-existence, of the world moving on in her absence.

Suddenly, the worms in her throat lined up in a more orderly fashion, allowing the movement of air once more. She filled her lungs to fullness with a deep, desperate gasp.

As she exhaled, a noise tore from her throat that was like nothing she'd ever heard. It was something the cry of a hungry baby, only deeper, like the howl of a coyote, or the wail of a wildcat. It was a long, deafening, drawn-out scream that caused the hands that pinned her to flinch.

It was the scream of a woman who had never even whispered. It was a howl that was the sum of countless days of silence. It was the cry of a woman who'd never laughed, never cursed, and bore in silence the pain of broken bones and a thousand cuts.

It was a sound she'd heard only in her dreams. There was no mistaking it. This noise was coming from her own mouth. It made her tongue itch and her teeth ache.

Slowly, the scream died away as the last thimble of air left her lungs. She took a deep breath, and screamed again.

One by one the hands that held her let go. She didn't move. She couldn't. All the anger and fear and shame of a silent lifetime had provided the tension that drove the springs of her clockwork heart. That tension was gone now, carried away by the primal howls. The last remnants of her unspoken agony seeped out as loud, choking, sobs.

"Ooo," she said, trembling. "Ooohhh, oohhhh, ooohhhhhh."

She possessed a voice, but she didn't know how to make words.

"Ooohhhh!" she groaned, as she curled into a tight, fetal ball. "Oooohhh... *Ooooohhh!*"

Gently, a pair of giant talons slipped beneath her and picked her up. She was cradled against Blasphet's enormous breast. She pressed her wet face against it. His scales felt cool in contrast to the heat of her tears. The drum-like beat of his heart filled her ears.

"Your screams are like music to me, child," Blasphet whispered. "They are the sounds of your body healing, so that your soul may heal. Soon enough, we'll teach you to talk. You shall be whole, child. You shall be healed."

"We shall all be healed," the chorus of women said in unison.

Anza opened her teary eyes. She didn't see an angry face among the women who looked up at her.

Beyond the women, however, was the sky-dragon she'd spotted earlier. He was standing near the back of the room, staring at her with a look that was best interpreted as a scowl. He didn't look pleased by what he was seeing, but he didn't look like a threat either. Nothing in the way the dragon carried himself suggested he was contemplating violence.

Feeling completely, truly safe for the first time in memory, Anza closed her eyes and cried herself to sleep in the cradle of Blasphet's wings.

JANDRA WOKE TO the sound of a woman screaming. Her eyes popped open as the echoes faded. She felt a flutter of panic; total darkness engulfed her. Was she blind? The disorientation faded and she remembered she was underground, deep in the mines.

She'd seldom encountered true darkness. Above ground, even a cloudy, moonless night still possessed some faint trace of light. Within the palace where she'd grown up, there were many shadows, but she was never far from a torch or lantern. When she'd had her powers, she could create light simply by sprinkling dust in the air. She sat up, tossing off the blanket that covered her, taking a deep breath to calm her racing heart. She felt stupid. She was too old to be frightened of the dark.

She groped for the visor she'd placed beside her rolled-up coat that she used as a pillow. The walls of the mine came into sharp focus as she slipped it on, not that there was much worth looking at. They were in a long shaft of black stone. Up was rock, down was rock, side to side was rock. The only living things to be seen were Shay and Lizard. Shay was sitting up, his back to the wall. He already had his visor on, hiding his eyes. The short braid he normally wore had come undone, and his red hair lay about his face in tangles. He hadn't shaved in a week, and the shadow of stubble around his mouth made him look older. Coal dust had darkened the creases of his skin. His shotgun was in his lap, grasped with both hands. Life underground was proving hard on Shay. He'd grown increasingly silent the deeper they moved into the earth.

The cool, dank tunnels were also taking a toll on Lizard. The little earth-dragon was pressed up against Shay, staring at Jandra with a wide-eyed gaze. He looked worried.

"How long have you been awake?" Jandra asked.

"You were talking in your sleep again," said Shay. "You woke up screaming."

"Did I?" Jandra cocked her head. She had a fleeting memory of a woman shouting, but it was ephemeral, the echo of an echo. "What did I say?"

"You were talking to someone named Cassie," said Shay. "Just before you woke, you screamed, 'It's mine!'"

Jandra brushed the hair back from her forehead, puzzling over this revelation. She thought about her tongue, how it could possibly speak without her mind controlling it, and grew aware of the bad taste in her mouth. "I need water," she said.

Shay held out the leather canteen. She uncorked it and took a deep drink. The water had a sulfurous taint to it. There were numerous streams and pools in the mine, but most tasted like rotten eggs. It wasn't pleasant to drink, but neither was it dangerous. Vendevorex had provided her with a thorough education in chemistry. Sulfur posed no harm to the human body when ingested. The main downside was that her spit was taking on the foul odor. In fact, she was starting to reek, period. When she'd still been in control of her nanotech, the tiny machines had kept her skin clean, her breath fresh, and her hair untangled. Low-tech grooming was tedious and almost pointless in a coal mine, where every surface she touched sullied her further.

She put the jug down and wiped her lips with the back of her hand, feeling the coarse grit that covered both her hands and her mouth. The black grit reminded her of the black sand of an oil-covered beach—one of Jazz's memories.

"Can you remember your dream?" Shay asked. "Who's Cassie?"

"My sister." Jandra cringed. "I mean, Jazz's sister. I don't remember the dream directly. I feel like my brain is sorting through all these extra memories. Jazz's life story is starting to make sense finally. All the random, disconnected memories are becoming a coherent sequence of events."

"A lot of slaves worshipped the goddess, but I wasn't a believer," said Shay. "It's hard to swallow the idea that she was real."

Lizard jerked his head upward when Shay said the word "swallow." The little beast's vocabulary was limited, but he knew all the words connected to food.

"Real is a relative term. Jasmine Robertson wasn't a goddess. She was a human, born a thousand years ago."

"I've read about that time," said Shay. "The Human Age. It must have been like paradise."

"Not quite," said Jandra. "Human civilization took a toll upon the earth. Vast areas of the globe had their native species plowed under and replaced with agriculture based on a few select plants, like corn. The soil had to be constantly replenished with petroleum-based chemicals. Poisons meant to fight pests worked their way into the groundwater. Water was also contaminated by runoff from digging into the earth for various minerals. To get at coal, humans would tear down entire mountain ranges. They burned that coal non-stop for two centuries, forever altering the atmosphere."

"Was the sky of the whole world like the sky over Dragon Forge?"

"Not quite. They constantly refined technology to make it cleaner. That's one reason Jazz's memories confuse me. She could have done so much to make the world better with her brilliance. Instead, she decided to tear the world down."

"Was she insane?"

"No. She was a genius, and something of an outsider, but not insane. Her sister, Cassie, had been born blind due to a side effect of a drug her mother had taken while she was pregnant. Cassie was an early recipient of artificial retinas. Jazz was fascinated by technology, and by biology, and, well, by everything, really. She wasn't insane—she was... overly confident. She thought she understood the world's problems and could fix them. Fixing the world, unfortunately, meant cutting the world's human population from eight billion to eighty million."

"I can't even imagine eight billion people," said Shay. "Where did everyone stand?"

"The world's bigger than you can imagine," said Jandra. "I don't think I really grasped just how big it was until Jazz took me to the moon."

"To the... you mean, you've been... *the moon?*"

Jandra nodded.

"How? I mean, not even dragons fly that high, do they?"

"Jazz knew a short cut. There's apparently a different kind of space that exists under our reality. Jazz called it underspace. She stole the technology for traveling through it from Atlantis."

Shay scratched his head. She sensed that her explanations were only making things worse. "Atlantis is an alien artifact that arrived on Earth at the tipping point of its environmental collapse. It was a machine intelligence programmed for almost perfect altruism—a living city designed to serve the needs of its citizens. It could have ushered in a true golden age... except, Jazz was one of the first people to encounter it. While the machine intelligence was far more advanced than anything she'd ever experienced, she was able to subtly alter its mission. She stopped its altruism at the edges of its immediate environment. The humans who went to live in Atlantis are effectively immortal. The city ignores the rest of the world. Jazz has since reduced mankind to a feral state, devoid of advanced technology. She thinks this is the wisest path for the long-term health of the world."

Shay nodded. If he didn't understand, at least he was humoring her. "You're still talking about Jazz in the present tense."

Jandra lowered her head as she realized he was right.

"What if I'm using the present tense because she's still alive?" Jandra whispered. "I need to get a genie back so I can fix my brain. I think... I think she's slowly pushing me out of my own memories." Despite her best efforts to hold them back, tears trickled down her cheeks.

Shay scooted over toward her. He placed his fingers gently on the back of her hand. Lizard's small claws fell next to them. She shuddered.

"Whenever... I go... to sleep," she said between sobs, "I'm afraid... I won't wake up as me."

Shay slid beside her. He wrapped his arm around her shoulders. "Shh," he said, in a soothing tone. "You're just getting scared by a few bad dreams."

"No!" she protested. "You don't understand. Nothing terrifies me more than losing my identity. I was raised by a dragon. I've always been confused about who I am."

Lizard looked up at her with a concerned expression. Shay squeezed her hand more tightly.

She wiped her cheeks. "I've always... I feel crippled because I didn't have wings, or a tail. I feel ugly when I look in a mirror and see skin instead of scales."

Shay stroked the hair back from her face and said, softly, "You aren't ugly, Jandra. You're the prettiest woman I've ever met."

Jandra rolled her eyes. "Inside, I'm all broken up and scarred. I'm a freak, raised by the wrong species. Now I've had my brain rewired by thousand year old egomaniac. I have to be the most screwed up person who's ever lived."

"Jandra," said Shay, "if you're screwed up, then the world needs more screwed up people. You're incredibly brave. My mind went blank with fear when Vulpine attacked, but you kept your wits. I was on the verge of peeing myself while you calmly reloaded your gun. You're amazing. You bossed around Bitterwood. You took away an earth-dragon's own axe and killed him with it. Could a brain-damaged freak do these things?"

"Why not?" She attempted to grin but couldn't quite manage it. "No wonder I wake up screaming. I'm a brain-damaged freak with a violent streak."

"You've also got a compassionate streak. You put your life in danger to save Lizard. You're kind and caring. Despite all the awful things dragons have done to you, you aren't consumed with bitterness and hatred. More than anyone I've ever met, you're trying to make the world a better place. Lizard's right... you're a good boss."

"Good boss," Lizard cooed. "Good, good boss." He stared up at her as she wiped the tears from her cheeks. The little dragon turned his gaze to her backpack. "We eat?"

Jandra laughed, then hiccupped. "Flatterer," she said. "Yes, we'll eat."

Shay released her hand. "If you want to talk more about this later, I'm ready to listen. You don't need to feel like the weight of the world is on your shoulders alone."

She looked at Shay, his face only inches from hers. Of the three people she'd ridden with from Dragon Forge, he was the last one she would have expected to still be with her when she undertook what was probably the most dangerous mission of her life. This seemed like an insane amount of effort for Shay to go through in order to get his hands on some books. A light clicked on in her head.

He hadn't come all this way for the books.

"By the bones," she whispered. "You like me!"

He grinned. "Of course I like you."

"I mean... you're... interested in me. As a potential, um, mate."

He looked away sheepishly and cleared his throat. "I haven't... I mean... I'm really..." his voice trailed off. He took a deep breath and looked back toward her. "Yes. I find you, as you say, interesting. On many levels. I've never met anyone like you."

"How long...?"

Shay shrugged. "It... it wasn't love at first sight. You are... you're a little intimidating, to tell the truth. But there's... there's something... something about the way you stand. Your shoulders are always pulled back. You hold your chin up. It's so... regal. I understand how a woman raised in a palace might find the interest of a slave... unwelcome."

"No!" said Jandra. "I mean... I didn't know. I hadn't been... I'm just... I've never been taught how to look for the, uh, signals. The only man who ever showed interest was Pet, but I always found his attentions… creepy. I felt like a mouse under the watchful gaze of a hungry cat. He may have given me a false sense of what indicates a man's interest. Since you weren't constantly leering, I just didn't suspect."

"I didn't… I don't know the signals either," said Shay. "Among slaves, we're usually matched with whoever our masters choose. Courtship isn't something I've had any experience with. When I look at you, I do feel… it's something like hunger, but nothing like hunger. It's… It's—"

"Lizard hungry," said the earth-dragon, tugging on Jandra's sleeve.

"We should eat," said Jandra, welcoming the change of subject. This wasn't a conversation she felt ready to have. She turned her back to Shay. She flipped open her backpack and reached in for the hardtack inside. "We have a long way to go."

CHAPTER TWENTY

SWIFT DECISIVE
ACTION

JEREMIAH'S HANDS TREMBLED as he cut away the watery black rot from the soft, lumpy potato. He dropped the remaining white chunk in the large iron pot he crouched over. He felt sick to his stomach. No doubt the stench of the mound of partially rotten potatoes he sat next to was the blame. It didn't help that his head was throbbing from his earlier "training," or that his arms and legs were covered with knots and bruises. These same knots and bruises had kept him from sleeping much at all the last few nights despite his exhaustion. His bed was a pile of empty potato sacks, and he was still using the same filthy blanket he'd been wrapped in by Vulpine. He wiped his brow with a burlap rag. He was sweating, despite the chills that shook his hands.

When Jeremiah had arrived at Dragon Forge, he'd been hungry, weary, and freezing. He'd possessed a half-formed dream that he would be welcomed into town by some kindly woman who looked like his mother. She would give him soup, clean clothes, and put him to bed in a big, soft mattress with clean sheets.

Instead of a kindly woman, he'd been met at the gate by a pair of thuggish teenagers who'd taunted his thin limbs and the tear-tracks down his filthy face. He later learned their names were Presser and Burr. They'd finally allowed him in, and brought him before a frightening man named Ragnar, who looked like a wild beast with his mane of hair and leathery skin.

Ragnar had made the rules of Dragon Forge clear: if you wanted to eat, you had to work, and, what's more, you had to fight.

"Can you do that, boy?" Ragnar had demanded.

"Y-yes sir," he'd answered. He'd never fought before, but he had Vulpine's knife still tucked into his belt. He imagined it might be satisfying to bury that knife into some dragon, though the exact details of how that might happen were fuzzy in his mind.

"Find a job for him," Ragnar had told the guards. "He looks too scrawny to be of much use, but get him outfitted with a sword, at least. Can you use a sword, boy?"

"I-I've never tried," said Jeremiah.

Presser chimed in, "There's a sharp end and a dull end. Once you learn which end to grab, it's not so hard."

Jeremiah wasn't sure if he was joking.

Burr added, "We'll get him trained, sir. Make a regular soldier out of him."

Ragnar grunted his approval, then dismissed the boys with a wave.

Presser and Burr had pushed Jeremiah before them out into the street. In the sunlight, the two guards' youthfulness was apparent—though both were taller than Jeremiah by a head, he doubted either was older than fifteen. They swaggered as they walked in their chainmail vests and iron helmets, sky-wall bows slung over their backs.

Once they reached the middle of the street, Burr said, "Presser, give me your sword. Leave it in the sheath."

Presser had complied. It was obvious that Burr was the leader of the pair. Burr gave the sheathed sword to Jeremiah. The weapon was only a short sword, two feet long at most, but it was still heavy. Jeremiah looked up quizzically, not certain what he was supposed to do next.

Burr removed his own sheathed sword from his belt and swung it, slapping Jeremiah hard on the back of his right hand, knocking the sword from his grasp.

"Ow!" said Jeremiah. "What did you do that for?"

"You heard Ragnar. We've got to teach you to fight. The first thing to learn is don't drop your sword. Pick it up."

"You'll hit me again!"

Burr swung his sword, attempting to slam it into Jeremiah's thigh, but Jeremiah jumped out of the path of the blow. He had good reflexes, and eluded Burr's next two swings as well.

Unfortunately, with his attention focused on Burr, he hadn't seen Presser slip behind him. Presser grabbed him, pulling him to his chest in a bear hug.

"Damn, this boy thinks he's a jackrabbit," said Burr. "You can't be a soldier if you're afraid of getting hit, Rabbit."

To prove his point, Burr punched Jeremiah in the stomach. After that, the lesson had devolved into a rather thorough beating that drew a crowd. No one intervened. In the end, they'd tossed Jeremiah, half conscious, into the kitchen and said, "This is your new home. We'll come around in a few days to train you some more. Next time, don't drop the damn sword."

LIFE IN THE kitchen wasn't completely miserable. It was warm, at least, with the wood-fired ovens churning out endless trays of cornbread. On the stoves, pots of beans and potatoes simmered night and day. Thankfully, no one tried to talk to Jeremiah other than the occasional grunted command. No one cared who he was or where he'd come from. Jeremiah took comfort in this, since he was certain that, if he did talk about everything that had happened to him since the night the long-wyrm riders attacked Big Lick, he would cry. That could only result in further beatings from Presser and Burr.

Even without talking, he still found tears welling up in his eyes, which was odd. He wasn't always the bravest boy in the world, but he wasn't a crybaby. The only times he normally felt weepy was when he was getting sick. Maybe it was more than the stench of rotting vegetables that made him queasy, or the heat of the stoves that made him feel feverish. His sweat smelled funny. He was so tired. He wondered if anyone would notice if he crawled into the back room and took a nap.

Before he could act on the impulse, the door to the kitchen burst open. He raised his hand to shield his eyes from the bright winter sunlight outside. The chill wind cut right through him. Two shadows stood in the doorway.

"Rabbit!" one of the shadows shouted. "Time for another lesson!"

Jeremiah blinked, bringing Burr and Presser into focus.

"I-I've got to peel potatoes," he said, his voice faint and quavering.

Presser stomped inside and grabbed him by the wrist. He dragged Jeremiah toward the open door and threw him into the street.

"Everyone fights! You don't fight, you don't eat!" Presser yelled.

Jeremiah lay on the cold, packed earth of the street. A crowd was already starting to gather. Burr's feet came round to his face. His boots were scuffed and worn. The right sole was peeling away at the toe, revealing a gray wool sock.

A sheathed sword dropped to the ground next to Jeremiah's hand.

"Get up," said Burr.

Jeremiah shook his head.

"Get up or I'll kick the snot out of you," Burr said.

"I feel sick," said Jeremiah.

"You feel chicken," said Burr. "Presser, help him up."

Presser leaned down and grabbed Jeremiah by the hair. He pulled and Jeremiah found the motivation to rise to his hands and knees, then to his feet. Presser let him go and Jeremiah stood, swaying in the bright sunlight, feeling the world spinning beneath him.

"Pick up your sword, Rabbit," Burr said.

Jeremiah didn't move. It wasn't fear that held him motionless. In truth, he didn't feel anything at all beyond the terrible dizziness. It took all his will to stay on his feet.

"He looks like he's about to faint," Presser said with a giggle.

Jeremiah felt like he was about to faint.

"This will wake him up," said Burr. He charged forward and delivered a powerful punch to Jeremiah's gut. Jeremiah instantly vomited, spraying a jet of thin yellow fluid as he doubled over.

Burr cursed as he staggered backwards, wiping the vomit from his face.

Presser giggled as Jeremiah fell back to the dust. He vomited again, heaving and heaving. He was stunned by the amount of liquid pouring from him. He hadn't eaten a thing all day, and had only taken a few sips of water.

Presser continued to giggle, but the rest of the crowd grew deathly quiet. The circle of men drew back further, dispersing. Some of the men took off running. Only as he watched the frightened reaction of the crowd did Presser's giggles trail off.

Jeremiah stared with unfocused eyes as a pair of black boots came up from behind the crowd. The crowd parted at their approach. The man who wore the boots fearlessly approached Jeremiah, kneeling before him, rolling him onto his back. The man was white-haired, his face dimpled with countless scars. His left ear was nothing but a mess of scabby ribbons. The white-haired man looked down with concerned eyes. On one of his hands, several of the fingers were set in splints. He pressed the back of this hand to Jeremiah's forehead. He pulled open Jeremiah's mouth with his good hand, tilting to better see inside, and frowned.

"Whose son is this?" the man asked the crowd.

"He arrived alone," said Presser. "Said he'd escaped from Vulpine himself. He's been working in the kitchen since."

"What's his name?"

"We've been calling him Rabbit."

Jeremiah swallowed, then whispered, "Juh...Jeremiah, sir."

"Where'd you come from?"

"F-from the m-mountains," he said, his teeth beginning to chatter as chills seized him. "B-Big Lick. I w-was sold into s-slavery."

"To which dragon?" the man asked.

"R-r-rorg."

A second pair of boots approached. These were the biggest feet he'd ever seen on a man. A deep voice asked, "What's happening, Frost?"

Frost shook his head. "Stonewall, you don't want to know."

"I'll be the judge of that," said the big man.

"This boy has yellow-mouth. Probably contracted it in Rorg's cavern."

"You're right," said Stonewall. "I didn't want to know that."

"And he's been working in the kitchen."

"Oh." Stonewall was silent as he contemplated this news. "Can yellow-mouth spread through—"

"Yes," said Frost. "Since he can still talk, he's not yet in the final phase. He won't live too many more days, though. I had the disease when I was his age, but I was healthy. He's half-starved and infested with lice. He won't make it."

Stonewall rubbed his eyes. "How widespread do you think—"

"He worked in the damn kitchen," snapped Frost. "Everyone in Dragon Forge is at risk."

"You've survived the disease," said Stonewall, sounding calm and thoughtful. "Others have, too. Spread the word that I want anyone who's survived yellow-mouth to gather at the kitchen. The men who this boy has been in contact with will need to be quarantined. We need to find out what his kitchen duties were. If he was in contact with the food before it was cooked, it may be that the grace of God has spared us. Not much survives the cooking here."

"This isn't something to joke about."

"Nor is it something to panic about," said Stonewall. "We have to have faith we'll get through this. We'll control the outbreak. We'll isolate those most exposed. We'll start a regimen of checking people's gums daily. Swift action is the key."

Frost scooped Jeremiah up and slung him unceremoniously over his shoulder. "Swift action works for me. You go update Ragnar. I'll take care of the boy."

Stonewall looked at Frost. "When you say take care of the boy...?"

"This isn't the time to argue."

Stonewall frowned. "After what you did to Biscuit, I—"

"I know what I'm doing. Go!"

Stonewall slowly turned away, then loped off in search of Ragnar.

Jeremiah kicked as Frost turned and walked in the opposite direction, but Frost only grasped his legs tighter. Jeremiah lifted his head, straining to see where they were going. They were heading toward the foundry. The double doors stood open—even in the dead of winter, the interior of the foundry was sweltering. The doors looked like the gates of hell. It was dark and shadowy within. White flames danced above a red stream of molten iron flowing into molds.

"Put me down," Jeremiah said. "I can walk."

"You can run, you mean," said Frost.

"I won't run. I'm sick."

"I know," said Frost. "Very sick. You're going to die, boy. Yellow-mouth is a bad way to go. It's not a quick death. So, I'm going to throw you in the furnace."

Jeremiah didn't believe him. "What are you really going to do?"

Frost chuckled, but didn't answer.

They passed through the door into the dark interior. The heat jumped dramatically—it was hotter than the kitchen, a dry, parched blast that sopped up the sweat beading on his skin. The noise of the foundry was as hellish as the swelter, with the constant roar of furnaces stoked by mule-driven bellows, and the banging of countless hammers against anvils.

"Y-you're really going to do it?" Jeremiah asked.

"I'll snap your neck first. I'm not cruel, boy. Only practical."

Jeremiah still felt dizzy, but panic sent a surge of strength through his limbs. He beat Frost's ribs with his fists. The man's broad back sounded like a drum. He kicked furiously, but to no effect. Frost didn't even flinch.

"Open the furnace door!" Frost yelled. "Then, get back! This boy has yellow-mouth!"

Slowly, the noise changed throughout the foundry. Hammers fell silent and men began to shout, "Yellow-mouth!"

"Don't panic, damn it!" Frost shouted. "Fear is more dangerous than the disease. We're taking swift, decisive action to stop the spread. Gather round. Watch me. This boy is the only one we know of who's sick. I want you all to see that we're stronger than any disease!"

There was a horrible groan as an iron door swung open. The roar of flames grew louder, and the back of Jeremiah's legs grew hotter. Red light cast a stark black shadow on the wall behind them.

Jeremiah screamed, "Please don't—" His hands flailed around. His fingers fell onto the scabby strips of flesh that had once been Frost's ear. He gripped these shreds of skin for all he was worth.

Frost screeched, pulled Jeremiah from his shoulder, and threw him to the hot brick floor. Jeremiah rolled onto his back, skittering and kicking to get away. He scooted backward until he was pressed against a low brick wall.

"Until now, I wasn't planning on enjoying this," Frost said, rubbing his ear nub with his good hand. He pulled his fingers away; they were orange with blood and puss. He reached toward Jeremiah's face. "Before I throw you in, I'm going to break every last damn fi—*NNNG!*"

Frost cried out in pain as an arrow erupted from his good hand. He drew back, staring at the missile that had entered the back of his wrist and passed through to the skin on the other side, pushing it out in a little pointy tent. The arrow was fletched with fresh green leaves that wilted in the sweltering heat of the foundry.

Frost craned his neck. "Who?" he screamed. "Who did this?"

From above, a voice answered. "The boy is mine. You may not touch him."

Frost and Jeremiah both looked into the shadows of the rafters. A human figure could barely be seen, the contours of his body distorted by a cloak. It was apparent, however, that he held a bow before him, with a second arrow aimed at Frost.

"This boy has yellow-mouth!" Frost protested. "He's dying anyway!"

"We're all dying," said the shadowy archer. "Some of us today, perhaps. Step away."

Frost walked backward, clutching his bleeding wrist with the thumb and splinted fingers of his other hand. The arrow swayed when he walked.

The archer dropped a pink rope down from the rafters. He slid down, landing at Jeremiah's feet. Jeremiah recognized the man; he'd traveled with his sister, Zeeky. It was the old man who'd claimed he was Bitterwood. But Bitterwood and Zeeky were dead, killed by the demons in the mines. Did this mean that Zeeky was also alive?

"I'm taking the boy," Bitterwood said. "We're leaving Dragon Forge. He won't spread the disease further."

"You can't leave," Frost said. "There's a blockade of dragons."

"They didn't see me come in," said Bitterwood. "They won't see me go." He looked down at Jeremiah. "Stand up. We're leaving."

Frost snarled. "Who are you to come here and start issuing demands?"

Bitterwood held his hand down to meet Jeremiah's outstretched grasp and help him to his feet.

"My name isn't important," said Bitterwood. "If you're going to order your men to stop me, do so. Their blood will be on your hands."

Frost glared at his assailant, studying his face. Bitterwood met his gaze with an icy stare. At last, Frost looked away.

"Let him go," he said to the men who'd gathered between Bitterwood and the door.

Bitterwood tugged at the rope in the rafter. The pink cord snaked down, shrinking as it fell into his gloved hand. He turned, prodding Jeremiah with a nudge between his shoulder blades. Jeremiah scuffled forward. When they reached the street, Bitterwood slung his bow over his shoulder then picked up Jeremiah. Jeremiah draped his arms around the old man's neck and was carried toward the city gates. He rested his head on Bitterwood's shoulder.

"Is Zeeky here?" he whispered.

"She's near," said Bitterwood. "Poocher, too."

"Will she catch yellow-mouth from me?"

"Don't know," answered Bitterwood.

"That man said I was going to die."

Bitterwood continued to walk, without saying another word.

SHAY'S FEET WERE sore. He'd lost track of how many days they'd been walking underground. He had no idea how many miles they'd covered. Since this morning when he'd confessed his attraction to Jandra, they'd walked without conversation. He followed behind her as she led the way. Lizard scrambled along like a faithful dog at her heels. The little dragon had a strange walk. He was bipedal, but he didn't really stand erect like a human. His torso leaned forward as his tail jutted out beside him. He bounced along in a gait resembling some flightless bird.

From time to time, Lizard would look over his shoulder, glaring at Shay with what seemed to be a newfound hostility. Did Lizard understand the conversation he and Jandra had shared earlier? Was the small beast jealous? Or did his muted hostility somehow reflect Jandra's own reaction? She certainly had been anxious to change the subject. Was she looking for a way to let him down gently? He'd been a fool to say anything. He'd never mention it again.

Or was he being a coward now? When he'd praised Jandra for her bravery, it had been a subtle confession of his own lack of courage. He'd run to escape from Chapelion while his master was away. A braver man might have waited for Chapelion's return and killed him. The biologian certainly wouldn't have anticipated it. No doubt, Shay would have been killed in the aftermath, but as a tactical move, killing the head of the College of Spires would have been a serious blow to the morale of all sky-dragons. But was courage only measured as a willingness to kill or be killed? Wasn't it also a type of courage to steal books and run so that he could teach others to read?

He'd read a thousand books on the subject of courage, and been offered a thousand different answers. The same was true of love. He'd read countless poems and essays on the matter, studied numerous plays, and could recite from memory a hundred lines where a man summed up his feelings and offered them to a woman like some gilded rose. And now that his moment of romantic confession had come and gone, what had he summoned up? *Something like hunger? Nothing like hunger?* A lifetime of working with words had left him with these inanities. Perhaps, in the end, Bitterwood was right. Books had never done the world any good.

He was pulled from his thoughts as the smell of the mines started to change. The damp, egg-scented air took on a saltier, more marine smell, as if they were nearing the ocean. It was like saltwater at low tide, a sort of soggy, methane-rich rot.

Jandra halted as she studied the tunnel ahead. The passage widened. The mine shaft led to a cliff, and beyond this he couldn't see anything. Jandra reached up and took off her visor. She turned, nodded her head toward the end of the tunnel, and said, "Light."

He removed the visor. He blinked in the darkness that swallowed him. Yet the darkness wasn't complete. The open end of the tunnel had a dull glow, like dawn just over the horizon. Jandra was a dark silhouette against this faint light.

"Something's changed," said Jandra. "When we left, the place had fallen into total darkness."

"We're here? This is the kingdom of the goddess?"

"Yes," said Jandra, walking forward at a rapid pace. "It's a world within a world. I only saw a small part of it when I was here with Bitterwood and Hex, but it stretches out for over a hundred square miles."

Shay hurried to keep up. They halted at the mouth of the tunnel, on a ledge overlooking a large underground lake studded with islands. The stench of rot was extreme. The light came from thousands of small bright pin points scattered across the roof of the endless cavern.

"To have been built by someone who loved nature, this has to be one of the least natural places on earth," Jandra said. "After the human age ended, Jazz withdrew to this underground world. She took her self-appointed title of goddess a bit too seriously perhaps, and began to populate it with life of her own design. She was fascinated by the limits evolutionary history had imposed on organisms. She wondered if she could create species that were more intelligently designed to fill niches left in the earth's ecology by the mass extinctions brought about by civilization."

"She thought the world needed long-wyrms?"

"And talking cats, and amphibious sharks, and zebra-striped winged monkeys," said Jandra. "She thinks of herself as an artist. She has the freedom to work on a canvas that no artist has ever truly been able to master... life itself. Some of her art is serious; some is whimsical. And, from the looks of things, some of it might still be alive."

Shay wrinkled his nose. "It doesn't smell like much is alive down there."

"Something or someone turned on the lights," said Jandra. "The other long-wyrm riders, perhaps? And... wow. Look at the walls." She pointed to the stone behind them. He turned and found that almost every surface was studded with pale yellow mushrooms. There was also something moving over his head. It was the size of a squirrel, but furless, slimy, like a long, pink frog with a tail. It crept along the rock face using sucker-toes, pausing to munch on mushrooms.

"I've never seen one of those before," said Shay.

"I haven't either," said Jandra. "But somehow I know that if you lick the hide, you experience psychedelic visions."

"My first instinct wouldn't be to lick it," said Shay.

"When you're immortal, even with all of creation as your plaything, there are times when you get a little bored," said Jandra. She looked back out over the saltwater lake. "Luckily, that big island a few miles away is where we need to go. That's where we buried the goddess's heart. It was a genie... the same sort of device I used. Vendevorex said his was designed to unlock upon his death so that anyone could use it. I'm gambling that hers acts the same, if it still works at all. We buried it with a flaming sword stuck through it. I'm not certain any technology, no matter how advanced, is going to survive that."

"How are we going to get over there?"

"That's an excellent question," she said. "Swimming is a bad idea if the ichthyosaurs are still alive. They were the apex predator of the lake and could survive quite a while by hunting one another. Any that are left are likely to be hungry."

"So what options do we have?"

Jandra pointed toward a stony path leading down the cliff side toward a black beach below. The beach ran along the outer perimeter of the cavern. About a half mile away, a waterfall spilled down over the rocks, crashing into an elevated pool before it spilled into the lake. A few sad trees stood beyond it, their leaves gone.

"Maybe we can build a raft?" she said. "I'll think about it some more in a little while. More immediately, I want to take a bath. There aren't any ichthyosaurs in that pool. I'll feel better and be able to think clearer once I get the grime out of my hair."

"I know what you mean," said Shay. "I've never been this dirty. Even my teeth feel gritty."

"There may be some small fish in the pool," said Jandra. "Won't it be nice to eat something fresh, instead of hardtack and jerky?"

"Good hardtack," said Lizard. "Good jerky."

"You'll like good fish even more," Jandra said. "You can use a bath, too. You used to be green. Now look at you."

Lizard looked down at his coal-darkened scales. "No bath," he said, firmly. It was the first time he'd ever said no to Jandra that Shay could remember.

Jandra gave the little dragon a good, firm stare.

Lizard looked down, avoiding her gaze, then looked up at Shay with big, pleading eyes.

"Don't drag me into this," said Shay.

CHAPTER TWENTY-ONE

THIS CLOSE TO HEAVEN

THE WATERFALL FELL a hundred feet into a pool twenty yards across. The water churned white at the point of impact, but most of the pond was crystal clear, revealing schools of silvery fish no bigger than Shay's thumbs darting through the water. On the rocks surrounding the pool, white crickets the size of mice jumped away as they approached. The insects chirped with a high-pitched rhythmic drone that provided a musical accompaniment for the thunder of the falling water. The whole scene was lit by a trio of bright lights high overhead. They looked like shards of moon set in stone. They emitted a steady radiance like nothing Shay had ever seen outside the heavens.

Through some lucky chance of geology, the water smelled like nothing more than water, free of the sulfur stink that had tainted their canteens ever since they'd moved underground.

Jandra dropped her pack on the rocky shore. "I've never wanted a bath so badly in my life," she said.

"No bath!" Lizard chimed in. He was perched once more on her shoulder.

"Fine. Don't take a bath," Jandra said, reaching up and stroking Lizard beneath his chin. "I like you the way you are."

Lizard tilted his head, looking skeptical.

Jandra pointed toward the pool. "Look at all those fish! I bet they'd taste delicious. Too bad we don't have anyone fast enough to grab them."

"Lizard fast," the small dragon said, sounding mildly offended. "Good hunter!"

"But see how they're darting around? Nobody could be fast enough to jump into the pool and start catching them by hand."

"Lizard catch!" The small dragon leapt from Jandra's shoulder with such force that Jandra stumbled backward toward Shay. Lizard looked like he was flying, sailing out twenty feet over the pool before splashing into the water.

Jandra lost her footing on the slick rock and Shay's hand darted out, catching her arm, giving her the added point of stability she needed to steady herself. She looked up at him. They stood there, still and silent. Jandra's eyes were fascinating, a complex mixture of hazel and amber flecked with mossy green.

"You have the most beautiful eyes," he whispered. It felt perfectly appropriate to kiss her.

She turned away as his lips approached, looking flustered.

"I'm sorry," he said, drawing back. "I didn't mean to embarrass you."

"You didn't," she said. "I... I want you to kiss me. But, not right now. I want everything to be right. I've never kissed anyone before. I mean, Pet kissed *me*, but it was sort of a sneak attack that I wasn't really prepared for."

"That's more experience than I have with kissing," said Shay. "But my impression is that it isn't all that difficult."

"I'm sure it isn't," she said. "But, we're both covered with mine grime and have breath that could wilt flowers. A kiss at this moment might not be a pleasant experience for either of us."

"I'm absolutely certain I'd enjoy it," Shay said.

"You can wait, can't you?" Jandra said, backing away. "We could both stand a dip in the water first."

"Oh," said Shay. "I … yes, of course. I'll go wait behind those trees while you bathe."

"You can wait there if you want," she said, shyly. "Or we could both go in the pool together. There's plenty of room."

Shay's mouth felt dry. "Of course," he rasped, as Jandra unbuttoned her coat.

Behind them, Lizard splashed up onto the shore, his mouth and all four claws brimming with bright minnows. "Big catch!" he said, spraying wriggly fish parts over the rocks before him.

Jandra knelt down to her pack and pulled out the tin pot she carried. "Good job! Put the fish in the pot. They're small, so you'll need to catch a lot. Can you do that?"

"Good hunter," Lizard said as he dropped his catch into the pot. He turned and leapt once more. He undulated beneath the surface as gracefully as an otter, his long tail whipping around like a rudder.

"That should keep him busy," said Jandra, continuing to fumble around in her pack. She pulled out a walnut-sized chunk of white soap, the only thing that remained of the fist-sized bar they'd started the journey with.

Shay had his coat, boots and socks off by this point and was fumbling with the buttons of his shirt. He peeled it off then reached for his belt buckle. He looked up, to see if Jandra was looking at him. She was. She had her hands on her own belt buckle. With a synchronized movement, each pulled their belts free. A few seconds later, each was standing before the other in their long-johns. The coal that had permeated their skin had sunk down to the once white cotton of their undergarments, leaving them gray. Jandra turned her back to him as she unbuttoned her long-johns.

Slowly, she peeled the gray cotton down her shoulders, revealing her bare back. She was slender, but not boney. Her pale skin glowed in the soft light. Her underwear bunched up at her hips for a moment. She took a slow, deep breath and pushed the long-johns over her hips until they dropped around her ankles. She stepped out of them. She was now naked save for the silver bracelet on her wrist. She wrapped her hands across her breasts and looked back over her shoulders.

"So," she said. "This is me. Scaleless, tailless, wingless, pale, and hairy."

"I give thanks to whatever gods there may be that you are scaleless, tailless, wingless, pale, and hairy. You are breathtaking. The most beautiful woman I've ever seen."

"Have you seen many naked women?"

"None."

Jandra smirked. "So the bar for comparison is fairly low."

"Have you seen many naked men?"

"Ragnar, obviously. Bitterwood when I cleaned his wounds. And I caught a pretty good look at Pet," she said. She paused, and he wondered if she was still searching her mental list. Apparently, however, she was remembering the last man on her list. "Pet was... well, honestly, he was like a work of art. He'd been bred to have a perfect body. It was only everything else about him that made my skin crawl."

"I suspect magnificent isn't the word about to spring into your mind," Shay said. He clenched his jaw. Jandra was all but naked. It was time for him to take the plunge. Since she'd turned her back to him to work up the courage, he did the same. He unbuttoned his long johns and pushed them down. They didn't bunch around his hips. Unlike Jandra's hourglass figure, Shay was built like a plank. His limbs were lanky and lean. His torso was so thin his ribs could be counted. If there was an ounce of fat on him anywhere, he was unaware of it.

His skin was as white as the soap Jandra held, save for stripes of freckles around his shoulders. His torso was mostly hairless, though his legs were covered in thick orange growth. Jandra was quiet. He wondered if she was repulsed. He looked over his shoulder and discovered she was only a few inches away, staring at his back. Her hand fell gently upon his shoulder blades, her fingers tracing the map of ropey white scars.

"By the bones," she whispered. "You said... you said you'd been whipped. But..." Her thought trailed off. Shay knew why.

His most severe beatings were best described as flayings, the whip peeling away flesh and muscle down to the bone. It was why he always stood with rounded shoulders and a slight hunch. Due to the scarring and muscle damage, he couldn't stand truly straight if he tried.

"You said I was brave," she whispered, her voice trembling. "I couldn't have survived this. I can't believe you're still alive, let alone still hopeful. So willing to risk everything to share what you know with the world. I don't know that I could be so defiant after what's been done to you."

"I was always willful," Shay said, managing the faintest ghost of a grin. "I read about things like freedom and justice and love, and I believed in them. I wanted to experience them. And if a world run by dragons didn't offer these things, then I knew from an early age I'd have to change the world. Chapelion did his best to beat my dreams to dust. I'm not brave, Jandra. I'd beg to avoid a whipping. I'd weep before the leather ever touched my back, and renounce every idea I'd ever believed in. When the beatings would stop, the slavecatchers would order me to drop and kiss their talons in gratitude for their devotion to my improvement. I've groveled, Jandra. It's not courage that drives me. It's fear. It's shame. I'll slit my own throat before I ever bow down to a dragon again."

Silently, she took him by the hand and led him toward the pool. They crept into the cool water together, their hands clasped for balance on the slick, smooth stones. Shay shivered as the water rose up his legs. They neared the white water at the edge of the waterfall and suddenly he slipped. He plunged beneath the water, pulling Jandra down with him. They both flailed about, their legs and arms entwining. They both grew still as Jandra pressed her breasts against his chest. They clung to each other tightly as they drifted back to the surface. Jandra's body was hot against his despite the chill of the water.

They bobbed above the surface of the pool. The water was deep here; Shay could barely touch bottom by stretching his toes. Jandra was floating, with her arms still clasped around his shoulders and her left leg wrapped around his hip. Gray water streamed out of her coal-tinted hair. Dark, oily spots lay upon her cheeks as the water beaded on the grime. Her face was only inches from his.

"Clean enough," she murmured, as she pressed her lips against his.

His assumption proved true. Kissing was simple enough to figure out. He closed his eyes as his toes curled and they drifted in the water, weightless.

"SCARY BIRDS," SAID Lizard.

Jandra's eyes fluttered open. The little green earth-dragon was perched next to her head. Behind Lizard, the fire had died down to a few smoking embers. Shay was still asleep beneath the blanket with her, his bony arm draped across her rib cage. It was warm under the blanket with the two of them pressed together. Jandra wasn't in the mood to get up and worry about breakfast yet.

"Go catch fish," she mumbled as she closed her eyes. She snugged the blanket tightly beneath her chin. She felt marvelous. For the first time since the goddess had altered her memories, she felt like she'd dreamed her own dreams. Shay's arms around her made her feel safe. He held her tightly enough that she couldn't be pushed out by the goddess.

Lizard's damp paw fell onto her forehead. He flexed his claws ever so slightly, pricking her.

"Scary birds!" he said, more emphatically.

She opened one eye. She didn't normally consider birds a threat, though she supposed a particularly robust eagle could have carried off Lizard. Still, for all she knew, there could be eagles the size of elephants down here.

"Where?" she asked.

"*Scary birds*!" Lizard shrieked, pointing skyward.

It wasn't birds. Three winged humans were flying across the lake. Their wings were metallic silver, similar to the wings Gabriel—the goddess's robotic angel—had flown on. While Gabriel had been designed as the pinnacle of human perfection, these winged men were a sorry looking bunch. They were wearing the once white uniforms of long-wyrm riders. All carried crossbows. Two of them still wore silver visors, but the third one's visor was missing and he'd recently suffered some horrible injury to the left side of his face. His eye was swollen shut and his lower lip dangled, streaming drool.

"Poor Meshach," she said, as Jazz's memories flashed the men's names into her mind. These were survivors of the goddess's long-wyrm riders. The wounded one was Meshach, the one with the thick black beard was Shadrach, and the last one, a short, balding man with a unibrow, was named Guido.

Shay sat up, stretching his arms. "Good morning," he said, his voice low and hoarse. "Waking up next to you is like waking up in heaven." He looked up, following her gaze. "Okay," he said. "Even this close to heaven, I didn't expect angels."

The winged men halted about fifty yards away, hovering in the air. Jandra vaguely remembered that the wings didn't need to flap to keep the men airborne. It was the sort of memory that might prove useful, yet, as often happened whenever she tried to actively access Jazz's memories, the details faded away before she could grasp them.

"Hide," she said to Lizard.

Lizard crept away, low to the ground, slithering into the pool with barely a ripple.

Shadrach, the highest ranking of the three guards, called out, "Intruders! You've violated the sanctity of the sanctuary of the goddess! The punishment is death!"

"Wait!" said Jandra. "You must know your goddess is dead! We're not violating the sanctity of anyone. There's no need for us to fight."

"She's right!" Meshach, the wounded one, snarled. "I told you the goddess was dead. Look around, Shadrach! The evidence is before your eyes!"

"Silence!" Shadrach snapped. "I'll bash in the other side of your face if you don't still your blasphemous tongue."

"But Shadrach," said Guido. "What if it's true? We don't need to follow the codes no more. We can make our own rules."

"We will obey the commandments!" Shadrach shouted. "Intruders are to be killed, not molested!"

"What if we molested her a little first?" said Guido. "We can kill her after we're done."

Shadrach spun around in the air, delivering a savage kick to Meshach's guts. Meshach doubled over, clutching his stomach.

"Guido suggested it!" Meshach whined.

"You were closer, and you were thinking it too," said Shadrach, completing his spin, halting as he faced Shay and Jandra once more. "Now, kill them!"

Shadrach lifted his crossbow. Guido did the same, though he didn't look happy about it. Meshach was still clutching his stomach. He looked a bit greenish.

Jandra flapped the blanket, jumping up as the crossbows rang out in simultaneous twangs. The crossbow bolt fired by Shadrach punched through the blanket, passed a few inches to the left of Jandra's belly, and buried itself in her backpack. The bolt fired by Guido was better aimed. It tore into Shay's left thigh, right on the inner edge of the skin a few inches above his knee. Shay's mouth opened as if to scream, but no sound came out. Jandra quickly analyzed the wound. The bolt had only cut the surface. His muscles looked uninjured, which was confirmed when he sprang to his feet.

Jandra dropped the blanket and dove toward the shotgun.

"Sweet goddess! She's naked!" Guido shouted. "Shadrach, you've got to—"

"Shut up!" said Shadrach, swinging out with the butt of his crossbow, smashing it into Guido's nose.

Guido did a loop in the air in response to the blow. He dropped down toward the saline lake, catching himself only five feet above the surface, with a massive down-flap of his silver wings that sent waves rolling toward the shore.

"Bastard!" Guido growled.

"The goddess is dead!" Meshach screamed, spraying spittle from his flapping lower lip. He was now the only guard with a loaded crossbow. He turned the weapon toward Shadrach. "I'll do as I please! There is no law!"

He fired, the crossbow bolt passing neatly through Shadrach's neck. The bearded man's eyes rolled up in his head as he tilted in the air. His body went limp, and his wings did as well. He plummeted toward the rocky shore, landing with a wet slap on the black beach.

"The woman is ours!" Meshach screamed, casting his one leering eye toward Jandra.

Jandra finished stuffing the shot bag down the gun barrel and pulled the ram rod free, dropping it onto the blanket at her feet. She took aim at Meshach. "I think I should have a say in this," she said, then pulled the trigger. Nothing happened. *Oh, right. The safety.*

Meshach dropped his crossbow and zoomed toward her, his arms open, on a trajectory to tackle her and carry her back into the sky. She fumbled to release the safety, but somehow her finger couldn't quite find it. Guido was now racing toward her as well, coming in low, skimming along only a few feet above the ground.

Suddenly, Lizard shot out of the pool, his claws extended, his jaws open wide, flying like an angry green bobcat into Meshach's path. Meshach's already tortured face collided with a smack into the little dragon's belly. Lizard's claws snapped around the flying man's head like a mechanical trap. Meshach zoomed skyward, shrieking. Jandra tracked him with the shotgun, her finger finally on the safety. There was no way she could be certain she wouldn't hit Lizard as she fired. She lowered her gun to target Guido, but here, too, her aim was blocked. Shay jumped into the path of the on-rushing guardsmen. The short, winged man smacked into Shay's lanky, naked form at the knees, flipping him into the air. The impact was enough to knock Guido off course. He smashed face-first into the rocky beach, tumbling head over heel before coming to a splashing halt in the pool. He lay limp, his head underwater.

Meshach, still under assault by Lizard, had flown back out over the water. He was about thirty yards off shore, his toes grazing the surface of the salt lake, as if he were dancing upon it. He had both hands on Lizard, trying to pull him off. Lizard had his turtle-like beak clamped down in a death-grip on the man's right eyebrow, and both his fore-claws buried into the scalp behind Meshach's ears. Meshach released a string of loud, incoherent yelps that might have been curse words.

Shay rose on his hands and knees following his collision. He shook his head. Except for the blood trickling from his bolt-wound, he looked okay. Jandra ran toward the shore, worried about what would happen to Lizard if Meshach flew further away.

Meshach gave a blood-curdling shriek as he finally tugged the little dragon away from his face, throwing him toward the water below. Lizard left a trail of blood as he fell. Meshach's face bled from countless wounds.

Jandra raised her shotgun. As she sighted down the barrel, her eyes were drawn to something odd. The once flat surface of the lake was mounding up behind Meshach, a moving hump of water almost a yard tall rolling toward his dangling legs.

Jandra almost shouted a warning—almost. The hump of water suddenly shot into the air, splitting open into a pair of toothy jaws that clamped around Meshach's legs. As quickly as it had appeared, the ichthyosaur plunged back down into the water, taking Meshach's legs and hips with it, leaving the guard's remains floating in the air, a winged torso from which entrails slowly spilled.

Meshach looked down, his face growing pale beneath the bloody wounds that crisscrossed it. He gave a breathless sigh and fell into the water with a splash.

Jandra stood on the shore, feeling a chill that ran all the way down to her bones.

"Lizard!" she yelled, lowering her gun. "Lizard!"

Meshach's winged corpse bobbed upon the waves. Aside from this, there was no sign of motion. She turned back toward Shay. He was in the pool, crouched over Guido. It looked as if he was making sure the guard's head stayed beneath the water.

"Lizard didn't come up for air!" she shouted.

Shay looked up, his eyes scanning the waves.

"He can hold his breath for a long time," said Shay. "You saw him in the pool."

"There's an ichthyo..." he wasn't going to know what she was talking about, "a sea monster out there!"

"A what?"

"It's a great big ocean-dwelling reptile! It can swallow Lizard whole!"

Suddenly, Lizard popped to the surface, gasping for air. His limbs flailed wildly as he splashed across the surface of the lake in a bee-line toward Jandra.

"Bad fish!" he shrieked as the water mounded up behind him.

Jandra ran to the edge of the shore. The ichthyosaur's mouth gaped open, creating a suction that drew Lizard back toward its teeth.

Jandra aimed at the top of the ichthyosaur's snout and fired. The explosion knocked her onto her butt as her feet slipped on the slimy stone. The scaly sea beast snapped its jaws closed with Lizard only inches from its teeth. Lizard shrieked as the monster flipped in a sudden u-turn. Bright red wounds speckled the ichthyosaur's snout. It dove beneath the water. The wave it left behind lifted Lizard, carrying him toward the shore. The wave broke over Jandra's legs, leaving Lizard sitting in her lap. Lizard swung his tail around and looked at it mournfully. The last four inches of it were missing.

"No more fish," he said, shaking his head.

"I'm comfortable with that," said Jandra.

Shay walked down the shore toward the still form of the first guard to fall. He poked the body with his foot, though it was pretty obvious from the angle of the man's head in relation to his shoulders that he was dead.

"This certainly wasn't the wake up I had in mind," he said.

Jandra chuckled grimly. "Me neither." She looked at the wings jutting up from Shadrach's corpse. The goddess memories stirred faintly and she realized she knew how to use the wings. "At least we don't have to build a raft now. We can just fly over to the island."

"Fly?" Shay asked, sounding skeptical. "I mean, yes, I saw them doing it, but it didn't look safe. None of these men had pleasant landings."

"The wings have an artificial intelligence that will do most of the flying for you. You'll be fine."

"If man were intended to fly, God would have given us wings," said Shay.

"The goddess corrected his oversight," said Jandra. She stood up. She was covered in slimy grit all the way down the back of her legs.

"Looks like we'll need another bath," she said. "As long as we've got a pool of fresh, clean water—at least, we will once we pull Guido's corpse out—we should take this chance to wash our clothes."

"I only have one set of clothes," said Shay. "I don't want to walk around all day in wet pants."

"We can spend the day under the blanket while our things dry," said Jandra.

"Oh," said Shay, brushing his curly orange locks back from his face. "Yes, then. Of course. That sounds like a perfectly acceptable plan."

CHAPTER TWENTY-TWO

HER DRAGON SOUL

SHAY'S PANTS WERE stiff after they'd dried by the fire. He carefully tugged them up his legs, wincing. Many of his body parts were somewhat tender. Beside him, Jandra hummed as she pulled on her boots. The worried look that normally haunted her face was completely gone. She stood, buttoning the fine blue coat she'd recovered at the palace.

"What are you humming?"

"It's called 'Original Air Blue Gown,'" she said. Instantly, her face fell.

"What?" he asked.

"It's one of her memories. This song is a thousand years old."

Shay moved to her side and took her hand.

"It's okay," he said. "You're here now. Don't worry about all that other stuff in your head."

Jandra leaned into him. "I hate it when the lines blur. Some of the things we did came so naturally. What if I was drawing on her experience?"

Shay kissed her forehead. "Don't let it bother you. No one is a clean slate. We all have other people's voices in our heads. After all the books I've been through, I have a hard time untangling my own thoughts from the things I've read."

Jandra nodded. "I hear Vendevorex inside me sometimes. Perhaps one day I'll accept these new memories as part of who I am. I'm afraid I'll get lost inside my own head if I surrender to these thoughts."

Shay squeezed Jandra's hand. "I'll be beside you to help you find your way back."

Jandra smiled. She took the bracelet off her wrist and slid it onto Shay's hand. "Take this," she said.

"You need it to turn invisible," he said.

"I need you even more," she said. "It's all I have to give."

Shay knew she had given him so much more.

In the dead tree near the waterfall, Lizard was still sound asleep, his limbs dangling from the tree branch. The bandaged tip of his tail twitched in response to dreams Shay could only imagine.

Jandra pulled her hand away, her fingertips lingering until the last possible instant. "As wonderful as this moment is, we should do what we came here to do."

"Lead on," he said.

Jandra reached down beside her pack and picked up one of the three metal plates laying there. She handed one to Shay. It was remarkably light for a grooved steel disk a foot across and two inches deep. He'd watched as Jandra pulled these from the backs of the dead guards. The huge wings had folded into these compact shapes. Looking into the edge-groove, hundreds of delicate metallic feather tips could be seen, all packed up in neat rows.

"It should weigh more," said Shay. "It's as big as some cast iron skillets I've used, and they're pretty hefty. This weighs little more than a quill."

"It's made of carbon nanofibers. It's like woven diamonds. The wings generate some lift with their shape, but an ion discharge provides the real thrust. That's why you can hover in these."

"I have no clue what an ion or a nanofiber is," said Shay.

"It's not important," said Jandra. "Just stick it between your shoulder blades. Hyper-friction will hold it. Then, think about the wings unfolding."

Shay stood up and reached behind his back. He didn't see how it was possible to get the disk centered directly between his shoulder blades, but when he got the disk near, he felt a tug. The disk leapt from his fingers and grabbed onto his back. His skin tingled as the disk adjusted itself to the correct position. The tingling stopped abruptly. He turned, expecting to find the disk behind him, certain it had fallen off. Seeing bare ground, he reached behind his back and found the disk was still there.

He imagined the wings spreading. Instantly, they did so, growing outward in an intricate unfolding pattern until they stretched from his body several yards in each direction. The feathers chimed like tiny bells. To his surprise, he could feel the wings as if they were part of his body. The wing nearest the fire was warm—the wing extending out over the pool was cool, and he felt beads of water dripping across the surface. All the tiny breezes stirred by the waterfall ruffled the feathers. It felt as natural as the breeze playing with his hair.

Until this moment, he'd been skeptical that the wings would lift him, despite having witnessed the flight of the guards. Now, flight felt like it could occur with only the slightest flick of his wing tips.

He flicked.

The sensation of his feet leaving the ground was one he knew would remain with him forever. He rose three feet in the air and hung there, holding his breath as his heartbeat pounded in his ears. When he finally allowed himself to breath, he found himself giggling.

Jandra rose into the air in front of him, leveling out. They both hovered on outstretched wings. The air smelled curiously fresh.

Jandra tilted toward him and drifted over. He leaned forward to meet her. This resulted in a sudden acceleration. Their lips met with what could fairly be called a collision. They each jerked back.

"We, uh, should practice before we try that again," Jandra said, her voice muffled by her hand over her mouth. She seemed to be checking for loose teeth.

"Scary birds!" Lizard screamed.

The little earth-dragon was awake on his branch now, looking ready to leap into the pool. His eyes narrowed when Jandra spun around in the air to face him. Shay had to duck to avoid her wings as they passed over his head.

"It's okay, Lizard," said Jandra. "It's just Shay and me."

"Good boss?" Lizard asked, sounding skeptical.

Jandra floated toward him, her arms outstretched. "Jump on," she said. Lizard scooted further back on the branch. "Don't be scared," she said. Lizard looked down at his tail tip and changed the subject.

"Tail hurt," he said.

"I know," said Jandra.

"Eat soon?"

"Breakfast is the next item on the agenda," said Jandra.

"New meat?" Lizard asked. This wasn't a question Shay had heard before.

"Same old beef jerky and hard tack for now," said Jandra.

"New meat!" Lizard insisted.

Jandra cast a puzzled glance back toward Shay. Shay shrugged. Lizard looked perturbed. He leapt down from the branch and skittered across the rocks like a small green monkey, traveling thirty yards in the space of a few seconds, until he reached the mound of stones that Shay had used to bury the guards.

Lizard sniffed the rocks. "New meat," he said, looking up at Jandra. Jandra grew pale as she realized what was on Lizard's mind.

"Lizard, we can't eat those men," she said.

Lizard cocked his head, confused. "Smell," he said, and drew a deep, whistling breath through the nostril slots in his beak. "New meat."

"Lizard, I wouldn't let the men back at Dragon Forge eat you. I'm not going to let you eat men."

Lizard tilted his head to the other side. It was as if thoughts were physically shifting around in his skull. "Lizard not meat," he said.

Jandra lowered herself onto the rocks beside the little dragon. He looked up at her with a mix of hunger and reverence. He reached to the grave and picked up a stone that looked too heavy for his small frame.

"Put that down!" Jandra snapped. Lizard dropped the rock and hopped backward, looking alert as he studied Jandra's face. "Who's the boss here?" Jandra asked.

Lizard lowered his eyes. "You boss."

"We eat hardtack. Any questions?"

"No boss," Lizard said softly.

"Now jump onto my shoulders."

The little dragon leapt as if gravity had no true claim upon him. He made it to her shoulders in a single bound and clung tightly as she glided back over the pond toward Shay. Together, they drifted down to a landing beside the fire. Her wings folded up with a soft, musical chiming. He willed his own wings to close and they did the same.

Lizard hopped down from her shoulder and sat before the pack with the last few bricks of hard tack, staring at it intently. Jandra glanced at Shay. The stern countenance she'd wore while bossing Lizard melted into a look of worry. Shay knew what she was thinking. If Lizard was hungry for human flesh now, with other food available, what would he be like if the food ran out?

THEY LIFTED INTO the air with a rush of ozone and the wind-chime tinkling of silver feathers. Jandra bent her head up to meet the wind. She closed her eyes, lost in memories. As a child, she'd traveled many miles with her face pressed against Vendevorex's breast as he flew with her strapped against him in a sling. She remembered the hard, smooth texture of his scales and the way his muscles had radiated heat as he beat his wings to soar across the miles. She remembered the sound of his heart, the powerful bellows of his lungs, and the whistle of wind whipping her hair against her cheeks.

She opened her eyes. Lizard clung to her coat, looking moderately terrified. They'd risen a hundred feet in the air and were now arcing out over the underground lake. Its waters were dark as crude oil. Ripples on the surface hinted at the monsters beneath. Lizard's fear was rational.

Yet, so was her happiness. All her life she'd dreamed she had wings. She'd wake in the night and ached at their absence. Her dragon soul felt as if it had reclaimed a birthright.

Shay was flying lower, slower. She curved and flew a broad, graceful circle around him. He flew straight and steady, his eyes locked on the island shore that was their destination.

"You look nervous," she said as she slowed into a path parallel to him. "Relax. The wings won't drop you."

"I'm sure the guards thought the same thing," said Shay.

"Those crashes were a failure of the men, not the wings," said Jandra. "The fact that the wings survived proves how tough they are."

"It's not the wings' survival that concerns me," he said.

She beat her wings and soared high above him, climbing toward the stone sky. "I feel so alive!" She did a backwards flip and dropped toward him. Lizard squeaked at the maneuver and dug his claws deeply enough through her coat that she winced. Perhaps the more daring moves should wait until she was flying solo.

Too swiftly for her satisfaction, the lake passed beneath them and they arrived at the shore of the island. Shay dropped down onto a beach of black sand flecked with countless specks of gold.

"I've never imagined there was this much gold in the world," he said as he surveyed the long beach.

"There isn't. This is fool's gold."

"Oh."

Jandra floated down beside Shay and folded her wings. The beach stank. The decaying jungle gave the place a garbage heap aroma. A few hundred feet away, the bones of two long-wyrms stretched down to the water's edge. They'd fallen victim to

Bitterwood during the final confrontation with Jazz. Crabs had picked the bones completely clean, leaving vertebrae, ribs, and claws scattered along the shore in a vaguely serpentine outline. Copper scales were strewn across the beach, gleaming in the dim light like newly-minted coins.

She picked up one of the scales. Deep inside her mind, a door opened and she recalled sketching out her plans for the long-wyrms.

"What's that?" Shay asked.

Jandra held out the copper scale in her open palm. It resembled in size and shape the petal of some strange rose.

"Jazz spliced genes found in beetles into reptilian DNA to give the long worms their metallic sheen. She was inspired by images of Chinese dragons."

"Chinese?"

"There used to be a country called China."

"Like the plates and cups the wealthy biologians use? A country named for dinnerware?"

"It was actually the other way around. We remember the porcelain, but we've forgotten the country."

Lizard hopped down and picked up one of the scales, testing it against his tongue. He dropped it, apparently deciding it wasn't food.

"There may be more gaps in my knowledge of reproduction than I thought. I didn't think it was possible to breed a beetle and a reptile," said Shay.

"It isn't. Not in traditional ways. Jazz came from an age where it was possible to insert the genetic material of one creature into completely different creatures. Dragons were created this way. They were made as exotic game animals, to be hunted for sport."

"Humans used to hunt dragons for sport?" Shay sounded skeptical.

"Ironic isn't it?"

"Did Jazz make the dragons?"

"No. She was against hunting as sport. Her opinions shifted, though, when... if you don't mind, I'm going to change subjects. I'm uncomfortable talking too much about her life. She had a thousand years of memory; I have seventeen. I don't want her memories washing mine away through sheer volume."

"I understand," said Shay. He looked concerned. "I know you have additional memories, but do you feel like you're losing your own?"

"How would I know? How do you remember the things you've forgotten?"

"Perhaps you should keep a journal?"

"I'd rather get a genie again," said Jandra.

As THEY HEADED away from the shore, the tree branches took on a ghostly white pallor, as if covered in cotton. It wasn't until Shay grabbed one to brace himself that he realized nearly every surface of the dead jungle was covered with a film of mold.

He rubbed the slime off on his pants, then hurried to catch Jandra. She was carefully stepping over fallen branches as she worked her way toward what looked like the vine-draped ruins of some ancient civilization. Jandra moved confidently toward it and the stones began to shift, forming a staircase leading down into the ground.

The air coming up the stairs was dry and fresh, a refreshing change from the odorous dank of the decaying jungle. An iron door at the bottom of the steps slid open as Jandra approached. The space beyond was brightly lit. "What if there are more guards," Shay asked in a loud whisper. "Is this safe?"

"There were only thirteen riders because I only made thirteen long-wyrms," Jandra answered. "This was their barracks. It's abandoned now."

Shay started to point out she'd said "I" when she meant "Jazz," but held his tongue, not wanting to upset her.

"We killed three yesterday, Bitterwood killed two on the beach, six were killed at the battle of Dead Skunk Hole, and Bitterwood told me he'd killed one at Big Lick. That's twelve. Adam's the only one left. If my math is right, there are still four long-wyrms unaccounted for. Maybe Adam knows where they are."

Shay stepped into the barracks, squinting as he adjusted to the light. The room was long and sparsely furnished with narrow cots. The walls were white brick. There were no windows. The ceiling was made of a translucent material like a large, uniform sheet of paper, glowing warmly. Toward the back of the room was a large desk. Behind it were shelves filled with books. Shay was afraid to approach them, given the recent ill fates of any book he touched.

"Oh look," said Jandra, as she peered over Shay's shoulder. "A map."

Shay gathered it was the island they were currently on, since there was a yellow arrow pointing to a spot that read, "You are here." Jandra placed her fingers on the map. The island got smaller as the area shown by the map expanded. Soon, a vast, perplexing network of white lines against a black background was revealed.

"This is her entire underground empire," said Jandra. "We're underneath what was once called West Virginia. It was absolutely riddled with mines." The image spun around when Jandra twirled her fingers on the image. "Ah. Just as I suspected. We took the long way here. We can make it back to the surface in just a few hours." One of the white lines began to pulse with pale red light.

Shay approached the frame. "A magic map. There are cartographers at the College of Spires who would kill for this."

"If you want to see magic, wait until we dig up the genie."

She walked over to the wall and pressed one of the white bricks. They slid back to reveal a large closet filled with tools. Shay spotted more of the wing disks on a metal shelf. Before he could examine the closet further, Jandra turned around with two shovels in her hand, as well as a small garden trowel.

She tossed a shovel toward Shay and the trowel at Lizard. "Everybody digs," she said.

JANDRA LED THEM to a clearing. The ground was blackened by a relatively recent fire. It was cool now, but the air still held the smell of a well-used fireplace. Charcoal crunched beneath Shay's boots as he stepped on what had once been a tree branch. Unlike the slimy ghost forest, the land here was bone dry. Jandra wandered over the ashes, her fingers outstretched.

"Can you feel it?" she whispered.

"Feel what?" asked Shay.

"The buzz in the air. It's a fine mist of nanites. Even without a genie, I can sense it. It feels like sunlight under the skin."

Lizard looked up at the stone sky. "Sun gone," he said, sadly.

"The sooner we get the genie, the sooner we get back to the surface," said Jandra. With a grunt, she thrust her shovel into the black dirt. "Once I have my powers back, we can fly out of here and bask in all the sun we want. Then... then I'll fix everything." She tossed away a spadeful of shiny black dirt. "I'll go back to Dragon Forge and heal Vance's blindness. I'll fix Burke's leg so well he'll be dancing." She plunged the shovel into the ground again.

Shay joined in the digging. Lizard approached and tentatively tossed aside a few scoops of earth with his trowel.

Shay pursed his lips and put his back into the task. Could this device they were digging for really give Jandra the power to heal the blind and the lame? If so... would that matter much in the overall scheme of things?

"I know you mean well," he said, tossing aside dirt. "But... doesn't the world have bigger problems than a few people's eyes or limbs? If this genie makes you as powerful as you say, couldn't you use it to fight dragons? Ragnar wants to drive all the dragons into the sea. Couldn't you actually do that?"

Jandra stopped digging. She bit her lower lip, lost in thought.

"What?" he asked.

"I just wish I could talk to Vendevorex," she said. "He had so much power, but he barely used it. He hinted that he was afraid that the Atlanteans might find him."

"And you're worried they might find you?"

"Not in the least," she said, with a cocky smile. "But... it's easy to sit here and talk about driving the dragons into the sea when we don't have the power to do it. Once I have my power back, though... I hope I'm wise enough to know what to do."

Shay brushed back the hair that was falling down into her eyes. He said, "The fact that you have thoughts like this is all the proof I need of your wisdom."

"Thank you," she said. She leaned forward. He closed his eyes and met her in a kiss. It was much more pleasant than their aerial lip smash.

She pulled back and gave him a wicked smile. Shay smiled back. "Would you like to take a break?"

She put a hand on her hip and rolled her eyes. "First work, then fun. Keep digging."

THREE HOURS LATER and six feet down, Shay's hands were blistered, his back was on fire, and sweat rained from his body with every thrust of the shovel. He'd removed his shirt and peeled his long-johns down, bunching them up at his belt. The deeper he dug, the harder the earth was packed. The hole was also becoming hotter.

Lizard had long since tuckered out. The little dragon lay next to the hole, his chin draped over the edge, looking down. Lizard was roughly at eye level whenever Shay tried to straighten up.

"I promise I'll make you feel better once this is done," said Jandra, who was sitting at the edge of the pit, her legs dangling. "Vendevorex had me study anatomy. I know what muscles to rub."

"If you're trying to motivate me, I appreciate it," he said. He stopped to wipe the sweat from his eyes. "But, honestly, I think I'm done for the day. I'm a scribe, not a ditch digger. If you need someone to sit at a desk and write for eight hours straight, I'm your man."

"You're my man anyway," said Jandra. "I like watching you dig. Your muscles are really bulging."

She handed him the canteen. He tilted it up and let it pour into his mouth and down his chest in a bracing gush. He glanced at his shoulders and biceps. They did look particularly chiseled after his efforts.

"Ten more minutes," she said, staring at him hungrily.

He swallowed another gulp of cool water. "For you, my love, I'll make it eleven."

He plunged his shovel toward the black earth, driving it with all his strength. The shovel blade barely scratched the soil. It felt like he'd hit bedrock.

"Ow," he said, pulling his hand away from the shovel. The abrupt halt had pushed a splinter into his palm.

He looked up, hoping for a sympathetic word from Jandra. Instead, her eyes were focused on the spot where he was standing.

"Out of the pit," she said, tossing off her coat.

"Do you think...?"

"I think there's not enough room for both of us in there," she said, holding out her hand. "Climb out."

She practically yanked him out of the hole. Before he could brush the dirt off himself, she'd grabbed Lizard's trowel and leapt into the pit. She knelt on the black dirt, her fingers tracing the outline of something he couldn't see.

"The sword," she said. "I can feel the heat."

Dirt flew up over her back as she hacked at the ground with the trowel. "Vendevorex and I wore our genies as helmets, but Jazz kept hers beneath her skin. It served as her heart. Bitterwood left Gabriel's flaming sword piercing her heart but it never melted, even when the rest of her body crumbled to ash. We buried her heart with the sword still in it."

Suddenly, orange light began to dance around the walls of the pit. Jandra stood up, holding a sword over her head. Faint flames flickered along the length of the weapon. Jammed against the hilt, pierced by the blade, was a lump of silver metal the size and shape of a human heart.

It was still beating.

CHAPTER TWENTY-THREE

GET READY FOR MAGIC

S HAY SWALLOWED HARD. He was ten feet away from Jandra but could feel the heat of the sword warming his face. The air smelled like a hot stove. Lizard, who normally clung to Jandra like a burr, scurried behind Shay and cowered between his legs.

"I'm not certain this was a good idea," he said. "I didn't expect the genie to look so… alive."

"It's not alive," said Jandra, her eyes focused on the reflection of her face in the silver heart. "It's only a tool. It's no more alive than a hammer."

"I've never seen a hammer pulse like that," said Shay. "I've stood by you Jandra. I believe in you and I've trusted your judgment this far. Now, I'm hoping you'll trust me. I think we should re-bury the heart and consider this further."

"You've got to be joking," she said. "After all we've been through to get our hands on this? You want to put it back in the ground?"

"I think—"

"When Bitterwood and I escaped from the Free City, he told me his hate was the hammer he used to knock down the walls of this world. That's all Bitterwood knows how to do—tear things down. I promised myself I would never walk that path. I don't want my life to be remembered for the things I've ruined. I want to be known as a maker, a builder, a healer. I need the power of this genie if I'm ever going to be the person I want to be."

"Jandra, you're already that person," said Shay. "You're a good woman. You're going to change the world with your kindness and wisdom. Put the heart back in the ground. There are other wonders we can take from this place. The wings, for instance. Tools that are a little less frightening."

"I'm not afraid of the genie," said Jandra.

"Aren't you afraid of the goddess?"

Jandra shook her head. "There're no such things as ghosts, Shay. Without a brain and a body, a person is gone forever. Jasmine Robertson is dead. You're covered in the ashes that were once her bones. She's not coming back."

"You still have her memories," said Shay.

"Those are, for better or worse, in *my* head," said Jandra. "It's my brain that will control the genie. Wearing this will help me make my own memories stronger, not weaker. I'm going to fix everything, Shay."

Jandra placed her hand upon the heart. Shay winced; given the unbearable heat of the sword, he expected a sizzling noise, followed by smoke. Her fingers skimmed along the surface. The metal pulsed more rapidly.

"It senses I'm here," said Jandra. "It's responding to my thoughts. I was right. It unlocked upon her death. And it's hurting. It's wounded. It can't heal itself while the sword is inside it."

"You're speaking like it's a living thing," said Shay.

"Sorry," said Jandra. "It's not really alive, but it's easy to slip into biological terminology. The nanocomputers woven into the heart are programmed to regenerate if damaged. Right now, they can't overcome the constant destructive effects of the sword."

She grasped the hilt. "There's no trace of her inside the heart," she said.

"How can you know?"

"I know," she said.

She pulled the flaming sword free and dropped it on the ground. The heart pumped in her palm, the jagged puncture wound pouring out a stream of black ooze.

"Get ready for magic," said Jandra. She furrowed her brow and the heart began to melt in her hand. The silver slid across her fingers and down her arms. It flowed like paint under her sleeves, disappearing under her clothes. A few seconds later, it appeared at the base of her neck and flowed upward, covering her throat, creeping across her chin, tinting her lips with a sheen of silver. She closed her eyes as the metal flowed across her cheeks and nose and climbed over her brow. Within seconds, every patch of visible skin was enveloped by the liquid metal. Shay held his breath as Jandra stood silently, her eyes closed, a look of intense concentration on her silvery face.

When she opened her eyes, they were no longer hazel, but were, instead, an intense jade green.

Lizard dug his claws deep into Shay's calves. "Good boss?" he whispered.

"Jandra?" Shay stepped closer, to make certain his eyes weren't playing tricks. "Are you okay?"

Jandra grinned. She stepped toward Shay and draped her arm across his shoulder. She pulled his face to hers and pressed their lips together. Her lips were cool, much smoother than flesh, yet still soft. Her tongue slipped between his teeth. It, too, was cold and slick, coated with silver.

Jandra made a purring noise as she ran her hands along his naked back. She grabbed his butt in a fashion he found unnerving, despite their previous intimacies. He stood still as a statue, not even breathing, as she groped him.

Her tongue stopped moving in his mouth. She pulled her head back, studying his face. She grinned again. She snickered and stepped away, giggling harder.

"What's funny?" Shay asked.

Jandra laughed wildly, clutching her belly as silver tears ran down her cheeks. Her laughing turned harsh, almost braying. Lizard's claws sank deeper into Shay's legs.

"Is it something I did?" Shay asked.

"She slept with you?" Jandra said, between gasps for air.

Shay scowled.

Jandra straightened up. She wiped the tears from her cheeks, and then motioned with her hands along her body. "I mean, look at me! I'm hot! Why am I wasting time with some skinny, freckle-faced slave boy? Any man in the kingdom would kill to touch me. Half the women too, probably."

Shay frowned.

"Nothing personal. I kissed you because, hey, you were convenient, and it was a nice way to celebrate the moment. Alas, I've outgrown you. I'm going to be more upscale in my partners from now on."

"Jandra?" Shay whispered.

The woman shook her head. "Guess again."

* * *

JASMINE ROBERTSON, GODDESS, hacker, geek, had always lived on the razor edge of risk. She'd topped the FBI's most wanted list when she was nineteen and had taken a paid tour of the White House to celebrate. She'd worked as an intern for Senator Coe the summer her Earth Liberation Army set off the bomb that toppled the Washington Monument. When she'd finally had to get out of town due to the tightening net, every member of the Senate woke up to a zero balance in their bank accounts and she'd been, on paper at least, the eighth richest woman in the world. Not that she ever cared about money. Money was only useful if you were the type of loser who actually bothered to pay for stuff.

Yet, despite her rebellious, devil-may-care nature, Jazz had always possessed one cautious, even conservative, trait: she never failed to back up her data.

Jazz stretched her new back. If felt as if Jandra had been sleeping on rocks, which was probably the case. Jandra's body was also scuffed and scraped and bruised in a variety of places, including some difficult to reach spots that hinted of interesting stories. She felt curiously... bubbly. Hormonal, even.

"Yowza!" she said. "I'm seventeen again!"

Across the pit, the lanky red-headed guy gawked at her. There was something trembling under the dirty long-johns that hung around his waist like a backwards apron. Either there was a frightened dragon hiding between his legs, or he was really unhappy to see her.

"Hmmm," she said, searching Jandra's memories. "You're Shay? Runaway slave. Would-be librarian. How pathetically noble."

"What have you done with Jandra?" Shay asked.

"I've evicted her," said Jazz. "My genie did a running back-up of my memories while I was alive. I've overlaid these onto Jandra's synapses, onto the sections of her brain I altered on the moon to make her more receptive. The preprogrammed urge to rescue my genie in the event of my body's demise must have worked. I've prepped a few hundred girls over the centuries, but this is the first time I've ever actually lost a fight."

Shay knelt and reached for a long leather pouch beside his backpack. He drew out a weapon, taking an oddly long time to free it. It was obvious the kid hadn't watched many westerns. Jazz looked down the barrel of the flintlock as he stood, a bit perturbed that it existed. She'd worked diligently to keep the world gun-free.

"Get out of Jandra's body," said Shay, in a low, hissing voice as he clicked off the safety. "Get out or I'll blow you to hell."

Jazz shook her head. "Kid, you really need to work on your threats. I've just spent a month buried underground as a bodiless intelligence with a flaming sword burning big holes in my personality. What was left of my senses was all digital, meaning I felt the full chemical subtleties of being buried in soil composed of my own cremated remains. Hell would be a vacation after that. Besides, we both know you aren't going to shoot your girlfriend in the face."

"You aren't her," said Shay. The muscles in his face twitched, but his hands remained steady on the flintlock.

"Jandra isn't dead, only dormant. I might give her back eventually. To be honest, she feels a little short. I'm sure I have enough DNA in my hairbrush to grow a new me. So put the gun... gun... guh... uh..."

Jazz's neck twisted. Her tongue cramped, bunching into a hard knot near the back of her throat. Her left hand jerked forward spastically, fingers wide, as if grasping for a rope just out of reach. Her jaw began to move of its own accord as she exhaled, *"Kiilll meee..."*

Tears trickled onto Shay's cheeks as he closed his eyes and squeezed the trigger.

Jazz was knocked from her feet by the force of the lead balls smacking into her. They tore at the cotton blouse Jandra wore, but failed to penetrate the silver shell of nanites that coated her skin. She hit the ground hard. The impact silenced the spirit that had temporarily grabbed control of some of her muscles.

"Son of a bitch," she muttered as she sat up. Her ribs felt like they'd been hit with a hammer. "This is why I hate guns."

She rose on shaky legs. Her toes didn't feel right. Was something wrong? This was Jazz's first experience with putting her mind into a new body. The Atlanteans did it all the time. No doubt there was going to be a learning curve.

Shay was busy reloading. While she was confident the gun couldn't do any real damage, she wasn't in the mood to get knocked on her ass again.

"I honestly hadn't intended to kill you until now," said Jazz.

Shay walked backward as she approached, still reloading the gun. He was attempting to pull the ramrod free as Jazz lunged forward and grabbed the gun barrel. It was still hot from the previous firing, but nothing like flaming angel sword hot. Almost pleasant, in fact. She ripped the shotgun from his hands, grabbed him by the collar, pulled him to her face, and whispered, "It was sweet of you to reload. Now, it's my turn to see if bullets bounce off *yoooooOOO!*" She cried out as something sank its beak deep into her inner thigh. She staggered backward, dragging a heavy weight on her left leg.

She looked down and found a twenty-pound earth-dragon with its mouth clamped firmly onto her leg just beneath her crotch. The little beast hadn't pierced the nanite shell, but it had pinched several inches of skin, muscle, and nerves between its powerful beak.

She banged it on the head with the shotgun. "Get off me, you damn lizard!" The small beast growled and shook its head, refusing to let go. She hit it again, harder. Still it held on. When she tried to strike again her swing went wide and the shotgun flew from her grasp. Her mouth moved without her ordering it too. "Run Lizard! She'll kill you!"

Jazz grimaced and retook control of her mouth. Tears welled in her eyes; the dragon bite hurt like hell, and the beast showed no signs of letting go. She said, her voice quavering, "You should have listened to your mama."

With a thought, she electrified her nanite shell. Lizard flew back and rolled across the burnt ground. White smoke trailed from his open jaws. She studied the dent on her inner thigh, half expecting to find that the little devil had drawn blood. It hadn't, though it had torn away a fair-sized chunk of Jandra's pants and long-johns. The silver thigh that shone through danced with reflected flame.

She looked up in time to see Gabriel's sword coming straight for her neck. She ducked as the blade passed overhead, trailing an arc of fire. Shay grunted loudly and fought to maintain his balance after the missed blow. The way Shay held the blade revealed that he wasn't terribly experienced with sword-fighting. The way he was standing so out of balance hinted he wasn't experienced at any sort of fighting, period.

Jazz straightened up before he could attack again with a backstroke. She raised her leg with all the power that her newly-youthful muscles could summon, planting the boniest part of her knee right into Shay's testicles. The young man's eyes bulged and the sword flew from his fingers. He dropped to his knees before her, unable to breathe.

She grabbed him by the hair. He had a skinny neck. Would Jandra's body be sufficient to break it? She grabbed his chin and the back of his skull and decided to give it a test.

Shay spoiled the moment by vomiting. A pale, fishy soup splashed all over Jazz's belly. Jazz jumped backward, wrinkling her nose. "Ewwww!"

She stared down at her ruined clothes and snapped her fingers, willing the fibers to disintegrate. Jandra's clothes fluttered away into dust. Except for black leather boots, Jazz was now wearing only the nanite shell. It flattered her. She looked at herself in the mirror of her inner arm. She would have been the heartthrob of any teenage sci-fi geek, if they hadn't all died off a thousand years ago.

She glanced up at Shay, who crawled across the ground toward the fallen sword.

"What, you aren't even going to gawk at me?" Jazz asked. "I'm practically naked and you're more interested in the sword? What's wrong with you?"

Shay's fingers closed around the hilt. "I've seen Jandra naked. She was beautiful. You're an abomination!"

Jazz snickered. "This sweet talk is doing nothing to delay your violent death."

Jazz stepped toward him. He pulled himself to his knees. A shadow fell across his face, a trick of the light that made it seem as if he knew death was approaching.

Except the shadow wasn't a trick of the light. There was a sound like a flag snapping in the wind as a powerful downdraft sent black ash swirling in all directions. Jazz looked up and found a familiar sundragon swooping toward her, his wings spread into parachutes, his long jaws open wide with twin rows of teeth aimed straight at her head.

"You again?" she said, or started to say as the jaws snapped down. She clenched her teeth and concentrated on her nanite shell to resist the impact and pressure of the bite. The teeth slammed into her ribs with a force greater than the shotgun pellets. Her face flattened up against the dragon's broad, hot tongue. His thick saliva smooshed through a gap in her lips, gagging her with the taste of some long dead mammal that still haunted his breath.

She turned her head and spat. "Gross!" She electrified her nanite shell. The stench of frying tongue was added to the unpleasant mix washing into her nostrils. Unfortunately, the sun-dragon proved a tougher opponent than Lizard. The brute refused to open his jaws. Instead, he jerked Jazz from her feet with a growl that nearly deafened her, given her proximity to his vocal chords. She was swung through the air until an abrupt collision with the hard-packed ground numbed her from the waist down.

He lifted her up to slam her down again. She was certain the points of several of his teeth had punched through the nanite shell and were now slipping between her ribs. She wanted to scream, but she couldn't even breathe.

She grabbed the longest tooth in his bottom jaw with both hands. It was time to test Jandra's strength. She grimaced until veins bulged in her forehead as she tried to push the tooth away from her ribs. All she accomplished was to drive the teeth at her back further in.

Fighting her urge to gag, and breaking her ten-century long commitment against taking a bite of meat, she opened her mouth as wide as she could and sank her teeth into the dragon's tongue. The dragon flinched. Blood spilled into her mouth.

She commanded a stream of nanites to swim into the open wound.

Seconds later, the beast's bite slackened. Jazz dropped from his saliva-coated jaws, slipping in the pool of drool beneath her as the sun-dragon staggered away. He shook his head violently, banging it on the ground, as if he were trying to smash to death a hive of bees that had somehow found its way into his skull.

She sat up, feeling woozy as she gasped in air. Several of her ribs were broken. A three-inch gash near her belly button bled profusely. Her old body would have already fixed this injury. Of course, her old body had more nanites in it than actual biological molecules. Jandra's blood was still mostly blood. She would have to fix that.

Before she could command the nanite shell to cover the wound, she went down again as the young earth-dragon tackled her, sinking his claws into her silvery hair, snarling as he bit at her right ear. "Bad boss! Bad boss!"

She grabbed the little dragon with both hands and jerked him free. Lizard wriggled in her grasp, kicking and scratching like a rabid animal, his eyes red with fury, his sharp beak snapping empty air.

"You are just so cute," Jazz said. She grabbed Lizard's beak with one hand, and his shoulder with the other. She gave a sharp twist, and the little creature went limp in her hands. "I really don't do cute."

She tossed Lizard's corpse aside as she tried to stand, but her legs wouldn't obey. Without warning, her left hand flew up and punched her in the eye.

"Kill you!" her lips snarled.

"Calm down!" Jazz shouted.

"Kill you!" the voice shouted again. The fingers of the left hand began to grow long, silver knives that slashed at Jazz's face. She grabbed her left hand with her right and pushed it away. Her breath came in panicked, sobbing gasps.

"Calm down!" she commanded again.

"Die!" a voice shouted. Only this time, it wasn't from her mouth. Shay ran toward her with the sword brandished in both hands. He lunged, chopping the sword down with a grunt. Jazz rolled to the side, but something fought her and kept her from moving as far as she could have. The sword cut a deep gash into her left shoulder. At least he'd hit the side she was having trouble controlling. She eyed the gaping wound in disbelief as blood spilled down her silver skin. A chill ran through her. This dumb slave boy might actually kill her. If Jandra's brain was burned to ash, she didn't have another back-up.

Shay raised the sword once more.

Jazz clenched her jaw and raised her right hand, willing the nanite shell to full strength. She caught the sword against her shielded palm with a satisfying *CLANG*. She closed her fingers and jerked the blade from Shay's grasp, tossing it as far into the forest as she could manage. He looked forlorn as the flaming sword flew away.

He never saw her foot flying toward his crotch again. She hated repeating herself, but this did seem to be his Achilles heel. Shay staggered backward, doubled over, until he tripped over the tail of the still thrashing sun-dragon. She was surprised the sun-dragon hadn't died yet. Of course, sun-dragons had the largest brains of any sentient organism on earth, and she hadn't exactly been concentrating on guiding her nanites to the important bits of his gray matter. If she stayed around to guide the attack she could finish him off in less than a minute, but sticking around felt like a bad idea. She was having enough trouble fighting the unwelcome ghost inside her without having to worry about external enemies as well.

Jazz reached out and traced an arch in the air. Her finger trailed a thread of pale white light that blossomed into a rainbow. A black crack of nothingness yawned between the bands of light. She crawled forward and fell, tumbling into darkness.

HEX ROLLED OVER onto his belly as the rainbow fizzled away. The bees buzzing in his brain slowly quieted. He was too weak to stand. His mind felt full of holes. He tried counting to ten. The numbers were still there, he hoped. If he was forgetting one, how would he know? What if there was some number between six and seven that was now absent from his brain?

Down near his tail, a human wept.

With a great deal of effort, Hex lifted his head and craned his neck around to better see the red-haired man who crawled across the dust toward the body of a small earth-dragon.

"Do I know you?" Hex asked. "I feel as if we've met. Why can't I recall where?"

The man didn't look back. He reached the small dragon and tentatively touched its shoulder. It lay perfectly motionless. The man dropped his head to the earth-dragon's chest. He kept his ear against the dragon's breast for a long moment, before rolling away to sit down, his hands on his knees. Tear tracks stained his soot-blackened cheeks.

"He's dead," said the man.

"I'm sorry," said Hex. He tried to rise, making it to all fours, trembling as he learned to control his muscles once more. Specks of light danced before him. He had the worst headache of his life.

"I'm Shay," the man said. He sighed heavily. "You're Hexilizan, Albekizan's eldest son. You know me because you were an aid to Dacorn and I was personal slave to Chapelion."

"Ah," said Hex, slowly rising onto his hind-talons, stretching his wings for balance. "You traveled with Chapelion to the Isle of Horses. I remember now. I take it you've escaped?"

Shay tensed. His eyes searched across the ground, perhaps hunting for a weapon.

"You've nothing to fear," said Hex. "I am a fervent opponent of slavery."

Shay nodded. He looked more relaxed now, but also more sorrowful.

"Jandra's gone," he whispered. "Lizard's dead. I warned her not to remove the sword from the heart."

"Did you help her dig it up?"

Shay nodded.

"Perhaps dissuading her from taking that step would have been more effective."

"I didn't know the heart would be alive," Shay said. "I thought it was some kind of machine. I imagined it like a heart-shaped clock." Then, his face hardened. He stared up at Hex. "You're the reason we came here! You're the dragon that stole her genie!"

Hex nodded. "It's true. Jandra was in possession of incredible power. I couldn't trust that the spirit of the goddess wasn't lurking somewhere inside her."

"You drove Jandra back into the kingdom of the goddess," said Shay. "You caused the thing you were trying to prevent!"

Hex kept his mouth shut. He wanted to argue that this wasn't his fault, but a significant part of his throbbing brain was shouting that he was, indeed, responsible. He decided to accept blame and move on to the next phase, finding a solution. "No matter where Jazz has gone, I'll hunt her down."

"And then what?" said Shay. "You'll kill her?"

"I have no other choice. Though, as we've both witnessed, that may not be an easy task."

"Jandra's still alive inside her," said Shay. "She was fighting to get back out. I don't understand everything that's happened here. But Jazz said her spirit had survived inside her genie. What if part of Jandra's spirit survives inside the genie you stole from her? What if we gave it back to Jandra? It might let her become the dominant mind inside her own body once more."

"Or it might add to Jazz's already formidable powers," said Hex.

"Just how much more powerful can she get?" asked Shay.

"You wouldn't ask that if you'd fought the goddess the first time. However, your idea is worthy. We'll go to the Free City."

"The Free City? Why?"

"That's where I buried Jandra's genie. The Free City has been abandoned in the aftermath of the atrocities that took place there. No human or dragon would want to call that cursed place home. I'd planned to keep the genie there until I could locate some force powerful enough to destroy it."

"After we get the genie, how can we find Jandra?" Shay asked.

Hex sat down. His legs were still weak. The dancing lights before his eyes were fading, at least. "We should find Bitterwood. He killed Jazz last time. She may seek revenge. More importantly, Bitterwood is now the guardian of Zeeky, a girl who possessed a power that the goddess greatly desired."

"What power?"

"I'll tell you what I understand, though when Jandra explained it to me I failed to grasp much of it. You witnessed the rainbow Jazz escaped through?"

"Yes. I've never seen anything like it."

"Beneath our own reality, there's a larger reality known as underspace. The rainbow gates let you slip through underspace to travel instantly to any other part of our own world. Apparently it's possible to become trapped in underspace. If you linger outside our reality, you gain the ability to see all points of space and time. You become omniscient."

"What does that have to do with Zeeky? She's smart for her age, but hardly omniscient."

"Jazz trapped Zeeky's family inside underspace, sealed inside a crystal ball. The goddess can't communicate with them, but, somehow, Zeeky can. From what Jandra told me, Jazz wanted to study Zeeky to discover what quirk of her brain gave her this ability."

Shay stood up. He walked over and picked up the flaming sword. "It sounds as if we have a plan. Recover the genie. Find Bitterwood. Guard Zeeky and hope the goddess still wants her."

He held up the sword, looking mournfully at the dancing flames. "This blade cut her. If I'd been a better fighter, she might not have escaped."

"Let me carry the sword. I trained extensively in my youth. When we find Bitterwood, we'll let him carry the blade."

Shay frowned. "How do I know you won't just fly off and bury this?"

Hex sighed. "I've done nothing to earn your trust. Keep the blade. Let us hope your mistrust doesn't doom Jandra."

"Let's hope your mistrust of Jandra, which led you to take her genie, doesn't doom us all," said Shay.

"We can argue later. We should leave. We have a long journey from this place back to the surface."

"Maybe not," said Shay. "We found a map at the barracks. It showed a shorter route out of here. We should stop and get it. There were other supplies that also would be useful."

"Lead on," said Hex.

Shay walked toward the fallen earth-dragon. The coat Jandra had discarded lay nearby. He knelt and wrapped the small body within it.

"I... I didn't like Lizard," he said. He shook his head slowly. "I thought Jandra was taking a risk in adopting him." He cradled the bundle to his chest as he stood. "When we make it back to the surface, I hope you don't mind if I pause for a while to bury him. He deserves better than to rot away down here in this sunless kingdom. I'd like to find a tranquil valley, or a sun-drenched mountain top. Some place... some place that..."

"Of course," said Hex. He wanted to ask more about Jandra's adoption of a dragon, but held his tongue. In truth, he wasn't surprised. Jandra had befriended Hex almost from the moment they'd met. She'd been, perhaps, the most trusting, open-minded individual he'd ever known. The burden of betraying her still weighed heavily on his soul.

Could all of this have been avoided if he'd extended her the same faith and trust she'd shown him?

CHAPTER TWENTY-FOUR

STRUGGLE AGAINST MONSTERS

JAZZ FELL FROM nowhere, face-down onto the white sands of a sun-washed beach. She rolled to her side, squinting as she looked around; the beach sparkled like powdered diamonds. She closed her eyes, letting the bright sunlight sink into her silver shell. The tiny machines that coated her hummed with pleasure as they ate up the free energy. All around her, the air buzzed with nanites not guided by her genie. She exhaled a thin swarm of machines, commanding them to acts of piracy. Given time, she could manufacture more nanites; right now, here in Atlantis, it was simply more expedient to steal them.

The ghost of Jandra's personality shouted somewhere in the back of her mind, but as the power levels of her genie increased, the faint remnant grew quieter. Jazz sat up, wincing from her wounds. The dragon had given her quite the workout. She ran her silvery fingers along the three-inch gash he'd torn in her belly, knitting the wound shut. She turned her attention to her shoulder. The heat of the sword had carbonized much of the tissue. It wasn't going to be as easy a fix. She set her nanites to work on it, then flowed the silver shell of her genie back over the wound to prevent contamination.

Satisfied that her new body was no longer in peril, she paused to look around. She was on the western shore of Atlantis. The sun hung over the waves. In another hour or two it would be night. The ocean lapping the shore was breathtaking, a bright shade of blue that would have looked perfect on the wings of a tropical butterfly. When all this was over, she'd have to whip up a batch of butterflies. She'd design them as flesh eaters the size of small eagles, but they'd still be beautiful. The required DNA chains uncoiled in her mind's eye.

Jazz stood up, wiping the sand from her silvery butt. She craned her neck to see as much of her new body as she could. She looked good in chrome, better than she would have imagined. Despite her high-tech talents, Jazz had always possessed simple, down-to-earth tastes in fashion—blue jeans, cotton blouses, hemp sandals. Her vegetarianism had extended to eschewing leather, but she had to admit that Jandra's calf-high black boots looked good against the mirror-smoothness of her legs. The fact that they were scuffed and worn provided a pleasing contrast to the machined perfection of the rest of her. The rationale for her longstanding vegetarian ethics rested on shaky ground, anyway. She was honest enough to admit she'd long ago lost the moral high ground when it came to killing the creatures who shared the planet with her. Jandra had eaten meat her whole life. Her brain brimmed with cells programmed to enjoy the taste of fish. Perhaps it was time to try sushi.

Jazz looked up and down the beach. Not a sushi vendor in sight. In fact, the beach was empty. Six billion people lived in Atlantis, and not one could be bothered to come down to the beach on this perfect day. Of course, this beach was perfect every day. That had always been the fatal flaw of the city. After a thousand years of paradise, even the most innocent souls grew bored.

She looked up at the towers behind her. The tallest spires stretched into the blue sky, vanishing in haze, their peaks somewhere beyond the edges of the atmosphere. She saw a shadow of movement race along the shell-pink surface of one of the towers, miles up. She had the nanites in her retinas reprocess the photons striking them and the image sharpened. It was a man, falling, flapping his arms like they were wings. He looked as if he was laughing. Quickly, Jazz spotted another man, then a woman, all falling on parallel paths. Now that she was aware of them, she quickly spotted a hundred more. Some were laughing like the first man she spotted, but others were weeping, and still others looked as if they were screaming in terror. One by one the bodies vanished behind the screen of the lower towers surrounding the spires. If anyone was walking below, Jazz hoped they were carrying heavy-duty umbrellas.

"If your friends jumped off a building, would you?" she asked out loud, remembering the question her father had put to her over ten centuries earlier. She shook her head in disgust. It was time to get to work. She said, "Find Cassie."

Her genie responded instantly, hacking the datastream that flowed along the beach like an invisible river. In Atlantis, every cubic centimeter of air was permeated with nanites, waiting to serve the inhabitants. Her eyes zoomed back up the tallest tower, the

Bethlehem Spire. A bright green circle of light flashed around a window too far away to be anything more than a speck, even with the fine tuning of the nanites. Still, she had the coordinates, which was all she really needed.

She waited a while longer, stealing more of the microscopic machines, turning in the ever-dimming sun to charge them to their fullest. Soon, her ribs felt better, with no evidence at all that she'd been a sun-dragon's chew toy. Jazz flexed the fingers of her left hand. They were fully under her control now that she'd fortified the nanites clinging to Jandra's nervous system. Her shoulder tingled as the nanites busily worked on cutting away the charred tissue they found there. On the whole, she felt back in control, not only of Jandra's body, but of everything.

She knew what she had to do to make sure she'd never lose control again.

Humming "Somewhere over the Rainbow," she opened an underspace gate before her.

A YOUNG WOMAN with golden skin looked up as Jazz stepped from the rainbow. The woman had glossy black hair that seemed to bubble up from her scalp like a fountain and flow down her neck and back in liquid smoothness. The woman frowned.

Jazz smiled, until she felt movement beneath her feet. She looked down. The white sand from the beach falling from Jazz's boots was causing tiny mouths to open in the onyx floor, swallowing the grains, leaving the smooth black tile immaculate.

The entire room possessed the same sterile cleanliness. It was as big as a museum gallery, yet barely furnished—its walls were clear panes of glass, free of any curtains or blinds. The golden woman sat at a black table, or at least a table top. The perfectly square polished wood hovered, unsupported by legs. A pearl-white cup and saucer sat before the golden woman, full of fluid as dark as the woman's hair. Jazz wondered why the woman was drinking ink. A memory stirred within her.

"Is that... is that... *coffee?*" Jazz spoke the last word with a reverential tone.

The woman's golden eyebrows scrunched together above diamond eyes. Her lips parted to reveal pearl teeth.

"Do I know you?" she asked.

Jazz walked across the floor, trying not to be distracted by the mouths gobbling up sand that fell with each step. The golden woman held her ground as Jazz approached until they were practically touching. Jazz grabbed the cup and sniffed it. The toasted, nutty odor of coffee filled her nostrils.

"Sweet merciful Jesus, I haven't drunk coffee in seven hundred years," she said.

She took a sip. Her lips puckered at the bitterness. The receptors in Jandra's tongue weren't mapped to the parts off her brain that would find the taste pleasant. She set her nanites to work fixing that. For now, there was a mildly pleasant surge of endorphins as the hot liquid scalded her tongue.

"Jazz?" the golden woman asked.

"How'd you guess?"

"One of your identifying traits is taking things that belong to me."

"Ah, Cassie," said Jazz. "Do we really have to launch straight into the old arguments?"

Cassie crossed her arms. Her chair drifted backwards, putting some space between her and her sister. A trickle of the liquid hair ran down the crease in her forehead, over her eyebrow, and down the edges of her nose. She blew it away and the liquid responded as if it was normal hair, falling to the outer edge of her cheek. She said, "I thought you died in that explosion on Mars."

"That's what I wanted you to think," said Jazz. She put the cup down and walked toward the window. Her chrome-plated skin was faintly reflected in the glass. She smiled as she realized how youthful her body looked. Her old body had been more or less frozen in development around the age of forty. Unlike the Atlanteans, she'd never had any particular fetish for looking as if she were barely out of puberty. She'd been comfortable with her body, with its stray hairs and generous curves and the familiar sags and wrinkles. It had looked, and felt, lived in. Still, there was something about this fresh, clean body that made her spirit shiver. It was the same artistic rush she felt when she picked up a sheet of fresh white paper.

Outside the window, the distant horizon curved in a perfect arc. They were on the threshold of space. The blue-gray ocean stretched out beneath them. At the edge of the horizon, the color changed as the ocean met land. She was looking at the eastern seaboard of what had once been the United States. These shores had once been studded with cities; now, it was a wild place, the abode of dragons. It was the crowning achievement of a long life.

Jazz leapt backwards as a man flashed past the window. He was naked, with bright red skin crisscrossed with black zebra stripes. He looked as if he was giggling as he plummeted toward the earth, many miles below.

"Jesus," said Jazz. "He scared the shit out of me. Is there a rash of suicides in Atlantis?"

"Don't be absurd," said Cassie, rising to stand beside Jazz at the window. Cassie was wearing a simple slip of sheer black lace that clung to her almost flat chest and barely noticeable hips. Save for Cassie's unnatural height—she was easily a foot taller than Jazz now—she looked no older than twelve. "The city won't let anyone die. The bodies of the jumpers will be destroyed when they hit the ground, but they'll awaken instantly in a back-up copy. The essential part of a person is nothing but information, and information is immortal."

"Ah, yes," said Jazz. "You Atlanteans change bodies more frequently than I change my hairstyle. Speaking of which, the last four times I've seen you, you've been female. You get that boy phase out of your system?"

Cassie shrugged. "The female body has… aesthetic advantages. It supports a broader palette of colors. The male body has never looked right to me in the brighter shades."

As if to prove her point, as second man fell past the window. He was dressed like a rodeo cowboy in a fringed leather vest and chaps, but had neon pink skin that looked dumb on him. A few seconds after he flashed by, his hat dropped past.

"It's like bungee jumping without the bungee," said Jazz, tracking the hat down as far as she could.

"They say it's the ultimate adrenaline rush. If you've gotten tired of a body and don't intend to use it again, why not dispose of it in style? It's less boring than going to sleep and waking up new."

Jazz shook her head. "This is what's so wrong about Atlantis. You've let the city remove all pain and fear and worry. You've devolved into beings so jaded you have to throw yourselves off buildings to get ten minutes of feeling alive. You've been given the gift of immortality, and except for the moderately ambitious folks who went off to new worlds, you've all turned into bored teenagers looking for the next distraction."

Cassie shrugged. Her hair flowed into a new trickle along her neck. "What great goals are left? There's no hunger. There's no death. There's no fear, or want, or sorrow. Every great challenge of mankind has been solved. How are we supposed to spend our days? There are no more battles to fight."

A leopard-skinned woman in a bathing suit darted past the window, her arms pointed before her in an arrow, her feet held in perfect balance. If they still held the Olympics, this would be a 10. But, of course, any dive—all dives—could be a ten. The muscle memory for doing anything perfectly could simply be borrowed from the Atlantean datastream. Atlanteans could know everything while literally learning nothing.

Cassie pressed her forehead to the window as she looked at the world far below. She sighed. "After the struggle's over, all that's left is entertainment."

Jazz nodded. She felt a flickering pulse of sympathy for Cassie. She thought of the empty beach below. Her sister was fated to eternity in paradise with the promise—or curse—of a billion years more of the same. The rebellious, fire-bombing ecoterrorist who'd once followed in Jazz's footsteps was long gone. How do you rebel against heaven?

As quickly as the sympathy welled up, it ebbed back. Jazz remembered the real reason for her visit.

"If you thought I was dead, why did you send people to kill me?"

Cassie raised an eyebrow. "Come again?"

"Don't act innocent. I'm wearing the body of a girl named Jandra. She had an Atlantean genie and a body full of nanite enhancements. She got them from a sky-dragon named Vendevorex. I don't think Vendevorex invented the technology on his own."

Cassie smiled. "Oh! Vendevorex. Wow. I haven't thought about him in years. How is he?"

"Jandra remembers him dying," said Jazz. "Of course, we both know that could be a false memory. Jandra doesn't have any memories of meeting you, but that could have been edited as well."

Cassie shook her head as she looked out toward the darkness of space that hung over the horizon. "I don't have a clue who Jandra is."

"But you know Vendevorex. How did he get the genie?"

"I gave it to him. I'm part of a debate committee to decide whether or not the dragon species should be regarded as hazardous bio-engineering waste and removed from the ecosystem."

"Atlanteans shouldn't care about that," said Jazz. "You shouldn't be *able* to care about that, because the city can't care about it."

"I know," said Cassie. "You hacked the city to keep Atlantean technology from spreading. You made the most powerful, benevolent force ever seen on this world turn a blind eye on the continents so they could go feral. But, while the Atlantean master intelligence doesn't care about what goes on beyond these shores, I still do, and so do some others. You didn't hack our memories, Jazz. Some of the people here were involved in creating the dragons. They're concerned about their spread. They were created as novelties. No one anticipated they'd become the dominant sentient species on the North American mainland."

Jazz leaned against the glass wall. "Unintended consequences are what make life interesting. But what does this have to do with Vendevorex?"

"Vendevorex was one of a handful of dragons the committee captured for study. Usually we keep them in laboratory settings, but Vendevorex was clever enough to escape. He eluded capture for three days, this on an island where even the air is sentient. I finally tracked him down. He was frightened, but also defiant. His fighting spirit stirred something inside me. He reminded me of the person I once was."

"I remember when you were a teenager. You were a real hell-raiser." Jazz grinned. "If you'd had a few more years, I bet you could have knocked me off the top of the most wanted list."

"Thanks," said Cassie, her golden cheeks blushing rose pink.

"I didn't say it enough back then, but I liked you," said Jazz. "You were fully committed to saving earth from mankind. You were a rebel to the bone."

"There's some of that still inside me," said Cassie. "That's why I gave Vendevorex a genie and trained him to use it. I helped him escape back to North America. It was a form of rebellion against Atlantis; more importantly, it was a form of rebellion against you."

"Me? How?"

"You prevented the spread of Atlantean technology by humans. Vendevorex would have no such qualms. I gave him the know-how to build other genies. I thought he would eventually spread the technology, and get around the block you placed on the island."

"Clever," said Jazz. "But there's no way he could have linked into the Atlantean networks to make full use of the genie's potential."

"Vendevorex was smart. Since he couldn't link to a database to guide his nanites, he devoted himself to the study of chemistry and biology. His mind would be the database."

"Ah," said Jazz. "That's why Jandra has the periodic table memorized and can name every bone in the body."

"It's not as efficient as the Atlantean mind, of course," said Cassie, "but it works."

"You said you were on a committee trying to stop the spread of dragons. Why give one such a powerful tool? This is only going to lead to more powerful dragons."

Cassie looked away. However, her reflection was clearly visible on the glass. She had the faintest hint of a smug grin.

Jazz added up all the clues. "Don't tell me. You've buried a code in those genies. Vendevorex was supposed to keep propagating the genies until they reached a critical mass. They'd form their own network, one that would communicate with Atlantis, and wipe out the shackles I programmed. Atlantis would turn all of Earth into a paradise for humanity, wiping out the dragons as an environmental pollutant left over from careless genetic tinkering."

Cassie raised her eyebrows. "Wow. That's quite a guess."

Jazz looked around the big, empty, dustless room. On the opposite wall, the earth was now in darkness, and the stars shone as perfect points, untainted by atmosphere. She spotted Mars and thought about the settlers there, and the good time she'd had two centuries ago intervening in their civil war. All the people worth knowing had long since fled the earth. "Do you remember how mom used to drag us to church?" she asked.

"I haven't thought about that in a long time," said Cassie.

"I recently had a reminder of the fire and brimstone sermons. I was buried in a pit of fire, neither dead nor alive, in constant agony. If things had gone badly, it might have lasted for all eternity. It's sheer luck that I escaped. Luck and my complete lack of any moral qualms about stealing another woman's body."

"Sounds rotten. Have you decided to mend your ways?"

"No."

"No?"

"Let me show you something," said Jazz. She opened her hand. The chrome coating her palm boiled, bubbling up into a silver marble an inch across. She rolled it forward and caught it between her fingers.

"What is it?" said Cassie.

Jazz held it out. "Take a close look at the writing on the surface."

Cassie frowned, leaned forward, and squinted. She picked it up, holding it only a few inches from her face, and turned it slowly.

"I don't see any wri—" she stopped in mid-word as the gold coating her face and lips begin to crack, flaking away like the shell of a boiled egg, revealing pale flesh beneath.

Cassie dropped the marble. It bounced on the floor. A small mouth opened to devour it, then froze. Jagged cracks ran across the surface of the onyx tile.

"What's happening?" The metallic shell that coated her fell away in fine flakes. Her black silk slip now sported a sheet of scaly dust, as if she'd just developed the world's most severe case of dandruff. Her black ink hair stopped seeping from her scalp, leaving her bald, missing even her eyebrows.

"Call for help," Jazz said.

Cassie glared at Jazz, her eyes full of hate. Slowly, her features changed; hate funneled away, leaving only fear.

"It's silent," she whispered. "You've made the city go silent."

"Not yet," said Jazz. "This is only a test run. The marble is a jammer. It emits a coded radio pulse that scrambles the Atlantean datastream. You've vanished from the city's awareness. You can't even use your own genie to communicate with your nanites. I'm immune because I encoded the pulse."

"This is… this is monstrous!" said Cassie, backing away, leaving a trail of dust. Her body looked pink and raw. Despite being taller than Jazz, she looked vulnerable in her girlish body, with the absurdly thin limbs that were the fashion in Atlantis. "Disabling my genie is like gouging out my eyes! You've made your point! Turn it off!"

"If I turn it off, you'll be back online, and Atlantis will know what you know."

"But… But…"

"Don't fight this. You had a good run. A thousand years. Try to appreciate the adrenaline rush."

Jazz willed an underspace gate to open in the air near her hand. She grabbed the edges of the rainbow, wrapping her fingers around it. Her nanites generated an electromagnetic field that let her fold the light. At the center of the rainbow, a slender black arc thinner than a human hair curved from her grasp like a scimitar.

"Have you ever seen what happens if you hit something with an underspace gate only a few nanometers wide?" Jazz asked.

Cassie clenched her fists. Despite the thinness of her limbs, Cassie's muscles would be finely tuned, and fast. Her nerves had been created cell by cell in absolute perfection, while Jandra's body still clunked along on the nervous system she'd been born with.

"Jazz, you can't seriously be thinking of killing Atlantis. There are six billion people here! Killing the city is the same as killing them. Not even you are that black-hearted."

"I snapped a baby's neck before I came here," said Jazz. "A scaly baby who bit the shit out of me, but still... I wouldn't go making bets about what I'm capable of."

"But... why? Why is it so awful to let the city help people? The city takes care of us."

"Atlantis turned mankind into a race of eternal children," said Jazz. "I'm tired of being the world's only grownup."

Cassie lunged forward, her fist aimed for Jazz's nose.

Jazz stepped aside, twirling the underspace blade into her sister's path. Cassie fell past her, landing with a wet smack on the stone floor. Jazz looked down at her sister's hands, which had fallen near her feet, severed by the world's sharpest scalpel.

Cassie twitched on the floor. Her exsanguination became a dark pool before her. Jazz had little appetite for gore.

She went to the black table, picked up the coffee cup, and took another sip. She was braced for the bitterness now. Jandra's tongue was no longer virgin; this time, the liquid washed across her taste buds with a mix of sharpness and heat that was almost pleasant.

Killing Cassie was an act of mercy. The centuries had left her sister soft; she would have been ill-prepared to face the world to come. The risk Atlantis represented was too great. Maybe Cassie had failed to undo her programming over a thousand years, but what of the next thousand years? Jazz had never learned the true origins of Atlantis. It was obviously an alien construct, but who had sent it here, and why? What would happen if they suddenly showed up to fix it? She had no choice but to kill the city.

Of course, Atlantis was probably a more formidable opponent than Cassie had been. If she was serious about doing this, she needed allies. Her long-wyrm riders had been laughably ineffective. Her best angel had been thoroughly trashed by a sour-faced little man with nothing more than a bow, an arrow, tenacity, and brains.

Bitterwood had killed her, true, but she didn't feel angry about this. Instead, she had a grudging admiration. The people of Atlantis were spineless hedonists. They reminded her of the world of her youth, an entire planet full of people with the mentality of locusts, devouring all the pleasures the world could grow, ignoring the wastelands left in their wake. Bitterwood, born and bred in Jazz's new world, was a true man; fearless, clever, and full of conviction. He was living proof that her world was a better environment for humans than this false paradise. There were more important things in the world than being safe and healthy and entertained.

For a man to be truly great, he must struggle against monsters. With the right weapons, Bitterwood would make a valuable ally.

Darkness crept across the ocean, lapping the shore of North America.

THE SUN WAS low over the hills to the west as Vulpine walked along the Forge Road, admiring the decaying scarecrows Sawface and his Wasters had placed along the highway. Word of the blockade had apparently spread quickly throughout the human population. In recent days, the stream of humans attempting to reach the fort had ended. This meant that humans were staying on their farms. Now that the earth-dragons that had been raiding them were organized once more into an army, home was the safest place for a human to be. In a few weeks, they would go out and plant their crops. Rebellions were easier to sustain in early winter, when food was plentiful following harvests. Once the crops were in the ground, the rebellion would effectively be finished. Few people would abandon crops to join a hopeless cause. By this time next year, the rebellion would be only a bad memory.

As pleasing as the results of the scarecrows were to Vulpine, the stench of the road was unsettling. He lifted into the air, climbing, climbing, till he was almost a mile high. In the dying light, it was difficult to be certain, but it appeared as if activity within the walls of Dragon Forge had greatly reduced. The streets were empty. Only a few spotters remained along the walls with the wheeled bows that caused such terror among the sun-dragons.

Most importantly, only one of the smokestacks of the foundry was spewing smoke. It was too soon for yellow-mouth to have manifested in many victims, but even one or two would be sufficient to spread terror. The foundry was faltering, no doubt because the workers were hiding in their bunks, afraid of encountering anyone with the disease.

Dropping from the sky back toward his camp, he saw the squad of valkyrie engineers still working on the thousands of iron bits spread upon the large tarp near his tent. These were the remnants of the war engine Sawface had destroyed. It was a shame—the machine had looked impressive in its short run. It obviously had design flaws—exploding after the bridge collapsed being chief among them. Still, he could only imagine what the valkyrie engineers and the biologians could accomplish if they'd gotten their talons on a working prototype.

Arifiel was present, speaking with her fellow valkyries. She broke away as she saw Vulpine, flapping her wings for a short flight to his landing target. Arifiel was a veteran of Blasphet's recent attack on the Nest. She still bore a rather unattractive festering burn wound on her shoulder as a reminder. It didn't slow her, however.

"How goes it?" Vulpine asked.

"My engineers are still analyzing the placement of the fragments. We've interviewed the earth-dragons who witnessed it up close, but their capacity for describing a device of this complexity is somewhat limited."

"I value Sawface for his ability to demolish a stone bridge with a hammer blow more than for his verbal prowess," said Vulpine. "Still, the report from Bazanel should be complete any—"

"Bazanel is dead," said Arifiel.

"What?"

"Chapelion's messenger arrived while you were visiting the other checkpoints. I was present when he gave the news to Sagen. A human assassin killed Bazanel and stole the gun. The secret of gunpowder had already been given to a valkyrie. She gave it to Chapelion, who shared the news with his advisors. A few days later, all of his advisors were slain by an assassin too—a young human female. Unfortunately, no copies of the formula survived, and Chapelion didn't bother to memorize the formula."

"Was poison used by the assassins?"

"No. This was my first thought as well. It doesn't appear to be the work of Blasphet."

Vulpine walked over to the tarp. He craned his neck down to see the gears and wheels laid out before him in the dim light that remained. He shook his head as he contemplated this turn of events.

"Why did he delay in sending me the formula?" Vulpine asked, speaking more to himself than Arifiel.

"I would have had gunpowder in production within a day."

"The greatest failing of biologists is that they debate all matters endlessly before taking action," said Arifiel. "Chapelion is the ultimate embodiment of this flaw."

Vulpine wanted to scold the female for making such disparaging accusations against his chief employer, yet in his heart, he knew it was true. As well as things were going here, it sounded as if things were in decline at the Dragon Palace. Every few days brought bad news. The Grand Library was burned. A dozen aerial guards and valkyries had abandoned their posts, in contrast to the mere four under his command. Now this.

"The valkyries were to aid in the protection of Chapelion and his advisors," said Vulpine. "Instead they've focused their attention on seducing members of the aerial guard and fleeing."

"I would argue it's members of the aerial guard who are leading the valkyries astray."

Vulpine ground his teeth. "The blame for our setbacks rests upon multiple shoulders, including my own. I've underestimated the humans in the fort. First the new bows, then the guns. Now they've built a war machine capable of rolling under its own power. There's obviously a genius hidden within the walls of the fort. He sent the assassins."

"What do you propose to do about it?"

"You valkyries are the ones who boast of being experts in war," said Vulpine. "What would you do about it?"

"I would load the catapults with barrels of flaming pitch and burn the city to the ground. We can build a new foundry on the ashes of the old."

"We could build a new foundry a few miles up the road without destroying anything," said Vulpine. "There's more to victory than mere destruction."

"Do you have a better strategy?"

Vulpine scratched his chin and gazed at the red sky left by the vanished sun. The black outlines of Sawface's scarecrows ran along the ridge.

"Ah," he said.

"Ah?" asked Arifiel.

"Tell your valkyries to ready their catapults. Have Sawface remove the scarecrows. They've served their purpose on the roads."

He looked toward Dragon Forge. The sky above it was dim in comparison to only a week ago. He said, "Whoever our mysterious genius is, he'll be working in unpleasant weather tomorrow."

Arifiel looked up. "The sky isn't all that cloudy."

"We won't need clouds for the rain I have in mind," said Vulpine.

CHAPTER TWENTY-FIVE

THIS LITTLE PATCH OF EARTH

SHAY AND HEX stood beside the tiny grave. They were near the peak of a rocky, rugged mountain, covered with a low, thick cover of rhododendron bushes. The stone shelf jutted out relatively flat for a dozen yards. Shay had made Lizard's grave by piling stones into a rough pyramid. From the cliff, the view was breathtaking, a narrow valley winding among steep-walled mountains. The sun painted the valley in vivid shades of green. The rhododendron leaves held their color throughout the winter.

The sun warmed the stone shelf. Birds sang in the bushes behind him. When his own time came, Shay could think of worse places for his mortal remains to rest.

Hex stood nearby. Shay hadn't spent much time around sun-dragons—even though Hex was friendly, it was still difficult not to feel small and vulnerable in his imposing presence.

"I should say something," Shay said. "It's traditional to pray."

"We dragons don't offer prayers to the dead," said Hex. "We speak mainly for the comfort of the surviving relatives and friends. We cremate our dead. The living inhale the smoke of the body. In this way, the deceased becomes part of our vital energy. It seems wasteful to bury a body."

"Humans prefer burial because we like to think of death as a type of sleep from which we'll one day awaken. The families of the dead visit the grave and talk to their lost loved ones."

"Not many people can visit him here, I fear."

"Lizard didn't have any friends other than Jandra. Zeeky, maybe."

"And you," said Hex.

"I wasn't much of a friend, I'm afraid," said Shay. His shoulders sagged. "I thought it was only a matter of time before the little beast tried to eat us."

"So why bury him?"

"Because Jandra loved him. And... he obviously loved her, or came as close to love as an earth-dragon can get. He fought to protect her." Shay straightened up, crossing his hands in front of himself as the wind whipped over the edge of the cliff. He faced the mound of stones.

"Lizard I don't know if you can hear me. I don't know if anything waits for anyone after we die, for men or dragons. But, if there is some great final judge who weighs the good we've done in life against the bad, I hope he judges that you were gentle, you were brave, and you were even wise. You accepted Jandra's love without question or hesitation. If there's a heaven, I hope you find a home there."

The shadow pointing from the pyramid led straight to Shay's feet. He felt as if the words he was saying were trivial, weightless noises that would vanish in the air. Yet, he had to keep talking.

"Maybe there is no heaven, and perhaps death is just another kind of sleep. Maybe someday you're going to wake up and look out over the valley. I hope this little patch of earth will make you happy when you see it."

Shay looked over his shoulder. "In a month or two, all these bushes are going to bloom with a million flowers. Maybe you'll wake up on a morning like that. It would have been fun to watch you hiding among them with your camouflage."

He searched desperately for more words to say. A faint smile crossed his lips as he found the words he'd meant to say all along. "Sleep well, Lizard."

Shay turned away from the stones. "I wish I'd had something to read."

"You took those books from the barracks."

"Those aren't for poetry," said Shay.

"Your words were quite moving," said Hex. "I think you've said what needed to be said."

Shay shook his head. "I think that with every day that passes, I'm coming to understand the inadequacy of words." He unfurled his metal wings. The wind played across his silvery feathers. In the valley, white circles of light danced on the dark leaves, reflections of the sun on his wings.

"Let's go," he said, tilting forward, his feet lifting from the earth. Now driven by the urgency of their cause, Shay had lost all fear of flying and was grateful for the twists and turns of fate that had provided him wings. They traveled a hundred miles in the span of a few hours.

Shay could have traveled further, faster. His mechanical wings were tireless. They also propelled him more swiftly than Hex could follow, a literally breathtaking speed at which the wind made it difficult to breathe. Hex required several breaks. The sun-dragon flew at a speed that could outpace any horse, but he couldn't keep up with Shay.

They paused to drink by a stream at the edge of a farm. Off in the distance, cows gave them nervous glances. Shay noticed the big dragon trembling when he lowered his head to the water. Hex's right limbs looked shakier than their counterparts.

"Are you all right?" Shay asked. "Are you still recovering from Jazz's attack?"

"Somewhat," said Hex. "Half of my body is numb. Perhaps it's my imagination, but my speech feels slurred."

"I never heard you talk before, so I can't judge. Have you always lisped?"

"I suspect Jazz's attack had the practical effect of a mild stroke," said Hex. "A more sustained assault might have killed me."

"We don't have to keep pushing on if you don't feel up to it. We don't know where Jazz is."

"We don't have the luxury of resting," said Hex. "It's difficult to counter the speed advantages of a foe who can traverse great distances in a heartbeat by taking a shortcut through unreality. I want to go to the Free City as swiftly as possible to recover the genie, then travel to Dragon Forge."

"Dragon Forge? Why?"

"Bitterwood was heading there to rescue Zeeky's brother, Jeremiah. He may linger there still. If he's moved on, no doubt someone can provide us with clues to their next destination."

"I'm not really welcome in Dragon Forge anymore. You *definitely* aren't welcome. They'll shoot you from the sky the second they see you."

"I'll approach on foot, fully armored. I hid my armor near Rorg's cavern to travel more swiftly. If needed, I'll recover it. I'm not afraid of archers."

Shay held up the shotgun. "Forget the archers. This is what you need to worry about. It can punch holes in armor. The earth-dragons we fought at Burke's Tavern had armor and we cut right through them."

"Hmm," said Hex. "I'm sure we can think of something. Perhaps you can enter the city in disguise."

Hex peered toward the western sky. "It will be dark before long. Perhaps we should rest. I don't like to fly after dark. Landing is often problematic."

"It's a shame the visors don't fit you," said Shay, pulling his own silver visor from the satchel that hung at his side. He looked down into the leather bag, at the many treasures within it he'd taken from the long-wyrm rider barracks. He had a second bag slung over his other shoulder—Jandra's pack. He'd stuffed her coat into it. It was probably pointless to hold on to her things, but it felt wrong to leave them behind. "If you could use the visor, we could fly all night."

"At some point, you'll need sleep as much as I do. You can't move forever on pure adrenaline."

Shay stretched his back. He ached all over from his earlier efforts in digging. "You're probably right. A couple of hours of sleep might do us both some good. At the first light of dawn, we'll split up. You go to the Free City and get the genie. I'll go to Dragon Forge and find Bitterwood."

Hex took another sip from the stream as he thought about this plan, lapping the water like a giant cat. His tongue looked awful, with a circular wound all purple and raw right in the center of it.

"Your plan is sound," said the sun-dragon. Water streamed from the right side of his mouth. "I only hope that the goddess doesn't find him first."

* * *

BURKE GROANED AS he stretched out on the burlap sack they'd spread on the chicken coop floor, a filthy mess of waste, feathers, and straw. They'd traveled to Nat Goodsalt's farm near Burke's Tavern and found the house and barn burned to the ground. The chicken coop had been the only building still standing, though it was blackened on one corner and the door lay on the ground a dozen yards away. All the chickens were gone. The spoils of war, no doubt.

It was dark outside; the wind whistled as it pushed through the cracks in the thin walls. Scratching noises within the straw told Burke he was sharing his bed with mice, but he was too tired and sore to worry about his bedmates. Covering ninety miles on uneven terrain with one leg had narrowed the focus of his world these last few days. It was difficult to think of anything other than the bloody, puss-filled blisters that the crutch had worked into his armpit.

Burke barely moved when a shadow fell across him. From the smell, he knew it was Thorny.

"Vance is hunting up some grub," said Thorny. "I looked around and can't find any bodies. Goodsalt must have fled before the dragons got here."

Burke nodded slightly, too worn out to speak.

Somewhere not too far away, there was a crisp, musical *zing* as a sky-wall bow was fired, followed by, "Woohoo!"

Thorny left the doorway and peeked around the edge of the coop. "Dang if that boy hasn't got us a possum!"

Burke's stomach gurgled at the thought of food. "Let me rest my eyes for a minute, then I'll help cook it."

Thorny said something in response, but the words sounded distant. Sleep yawned before him like an open pit. He slipped into its depths.

When he woke, there were voices outside the door. It was still dark outside; he could smell a campfire and charred meat, and something else, something he couldn't identify at first.

It smelled musty, slightly sour, almost like... a dragon? He sat up, his eyes wide as they probed the darkness. He bit his lower lip to keep from crying out in pain as he tried to move his left arm. The blisters had scabbed over as he slept; it was like his upper arm had been glued to his rib cage. His eyes watered as he peeled his arm free.

Burke was freezing. They'd escaped Dragon Forge with only the clothes on their backs, plus the few meager supplies they'd stolen from the cabin. His toes were full of tiny little knives of ice. His phantom leg shared the symptoms. He reached down and rubbed the toes of his remaining foot through his boot. Though he knew it was irrational, he moved his hand to where his nerves told him his other foot lay. On some instinctive level, he was disappointed when his fingers closed on empty air. On a more rational level, he was relieved that he still had at least some tenuous understanding of reality.

He scooted closer to the wall and carefully peeked through a crack to see what was happening. That tenuous understanding of reality took a sharp blow as he found himself staring at the side of an impossibly long, multi-limbed dragon covered with overlapping copper scales. The head of the beast reminded him of old prints he'd seen of eastern dragons—purely mythological creatures, unlike the flesh and blood dragons he was used to fighting. For a mythical beast, it looked solid enough. Its breath came out as great puffs of steam in the frosty night.

The beast turned its giant head toward the chicken coop. Burke jerked his eyes from the crack and pressed his back against the wall, his heart racing. He searched the blackness of the chicken coop for a weapon. The shotgun must be outside with Vance.

As the seconds ticked past, he began to assemble a theory about the oversized lizard waiting at his door. Jandra had talked about a new kind of dragon, a long-wyrm, that fit the description. More importantly, she'd told him about the long-wyrm riders. These creatures weren't as smart as other dragons and were closer in intelligence and temperament to horses.

He could still hear Vance and Thorny talking. They didn't sound particularly nervous. From time to time a little girl's voice chimed in. And, there was an older male voice, gruff and gravelly. Bitterwood?

He steadied himself with a hand against the wall and rose. He didn't bother trying to find his crutch. He hopped into the doorway and studied the scene once more. Beyond the long-wyrm, there was the glow of a fire. This is where the voices were coming from.

The long-wyrm turned its head to him once more, but didn't show any signs of attacking. It seemed merely aware.

"Thorny?" Burke called out.

Thorny stood up on the other side of the long-wyrm. "Burke! Sorry. We didn't mean to wake you. We have visitors."

"I see," said Burke.

A second man rose up beside Thorny. He wore a heavy cloak, his face hidden in the shadows of the cowl. "You look like hell, Kanati," the man said.

"It is you," said Burke. "Now I see why you didn't want a horse. I take it this beast is yours?"

"He belongs to Zeeky, actually."

The little girl's voice called out, "No he doesn't! Skitter's my friend, not my property!"

Burke hopped out of the chicken coop, keeping his hand on the wall for balance. Vance ran to his side to help him hop to the fire.

In addition to Bitterwood and Thorny a boy slept on a blanket by the fire, and a small, blonde girl he assumed was Zeeky sat next to him. There was also a pig, wearing a metallic visor and a sneer.

Vance helped lower Burke to the ground only a few feet from the fire. Burke welcomed the heat. He hadn't been truly warm since he crawled out of the river. Not so long ago, whenever he closed his eyes, he would see visions of new weapons he might design. Now, he kept imagining bath tubs continuously filled with hot water, regulated by a finely-balanced system of pipes and gauges.

"This is Zeeky," said Bitterwood. "The pig is Poocher."

"I've never been introduced to a pig before," said Burke.

"Poocher's family," said Bitterwood. "Sleepyhead over there is Jeremiah. Keep your distance. He's got yellow-mouth."

"Oh," said Burke. He'd never had the disease. He wasn't certain in his weakened state he'd survive it. "How'd you find us?"

"Skitter smelled cooking possum," said Zeeky.

"Skitter?"

"The long-wyrm," said Bitterwood.

Zeeky said, "Normally, I would have had him ride past the campsite, but the villagers whispered that a friend of Bitterwood's was nearby, so I let him follow his nose."

"The villagers?" Burke asked. "From Burke's Tavern?"

"No. From Big Lick."

"They're ghosts," said Bitterwood.

Burke frowned.

"You don't believe in ghosts, do you?" Bitterwood said. "I remember back at Conyers—you didn't believe me when I told you I'd seen a devil get his head chopped off and keep fighting, sticking his head back on and killing the dragons that had decapitated him. You didn't believe in gods or ghosts, angels or devils. I've since fought all these things and worse. There's more to this world than you understand, Burke."

The toes of Burke's phantom foot thawed as the fire penetrated into his phantom boot. He wasn't in the mood to reopen this old debate.

Zeeky opened it for him. "They ain't ghosts," she said. She held out a crystal ball. The firelight danced across its surface. "They never died. They just don't have bodies no more. The world inside this crystal ball isn't like our own. There's nothing solid there. Everything exists like a dream. The villagers can see into our world if they try, but, for the most part, they're learning to get by in their new world."

The hair on the back of Burke's neck rose. "Are you talking about underspace?"

"That's what the goddess called it," said Zeeky.

"That's Atlantean science," said Burke. He scratched the stump of his leg as he pondered this. His training was in metallurgy and engineering. Over in Tennessee, he'd had relatives charged with solving the mysteries of extra-dimensional space, but Burke had always preferred to study things he could do something about.

"I met an Atlantean once," said Bitterwood. "She healed my hands after they'd been bit off by a dragon."

"Your hands were... of course. Atlanteans were masters of technologies far beyond our imagination. Jandra said she used to have healing powers." He looked toward Vance. "Could that seed you ate have been from Atlantis?"

Vance shrugged, looking as if he didn't understand the question.

"Jandra's healing powers are the reason we're traveling this way," said Bitterwood. "Hex stole the source of her powers—"

"The genie," said Burke, feeling like his mind was suddenly full of jigsaw pieces that he could almost, but not quite, fit together.

"When I met Hex in Rorg's cavern, he told me he'd buried the genie in the one place humans would never look for it. The way I figure, the last place humans would go look for anything would be the Free City. So we're going there to hunt for the genie. I don't know how to use it, but it's something I have to try. It may be able to cure Jeremiah."

Two puzzle pieces clicked together in Burke's head. "Shanna said she'd come from the Free City. She had healing seeds. Her body had been repaired to the point that she no longer had tattoos. It suddenly makes sense. Someone has found the genie in the Free City and is using it to heal people. Jandra told me the genie wouldn't work for anyone but her, but it looks like she was wrong."

"There are humans at the Free City?" Bitterwood asked. "When I was there a few weeks ago, I saw earth-dragons around it. I figured refugees from Dragon Forge were using it."

Burke looked down at his missing leg. His armpit throbbed. He thought of Vance's restored vision and Bitterwood's regrown hands. Could he one day walk again?

Zeeky looked up from the crystal ball with a serene smile upon her lips. "We shall all be healed."

CHAPTER TWENTY-SIX

RESPONSIBILITY TO MANKIND

BURKE GRIPPED THE edge of the saddle so hard his knuckles turned white. The long-wyrm flew across the landscape at a breakneck speed. They avoided the main road, splashing along the twisting beds of a stream as they raced eastward toward the Free City. The creature veered up a steep river bank, running perpendicular to the water below. Given the speed with which they traveled and the ruggedness of the terrain, Burke couldn't believe he hadn't been thrown off the beast. His butt stayed planted firmly on the smooth saddle, as if it were a powerful magnet and the seat of his pants were steel.

As strange as the circumstance of his ride were, there were stranger things still on his mind. Bitterwood rode on the saddle before him carrying Jeremiah in his arms. The boy's face was corpse white, glistening with sweat. The boy somehow slept through the convolutions of the long-wyrm, his mouth hanging open. His gums were pus yellow.

Bitterwood risked his life by carrying the boy. Yet, not only did he hold him, he cradled him. He stroked the boy's brow and whispered encouragements.

"This is a side of you I've never seen, Bant," said Burke. "I didn't know you had such fatherly instincts."

"I wasn't always the Ghost Who Kills. I had a family once, long ago. I would rather have lived my life as a father than as an avenger."

Burke shook his head as his own regrets welled up. "I've had the opportunity to live as both and I've failed at both. I have no idea where Anza is. You tell me she's gone off to try to recapture the shotgun Vulpine stole, but that could be anywhere, and it will be heavily guarded. It's a terrible risk to chase after it. She'll keep trying to retrieve it until she succeeds, or she's killed. Why didn't I tell her that her life means more to me than the gun does? What if I never learn of her fate?"

"Anza struck me as a woman who could take care of herself," said Bitterwood.

"Maybe. But then what? She'll return to Dragon Forge looking for me, and Ragnar's men will ambush her. Ragnar has a whole army to throw against her, all armed with the guns I designed. Anza's fast, but not faster than a shotgun blast. I can't believe how badly I've let things spin out of control."

Bitterwood narrowed his eyes. "This has always been your great flaw. You treat the world as if it's a giant machine, and if you can only find the right screws to tighten, you can make the whole thing hum."

"Someone's hand needs to be on the controls," said Burke.

"*There are no controls*," said Bitterwood. "There is no mainspring. Your pride blinds you to this simple truth."

"What have I done to piss you off?"

"You started another revolution you couldn't finish," said Bitterwood.

"Technically, Ragnar started it," said Burke. "One might even argue that you started it by killing Albekizan."

Bitterwood turned his back on Burke.

Burke reached out with his crutch and poked him on the shoulder. "I'm not done talking."

"I am," said Bitterwood.

"I've listened to your criticism. You're going to listen to mine. I'm not angry that you killed Albekizan. Your guerilla warfare tactics of the last twenty years have been far more effective than I would have guessed. But I've never figured out what it was you were hoping to accomplish. Ridding the planet of one dragon at a time isn't going to save humanity."

Bitterwood looked back. His face was in shadows beneath his hood. "I care nothing for the fate of humanity. I only want to make certain that dragons suffer at least a fraction of the pain they've caused me."

"That's where we differ. All I've ever wanted was to give humans an equal footing—or better still, an upper hand—when dealing with the dragons. That's never going to happen while men choose to follow fanatics like Ragnar. Mysticism and charisma have a way of trumping logic."

"'Choose' is an interesting word," said Bitterwood. "Did you ever offer the men of Dragon Forge a choice? Did you ever say to them, 'I lead, or Ragnar leads, decide?'"

Burke shook his head. "Ragnar gathered the army. They were loyal to him. They cheered his firebrand speeches. What did I have to offer anyone other than gadgets and advice on sanitation?"

Vance, on the saddle behind Burke, spoke up. "I would have chosen you as the leader in a heartbeat. So would any of the sky-wall team."

Burke shook his head, rejecting Vance's words. "The members of the sky-wall team cheered Ragnar on during his little fire-sermon before the invasion. They lift up their hands in rapture whenever he preaches of war."

"That's because he's making a stand," said Vance. "We're all tired of living under the shadow of dragons. We'll cheer any man who fights them. Ragnar has been willing to get out in front of us. You haven't. You've worked behind the scenes, a plotter, a planner, but never a leader."

Burke grit his teeth as the long-wyrm splashed across a narrow ford in the stream. Vance was right. He was a planner at heart. He'd never thought of this as a character flaw. Nor had he thought that wanting to remain in control of events was a negative trait. This was why he liked machines. He could control all the variables. If one part of the machine failed, he could toss out that part and design a replacement. But the mob Ragnar had gathered... how could he control such a motley collection of variables? They were people with unknown abilities, fighting and acting with unknown motivations.

With a shiver, he sat bolt upright in his saddle. This is why he'd raised Anza in such a mechanistic fashion. He'd programmed her to behave the way he thought a rational being should behave. She was his ultimate exercise in controlling all the variables in a human life.

He'd taught her that maintaining control by tracking down and recovering the stolen shotgun was more important than her own safety.

Even Bitterwood was a better father.

* * *

SHAY RODE THE wind high above Dragon Forge. Far below, the fortress was a small gray diamond set in a broad circle of red clay. He was so far up that he could hold out his hand and cover the whole town. It was midday, with a clear blue sky above him; the air was clean enough that he could see Talon Lake and the Nest thirty miles to the west. The distant waters gleamed like a mirror.

The blue sky filled him with despair. All three of the smokestacks in Dragon Forge were lifeless. The fires of the revolution had gone out.

Shay shivered and pulled his collar higher. The air up here was frightfully cold. He wasn't sure how high he was flying. He was certain it was over a mile, perhaps even two miles. The few guards moving along the walls of Dragon Forge were nothing more than specks. He doubted anyone below could see him. He suspected the wings would fly even higher, though his lungs kept him from testing the notion. Beyond this height, he grew lightheaded due to the thinness of the air.

Sky-dragons circled far below, patrolling in a rough circle around Dragon Forge. Shay could also see dragon troops encamped along the roads leading to the city. It looked like a blockade, a fairly obvious tactic for dealing with an entrenched enemy. Surprisingly, none of the sky-dragons appeared to have seen him. He was high enough that they were the size of flies. No doubt he was only a speck to them as well. Or perhaps dragons simply didn't bother with looking up. They had no predators in the sky; all their threats were on the ground.

Shay wasn't happy about the events that had caused him to be the world's only winged human. He'd rather have Jandra than the wings. But perhaps there was some good that would come from his sorrow. With his wings, he could fly higher, faster, and further than any dragon. He was still firmly committed to the cause of human liberty, despite Ragnar's rather chilly reception. Burke would definitely understand the tactical importance of humans having control of their own wings. He hoped Jandra was right about the technological origins of the wings; if they were nothing but machines, then perhaps Burke could reproduce them. If they were magic, then they would be beyond even the Machinist's understanding.

Getting down into the fort was no easy task, given that the sky-wall archers were likely to fill the sky with arrows the second he approached. The dragons might not be looking up, but the humans almost certainly were. Could he dive fast enough to avoid the arrows, and then pull from the dive quickly enough to survive the drop? If only there was some way of doing this... invisibly.

He looked at Jandra's bracelet on his wrist. When she'd used it before, she'd simply struck it hard against the stone. She said a strong jolt would activate the tiny machines that could produce invisibility.

Shay pulled the angel's blade from beneath his coat. He'd learned that he could control the heat of the weapon with but a thought. Right now, the blade was merely warm. The broad side of the sword provided a flat, hard surface. He banged Jandra's bracelet against it and the light around him dimmed.

HEX'S NOSTRILS TWITCHED as he caught the distinctive smell of a long-wyrm. As quickly as he'd detected it, the odor vanished. He circled back, searching for the tendril of breeze that had carried the aroma. Long-wyrm scents were an intriguing mix—snake mixed with sulfur mixed with crushed beetles. Ten minutes of searching the air proved fruitless. Had it only been his imagination? He hadn't eaten anything in over a day—his tongue was sore and swollen. Even sipping water was painful. Maybe his mind was playing tricks on him.

Fortunately, Hex was almost at his destination. Off in the distance was the Dragon Palace. His eyes were instantly drawn to the black jagged spire that had once been the Grand Library, now gutted by fire. His heart ached as he thought of all the history and wisdom within its walls, forever lost. Yet, perhaps it was for the best. The books within that tower told of a history of conquest and oppression. It was an age he was happy to see at its end. The era of kings was truly past.

As he studied the burnt tower, he noticed the wooden fortress a few miles beyond. This was the Free City—a clever death-trap designed by his uncle Blasphet and built using the wealth and armies of his father, Albekizan. When last he'd visited the structure, it had been abandoned. Now, it was bustling. Thousands of tents dotted the fields around the city. Within the walls, countless bodies swarmed over the dozens of large buildings under construction.

His mouth went dry. He'd chosen the Free City to hide the genie because he was certain no one would search there. He hadn't expected it to grow overnight into one of the largest human cities he'd ever seen. Or was it a human city? He strained to make sense of the moving figures. There were definitely earth-dragons side-by-side with the men. Here and there, the bright blue form of a sky-dragon flitted from one side of the city to the other.

He squinted harder. Always in the past, when he'd seen the various races gathered like this at construction sites, the division of labor had been clear.

Sky-dragons were architects, earth-dragons were bosses, and humans did the actual work. Here, everyone was working. None of the earth-dragons wore armor or carried weapons. Most were dressed in simple white tunics, as were the humans. There were no glowering slavecatchers watching over the scene. What was going on?

His nose once more picked up a few stray molecules of long-wyrm stink. He flared his nostrils, seeking the trail, his head snaking from side to side as he tested the relative strength of the aroma.

It was unmistakable now. He dropped lower in the sky, his eyes darting across the landscape, seeking the flash of copper that would reveal a long-wyrm's presence. There! The bright scales of a long-wyrm shimmered through the leafless thickets by the river. The beast raced along with sinuous grace, seeming to fly as its many limbs worked in perfect harmony. Hex tilted in the sky, the cool wind soothing his aching muscles as he fixed his wings to glide on an intercepting pass.

The long-wyrm was absolutely studded with riders. At the rear-most saddle sat a young girl with flowing blonde hair—Zeeky, no doubt, though at this distance, with her back to him, he supposed there was a tiny chance he could be wrong, and that this could be some other girl riding a long-wyrm with a pig seated in front of her.

In front of the pig were three men Hex had never seen before, and, in the forward saddle sat a man in a familiar cloak. Bitterwood! He carried someone in his lap, a sleeping girl with similar blond hair. Or was it a girl? More logically, this was Zeeky's brother, Jeremiah.

Hex was almost at the level of the tree tops and only a few hundred yards behind the long-wyrm. He beat his wing to accelerate. The sound caught the ears of one of the humans—the young man sitting two saddles back from Bitterwood. The man turned, revealing a face covered with wispy facial hair. His eyes bulged somewhat comically as they fixed on Hex's approaching form.

It was much less comical when the man leapt up to stand on his saddle and produced a sky-wall bow, placing an arrow against the string with lightning reflexes. Hex was too close to climb out of the bow's range, but not close enough to charge the man and reach him before he fired. At this distance, the man would have to be a horrible marksman not to place an arrow somewhere within Hex's forty-foot wingspan. He braced himself for the impact.

Before the man could release his arrow, however, Zeeky jumped up in her own saddle and shouted, "Stop! He's a friend!"

The long-wyrm undulated to a graceful halt. The bowman leapt from his saddle to the ground, arrow still against the string, wary as Hex swung his legs forward to land. Hex hit the gravel of the riverbank with a lopsided stance. He flapped his wings to keep his torso from smashing into the rocks. His huge wings snapped the branches of the bushes lining the banks as he skidded to a halt. It wasn't graceful, but in his present condition anything that brought him to the ground in one piece was a good landing.

"Thank you, Zeeky," said Hex. His tongue felt swollen and stiff. "I'm happy you consider me a friend."

Bitterwood carefully dismounted, cradling Jeremiah in his arms. The boy's pale face glistened with sweat. Hex instantly recognized the scent of yellow-mouth.

Bitterwood said, "This boy is dying. We need Jandra's genie now. Go to the Free City and bring it to us."

"I... how did you know it was at the Free City?"

"You sun-dragons never really accept that people are as smart as you. You practically told me where it was buried, thinking I wouldn't be clever enough to figure it out."

Hex pressed his damaged tongue against the roof of his mouth, sucking to soothe the pain as he thought about how much he should reveal to Bitterwood. "You're right," he said. "I buried the genie in the Free City. It was a foolish choice of hiding places. Have you seen what's happening there?"

The one-legged man who was still seated on the long-wyrm spoke up. "Let me guess. A couple of hundred women are running around in white robes." The man was about Bitterwood's age. His skin was darker than Bitterwood's, and his gray-streaked black hair was pulled into a braid decorated with bright red sun-dragon feather-scales. His face had the balance of a sculpture—a square jaw, and a sharp, angular nose—though the symmetry was broken by three parallel scars that graced his right cheek. "Apparently, they've gathered there to worship some sort of healer. We had one of their disciples visit Dragon Forge."

"There are more than a few hundred," said Hex. "I saw thousands. And not only women. Men, as well, plus earth-dragons and sky-dragons. They're working together to expand the Free City. I'll dig up the genie if it's undisturbed, but if a mob tries to stop me, I'm not certain what I can do. My encounter with the goddess has left me weakened."

"The goddess?" Bitterwood said.

"My suspicion that she survived inside Jandra has proven accurate," said Hex. "Her mind controls

Jandra's body. It's lucky I've found you; we think our one hope of capturing Jazz will be if she tries to kidnap Zeeky again, or take revenge on you."

"We?" asked Bitterwood.

"Shay also survived the encounter with the goddess. He's gone to Dragon Forge to find you, in fact."

The dark-haired man frowned. "The goddess will go to Dragon Forge once she learns about the guns. Once she's done there, she'll no doubt come looking for me. She's had a thousand year agenda to keep the world free of guns. I doubt she'll give up now."

Hex furrowed his brow. This human was curiously well-informed about the goddess. "Who are you?"

The man crossed his arms. "You can call me Burke," he said. "I think it's time we found a good hiding place and stopped to compare notes. I'm pretty sure Jandra's genie has already been found. Jandra said it gave her healing powers. Not that long ago, our friend Vance"—he nodded toward the young man with the sky-wall bow—"was blind."

"He's been healed?"

"He ate a seed left behind by a woman who said she was a disciple of a healer in the Free City."

Vance lowered his bow, apparently content that Hex wasn't a threat. He said, "It wasn't only my eyes that got better. All my scars healed up. I used to have a doozy on my left foot from a bad swing chopping wood. It's gone now."

"We don't have hours to sit around and talk," said Bitterwood. "Jeremiah is growing weaker by the minute."

Hex nodded. "We'll talk as we travel. If the denizens of the Free City are offering healing, it looks as if several of you can make use of them."

Burke raised his hand to his cheek and traced the scars there as Bitterwood and Vance climbed back onto the long-wyrm.

The last man on the copper serpent nodded toward Hex. He was older than Burke or Bitterwood; snaggle-toothed, with a wild mane of gray hair and hands knotted with arthritis. "If no one else is going to bother to introduce me, I'll do it myself. Thor Nightingale. Most folks call me Thorny."

"Hexilizan. My friends call me Hex."

Thorny grinned. "What do your enemies call you?"

"I call him Hex, too," said Bitterwood.

"It's probably best if I approach on foot. They'll quickly spot me if I'm airborne." In truth, Hex wasn't certain he had the energy to get airborne. Flying was demanding work. Sun-dragons normally ate voraciously to fuel the muscles that allowed them to lift their massive bodies into the sky. With his damaged tongue thwarting his appetite, he was quickly exhausting the last of his strength. It was probably best that Bitterwood did not suspect this.

Hex noticed as Bitterwood settled onto his saddle that the living bow strung with the goddess's hair was intact once more, and Bitterwood's quiver was full. Hex wasn't certain he could successfully fend off an attack if Bitterwood's bloodlust returned. Yet, the hatred that normally burned in Bitterwood's eyes was missing. Instead, all that remained was worry. The aging dragon-hunter wiped the sweat from Jeremiah's brow with the edge of his cloak. The boy murmured softly in his feverish slumber.

"It's going to be all right," Bitterwood whispered.

SHAY FLOATED DOWN to a landing in the middle of the main street, near the foundry that housed Burke's loft. His landing stirred up the sooty dust that covered the road. The bacon and egg smoke that had hung thick in the atmosphere was gone, replaced with the stench of raw sewage. He'd noticed while in the sky that the dragons had built a dam on the canal that emptied the city's sewers.

The town was eerily silent, absent of the sounds of hammers and foremen shouting. The handful of people left on the streets wore handkerchiefs over their mouths. It was as if most of the town had left and only a few bandits remained behind.

Shay folded his wings and wondered what it would take to turn off the invisibility that had allowed him safe passage into the town without attracting the attention of the sky-wall. Glancing toward the nearest wall, he saw only three bowmen. When he'd left, the walls had been thick with guards. As he pondered the control of his invisibility, he noticed a slight shift in the light. He once more had a shadow.

He bowed his head as he headed into the building that housed Burke's loft. Perhaps no one would recognize him; he'd certainly not been in town long enough to leave much of an impression.

Within the foundry, it was cold and dim, with only the occasional lantern piercing the gloom. The building wasn't completely uninhabited. A handful of workers were gathered at various stations along the work flow, tinkering with machinery. Had the production line encountered some mechanical failure?

He didn't dare risk speaking to anyone until he talked to Burke. He didn't know who might be loyal to Ragnar. His eyes searched the dim light for the elevator cage. Spotting it, he strode briskly toward it.

He was brought to a halt by a big, calloused hand that fell on his shoulder, and a voice that said, "Shay? What are you doing back?"

Shay looked behind him and found, to his relief, that the hand belonged to Burke's friend Biscuit. He recognized the rotund, bald man even though Biscuit had apparently suffered misfortune in his absence. He now wore a leather patch over his right eye. "I'm glad it's you. I need to see Burke."

Biscuit's jaw tightened. "Burke isn't here any more."

"What?" Shay said, louder than he should have. All the other workers were staring at him now. He lowered his voice as he asked, "Where is he?"

Biscuit frowned. "Burke was disloyal to the cause. He fled town when confronted. We think the dragons killed him at the southern bridge."

"Disloyal to the… Burke *was* the cause! He was the whole reason this rebellion stood a chance!"

Biscuit shook his head, looking sad. Before he could say anything, a new voice interrupted: "Boy, this rebellion succeeded because of Ragnar and his faith."

Shay turned to find the white-bearded blacksmith called Frost behind him. The ear Jandra had shot off was a mass of white scar tissue clinging to the side of his head, dotted with brown, peeling scabs. Frost approached until he was inches from Shay's face and said, "Burke was trying to sabotage us. He killed a dozen men. If he's dead, good riddance."

Shay wanted to back away from Frost. His eyes were bloodshot and his breath stank of goom. He was looking for an excuse for a fight. Shay clenched his fists and held his ground. He was taller than Frost. He straightened to his full height and looked down into Frost's eyes. "How about Bitterwood? Would he be welcome here? Because that's who I'm really looking for." Frost's left cheek twitched at the mention of the name.

Biscuit said, "A man claiming to be Bitterwood was here a few days ago. He took the boy with yellow-mouth and left."

"Yellow-mouth?" said Shay. "Is that why the streets are so empty?"

Biscuit nodded. "The men are all staying indoors."

"To avoid those with the disease?"

Biscuit stared at Frost. He looked afraid. Frost carried a weapon resembling a short shotgun tucked into his belt. The barrel was less than half the length; it looked as if it could be held in one hand. Frost's palm rested on the butt of the gun. Shay noticed the bloody bandage on his wrist.

Biscuit chose his words carefully. "Avoiding the disease is one theory."

"You've let the foundries stop running because of this?" Shay asked, incredulous. "The disease is dangerous, yes, but with proper sanitation and a little—"

Frost yelled, "The disease is under control!" His spittle flecked Shay's cheeks. "The furnaces have stopped 'cause we don't wanna run out of coal. We can't get any more."

"I see," said Shay, wiping his cheeks as he backed away. Standing his ground wasn't as important as not getting goom-spat. He knew there was still a sizable mound of coal out back; he'd seen it from the air. Of course, there had also been hundreds of coal wagons backed up along the Western Road.

"How did you get in?" Biscuit asked. "The only people the dragons have let slip past have been the sick and the disabled. You're the first halfway healthy man I've seen get past the blockade."

Shay decided that mentioning the wings—or Jandra's bracelet—would be unwise. If Bitterwood had already been here and left, and Burke was dead, his immediate reason for staying was gone. On the other hand, with or without Burke, Dragon Forge was too important to the human cause to fail. Jandra was his top priority, but he had recovered items in the long-wyrm barracks that could give humans the upper hand in this war.

He closed his eyes. The vision of *The Origin of Species* crumbling to ash flickered before him. The last person he wanted to talk to was Ragnar. Yet, like it or not, Ragnar was the power in Dragon Forge. It was Shay's responsibility to mankind to see that he did not fail.

"I can help break the blockade. I need to speak to Ragnar."

CHAPTER TWENTY-SEVEN

THUNDER ON A CLOUDLESS DAY

JEREMIAH SHIVERED AGAINST Bitterwood's chest. "I-it's c-c-cold," he whispered through cracked lips.

The boy's breath was as hot as a furnace. Bitterwood pulled the filthy blanket that swaddled Jeremiah higher up on his chin. He knew that a thousand blankets wouldn't be enough to make the boy feel warm.

"We'll be inside soon," Bitterwood said softly, brushing the boy's matted hair away from his eyes. "I promise we'll find you a proper bed, and some hot soup."

"I-I'm n-not h-hun…" Jeremiah's voice trailed off.

Jeremiah was slipping in and out of sleep without bothering to open his eyes. Bitterwood wasn't certain if the boy was even aware that Hex had joined them. He showed no awareness of their odd surroundings.

They rode through the forest of tents that surrounded the Free City. Flaps were pushed aside as men and women peeked out to stare at the gleaming long-wyrm and the sun-dragon walking beside it with a noticeable limp. Here and there among the crowd, the dark green turtle-faces of earth-dragons could be seen. They were as curious as the humans, and showed no signs of hostility. The last time Bitterwood had approached the Free City, the only earth-dragons in sight had been armed soldiers, pushing their captives along at spear point.

"I didn't know there were so many people in the world," Vance said softly.

Bitterwood remembered how small the world had seemed to him back in his own youth. Until the dragons burned Christdale, he'd never journeyed more than thirty miles from his birthplace. The true scope of the world had been impossible to fathom.

"There are far more people here than at Dragon Forge," said Burke as he surveyed the crowd. "Are these refugees who were turned away by the blockade? Or perhaps chaos is spreading further through the kingdom than we knew?"

Hex's scales bristled at the use of the word "chaos." "It isn't chaos that's spreading," the sun-dragon said. "It's freedom. The authoritarian regime that enslaved these people is gone, leaving them free to follow their own destinies."

"If following their own destinies means abandoning their homes to live in tents, I fear their destinies will be short and sad," said Burke. "Think of all the abandoned villages we've seen. Spring is coming. Who will plant the crops? Where will the food to feed everyone come from by next summer?"

"The beasts of the forest survive without farming," said Hex. "The world is bountiful."

"Hex, as I understand it, you've lived most of your life in a library on the Isle of Horses. You have an overly romantic view of nature, I fear. I've spent a fair amount of my youth in the forest. It's not as full of food as you might think."

"My views aren't romantic," said Hex. "I'm simply able to see the evil that has been inflicted on both men and dragons in the name of order."

"I'll take order over chaos any day."

"This is a curious argument for a revolutionary to make."

"Seizing Dragon Forge was the first step to imposing a new order," said Burke. "Anarchy was never the goal."

"*Impose* is a telling verb," said Hex. "If the rebellion at Dragon Forge is intended to be the first step toward a human war of genocide against dragons, rest assured I will destroy your rebellion. I haven't helped take the slavecatcher's whip away from the dragons in order to give it to humans."

"Someone's hand is always going to be holding the whip," Burke said. "It's the way the world works. It's the lesson of history."

"I intend to bring an end to history. I want to live in a world where the strength of ideas has more power than the strength of arms."

Bitterwood had heard enough. "You're a hypocrite, Hex. You didn't persuade Rorg with the force of your ideas. You didn't change Shandrazel's mind with an argument. Everything you've accomplished of note you've done through violence—you slaughtered Rorg and you allowed your own brother to die. You call yourself a warrior philosopher, but you're nothing but a long-winded bully."

Hex looked around at the throng of refugees who stared at them. "Bullies use their strength against those who are weaker. I've stood up to would-be kings and would-be gods. These humans have nothing to fear from me."

"Unless they join the rebellion under their own free will, and you try to crush it," said Burke.

Hex shook his head. "If they don't become oppressors, they have nothing to fear. Any hand that would reach for a whip, however,"—he turned his gaze toward Burke—"will find itself bitten off."

By now, they reached the gates of the Free City. A quartet of young women in white cloaks, their faces shadowed by large hoods, approached cautiously.

One held out her hand and said, "Greetings, brothers," then spotting Zeeky near the back of the long-wyrm she added, "and sister. Welcome to the Free City. Many among you appear injured. You shall all be healed."

"We need to see the healer now," said Bitterwood.

The woman pushed back her hood, looking sympathetic to Bitterwood's need. She patiently explained, "The increase of supplicants in recent days is placing great demands upon the healer's time. He only attends to those with the gravest needs. The rest of you will be cared for by his disciples, who will administer the dragonseed."

"'Disciples' is a word with religious overtones," said Hex. "Does this healer claim to be a god?"

The woman smiled gently. "He makes no claims to godhood. He says he is, instead, a servant to us all."

"He's the servant?" Hex asked, sounding skeptical.

Bitterwood sensed that Hex might be on the verge of a diatribe on the political implications of a servant/master relationship and decided to nip off the argument before it began.

"This boy has yellow-mouth," said Bitterwood. "He may not survive the day. Can your healer save him?"

The woman approached the long-wyrm. She reached up and stroked Jeremiah's sweat-beaded brow, frowning with concern. She said, "We shall take him to see the healer immediately. Give him to us."

"I'll carry him," said Bitterwood. "I want to stay with him."

"We'll all stay with him," Zeeky said.

The woman looked back toward her three companions. Some unspoken communication took place, ending with a nod by all four.

"Very well," said the woman. "We'll lead you to the healer. Dismount and we'll tend to your steed, seeing that it has water and food... though, I confess, I'm unfamiliar with this beast. What does it eat?"

"Pretty much anything," said Zeeky, hopping down from her saddle. "Oats would be great. Don't leave him alone around any small animals, though. He'll gulp down a chicken before you can blink."

Bitterwood was surprised that Zeeky was surrendering Skitter to the women. From her body language, Zeeky didn't appear worried about their intentions. Bitterwood wasn't as certain, though he couldn't say why. There was nothing overtly sinister about these women. That only added to his sense that they were walking into a snake pit. But, if he had to walk into hell itself to save Jeremiah, he would. He slid down from his saddle as the others dismounted.

Hex extended his fore-talon to help Burke balance himself. Burke looked skeptical, then placed his hand on the claw and lowered himself to the ground.

"Thanks," he said.

Skitter followed one of the women toward the stables as the first woman led the motley collection of men, sun-dragon, girl, and pig through the busy streets of the city. The scent of fresh-cut pine hung heavy in the air. Hammer blows echoed from all directions.

Burke limped more rapidly on his crutch until he was just behind the woman. "How are they feeding all these workers?"

"Our healer is also our provider," said the woman. "I've witnessed him take a bag of grain, and pour it into an empty bag. Once that bag is full, another is brought, then another, then another. From a single bag, he may fill forty of the same size. There is no hunger here."

"That's what was said about the Free City when Blasphet ran it," said Burke. "This city was sold as a sanctuary where all human needs would be met. But once everyone was inside the gates, the true plan was for it to become a mill of death."

"You speak of the time when Blasphet was known as the Murder God."

"Yes," said Burke.

"Blasphet, the Murder God, is dead," said the woman. "According to the healer, a new Murder God has taken his place."

"A new Murder God?"

"Yes. The beast who murdered the Murder God. His unholy name is…" the woman paused, frowning, as if the name were sour on her tongue. When she finally spoke, her voice dripped with contempt. "He is known as the Death of All Dragons. He is called the Ghost Who Kills. His unholy name is Bitterwood."

SHAY WALKED WITH Biscuit on one side of him and Frost on the other. Biscuit looked disgusted as Frost stumbled on the steps of one of the nicer buildings Shay had seen in Dragon Forge, a stately two-story house built of brick, with slate shingles and glass windows.

"This was Charkon's residence," said Biscuit.

"Ah," said Shay. Charkon had been the boss of Dragon Forge. It made sense that an earth-dragon of his reputation would have a better home than the dragons who worked beneath him. It made sense, as well, that Ragnar should claim possession of the house. Shay guessed that, inside, he would find many of the spoils of war being used for Ragnar's comfort.

Instead, when the door opened, pulled from within by the giant bodyguard Stonewall, Shay saw that the interior of the house was almost empty. The large central room had been stripped bare, with the only furnishing present being an iron cross forged from the blades of four swords leaning against a brick wall. Ragnar knelt before this cross, his head lowered so that his bushy mane touched the floor.

Stonewall stepped outside and closed the door behind him.

"This boy wants to see Ragnar," said Frost. A slight belch punctuated his sentence.

"Ragnar's praying," Stonewall said. "He's not to be disturbed. I saw your approach from the window." Stonewall looked at Shay with a thoughtful gaze. "You're the escaped slave who brought the books. I don't believe I ever learned your name."

"Shay. It's important I talk to Ragnar."

Stonewall shook his head. "I'm sorry. The prophet's present conversation is with someone more important. He's praying for divine assistance to deal with the rumors of yellow-mouth."

"Rumors?" said Shay. "I thought there were people actually sick from the disease."

"There was a single boy who vomited," said Stonewall. "Bitterwood took him. We quarantined two dozen men who had contact with him. So far, there have been no symptoms."

"Then why have the foundry fires died?" asked Shay. "You're surrounded by dragons on all sides. I would run the foundry until every man in Dragon Forge had a gun, or even a dozen guns. From my vantage point, I spotted catapults ringing the city. It looks as if the dragons may be preparing an attack."

"The foundry workers are damn cowards," muttered Frost.

Biscuit ground his teeth loudly enough for Shay to hear. He grumbled, "No man wants to be seen in public if the next time he coughs he's going to be thrown into the quarantine barracks—or the furnace."

"Are you trying to start something?" Frost asked, his hand falling back to the modified gun on his belt. "Speak carefully. You still have one eye." He hiccupped.

"Have you been drinking?" Stonewall asked before Biscuit could answer.

Frost turned pale. "Of course not. Ragnar forbids all alcohol."

Shay said, "What happened to Burke? He could have managed an outbreak of disease. He wouldn't have let the foundries shut down."

Stonewall crossed his arms. "Burke also wouldn't share his knowledge freely with his fellow men. His pride prevented him from telling Ragnar all his secrets. In his disbelief, he lacked a moral compass to guide him to the greater good. In the end, he killed a dozen men as he fled the city. He destroyed the southern gate, exposing us to the risk of attack; we've set up a barrier, but it's impossible to describe the harm Burke has done to our cause."

Shay clenched his fists. He wanted to scream at the stupidity of Stonewall's words, but fought to keep his cool. "Don't talk to me about sharing knowledge. I came here with books filled with information and ideas that could have helped launch a new human age. Ragnar took those books and flung them into the fire. Ragnar gave Burke every reason to be cautious about sharing what he knew."

Stonewall said, "Ragnar threw only one book into the fire. He had me gather up the rest. I still have them. He forgot about them five minutes after we left the loft. The prophet has many things on his mind."

"You have the books?"

"I'm a voracious reader. I was curious as to their contents," said Stonewall. "The Drifting Isles are remote and lonely. Books are highly valued there."

Shay was confused. It must have shown in his face, because Stonewall said, "You seem to think that because I'm a man of faith, I'm also a man of ignorance. It's a prejudice that Burke shared, I'm afraid."

"According to Chapelion, faith is the opposite of knowledge," said Shay. "It's difficult, I admit, to think that you can be well-read and still believe that Ragnar speaks directly with God."

Frost let loose a low growl as his fingers fondled the butt of his gun. "You're getting mighty close to blasphemy, boy."

Stonewall's eyes twinkled. He didn't look offended by Shay's argument. "You aren't so different from me, Shay. You place your faith in books. You've read things written long ago and believe them, even though these events unfolded centuries before your birth, and there's no direct evidence that they actually occurred. How am I any different? I've read a book that taught me that God chooses men from time to time as his prophets, to guide his people through periods of darkness. Ragnar is one of these men."

Shay started to speak, but held his tongue. He was getting sidetracked from his main mission. Stonewall evidently mistook his pause as an invitation for further explanation. "Some force spared Ragnar when dragons slew his family. Some force gave him the gift of persuasion that has allowed a man so young to gather so many followers. Some force placed Ragnar at the Free City, where he helped defeat Albekizan and Kanst and Blasphet. This same guiding force led Ragnar to gather the refugees into an army and seize control of this fortress. You weren't here to see him fight. With no armor, Ragnar plunges into the thick of battle and emerges with nothing but scratches. If you cannot accept this as evidence that he's God's chosen, then no evidence in the world will ever lead you to the truth."

"He could also just be lucky," said Shay. "I should have been killed a half dozen times in recent days. I'm alive more due to chance than to my own efforts. But I don't regard a little luck as evidence that I'm one of God's chosen. I've also had my share of misfortune." He felt a cold, hard spot in his belly as he thought of Jandra.

"One of the books you brought spoke of an invisible hand that guides the economies of mankind," said Stonewall. "I believe in an invisible hand that guides all men in all actions. Even you, Shay."

Shay grimaced. He hadn't come here to debate philosophy. "We're wasting time," he said. "I have to find Bitterwood, before the goddess finds him."

"The goddess is only a false idol, Shay," said Stonewall.

"This false idol almost killed me and she's currently possessing Jandra, whose life means a great deal to me. I can't stay here until Ragnar finishes talking to his invisible hand. I have a secret that can help you break the blockade."

"Let's hear it."

"When we were in the kingdom of the goddess we found wings that let a man fly. I gave them to... to a friend to carry. I have six pairs, not counting my own. With them, you can outfly dragons. It's how I got here. You could fly over the blockade in the dead of night, since I have a device for seeing in darkness as well."

"Only witches see in the dark," grumbled Frost. "I think Jandra's enspelled you, boy."

"Jandra's not a witch," said Shay.

"I know a witch when I see one." Frost spat to punctuate his sentence.

"Shouldn't you go somewhere to sleep off your goom?" asked Shay, finding Frost's presence tiring.

While Frost looked hostile, Stonewall looked concerned. "Are you claiming to have flown? With wings? Shapeshifting *is* a sign of witchcraft."

"I'm not shapeshifting," said Shay. "They're a machine."

With a thought, he willed his wings to unfold. They unfurled, glinting silver in the sun, tinkling like a thousand tiny bells.

He smiled, expecting this to provide convincing proof for his argument.

Instantly, he realized the error of this assumption.

Frost yanked the short shotgun from his belt and held it inches from Shay's face. The blacksmith's bloodshot eyes narrowed as he squeezed the trigger. Shay flinched.

Nothing happened.

Biscuit leapt forward, tearing the gun from Frost's fingers. He said, in a voice trembling with pent up anger, "A sober man wouldn't have forgotten the safety."

Frost looked at Biscuit, his mouth hanging slack, staring down the barrel of his own gun. Biscuit's thumb flicked the safety.

Shay turned his face away as Biscuit pulled the trigger. In the flash and bang that followed, he almost didn't see Stonewall leaping from the brick steps, drawing his sword.

With a thought, Shay launched thirty feet into the air in the half second it took Stonewall to land where he'd just stood.

Frost dropped to his knees. Half his head was missing. His body slumped forward, landing against Biscuit's trousers. Biscuit snarled, "An eye for an eye you bastard!"

Stonewall was staring up at Shay. Shay hesitated. Was it too late for reason? Five seconds ago, they'd been talking civilly. How had events turned so sour so quickly?

There was a *clang* at his back as something bounced from the broad circle from which his wings unfolded. He spun, and an arrow suddenly jutted from the bag over his shoulder that held Jandra's coat. A third arrow whizzed past his head, close enough that he could feel the wind that trailed it.

It appeared the debate was over.

Shay turned his face skyward, then zoomed toward the blue above, swifter than arrows.

BISCUIT'S ONE GOOD eye was full of hate as it glared at Stonewall. The man's hands were trembling as he rammed the bag of shot he'd snatched from Frost's belt into the barrel.

"Put the gun down," Stonewall said.

"You might not have been with them," Biscuit said. "But I know your hand was on the knife just as sure as Frost's."

"I've never tortured any man," said Stonewall. "Had I known what Frost was capable of, I wouldn't have told him my suspicions that you were Burke's confidante. Put the gun down."

"Not until I put down you and Ragnar and the rest of the monsters!"

Never once as Stonewall looked down the barrel of the gun did he fear death. Faith, however, wasn't the reason for his confidence. Shay had escaped so swiftly he'd been difficult for the eye to follow. Biscuit was a stationary target.

The first arrow struck him in the shoulder of the arm that held the gun. As the gun fell to the dirt, two more arrows struck Biscuit in the back, and another jutted from his neck. By the time he hit the ground, he looked like a pin-cushion.

Stonewall shook his head, saddened by the loss of two fine blacksmiths. He was sad, as well, that Shay was gone. He'd enjoyed their discussion. Since leaving the Drifting Isles, he'd found precious little in the way of informed debate. Still, Shay's wings were difficult to ignore. What spell had Jandra cast on him? Or could it be true? Were the wings simply machines?

The blood that flowed from Frost and Biscuit merged into a single pool. Stonewall stepped into this pool and picked up the handgun. It was a fairly clever invention. Was it Burke's design? Or had Frost taken the initiative to modify the weapon on his own?

His musings were cut short as the door to the brick house opened. Ragnar stood on the stairs, dazed. The prophet's forehead had a red dot from where he'd been pressing it against the floor. He didn't appear to notice the two dead bodies on his doorstep.

"The Lord answered my prayers with a voice of thunder on a cloudless day," said the prophet.

Stonewall started to mention the fight, but decided it might be blasphemous to imply the prophet had mistaken gunfire for the Lord's voice.

"I have a message for the men," said Ragnar. "Gather them. Everyone."

"Even those under quarantine?"

"Everyone. Now."

The hairy prophet spun on his heels and marched back into the house.

AN HOUR LATER, Stonewall had overseen the removal of the bodies. Straw had been spread to hide the blood that stained the hard-packed soil. The Mighty Men had gone from building to building, dragging men from their bunks and, in some cases, from beneath them. Two thousand men crowded onto the street before Ragnar's house. At the front stood the men who'd been placed in quarantine. They were a sorry-looking lot, disheveled and dirty, with oily hair and scraggy beards. They'd not been allowed near the baths since their confinement.

It was mid-afternoon. With the bright sun, the day was warm. It was the sort of winter day that promised that spring was near.

Soon, everyone in the fort was present, save for the men on the sky-wall team. They'd been boosted back to their full numbers. They made an impressive sight upon the walls.

The door to the brick house opened.

Ragnar stepped out, the cross of swords in his left hand. He slammed it onto the brick steps. The iron blades sang out like bells.

"There is no disease in Dragon Forge!" Ragnar shouted.

Stonewall furrowed his brow. There were whispers in the crowd.

"There is no disease in Dragon Forge!" Ragnar again cried out. "The Lord spoke to me in thunder! He said we have no reason for fear! Our righteous cause will not be brought low by illness. He shields us from plague and fever. Any who were sick are now healed by the power of our faith!"

Stonewall looked over the ragged men who'd come from the quarantine barracks. While none of them were the picture of health, none of them were incapacitated either. None even looked feverish, save for one of the younger men, a boy really. Stonewall felt as if he should know this boy's name. At last, it hit him. This was Burr, the boy Jeremiah had vomited on. When he'd gone into the quarantine barracks, Burr had been a big lad, his face ruddy and plump. Now, his cheeks were pale and hollow. Could worry alone have produced this change?

"Every man is to return to his work when he leaves here," said Ragnar. "Let the dragons tremble when they see the smoke rising from Dragon Forge once more. The archers on the walls report they've seen the movements of catapults. Their pitiful engines of war are nothing compared to our cannons! Tonight, we will demonstrate our power! I want all the cannons currently ready placed upon the walls. We begin our barrage of the blockade tonight!"

Stonewall cleared his throat. He leaned over to Ragnar and whispered, "Sir, there are only five spots along the wall that can support the biggest cannons. We've been working to reinforce the wall for more, but…"

Ragnar answered him by shouting to the crowd. "By nightfall, we will have fifty large cannons upon the wall. Every man here is rested and ready! Our task is clear! Our cause is just! Remember the Free City!"

The crowd cheered at these sacred words.

"Remember the Free City!"

Again they roared.

"Remember the Free City!"

Now even the sad-looking men from the quarantine barracks pumped their fists in the air and shouted.

Save for Burr. The boy, already pale, grew paler still. His eyes rolled up into his head and he fell forward onto the brick steps at Ragnar's feet.

The men closest to the Ragnar who'd witnessed the boy fall stopped shouting. Like a wave, the cries of war faded and confused, hissing whispers spread from the front of the crowd to the back.

"The boy is overcome with excitement!" Ragnar shouted. "There is no disease in Dragon Forge."

Every man pushed away from Burr's unconscious form, deeper back into the crowd, standing as if there was an unseen wall that wouldn't allow them to be closer than twenty feet to the boy.

Stonewall stepped down and rolled the boy over. He felt as hot as a just-fired gun barrel. Steeling himself, Stonewall pushed back the boy's lips. His gums were puss yellow.

From the man standing nearest, he heard the whisper, *"Yellow-mouth!"*

Ten seconds later, there was full bore panic through the streets. Men were shouting. There was a shrill cry of pain near the back of the crowd as a man was trampled.

"Be still!" Ragnar shouted. "Have faith! Remember the Free City! *Remember the Free City!*"

The screams of fear only grew louder as the crowd streamed away.

"There's… there's no disease in…" Ragnar's voice trailed off as he looked toward the heavens. His fingers went limp and the iron cross slipped from his grasp.

Stonewall looked up as the bright sky dimmed.

The sky was full of rotting human corpses, flying over the walls of Dragon Forge in long, graceful arcs.

CHAPTER TWENTY-EIGHT

THE PATH OF SCARS

ALTHOUGH IT WAS still light outside, the interior of the barn in which Bitterwood and his companions stood was full of flickering candles that gave the air the scent of tallow and beeswax. They waited in silence as the woman who'd led them to the barn knelt in front of a canvas-covered platform.

Bitterwood was growing impatient with the woman's lengthy prayer. Jeremiah was heavy in his arms, but he didn't dare put him down. He felt that, as long as he was holding the boy, he was holding onto the last spark of life that still glowed inside the child.

Hex had settled into a seated position. Bitterwood spotted the weakness in the giant dragon's limbs. Normally, when he witnessed weakness in a dragon, it triggered the same instinct a dog feels when seeing a wounded rabbit. Now, Bitterwood felt something approaching sympathy for the sun-dragon. After cradling Jeremiah for so long, he no longer took any pleasure at seeing even a dragon suffer.

Burke joined Hex on the floor, as did Thorny. Vance and Zeeky were still on their feet, as was Poocher, who paced back and forth nervously.

"Can't you make him sit still?" Bitterwood grumbled.

Zeeky shrugged. "This is the barn where he was penned up with the other animals the last time we were at the Free City. He remembers the smell of the place. Smells get him agitated."

Poocher looked at her and grunted.

"For instance," she said, "he smells a sun-dragon here."

Bitterwood looked at Hex, who possessed the distinctive draconic odor of rotten fish.

"I mean he smells a second sun-dragon," said Zeeky.

Before they could discuss this further, a throng of young women in white robes, their faces hidden by hoods, filed into the barn. They quickly lined the walls.

Bitterwood was assessing their potential threat when Vance, Burke, and Thorny all gasped. Hex's scales suddenly bristled. Poocher squealed. Bitterwood turned to the canvas platform and found Blasphet seated before him, not twenty feet distant. Hovering a few inches above Blasphet's ebony brow was a glowing circlet of silver he knew well: Jandra's tiara.

Blasphet eyed him with an unblinking gaze. The great beast's mouth opened as he said, "The light is better than when we first met, oh Ghost Who Kills." He narrowed his eyes. "You're shorter than I remembered."

Bitterwood dropped to one knee before Blasphet. He leaned forward and carefully placed Jeremiah onto the straw-covered floor. He stroked the boy's cheek to brush the hair from his face. He turned his head toward Hex, who looked dumbfounded by Blasphet's sudden appearance. Vance, too, was standing slack-jawed, oblivious to Burke and Thorny, who were trying to stand.

The only ones nearby who still had their wits about them were Zeeky and Poocher. With the bristles along his spine raised like little spears, and his head tilted forward to turn his small tusks into weapons, Poocher looked ready for battle.

"Protect the boy," he said.

When he rose, all his gentle, fatherly instincts were gone. His bow was in his hand as if it had always been there. He plucked an arrow from his quiver with as little thought as he gave to commanding the beat of his heart.

Blasphet rose, his serpentine neck snaking toward the beams of the loft. The light from the tiara cast shadows down his torso. "Put down your bow. There's no need—"

Before he could finish his sentence, Bitterwood fired. The arrow raced straight toward Blasphet's eye. A full foot from its target, a gleaming tomahawk flashed across its path, knocking it away. Bitterwood didn't pause to ponder its source. He already had another arrow aimed. With a *zzzmmm*, his second arrow flew, flashing toward the black beast's gut.

With a speed that was difficult for even his eyes to follow, one of the white-robed disciples leapt into the arrow's path, her slender arm whipping out. She caught the shaft in mid-flight. Her hood fell back, revealing a woman with deeply-tanned skin and jet black hair.

"Stop!" Burke shouted.

Bitterwood had no intention of stopping. He'd been caught off guard by the impressive reflexes of Blasphet's protector, but now that he was aware of her, she could be neutralized. His third arrow targeted her, on a trajectory that wouldn't hit Blasphet. As expected, she leapt from the arrow's path, landing with a roll that would bring her back to her feet. Bitterwood already had another arrow nocked. She was reaching her feet when he let the arrow fly, aimed at Blasphet's heart.

A sword appeared in the woman's hand as if by magic. She threw the sword into the arrow's path, so that the razor sharp edge of the blade bisected the thorn-tip of the arrow. The wobbling twin shards of arrow that continued past bounced harmlessly from Blasphet's scales. The woman somersaulted across the front of the platform and landed with her hand outstretched. The sword she had thrown fell into it.

Bitterwood narrowed his eyes. The woman looked at him with a calm gaze. There was something familiar about her. She moved like the mechanical men he'd fought, Hezekiah and Gabriel, ancient engines designed to look human.

The woman held an upturned palm toward Bitterwood and crooked her fingers, as if daring him to attack. Bitterwood took careful aim, intending to take that dare.

A steel crutch whacked him across the side of his face, knocking him off balance. Stars danced before his eyes and he stumbled. His ears rang, but not from the blow. Instead, Burke was inches from his ear, shouting at the top of his lungs.

"I said stop!" Burke grabbed Bitterwood by the collar and pulled their faces together. "That's Anza!"

"Anza?" Bitterwood said, casting a glance back at the woman. Now he knew why she'd seemed familiar. He'd only met her briefly during their escape from the Dragon Palace. He hadn't recognized her without her black buckskins. Her hair hung loosely around her face instead of being pulled back in a severe braid.

"There's no need for violence," said Blasphet in his smooth, well-mannered voice, as he lowered himself back down to a seated position. "I hold no grudge against you, Bitterwood."

"Who are you really?" Bitterwood growled. "I killed Blasphet. You can't be the real Murder God."

"Indeed," said Blasphet. "You brought an end to my reign as the Murder God. You are the Ghost who Kills, the Death of All Dragons. You, Bitterwood, are the true Murder God."

Bitterwood felt as if he'd slipped into a nightmare. It was the only explanation. Even if Blasphet had survived, how could he be talking? His anger faded into confusion. "I ate your tongue."

"How appropriate," said Blasphet. "Devouring the remains of a defeated foe is a way of taking on their power."

"It was only dinner," said Bitterwood, shaking his head.

Hex said, "This is why the valkyries never found your body, uncle. Once more, you've made an impressive escape."

"No!" Bitterwood protested. "He had no heartbeat! He wasn't breathing. When I sawed his tongue out, he didn't even flinch."

Blasphet nodded. "All true. I've lived many years with the threat of execution over my head. I long ago developed a poison that would plunge me into a state indistinguishable from death. Colobi found me and administered the antidote only moments after you departed. We limped away from the Nest. My wounds were grievous. You butchered me most effectively."

"You… weren't dead?" Bitterwood found this difficult to believe, despite the evidence before him.

"I was as close to death as any mortal being may come. As the poison spread within me, I felt as if I were falling from my body, into a great, unending nothingness. I have been to the abyss, Bitterwood. What I found there changed me. When Colobi revived me, I returned to a world where every breath was agony. And yet, I now bear witness to the fact that one painful gasp is far, far sweeter than the nothingness of death. I left the dark tunnel repenting my wicked ways, vowing never to cause harm to a fellow being. I have turned my intellect, once so enamored with murder, to the protection and improvement of life."

Hex shook his head as Blasphet spoke. "You'll forgive me if I'm skeptical, uncle."

"Judge me by my deeds," said Blasphet. "Look around you. I give sight to the blind. I allow the lame to walk. I feed the hungry and clothe the poor. When I designed the Free City, the false promise spread that it would be a paradise where all needs were met. Now, I intend to keep that promise. All who seek comfort will find it."

Hex's eyes focused on the tiara above Blasphet's head. "How did you come to be in possession of Jandra's tiara?" he asked. "I've experienced her healing touch. I know that its power would be sufficient to regrow your tongue."

"When I returned to my temple with Colobi, the sisters who stayed behind presented me with treasures they had collected during their raids on the

Dragon Palace. Among their gifts was this tiara. I recognized it instantly. I'd long studied Vendevorex and
Jandra, suspecting their headgear might be the source
of their abilities. I placed it on my brow... and felt
nothing. The device was lifeless."

"Obviously, you figured out how to activate it,"
said Hex.

"That was due to another looted treasure," said
Blasphet. "The sisters had stolen Vendevorex's corpse
before they freed me from my confinement in the
dungeon. I'd long wanted to study Vendevorex to
find out if his magic was, indeed, the result of his
skull-cap, or perhaps flowed from some strange
mutation. I hoped his body would reveal his secrets.
Alas, I was occupied with the plot to destroy the
Nest, and had little time to perform a dissection.
When I returned from the Nest, with my change of
heart, I regarded dissecting Vendevorex in a different
light. Desecrating his remains further seemed distasteful. I went to the morgue where I had laid his
body upon a slab. I discovered, to my amazement,
that his body hadn't decayed since. Indeed, he
showed signs of continued life. The broken and twisted bones of his wings looked straight and whole once
more."

Bitterwood watched Anza carefully as Blasphet
told his story. She, in turn, watched him. Burke still
held his collar. Bitterwood glanced toward the tiara
floating like a halo above Blasphet. He needed this to
save Jeremiah. Burke would never forgive him if he
hurt Anza. But what choice did he have? Blasphet
possessed poisons that would alter the mind. Anza
must be under the influence of such a drug.

Blasphet continued his tale: "I leaned close to the
wizard's body, listening for a breath. I heard nothing.
I placed my head on his chest to detect a heartbeat.

Not a single sound stirred beneath his azure scales. Yet, as I concentrated, the tiara, which I still wore, began to glow faintly. I slowly grew aware of a multitude of microscopic machines permeating Vendevorex's body. These invisible constructs whispered pleas for my guidance. They had reversed his decay, repairing him from the cellular level up, yet lacked the initiative to restore the spark of life. The more I concentrated, the more clearly I understood the whispers of the machines."

Hex rose on his shaky legs. "So. You owe your new-found abilities to a tiara you admit to stealing and to a corpse you admit you planned to desecrate. I'm a friend of the true owner of the tiara. Jandra was haunted by the mystery of Vendevorex's missing body. If you're truly an honorable being now, you'll give me the tiara."

Blasphet sagged as he shook his head mournfully. "I cannot defend the actions of my previous self. The dragon I was died in the darkness, slain by the hands of the true Murder God. The dragon who limped out of that tunnel, and now stands before you, is a reborn being. Possession of this tiara is my greatest hope for repairing the evil I've done."

"You slew eight hundred valkyries," said Hex. "No amount of good deeds can balance this villainy."

Burke still had his hands on Bitterwood's shirt. He'd been glancing back and forth between Bitterwood and Anza. Increasingly, his eyes were upon his daughter. Finally, he asked, softly, "Are you all right, Anza? Why are you protecting this monster?"

"Fah-der," she said, in slow, halting syllable. "Dis drak-on haz..." She paused, her mouth open, a look of intense concentration in her eyes. She uttered the final words of her thought carefully, in syllables that were more on the mark. "He... healed... me."

Burke's hand went slack and dropped from Bitterwood's collar. "You can talk?"

"Yas," she said, nodding for emphasis.

"Your daughter suffered from a calcified tumor near her vocal chords," said Blasphet. "I removed it, repairing the damaged nerves and reviving atrophied muscles. She is still training her new voice. In time, she will speak as well as any other human."

Anza pursed her lips once more. "He... can heal... you."

Burke's crutch slipped from his fingers. He dropped to the floor in a motion that was half falling, half sitting. He held his hands in his head as he whispered, on the verge of tears, "All my life, I've had dreams that you could talk to me." He let out a long slow breath. "I trust Anza. Let Blasphet heal Jeremiah."

"You're insane!" Bitterwood said.

"No he's not," said Vance, stepping up. "I ate the dragonseed and it cured me. Let Blasphet help Jeremiah."

Bitterwood furrowed his brow. This was, in a way, such an obvious thing to try. Why had his first approach to this problem been to kill Blasphet and take the tiara? Would there ever be a problem in his life he wouldn't attempt to fix by killing something? He shook his head, disgusted that he was having these doubts, especially here, in the Free City. Blasphet was a monster. Was he the only sane person in the room?

Before he could decide on a course of action, Thorny walked toward the huge black dragon, holding his gnarled hands before him. "If you've done right by Anza, I'll trust you. Can you fix my hands?"

"Of course," said Blasphet. He raked his fore-talon along his chest. His feathery scales were bunched into small polyps. He plucked one free, and held it toward Thorny.

"The seeds grow from your body?" Burke asked.

"Yes," said Blasphet. "They are full of the same tiny machines that swam in Vendevorex's blood. They now thrive within me. When you ingest the seed, the microscopic engines will spread through your body, seeking out damage and repairing it."

Bitterwood felt nauseated as Thorny bent his head down to Blasphet's talon and took the seed between his lips. Thorny swallowed as he stood up. He looked down at his hands as he asked, "How long will it take to work?"

"Unguided, the machines need several hours to analyze your body for flaws," said Blasphet. "I can guide them more quickly. My... familiarity... with corpses has left me well prepared as a healer. I know what all the bones in a healthy human hand should look like. I know how thick the cartilage between them should be, and where the tendons should attach. If you choose to have me guide the process, there will be a certain level of pain involved."

"I've not had a moment free of pain in thirty years," said Thorny. "Do it."

"As you wish," said Blasphet. He fixed his gaze upon Thorny's hands. Thorny suddenly drew a sharp breath and dropped to his knees, leaning against the canvas-covered platform.

Around the room, the white-robed disciples began to sing as Thorny cried out in incoherent, babbling agony. His fingers twitched and writhed. Even Anza's gaze was drawn to the sight of Thorny's useless, knotted claws changing into something that looked like healthy hands.

Bitterwood knew this was the moment. He reached over his shoulder, his fingers brushing against the leafy end of a fresh arrow. Before he could pluck it from the quiver, a small hand touched him on the hip. He looked down and found Zeeky looking up at him.

Beneath the din of the singing and Thorny's screams, she said, "Let him help Jeremiah."

Bitterwood drew the arrow.

"If Jeremiah dies, you'll never forgive yourself," said Zeeky.

Bitterwood clenched his jaw. Every instinct wanted to place the arrow against his bowstring. However, just as Burke trusted Anza, Bitterwood trusted Zeeky. He'd been friendless for twenty years. This mysterious little girl had liked and trusted him from the moment they'd met. He wanted her approval more than he wanted Blasphet's death. With a sigh, he returned the arrow to his quiver.

The song of the disciples fell off and Thorny stopped screaming. The old man breathed heavily, his face dripping tears. He stared at his restored hands, opening and closing them slowly.

He wiped his cheeks. He pursed his lips tightly and took a long, calming breath through his nose. He grabbed the edge of the platform and supported his weight on his hands as he stood. He looked up at Blasphet.

"Thank you," he whispered, his voice raspy from screaming.

"You're welcome," said Blasphet. "The dragonseed will continue to work, slowly restoring further infirmities. Soon, you'll eat your meals with a full set of teeth once more. And your overall health will improve as the damage that alcohol has done to your liver is reversed."

"Will I be young again?" asked Thorny.

"No," said Blasphet. "Age is not a disease. You will, however, be strong and healthy. A well-maintained human body should last nearly a century.

See to it that you are careful in your habits, and you will at least feel young."

As Thorny nodded and walked away, Blasphet looked at Hex. "How about you, nephew? I see that you've suffered trauma to your brain. Will you allow me to restore you?"

Hex scowled. "Uncle, if you attempt to alter my brain with your invisible machines, I'll alter your brain with my jaws."

"So be it. I understand the reason for your scorn." He then looked to Burke. "You, human, have seen the good I've done for your daughter. Will you let me make you whole? Life has left you with many scars."

Burke stared down at his missing leg. He lifted his hand and traced the three scars that marred his cheek. Bitterwood could tell from the way the machinist held his body that the blisters beneath his arm were still a source of pain. When Burke inhaled to answer, Bitterwood knew Burke, too, would accept Blasphet's help.

"No," said Burke.

"No?" said Blasphet.

"No?" said Anza. She walked toward him, kneeling to look into his eyes. "Fadder, he can fex yuh leg." Her words were more difficult to follow when she tried to speak quickly.

"I believe he can," said Burke. "But I lost my leg due to a tactical error; I didn't use sufficient armor on my war machine. And, these scars... I've had these scars on my cheek since the battle of Conyers. Every time I've looked into a mirror for the last twenty years, I'm reminded of all the men who died because they believed I could lead them to victory."

Anza shook her head as she listened to her father's words.

"I don't regret my bad memories," he said, taking her hand. "I can't claim they've left me wiser, but they define me. These scars, Anza, they aren't flaws. They're part of me. Erasing my scars is like erasing my life."

Anza nodded, her dark eyes full of understanding. She helped her father rise again on his one good leg. Vance handed Burke his crutch.

Blasphet turned toward Bitterwood.

"The boy at your feet is dying from yellow-mouth," he said. "With your permission, I shall heal him."

Bitterwood clenched his fists as he turned away, unable to look at Blasphet. He gazed at the candles guttering among the rafters, and at the thin rays of a declining sun that poked through the gaps in the barn wall. He saw dust dancing in that light, gleaming like tiny flecks of snow. Jandra had said that all her magic came from dust. Hezekiah had taught him that man came from dust, and returned to it. His shoulders sagged. There were mysteries in this world far beyond his grasp.

"Save him," he whispered, walking toward the door they'd entered.

He didn't know if he was doing the right thing, despite Zeeky's reassurance. He needed to step outside and get some fresh air to clear his thoughts. When he pushed open the door, he stepped onto a broad avenue where men and dragons were crowded together, all looking toward the western sky. He shielded his eyes as he, too, looked toward the sunset and discovered an angel. A winged human was plainly visible as a silhouette against the red sky. The entity drifted down toward the Free City. Bitterwood tensed. Was this another of the goddess's machines, like Gabriel? What was its connection to Blasphet?

He reached for an arrow. The flying figure altered his descent slightly, now plainly heading for the ground where Bitterwood stood.

A voice called out, "Bitterwood! I didn't expect to find you here!"

Bitterwood squinted. "Shay?"

Shay flapped his wings and he slowed to a halt a few yards before Bitterwood, hovering several inches above the ground. The wind stirred the folds of Bitterwood's cloak. "I'm here to find Hex. I didn't expect to find you. And who are all these people?"

"Worshippers of Blasphet," said Bitterwood.

"The Murder God?" Shay asked, looking around at the crowd that gathered to gawk at him. "I expected his followers to look more... sinister."

"He's renounced the title of Murder God," said Bitterwood.

"Can you do that?" Shay sounded perplexed. "Just decide one day you're no longer a god?"

Bitterwood shrugged. "Who makes the rules?"

"Is Hex here?"

"He's inside with Burke and the others," said Bitterwood. "We all arrived together."

"Burke?" Shay ran his fingers through his hair. His orange locks were disheveled and tangled to an absurd degree, as if he'd spent time inside a tornado. "I can't believe it! I was told he was dead."

"Death is apparently not as permanent as it used to be," said Bitterwood.

"This is good fortune. I needed some luck after the last few days. Did Hex tell you about Jandra?"

"Some," said Bitterwood. "We haven't been together long. He failed to mention you'd sprouted wings."

Shay glanced back at his silvery appendages, as if he was almost surprised to find them there. He stretched them out and gave them a gentle shake. The metallic feathers chimed softly. "You like them? You're in luck. I have more of these in Hex's bag."

Just then, Burke limped out the door, supported by Anza. They both stopped in their tracks as they followed the gaze of the crowd upward.

"Hallo, Sheh," said Anza.

Shay's eyes widened. "You can talk?"

Burke said, dryly, "I think the more surprising development here is that you can fly."

Shay grinned; then just as swiftly, his grin vanished.

"Burke, Dragon Forge is in trouble. There's an outbreak of yellow-mouth. Or, at least, there's fear of an outbreak. The foundry has come to a standstill. The walls were barely manned."

Burke shook his head. "I'm sorry to hear that. But it's not my problem anymore."

Shay's eyes flashed with the same rage Bitterwood had witnessed when he'd announced he'd set fire to the library. "Not your problem?" Shay shouted. "Dragon Forge promised the rebirth of the Human Age. The revolution was the light of a new human dawn, the hope of the slave! You were the brains that made it possible!"

"I may have been the brains, but Ragnar was the heart. And that heart was corrupted. The two of us never trusted each other. We were doomed from the start."

"You have to become the heart as well as the brains," said Shay. "You know you have the dream to make men free once more!"

Burke sighed. "I've already caused too many people to die."

Shay made several exasperated grunts as he tried to find the words to respond to this. "Wha... but... it's not your fault people have died fighting to take

Dragon Forge! You're not a king, pressing slaves into service. Those men at Dragon Forge were volunteers. Everyone who died, died for a cause. Giving up now means they'll have died in vain."

Anza nodded. "Lissen ta hem."

Burke raised an eyebrow. "You agree? I thought you were a pacifist now that you were worshipping Blasphet."

Anza cast off her white robe, revealing the weapon-studded buckskin beneath. She drew her sword and said, "Ah ahm a waryor. Ah belif in de cause."

"You're a warrior because I robbed you of a normal life," said Burke. "I had no right to turn you into a weapon. All those years, Blasphet gathered young women around him and taught them to kill. They called him a monster. How much more of a monster am I to do the same thing to my own daughter?"

"Father," she said, slowly, carefully. "I... don't... want... a normal... life. Ah am ... not a muh-sheen. Ah am your daughter. Ah love... my life."

"You should hate me," Burke whispered.

Anza pressed her lips into a thin, straight line. The muscles in her jaws flinched as she worked out the next movements of her mouth in her head.

"You can use your hand signals to talk if it's easier," said Burke.

She frowned. It was obvious, from her expression, that she was determined to make the muscle of her tongue obey her will with the same precision that it commanded all her other muscles.

"I love you, Father," she said, slowly and deliberately. "I'm happy... to fight... because I fight for you."

"Thank you," he whispered.

Anza returned his gaze with intense seriousness. "We must fight... for Drak-on Forge."

Burke nodded. He straightened his shoulders. He looked toward Bitterwood. "How quickly can Skitter carry us back to Dragon Forge?"

Shay said, "Not as fast as wings will carry us. I've got more of these in Hex's bag."

Burke nodded, then jerked his head up, as if he suddenly remembered the reason he came out to the street in the first place. "Bant, Jeremiah's awake."

Bitterwood stepped out of the crowded street back into the candlelit barn, leaving Shay to fill in Burke on what he'd discovered at Dragon Forge. Jeremiah was sitting up now. The corpse-like pall that had gripped him was gone; his cheeks had color again. Zeeky sat beside him, her arms wrapped around him, hugging him tightly. Poocher was next to him also; Jeremiah had one hand on the pig's neck and was scratching him behind the ears. The big pig looked content.

Bitterwood walked toward Jeremiah. Before he could reach the boy, however, a vertical rainbow appeared in the air in the center of the barn. Several of Blasphet's followers gasped at the strange apparition.

A woman, dressed in a gown that resembled the red scales of a sun-dragon, appeared. She had a silver helmet atop her head. Bitterwood recognized her instantly.

"Jandra?" he said.

Jandra smiled as she spotted him. "Bant!" she said, sounding genuinely pleased to see him. She turned her head and said, even more joyfully, "Hex! Zeeky! Poocher! You're all here!"

Hex snaked his head toward the woman. At first, the swiftness of the motion led Bitterwood to think he was attacking her. Instead, he stopped inches from her face and sniffed, his nostrils flaring. Her hair fluttered as he inhaled as deeply as his dragon lungs could muster. He stared into her eyes, and she stared back.

He exhaled slowly and said, "It smells like you. But, of course, with the goddess in your body, I don't know that I could tell a difference."

"Sometimes you have to trust your nose," said Jandra. "You saw me fighting to regain control. I won. I've pushed the goddess out of my brain at last."

Hex looked skeptical. "Jandra didn't know how to form an underspace gate."

"I do now," said Jandra. "I got rid of Jazz's personality, not her memories. I've learned something amazing while I've been away. I've been to Atlantis."

The hair raised on the back of Bitterwood's neck. He'd encountered Atlanteans before. The technology Jazz had used came from there. Jazz had been his most dangerous fight, ever. It was difficult to imagine a whole city of people with her power.

Jandra continued, "Now that I've been there, I have to go back. I need allies. I plan to destroy the city, and I don't know if I can do it alone."

"Why would you want to destroy the city?" asked Hex.

Bitterwood was more puzzled by something else. "How did you know we would be here?"

"Jazz could track her nanites in your quiver, and now so can I," said Jandra. "Speaking of nanites, I see my original genie has a new owner." She looked at Blasphet. She didn't look particularly concerned by his presence. "And who's using Vendevorex's genie?"

"The genie I buried?" Hex asked.

"It's not buried anymore," said Jandra. "It's here, and it's in use. I can detect its radio pulses."

Her eyes fixed on seemingly empty air beside Blasphet. "Come out. If you can use the genie well enough to make yourself invisible, we should talk."

For a moment, nothing happened, and then a calm voice said, "Very well."

The air beside Blasphet cracked as an unseen mirror began to vibrate. The silvery barrier broke into a shower of sparks and dust that fell to the earth in a perfect circle.

Standing within that circle was a sky-dragon wearing a skull cap. He spread his dark blue wings, which were studded with diamonds that twinkled like stars. He stared at Jandra with golden eyes that glowed as if small suns were hidden behind them.

"Greetings," he said, taking a bow. He straightened up and looked around the room. "Some of you are no doubt wondering why I'm no longer dead."

Vendevorex, Master of the Invisible, had always appreciated the value of a dramatic entrance.

CHAPTER TWENTY-NINE

THE GATE TO ATLANTIS

THE MOMENT JANDRA appeared, the voices from the crystal orb Zeeky carried in the cotton satchel slung over her shoulder began to howl. She couldn't believe that everyone in the room didn't hear them. Yet, the only reaction was from Poocher, who tilted his head and fixed his eyes on the bag. He rose from sitting on his haunches and stepped away from Jeremiah, who'd been petting him. The hair along his back once more stood in bristles as he faced Jandra.

Zeeky reached out and placed a hand on his muscular shoulder. "Not yet," she whispered. The pig looked at her with an expression approaching pleading.

"I know," Zeeky whispered, squatting down to his side. "You want to see some action. I promise, you'll get your chance soon."

As they spoke, the shower of sparks caught her eyes. A sky-dragon with a silver skull cap and starry wings stood next to Blasphet, bowing as he greeted the room. She recognized him as Vendevorex from the battle of the Free City—the dragon Jandra thought of as her father.

Bitterwood stood next to her and Jeremiah, but had his attention on Vendevorex. He grumbled, "Doesn't anyone stay dead anymore?"

"It's a pleasure to see you as well," said the sky-dragon.

Jandra crossed her arms. Zeeky knew this wasn't the body language of a daughter reuniting with her father. Jandra said, "So that we can hurry things along and get back to my news, let me fill everyone in on what's happened."

"Please do," said Hex.

Jandra looked at Vendevorex and said, "You died, but with your nanites already programmed to repair your wounds. Unguided after your skull cap was removed, they kept your body in a state of cellular stasis until Blasphet revived it. But he couldn't have restored your mind, could he? Somehow, he brought you back in contact with your old skull cap—the one Hex stole from me."

"And buried here in this barn," said Hex.

"When I brought Vendevorex to the Free City, he was a soulless shell," Blasphet said. "He possessed all the motions of life—he breathed on his own, and if you gave him water, he would swallow—but he was completely devoid of will. I hoped that, as my understanding of my new abilities grew, I might one day restore his mind. Yet, when I brought him into this barn, he slowly began to recover on his own. At first, he possessed no memories, but within days he was fully restored."

Jandra nodded. "That's because you'd brought his body into the control range of his old genie. The device possessed a map of his brain at the time of his death, and guided the nanites in reconstructing Vendevorex's personality."

"How can you know all of this?" Hex asked Jandra.

"It's simple enough to put together," Jandra said. "Obvious, really."

"Your powers of deduction are impressive," said Vendevorex. "I was planning to find you soon. I know that my death must have caused you a great deal of emotional stress."

"Oh," said Jandra, nodding. "Totally."

Vendevorex narrowed his eyes.

Jandra uncrossed her arms. "Now that everybody's up to speed, let's focus on me again." She waved her hand in the air and a flat white disk of spinning light formed before her. Quickly, the light took on the shape of a green island surrounded by a bright blue ocean. The spires of impossibly tall buildings thrust up from the greenery.

"This is Atlantis," said Jandra. "It's a city of six billion people, who all have the same technology used by the goddess. They made the genies Vendevorex and I—and now Blasphet—draw our powers from. These people have powers best described as godlike—but, in one special way, they possess a weakness that leaves them exceedingly vulnerable to attack."

Blasphet craned his long black neck toward the image of the island for a better look. "Why would you wish to attack such a place? Think of the good I've accomplished with my limited understanding of their tools. If they shared their secrets, we could end all suffering."

"But they don't share," said Vendevorex. "They guard their secrets jealously. When Atlantis first came to earth, it decreed that anyone who wanted to experience its bounty would have to live upon its shores. Anyone who didn't would lose access to its miracles."

"Why?" asked Blasphet. "Why possess such power if you don't intend to use it?"

"At the time, the world had gone over the precipice of environmental collapse," said Jandra. "Vast swathes of the ocean were dead zones. The world was experiencing a mass extinction that rivaled the disappearance of the dinosaurs. The cause was human civilization. The goddess was clever enough to constrain civilization to this remote, artificial island. She allowed the continents to return to a state of wildness, or near wildness. Atlantis provided a way for her to cut out the cancer of humanity so that the body of the earth could heal itself."

Vendevorex scowled. "This meshes with the story I was told, though with somewhat different motivations attributed to the goddess."

"That's because, while I was in Atlantis, I discovered you were a pawn," Jandra said. "You were given your genie by a woman named Cassie, who was Jazz's sister and lifelong rival. Cassie wanted you to spread the technology among dragons, so that Atlantis would regain its awareness of the outside world and wipe out dragonkind. Cassie views dragons as biological contaminants—leftover relics of genetic engineering that don't belong in the ecosphere."

"It's fortunate I didn't behave as expected."

As Jandra and Vendevorex talked, Bitterwood crouched next to Zeeky. He whispered, "Is that really Jandra?"

"It's her body," said Zeeky. "But not her mind. Right now, if you kill Jazz, you'll kill Jandra."

"I'm willing to make that sacrifice," whispered Bitterwood. "You saw what the goddess can do."

Zeeky shook her head. "Jandra's still alive inside her. We can save her."

"How?"

Zeeky motioned for Bitterwood to pay attention to Jandra/Jazz once more.

"So, here's the plan," said Jandra. "Hex, Bitterwood, and Blasphet: you all have a passion for breaking things. I want you to help me break Atlantis. We can steal the wonders there and share them with everyone. Vendevorex, I wasn't expecting you, but you'll be useful as well. Once I trigger the jammer, you'll be one of the few minds on earth that will be able to use the Atlantean tech to its full potential."

"So you know their weakness," said Vendevorex.

"Yes," said Jandra. "This is why you had me study all those books on chemistry and physics. If I want to make an antidote to a poison, I need to understand the physical properties of the molecule I need to counteract it. I have this knowledge for the same reason you and Jazz did—I spent years with my nose buried in books memorizing a lot of boring stuff."

"This is also why Blasphet adapted so quickly to the genie," said Vendevorex. "He's spent decades studying the workings of the body and the chemistry of countless poisons."

"Unlike the Atlanteans who haven't had to study anything for the last thousand years," said Jandra. "They have instant access to the city mind, a repository of all shared knowledge. They don't need to memorize the chemical and physical changes needed to turn water into wine. They don't even need to remember their own names. Whenever they want to know something, they ask the city. If they were cut off from the city mind, they'd be helpless."

"The city mind is too sophisticated for simple radio jamming, however," said Vendevorex.

"Wrong," said Jandra. "The goddess developed algorithms for jamming signals that will cripple the Atlantean network. The city mind will be able to crack the code in a matter of minutes, but we aren't going to give it minutes. Are you with me?"

Hex nodded. "Jandra, you have my promise I won't let you out of my sight."

Zeeky could tell from the sound of his voice that Hex suspected the woman before him was more Jazz than Jandra.

"I knew I could count on you." She looked toward Bitterwood. "How about you?"

Before Bitterwood could speak, Zeeky blurted out, "He'll go. I will too."

Bitterwood jerked his head toward her. "No," he said. "I'll go if you wish, but I'm not taking you and Jeremiah into a battle with gods."

Zeeky shrugged. "Okay," she said. Bitterwood frowned at her easy agreement.

Jandra, meanwhile, had turned to face Blasphet. "I assume I can count on you? Killing a city is certainly worthy work for a Murder God."

"No," said Blasphet.

"No?"

"I'll never again act to harm another living being."

Jandra sighed as she motioned toward the model city constructed from light. It bubbled away. She said, "I don't know who you're trying to fool with this good guy act, but you weren't part of my original plan anyway."

Vendevorex said, "I shall go. My familiarity with Atlantis could prove useful."

Jandra nodded. "Good enough. Let's roll."

She traced a half circle in the air and a rainbow formed in the wake of her motion, slowly opening into a yawning void.

"Next stop, Atlantis," she said, stepping toward the gate.

Suddenly, a man shouted, "Wait!"

It was Shay, sporting silver wings, floating in the doorway next to Burke. His wings folded behind him as he dropped to the ground and ran toward Jandra.

Jandra flinched as Shay threw his arms around her. "You're back!" he cried, hugging her with all his might. She awkwardly lifted her arms to pat his back.

"Yeah," she said, pushing away from him. "But, as much as I'd like to catch up, I'm kind of busy right now. I have a city I need to go wreck."

"Jandra?" Shay asked, sounding confused. "It is you, right?"

"Of course," she said, smiling. "I pushed Jazz out of my brain. But, you know me. I'm always rushing off on some new mission."

"Then I'm coming with you," said Shay.

"I don't know that that's a good idea. You're not really the warrior type. Bitterwood and Hex are more the firepower I need."

Poocher snorted indignantly. Zeeky knew he felt slighted not to be included on the list of great warriors present.

"Shay," said Burke, laying his hand on the redheaded man's shoulder. "I know your reunion with Jandra is important, but if we can get the items you mentioned, I'd appreciate it. I've been away from Dragon Forge too long."

"Of course," said Shay. "Hex, do you still have your pack?"

Hex nodded, placing the large leather bag onto the straw-covered floor. Shay opened it and pulled out several silver disks like the one that sat between his shoulder blades.

"Stick these on your back and think about flying. You'll sprout wings. I have six more sets," Shay said. "That's enough for you and Anza, plus Vance and Thorny if they want to go with you."

"And me," said Jeremiah.

All eyes turned toward the twelve-year-old. He stood up from where he'd been sitting. He pulled out a knife that had been tucked into his belt. "This is Vulpine's knife. It's not his only weapon here. He gave me yellow-mouth so that I'd make everyone at Dragon Forge sick. If you're going back, I want to come. I want to take a big handful of the dragonseed back to heal anyone who got ill because of me."

"Boy, I didn't drag you all this way to heal you so that you could go off and get yourself killed," said Bitterwood. "Let someone else take back the dragonseed."

"You're going off to fight in a city of gods. Zeeky's stood up to dragons and angels. If my younger sister can fight these battles, so can I."

"I don't want Zeeky fighting these battles," said Bitterwood. "But your sister has powers. She can control the minds of animals. She can talk to ghosts and see the future."

Zeeky didn't think Bitterwood described what she could do correctly, but she held her tongue. She knew exactly how the next ten minutes were going to play out. In ten minutes, she would follow Bitterwood through the underspace gate to Atlantis. That's where her knowledge of the future ended. Whatever waited in Atlantis, the voices either couldn't see, or wouldn't say.

Jeremiah walked over to the disks and picked one up. "You're right. Zeeky was born with powers. She's the one who could talk to animals. She once talked a bear out of eating our grandma." He stuck the disk on his back. He scrunched up his face, as if he were about to sneeze. Whatever mental signal he sent the disk worked. Silver wings unfolded from his shoulders, flashing in the candlelight.

"I should at least have wings," he said, as his feet lifted from the ground.

Zeeky had to admit, the wings looked good on him.

Bitterwood, however, wasn't convinced. "Jeremiah, you ran when the long-wyrms raided your village. You ran from the battle at Dead Skunk Hole. Why are you suddenly so brave?"

Jeremiah gave Bitterwood a serious look. "I heard Blasphet tell you how it feels to die. It's the same way I felt fifteen minutes ago, before he healed me. As horrible as death feels, it's not as bad as being afraid. It's time I grew up."

Vance butted in. "There are other rebels his age at the fort."

Bitterwood clenched his jaw. Zeeky placed her hand on his fist. "Let him go," she said.

"Will he be alright?"

"Yes," she said, though she didn't know his fate beyond the next few minutes. But he wasn't going to be killed in that small window of time, so it wasn't really a lie.

Vance and Thorny took their wings and Anza grabbed a disk for both herself and her father. In the aftermath, only one disk remained.

With an excited snort, Poocher trotted up, staring at Shay with a look somewhere between pleading and demanding.

Burke looked curious. "Would they even work for him?"

"I don't see how," said Shay. "They're controlled by thought."

"Hey!" Zeeky snapped. "Poocher thinks! He's as smart as you, just in different ways. Can you find edible roots by sniffing around? He's not even a year old and I bet he could survive alone in the woods better than you. Don't tell me he doesn't think."

Shay looked suitably chastised. "Fine. It can't hurt to try."

He sat the silver disk between Poocher's shoulder blades. The pig turned around in a circle, as if he were trying to see the disk on his back, which his fat neck wouldn't allow. After his third revolution, he closed his eyes and scrunched up his snout. His wings unfolded. He floated off the ground, looking smug.

Everyone in the room knew there was something that needed to be said. But not even Hex, who'd never shown any fear of an obvious joke, dared say it.

BURKE SOARED INTO the night sky. Shay led the way, shouting out advice on how to control speed, how to maneuver, and how to hover. Burke found most of the advice unnecessary. The wings responded to thought. He was good at thought.

It felt wonderful, slipping free of gravity, taking the weight off his exhausted leg and the pressure off his aching armpit. He experienced a sense of something approaching deja-vu—it was as if he had flown before. It felt perfectly natural. Just as he could feel the ghost of his missing leg, he now felt a different sensation: the presence of phantom wings that spread from his shoulders and occupied his new metal limbs. He, like most people, had experienced dreams of flying. What did it mean? Why did he feel so at home in the sky? Was it feedback? Since his thoughts guided the wings, did the wings somehow affect his mind? Or was there some deeper mystery at work here? The dragons believed in a myth that the world had once been ruled by angels who were then overthrown by dragons. His people believed the myth was a metaphor for dragons overthrowing humans. But, what if the myth was true? What if mankind had once possessed wings?

As comfortable as he felt in the air, Jeremiah and Anza looked even more at home. They were zooming around like sparrows at play, flitting about in tight loops that Burke doubted he'd have the stomach to attempt.

Vance looked stable in the air, though he avoided the daredevil antics of Anza and Jeremiah. Poocher floated without flapping his wings, as if he were some oversized black and white balloon. The pig didn't look nervous, but he no longer looked as cocky as he had earlier now that they were hundreds of feet off the ground. Thorny was the only member of their group who looked frightened. His newly-restored hands were held out stiffly to each side, as if he was balancing himself on unseen stair rails.

Shay said, "I flew here in about two hours. I think the wings could go faster, but the wind takes your breath away. Also, in daylight, it was easy to follow the Forge Road. You'll probably need to fly slower so you won't lose it."

Poocher snorted. Shay looked at him, and saw the silver visor sitting on his snout. Shay could see in the dark with his visor; he supposed Poocher could too. He took the visor from his eyes and handed it to Burke. "Wear these. You won't lose the road then. The others can follow you. And, you may as well have this too." He loosened the long leather holster than held his shotgun and ammo. "It doesn't sound like it's going to be much more effective than a pea-shooter where I'm going."

Burke took the visor and the gun. He'd given Thorny the shotgun he'd fled Dragon Forge with now that he had working fingers again, so the additional firepower was welcome. "You're going to follow the others to Atlantis?"

Shay nodded, looking apologetic. "As much as I want to fight for Dragon Forge, my heart lies with Jandra. I'm afraid she's still possessed by the goddess."

"And what if she is?" said Burke. "How will you free her?"

Shay placed his hand on the hilt of the angel sword. "I don't know if she can be freed. If she can't, I have the only weapon that can hurt her."

"Understood," said Burke. "I'd make the same choice."

Shay floated over to Thorny. He slipped his satchel off and said, "You're a man who knows the importance of books. I found these in the kingdom of the goddess. They aren't interesting reading on their own, but they provide a key to understanding a lot of the books that survived from the Human Age. Try not to let them get around any open flames, okay?"

Thorny took the bag. "When all this is over and you get back to Dragon Forge to start your school, count me in as one of the teachers."

"Thanks," said Shay. He looked at the barn down below. "I should go. You all have a revolution to save."

"You're a good man, Shay," said Burke. "We won't let you down."

SHAY SWOOPED BACK toward the barn. Now that the sun had set, the night was biting cold, with a steady wind blowing from the north. Despite this, the streets were full of men, women, children, and earth-dragons dressed in white, crowding together, watching as he came to a gentle landing on the packed earth of the street.

Someone in the crowd said, "Our healer denies his divinity, but who else would be visited by angels?" There was a general murmur of agreement.

Shay knew nothing of Blasphet save that he was a mass murderer of both men and dragons. He didn't like the idea that his presence might somehow be helping Blasphet's reputation. For the moment, however, he had bigger things to worry about.

Within the barn, the underspace gate was still open. Jandra, Hex, and Bitterwood were gone, as was Jandra's mentor, Vendevorex. Skitter, the long-wyrm, was now in the barn, his copper-scales reflecting the various hues of the rainbow. Zeeky sat alone upon his back, cross-legged, with a glass orb roughly the size of a baby's head perched in her lap. The surface of the orb reflected the shimmering rainbow edges of the gate. Zeeky didn't take her eyes off the orb as Shay walked toward her.

"We're at the end," she said. "After we go through the gate, I don't know the future."

Having lived his life so far without knowing the future, Shay didn't feel as nervous as Zeeky sounded. He wondered how Skitter had slipped into the barn without him noticing. He must have been more preoccupied with getting Burke and the others on their way than he thought.

Zeeky said, "You know that Jazz is still in control of Jandra."

"I know," said Shay. "When she wasn't coated in silver any more, I had a flicker of hope that Jandra was back, but knew it was too good to be true. But I can't just give up. Is there no way to save her?"

"I don't have any idea. The villagers won't tell me. They've stopped using words. All I hear are howls of rage. They want vengeance against the goddess."

Shay grew closer. In addition to the rainbow reflected on the surface, there was a tiny rainbow floating inside the orb. When he'd first met Zeeky, he'd been skeptical of her claims that she could hear the voices of ghosts predicting the future. Now that he had wings and a flaming sword, he found it difficult to be skeptical of almost anything.

"I don't understand how this works," he said. "How can people be trapped inside this glass ball? Even if they are, how can they see anything other that what's right here around us?"

"The ball looks solid," said Zeeky. "But, it's not, really. Touch it."

Shay moved his hand toward the glassy surface. His fingers stopped as they encountered a pressure. It reminded him of the magnets that Chapelion had kept for study. Turned one direction, the magnets would pull toward one another. But, if you flipped one of the magnets and tried to force them together, they wouldn't touch. Some unseen force held them apart. The orb produced a similar sensation on his finger tips.

"There's a whole world inside this ball," said Zeeky. "In underspace, people exist as pure thought, ghosts without bodies, forever looking out at the world. Past, present and future are all visible. The villagers tell me that, even though they don't have bodies, the things they imagine become real inside the void. It's like they're gods, creating a new world with their minds." She looked up at him. "Gods don't like to be trapped. If they could get out, they'd punish Jazz."

Shay looked at the gate to Atlantis. The black rip in reality yawned like an open mouth. "If they're in underspace, can't they get out through that portal?"

"No," said Zeeky. "The goddess has trapped this sliver of underspace in the orb. It's like a loop of space folded in on itself. Until this ball is broken, they can't get out. Jazz said nothing on earth can hurt it."

"Really?" asked Shay, his hand falling to the hilt of the angel sword. "Mind if I give it a try?"

Zeeky handed him the orb. "Be my guest."

The ball was strangely heavy for something that wasn't solid. He squeezed it with both hands; it was hard as stone. Shay sat the orb on the floor and pulled out his sword, willing it to burst into flames. Skitter jerked backwards as a hot wind washed across the room.

The white-robed women around the room stepped toward him, looking highly alert. Blasphet, who had been watching attentively, said, "Have a care. I'm committed to non-violence, but my followers are zealous in defending me."

"Lucky for me I'm not planning to attack you," Shay said, as he willed the blade to white hot intensity. Smoke rose from the frayed edges of his coat sleeve. The hilt of the sword protected his hand, but the air was so hot he could barely breathe. Gritting his teeth, he took a powerful swing at the orb.

The sword bounced off. Needles of pain shot up his wrist from the force of the blow.

Feeling dizzy from holding his breath, he lowered the heat of the blade back to a dull cherry red. The air swirled around him as the temperature dropped. He frowned as he looked down at the orb. The straw around it was burning, and there was a black, glassy gouge on the earth beside it where his sword had hit. The orb wasn't even scratched.

He stamped out the straw, and then picked up the orb.

"That was my best shot," he said. "Could Skitter bite it open?"

"I'm pretty sure he can't," said Zeeky. "And if he swallowed it, it might take weeks until it, um, came out."

Shay nodded. "Maybe there's something in Atlantis that can free them. I should go. I need to chase after Jandra and the others. I mean, Jazz and the others."

"I'm coming with you," said Zeeky, uncrossing her legs and taking on a more traditional mounted position astride her saddle. "Bitterwood is probably already fighting the Atlanteans. Let's hope we find Jazz before they finish the job."

"You're right. Once she no longer needs Bitterwood and Hex, she'll kill them." He offered her the orb.

She shook her head. "This is the last part of the future they told me. They said you would carry them through the gate."

Shay frowned. If the fortune-telling ghosts had seen that he would be taking them through the gate, had they seen Jazz possessing Jandra? If so, why hadn't Zeeky warned him? All of this might have been avoided. But, he decided it was the wrong moment to confront Zeeky on this. He placed the orb into the last bag he carried, Jandra's backpack, resting it on top of her coat. He ran his finger along the silky fabric. Though it was smudged with soot from their work digging up Jazz's heart, it still had the smell of the crystal clear pool beneath the waterfall.

His heart caught in his throat at the memory.

He willed the sword to bright yellow flame once more and held it toward the portal. The void within the rainbow devoured the light, revealing nothing, not even shadows. He breathed in slowly through his nostrils, staring into the darkness. Even his bones felt cold, despite the heat of the sword.

Leaping into the unknown was the job of heroes. He was only a skinny former slave with an aching heart and unusually crisp handwriting. It was just as well he didn't know the future. Closing his eyes, he leapt. The last thing he heard before the void swallowed him was Skitter clattering at his heels.

CHAPTER THIRTY

PARLOR TRICKS

AVING BEEN THROUGH an underspace portal before, Hex was braced for the disturbing sensation of nothingness that enveloped him as he stepped into the gate. Blasphet's description of death as feeling as if he was falling from his own body echoed the experience, though not fully. For the briefest flicker of time, Hex simply ceased to exist, and all his senses ended.

When he emerged on the other side, the first sense to return was touch. He stepped into air that was positively balmy. It was night; he stood in a well-manicured garden full of statues, male and female nudes of exquisite perfection, their skin and hair crafted from precious metals, gold, platinum and palladium. Bright pink and white flowers filled large terra-cotta pots, lending a sweet scent above the sea breeze that swirled gently around him. In the center of the garden was a fountain made of glass with a central spike taller than Hex. Water poured from a large golden disk atop the spike in an unbroken circle and fell in a shimmering column to the pool below. Goldfish that looked crafted from actual gold darted about in the softly-lit pool.

Beside him, Bitterwood tilted his head upward, then higher, then higher still. They were surrounded by towers that rose until they vanished among the stars that shimmered in the cloudless sky.

When he looked down, he found Vendevorex and Jandra standing on the broad glass rim of the pool. She said, "Gentlemen, if you're done gawking at the architecture, we need to get to work. The second I start construction of the antenna, the city mind will know something is happening. We need to get you ready for the fight."

"I'm as ready as I'll ever be," said Bitterwood.

Jandra smirked. "Your thorn-tipped shafts aren't going to scratch the guards here in Atlantis. You need an upgrade. Draw an arrow."

Bitterwood frowned. Hex sensed that the hunter didn't like being ordered around so brusquely. Bitterwood was here for the same reason he was; not to fight the city, but to stay close to Jandra. He was almost certain that Jazz was the controlling personality within her. The barest sliver of doubt was enough to keep him from lunging out and snapping her skull between his jaws while he still had the strength. On his empty stomach, he felt every muscle in his body trembling.

Bitterwood drew an arrow from his quiver and stared at the tip, perplexed. The shaft now ended in a tiny rainbow, with an almost invisible spot of black at the point.

"Now when you draw an arrow from the quiver, it will be capped with an electromagnetic field encompassing an underspace gate only a millimeter across,"

Jandra explained. "This tip can carve through any matter it encounters and send it on a one-way trip to the Mare Ingenii."

"Where's that?" asked Bitterwood.

"The far side of the moon. There's a city there now. If you shot Hex with that arrow, some moon man would no doubt be mystified as to why a long spaghetti-shaped strip of dragon entrails had fallen on him."

"Spaghetti?" asked Bitterwood.

"Moving on," said Jandra, turning to Hex. "You've suffered brain damage. It's slowing you down, and I don't have time to fix it. Luckily, I have a sort of whole body crutch you'll find useful."

Hex shook his head. Jandra might be about to put underspace gates on the tips of his teeth, a prospect he found worrisome. "No thank you. I've fought with more severe injuries than this." He hadn't.

"This really isn't a situation where you get to choose to accept my help or not," said Jandra, casting her gaze toward the statues. Suddenly, the gold that coated them began to drip to the ground, exposing naked flesh beneath. Around the garden, men and women fell to their hands and knees gasping as the nanite shells that supported them flowed into a large golden river that snaked toward Hex. Hex flapped his wings and hopped backwards, avoiding the liquid metal.

He landed in an even larger pool of gold. Flecks of the cold metal splashed onto his belly and wings. Instantly, they began to slither and expand, coating his scales. He flicked his wings sharply to fling the metal off, to no avail. The gold crept upward. He craned his neck and held his breath as it reached his jaws. He instinctively closed his eyes as the gold washed over his face. When he opened his eyes, he was completely encased in a flawless sheet of gold.

"Gold seems ill-suited for armor, daughter," said Vendevorex. "It's too soft, and too heavy to allow him to move freely."

"Gold is merely an aesthetic component," said Jandra. "The armor actually incorporates several different elements, including titanium. There aren't many things that are going to be able to cut through it. The added weight is offset by the exoskeleton's power, which will multiply Hex's strength by a factor of ten."

Hex spread his wings. She was telling the truth. He didn't notice any additional weight. He still didn't feel good, but he no longer felt as if he were about to collapse.

He looked around at the score of men and women who lay on the ground, groaning in agony. Some of the statues still stood, unaffected by Jandra's spell.

"Were they prisoners of the shells?" he asked.

"No. The statue act is a kind of art. They stand out here for years at a time. Visitors to the garden try to figure out the real statues from the living ones. They're like very, very, very slow and focused mimes."

"Why are they in pain?"

"Severe nanite withdrawal," said Jandra. "The city knows we're here by the way. Heads up."

Hex looked toward the sky. The stars were blotted out by an army of onrushing angels.

"Keep them out of my hair," said Jandra. "I've got an antenna to build."

BITTERWOOD KNEW HE was being manipulated into this fight. He pondered Zeeky's counsel that Jandra could be saved. He placed his new arrow against his bowstring. If the shafts were as powerful as Jazz said they were, would they slay even her?

Unfortunately, this wasn't a moment for contemplation. A throng of bright angels swooped toward him. Despite their wings, they were objects explicitly out of place in the sky. They appeared carved from polished marble, too heavy to do anything but plummet.

If these creatures were like Gabriel or Hezekiah, the danger they represented through their sheer numbers made them more of a threat than the goddess for the moment. Yet, the angels weren't bearing any obvious weapons. Their faces were placid, devoid of emotion. They looked as if they were here to investigate, not to fight.

Against foes this powerful, the element of surprise was something Bitterwood couldn't afford to lose. As so often happened in his battles, he would draw first blood... though he doubted they had blood. A rainbow-tipped arrow launched from his bowstring in a glowing streak, punching into the brow of the nearest angel. The winged statue lost control of its flight, its body wracked with spasms as it dropped, crashing onto the granite tiles that surrounded the fountain, sending a shower of gravel and dust skyward.

The other angels instantly halted their descent, their eyes narrowing as they turned their gaze to Bitterwood, assessing the threat. Bitterwood needed no time to think. A second arrow raced skyward, then a third, then a fourth, his bow singing a song of one-note staccato plucks. Three more angels dropped from the sky, silently, with no sign of pain on their faces. They crashed into the ground, shattering.

A strong wind suddenly swept over Bitterwood as Hex beat his wings, launching himself at the angels. They were only a hundred feet overhead, barely two body lengths for the giant dragon. They had no time to focus on him before he grabbed the first angel in his toothy jaws. He whipped his head about, tossing the angel into his nearest brethren. The wings of both shattered from the impact and they plummeted.

It had been almost twenty years since the first time Bitterwood had shot a sky-dragon in flight and watched it fall to earth. Watching the angels fall, he felt the same pulse of adrenaline wash through him. He didn't know if he was on the right side in this battle. He didn't know if Jazz was manipulating him into an act of unspeakable evil here in the city of gods.

Mere moments ago, all he had wanted was to save Jeremiah and take him and Zeeky far away, to a place where war was only a distant whisper, to live in peace as something almost a family. He had wanted to put his life as a killer behind him. Yet, as he watched his opponents fall from the sky, all these desires faded, washed away by the battle lust that surged through his veins. He targeted the next angel with a feeling approaching glee, and let his arrow fly.

JAZZ PAID NO attention to the throng of angels. Her experience with the two warriors at her back left her confident that the next sixty seconds would pass in relative quiet. She clapped her hands and the water falling into the pool trickled to a halt. The golden disk atop the fountain would make an excellent conductor for her transmitter.

She needed to concentrate. She allowed the shell of light that clung to her like her third skin to fade away, revealing her second skin, the silver genie that was affixed to Jandra's pores. It had been an obvious mistake to wear her genie in such a compact form inside her old body. Balling it up like that had left it vulnerable to Gabriel's sword. By spreading it out along the full surface of her new body, she had a greater chance that, should any part of it be damaged, the rest of it would survive. Her personality was still mostly located within the computer memory of the genie. Once all the excitement was over, she'd spend a few days relaxing on the beach, soaking up some sun, and rewiring the synapses of her new brain so that it would be truly her own extinguishing Jandra forever.

Threads of silver shot from her fingers and wrapped around the glass spire at the center of the fountain, twining upward around it, sinking into the gold at the top, etching elaborate maps across its surface.

An angel crashed into the fountain on the other side and the glass rim shattered. The pool water surged out the new opening, leaving goldfish flopping about beneath her. She didn't mind that she was about to kill or cripple six billion people, but she felt bad that the fish had to suffer.

She was vaguely aware that Vendevorex was standing right beside her. She was a little perplexed as to what she should do with him. He wasn't part of her plan. If she'd killed him back in the barn, it would have made her Jandra act less convincing. On the other hand, Hex, Bitterwood, and all the others were recent acquaintances according to Jandra's memories. They were easy to fool. Vendevorex had known Jandra her whole life. Was he buying her act? She'd called him by his full name earlier, which was a slip up. Jandra had a more affectionate term for him.

"Ven," she said. "The key to talk to your nanites once the pulse is activated is 17351. It's about twenty seconds in coming. Since you're not doing anything in the meantime, could you save the goldfish?"

Vendevorex nodded. He swept his wing over the shattered pool with a dramatic flourish, sending out a shower of silver dust. The shards of glass began to dance, hopping and popping until they formed bowls around the gasping fish. He closed his fore-talon, and the water that clung to the bottom of the pool rose in a mist. He opened his talon, and the water rained down in precise rain clouds, filling the fishbowls.

If Jazz had known he'd complete the task so efficiently, she wouldn't have shared the key. Not that it was important. Vendevorex might have been a wizard among more primitive minds, but he was little more frightening than a birthday party magician to her. He could push a few molecules around, bend a little light, and knit together a bad cut. Parlor tricks compared to the technology's full potential. Jazz configured the last circuit.

"Omega," she whispered, activating the signal. Instantly, the angels remaining in the air exploded into clouds of dust.

Seconds later, a howl that could have come from the depths of hell itself echoed through the city, as six billion souls that had felt the touch of a shared mind for a millennium suddenly found themselves alone with their own thoughts.

In the rain of dust, it was impossible to see more than ten feet. Hex and Bitterwood couldn't see her right now. Jazz turned to Vendevorex. She twisted the electromagnetic field around her fingers as she once more opened the razor-thin underspace gate that would form a rainbow blade. "Thanks for helping with the goldfish. Now, no hard feelings, I'm going to kill you."

She slashed the blade across his throat. She waited, watching for his neck to slide from his shoulders. His eyes, rather than rolling back into his head, glared at her with a stern look of disapproval.

He said, with a voice unmarred by trachea severing, "You've taken something from my daughter. It's time you give it back."

The underspace blade was so sharp that perhaps the surface tension of the water in his cells was holding his neck. Jazz stretched her silver-plated fingers forward to give his head a nudge and knock it loose.

Her fingers passed through thin air.

Her feet were suddenly locked in place as the thick glass rim of the fountain began to climb up her legs. She went blind as twin phosphorous flares erupted inches from her face. A dragon's fore-talon fell upon her shoulder from behind.

Parlor tricks.

FROM THE MOMENT she'd stepped from the rainbow gate, Vendevorex had suspected that Jazz was the mind animating the body of Jandra. When he'd come back into contact with his genie, he'd discovered something curious: nearly a month of Jandra's recent memories were stored within the device, recorded during the time Jandra had worn his genie. Jandra apparently hadn't discovered this was a function of the device, since she hadn't encoded her memories so that other users couldn't access them. Thus, he knew in great detail the events of Jandra's life from the moment she'd put on his skull cap to the moment that Hex had ripped the genie from Jandra's spine. He knew who Jazz was, and the threat she represented.

He wondered if Jazz was aware of the threat he represented.

The ground beneath them rumbled as an earthquake wracked the island. He had no time to ponder the cause.

By now, the glass of the fountain had climbed to Jazz's waist, immobilizing the lower half of her body. Jazz twisted her neck around, trying to see him, but it wouldn't have mattered if she'd swiveled her head in a complete circle. With the flares before her eyes, she couldn't see a thing. He fashioned a long staff of glass with a head in the shape of his fore-talon, and lowered it to her shoulder. As anticipated, she whipped her arm over her back, stabbing the rainbow blade into the space where he should have been standing in order to touch her. He dropped the staff and leapt forward, grabbing her wrist, pushing it against her back so that the impossibly sharp sword cut away a thin slice of the nanite shell along her spine, exposing Jandra's skin.

He needed both his talons to control the blade as she struggled to free herself. He bent his serpentine neck forward and caught the torn edge of the silver shell with his teeth, peeling it out from her skin. Then, though it would cost him his powers, he willed his genie to reconfigure itself, turning into a stream of silver liquid that raced down his scaly snout and leapt onto the patch of skin he'd exposed.

Instantly, the flares vanished. He leapt back, flapping his wings, getting out of the reach of the blade. The glass around Jazz's legs cracked and shattered, as Jazz overpowered his unguided nanites.

Jazz spun around, her face distorted with rage. "Flying won't protect you, you bastard," she snarled.

Before Vendevorex could fly higher, the glass of the shattered fountain reshaped itself into an enormous hand that reached up and plucked him from the sky. The fingers closed upon his ribs with an unearthly swiftness and pressure. The sound of snapping bones reached his ears a fraction of a second before the bolts of pain.

Suddenly, Jazz shouted out. "No! Noooo!"

The glass hand went slack. Vendevorex lost awareness as he tumbled into the flowers below.

SHAY FELT AN odd sensation in his wings, a new sense he hadn't known he possessed until this moment. There was an unseen wave of energy in the air as he emerged through the gate, and his wings tingled with each pulse.

His arrival was badly timed. He seemed to be in the middle of an earthquake. The air was thick with dust. The ground beneath him shook violently. Yet, instead of buildings toppling, the opposite was happening. A structure was rising from the earth nearby. He recognized it from the books he'd studied at a Greek temple, with walls formed by gleaming white columns of marble. In scale, it rivaled the Dragon Palace. Within its shadowy confines, a giant man, two hundred feet tall, glared out. He wore a shimmering toga and sported a thick white beard and a mane of long white hair. He carried a trident, like the image of the god Poseidon.

The god did not look happy.

Thunder rumbled through the air, loud enough to rattle Shay's teeth. It took a second to realize the thunder formed words: "Who dares silence the voices of my children?"

A golden dragon that bore some slight resemblance to Hex darted through the air toward the god. In scale, it was like an eagle attacking a bear. The god lifted his hand in a dismissive swat. The golden beast flew off in a streak and smashed into one of the impossibly tall towers. The force drove the dragon through the wall. Shay couldn't see if he emerged from the other side.

Skitter slithered from the gate beside him. Zeeky craned her neck upward toward the god's angry face. She sighed. "I guess I'd better go talk to him."

"Talk to who?" Shay asked.

"Him," said Zeeky, pointing to the giant.

"Him?"

Zeeky nodded. "I can talk to pretty much anyone. It's my gift."

By now, the dust was starting to settle. Jazz stood beside a large spire topped with a golden disk. The granite-tiled walkway she stood on was sopping wet. For some reason, she was surrounded by hundreds of goldfish bowls.

Jazz looked as if she were dancing. Her skin was silver once more. She was whipping back and forth, her silver hair flying, raising her hands over her shoulders to claw at her back.

Shay rushed toward her and raised his sword to strike. Yet, as he neared, he realized Jazz wasn't dancing. There was something moving beneath the silver shell that coated her back, and she was trying to claw it off.

"Get out!" Jazz screamed. Or was it Jandra?

Knowing he might forever regret his decision, he swung his angel sword. The flat of the blade smacked squarely across Jazz's ear. The force of the blow tore the sword from his grasp and sent him spinning through the air.

When he stabilized, he turned to see the results of his blow. The silver-shelled woman stared at him. She didn't look injured.

"Shay," she said, in an utterly neutral tone. "Thanks for helping me focus."

"Jandra?" he asked.

"Guess again," she said. She turned her back to him and slammed her foot down onto the hilt of the flaming sword. In the center of her back there was a bulge. It looked almost like a woman's face, criss-crossed with chains. Jazz looked up at the Atlantean god, who glowered down at her.

"To answer your earlier question," she shouted to the giant, "I dare!"

The god shook his head slowly, as if pitying her. He crouched and reached toward Jazz with his impossibly huge hand.

"You no doubt thought I'd attempt to crack the jamming code of your signal," the god said, his thunderous voice causing the flowers of the bushes to tremble. "A more elegant solution is simply to destroy your antenna."

The god's fingers closed upon the golden disk.

Instantly his fingers vanished, then his arm, then his torso and shoulders and head. Shay was again aware of a tremendous surge of energy in the air.

"Sucker," said Jazz. "I knew you could still control the nanites you were in contact with, since you could transmit your commands through physical connections. Touching the disk gave me access to these physical connections. I've knocked you back to your core form. And now, I'm going to flush you."

Shay had no idea what had happened, but he was pretty sure it wasn't good. From his vantage point in the air, he could see into the giant temple. Where the god had stood, there was now a small, naked, white-haired boy, perhaps no older than five, slumped on the ground. He looked dazed.

Jazz suddenly appeared next to the boy, even though she also continued to stand by the fountain. The Jazz by the fountain looked down, as if the boy was standing right at her feet, and said, "Underspace gates have so many uses." The boy looked up at the Jazz in the temple, a frightened look in his eyes. "Traveling to the moon in a blink is one. Disposing of unwanted gods in the reaches of interstellar space is another."

She snapped her fingers. A perfectly circular rainbow appeared around the boots of the Jazz standing in the temple. A black pit opened beneath her, expanding outward. The white-haired boy opened his mouth as if he were screaming, but Shay couldn't hear him. The boy tried to crawl away, but made little progress. The only sound coming from the temple was a terrible howl of wind. The circle expanded ever outward. Shay was tugged toward the temple by a sucking wind. The black circle was now fifty feet across, and stars shimmered in its depths.

The flowers in the courtyard beneath him all leaned in the direction of the yawning pit. The boy's desperately grasping hands found no purchase on the marble. He splayed his body out, searching for any handhold, as his small form was dragged by the air rushing to the gaping void.

Shay ground his teeth and tilted toward the temple. The boy would reach the edge in mere seconds. Could he fly fast enough to save him?

Before he could find out, there was a flash of copper as Skitter raced up the steps at the side of the temple. Zeeky leaned down from her saddle, extending her hand. The boy's legs tilted over the side of the space pit and he closed his hand around Zeeky's.

The force ripped Zeeky from her saddle. Skitter slid to a halt on the polished marble floor, whipping his head around, snapping his mighty jaws shut on the back of Zeeky's tunic as she, too, tilted over the edge of the space pit. Skitter's claws left scratch marks in the marble as the wind caught him. The boy dangled from Zeeky's grasp as she dangled from Skitter's jaws.

"Oh, the suspense," said Jazz, giggling.

Skitter's first pair of claws slipped over the edge, then the second. There was a flutter of dark motion in the shadows at the rear of the temple. Shay's heart leapt as he realized it was Bitterwood's cloak. The archer was perched in a tree on the other side of the temple, his legs securely wrapped around a branch to resist the wind. He glared at the Jazz over the black pit.

He let an arrow fly.

It sliced straight through Jazz's head and kept flying, burying itself to its leafy feathers in a marble column beyond.

The Jazz near the fishbowls winced. "Ooh, that would have stung. Good thing Ven wasn't the only one who knew parlor tricks."

The way Jazz turned her head as she spoke drew Shay's eyes. She was looking at the fallen body of a sky-dragon who was tangled in the twisted branches of a thorny bush. He couldn't tell if the dragon was breathing.

Jazz began to twitch.

"Calm down," she growled.

The face on her back bulged out further, its mouth opening to scream, "Vennnn!"

Jazz closed her fists and clenched her jaw, concentrating to push pack Jandra's ghost.

Shay was torn. Should he attack Jazz again? Last time, physical pain had helped her focus. He decided to rescue Zeeky. But when he looked back to the temple, he saw a long bright pink rope tied to the tree where Bitterwood had stood. The hunter himself was gone, but the rope stretched in a straight line to the edge of the pit, where Skitter had his claws wrapped around it. The giant beast had inched himself out of the void, dragging Zeeky, who still held the boy. They were only feet from the pit, and the wind was beating them mercilessly. Still, for the moment, they were safe.

A physical attack on the goddess hadn't done him any good. Could an emotional appeal make a difference?

He dropped from the sky, coming to rest before Jazz, who had her eyes closed. The turmoil on her face was gone. She looked almost peaceful.

"Jandra," said Shay, barely a yard from Jazz's face.

Jazz opened one eye to glare at him.

"Remember Lizard," said Shay.

Jazz fell to her knees as a howl rose from the face on her back.

HEX PICKED HIMSELF up from the sandy beach where he'd come to rest. He was astonished to find he had no broken bones. There were scratches on his golden shell from his flight through the buildings, but no cuts or gouges. Just how tough was this armor?

He tried to flap his wings, but found he didn't have the strength to lift into the air. The fault wasn't his golden shell. He was still too weak from having had nothing to eat or drink. Jandra—or was it Jazz?—had said the shell would multiply his strength by ten. Unfortunately, ten times nothing was nothing.

He limped back into the city of towers. All around him, men and women in exotic hues wandered around, looking dazed. Many had simply collapsed where they stood, staring into the night sky, paralyzed by fear. He could hear the cries of men and women rising from unseen chambers beneath the earth as the lights of the city fell dark.

He came to a fountain. He lowered his jaws to drink, then halted, focused on the strangeness of seeing his countenance in gold. His green eyes weren't coated by the metal. He opened his mouth. His teeth were covered, but the metal stopped just inside his gums. His tongue was unprotected, still purple and raw.

He didn't care about the pain. He thrust his snout into the water and gulped until he'd had his fill.

When he lifted his head once more, he heard a howling sound, like wind rushing through a cave. The flowers in the garden around him fluttered as the breeze picked up.

With his belly full of water, he felt even more sluggish than before. Yet, he couldn't afford this weakness. He, more than anyone, was responsible for Jandra's condition. This meant he, more than anyone, was now responsible for the fate of the world.

Digging into the deep reservoir of strength that only guilt can provide, he beat his golden wings and took to the air. Quickly, he gained his bearings. He could see the temple in the distance, though he couldn't tell what was happening in its shadowy interior. As he weaved his way among the towers, he soon spotted the silver form of Jazz, down on her knees beside the shattered fountain. A winged man stood before her. One of the angels?

He dove closer and realized it was Shay. He was talking to Jazz. Jazz was shaking her head. Her silver shell was bubbling up on her back. What was happening? He had only seconds to decide on a course of action. He knew his strength would fail any moment.

Shay's eyes grew wide as he saw Hex.

Jazz looked over her shoulder at him.

Hex made his decision. Just before his jaws clamped down onto Jazz's silvery body, he realized that the bulge on her back looked a bit like a woman's face.

He dug his teeth into Jazz with all his might. It sounded as if two voices screamed inside his mouth. He spread his wings to come to a halt before he crashed into the columns of the temple. He stumbled as he hit the ground. The wind at his back was like a hurricane. He tumbled and rolled, losing his grip on the silver woman. He bounced up the steps of the temple, pushed by the incredible wind. He dug his golden claws into the polished marble as he continued to slide. He craned his neck and saw Skitter struggling to keep from being pulled into an enormous black pit over which a second Jazz stood.

While his golden shell was stronger, and his claws were sharper, his metallic scales did lack one important quality: friction. Nothing he did halted his slide toward the void.

A sharp pain punched into his left wing. He came to a sudden and complete halt. He looked toward the source of the pain.

One of Bitterwood's arrows jutted from his wing. Half the shaft was buried in the marble floor. The force that tugged on him would no doubt have torn his ordinary flesh, but the golden shell held firm against the arrow. He was pinned.

"Take her down!" Hex growled.

Somehow, even above the howl of wind, he suspected the Murder God heard his prayer.

CHAPTER THIRTY-ONE

LOST CITY

THE SILVER-SHELLED WOMAN at the foot of the temple steps rose on wobbly legs. Deep, ugly puncture wounds seeped dark blood from both sides of her rib cage. Shay approached her carefully, having retrieved the angel sword. Yellow flames reflected on her metal cheeks as she stared at him with eyes full of murder.

"She killed Lizard," said Shay.

The woman's left eye twitched.

"N-nice t-try," she said, wiping her silver lips with a bloodied hand. "But your f-friend's attack put me back in the d-driver's seat."

"She killed Vendevorex," said Shay, though he wasn't certain this was true.

Jazz's silver skin literally crawled as is it crept over her wounds.

"A-attacking me... only reinforces... the defensive programs in my genie." She sounded winded. She grew more stable on her feet as she took a long, slow breath. "I'm the living embodiment of the concept that whatever doesn't kill me makes me stronger. I've silenced Jandra forever. I've flushed Atlantis into orbit around Proxima Centauri. You can't win this, Shay. Do you think they call me *goddess* because I have a fabulous body? This is my world now."

Shay willed the flames of the angel sword even brighter. "You've been beaten before."

"You want to sword fight?" Jazz giggled. A rainbow sword grew in her left hand. She planted her black boots in a fighting stance. "Let's do this thing!"

Shay gripped his sword with a sweaty hand. He watched Jazz's face intently. He had to know. "Remember Lizard!" he pleaded.

"I remember," she said, as a smile played upon her lips. "His neck made the most satisfying snap when I twisted it."

Shay lunged. The goddess leapt.

There was a flurry of motion that Shay found difficult to understand. He felt suddenly light-headed. He looked down. His sword was lying at his feet. His right hand was still wrapped around the hilt.

"You might be worse at this than anyone I've ever seen," said Jazz.

Shay grabbed the stump of his wrist with his left hand, pinching off the blood flow.

"You might not have got the memo that my sword can cut through anything," said Jazz, as Shay dropped to his knees. "Still want to fight?"

He shook his head mournfully. "I never wanted to fight you," he said. He looked into Jazz's eyes, into whatever tiny echo of Jandra remained, "I love you."

Jazz's left eye twitched shut. Her head twisted until it pressed against her shoulders. Her lips trembled as she whispered, "I love you too."

Seconds later, she screamed, "Shutup*shutup*SHUT-UP!"

"*Nooooo!*" a second voice howled from her back.

"If you like him so much, we'll keep the head!" Jazz snarled. She lunged forward once more, swinging her rainbow sword in a powerful arc.

Shay fell backwards, pulling Jandra's pack off his shoulder with his left hand. He let go as the sword sliced through the bag. He prayed it would slice open the impenetrable crystal ball within it.

When the severed pack fell to the ground, the only thing to tumble out was Jandra's blue silk coat.

Above the roar of wind came the howl of ghosts.

Jazz was plucked from her feet by an unseen hand and thrown into the temple. Shay clamped the severed veins of his wrist shut again and rose on wobbling legs to follow her.

Jazz bounced across the marble floor, sliding past Hex's sprawling golden form. Her face and shoulders were no longer silver. The shell coating her skin was being peeled away by invisible fingers.

"Shay!" Jandra screamed as she was sucked toward the pit.

Shay didn't need his hands to use the wings. He shot forward, letting go of his bloodied stump, reaching out with his left hand. Her right hand closed around it. He tried to lift off, but the wind was too strong and he felt too light-headed as even more blood gushed from his wrist.

Jandra looked at him, fear and confusion in her eyes as they continued to slide toward the pit. Her feet went over the edge, then her body. He clamped onto her hand with all his dwindling strength as his arm and shoulder slid over the edge.

They suddenly halted. Shay felt pressure on the tip of his left wing. He looked and saw that Hex had snagged his wing with his hind-talon, piercing the metal feathers with a single golden claw.

The ghosts continued to howl around him, even louder than the wind.

Below him were stars. The cold within the pit was far worse than any winter. Jandra looked up at him. The silver skull cap that Vendevorex had worn had crawled onto her brow. She reached out and grabbed the stump of his right hand. There was a sizzling sound and the bleeding stopped.

The ghosts slowly fell silent. They'd had their chance to tear Jazz free from Jandra and banish her into the far reaches of space.

And they'd failed.

A silver-skinned woman, an exact duplicate of Jandra, had the metal nails of her left hand sunk deep into the flesh of Jandra's calf. Her eyes were utterly empty. It was the hollow shell of Jazz's genie, still clinging to her new body. She swung her right arm up and sank it into the flesh of Jandra's thigh.

Tears welled in Jandra's eyes as the goddess clawed further up her body. The hollow woman pulled the nails of her left hand free and swung them higher, sinking them into the dimples that sat at the base of Jandra's spine.

Jandra screamed as the goddess advanced another foot.

"I'm sorry," Jandra cried, as she let go of Shay's stump. Her fingers loosened in his left hand. He squeezed with every fiber of muscle remaining to hold on to her.

"Let go!" she begged. "We can't let her climb back!"

The shell's hollow eyes gazed at Shay. Its lips curled into a smirk.

He turned away. He knew he would save the world if he let Jandra go. He knew that she was willing to make this sacrifice. But he couldn't release her, and he couldn't meet her gaze to let her know this.

He saw, as he glanced across the pit, that Skitter and Zeeky were safely out of the temple, clinging to the trees.

The goddess sank her claws into Jandra's shoulders.

He couldn't let the Goddess back into the world.

He couldn't let go of Jandra.

His wings responded to his thoughts.

So he told the wings to let him go.

As the hyperfriction field between his shoulders shut off, he was sucked over the edge. A rough-knuckled hand brushed his neck as it closed around the collar of his coat.

A white-hot flaming sword thrust down, sinking to the hilt between the goddess's empty eyes. The goddess hissed as her body began to twist and warp, distorted by the sun-like flame within her. Her hands pulled free of Jandra's shoulders.

She fell the length of Jandra's body, catching Jandra's right boot with hands tipped with tentacles instead of fingers. She dangled there as she swung her arm to climb again.

Jandra kicked down with her left boot, planting the blow on the hilt of the sword, shattering what remained of Jazz's face as the weapon sank deeper into the hollow of her body. The silvery tentacles loosened and Jazz tumbled free, limp and lifeless, trailing smoke.

As Jazz fell, her silvery form folded in on itself, looking less like a woman, and more like a heart pierced by a flaming sword. It fell, further and further, until the white hot flame of the sword dimmed in the thinning air. At last, the speck of her heart was lost in the yawning darkness.

Shay finally looked up. He was dangling in the grip of Bitterwood, who had a bright pink rope tied around his waist.

Jandra shouted above the wind, "Bant, as always, your timing is flawless."

Shay pulled Jandra closer as some force pulled the rope upward. They were locked in an embrace when they passed back over the lip of the pit onto the marble floor.

"I don't suppose you know how to close that hole, do you?" Bitterwood asked Jandra as they reached the marble pillar to which the other end of the rope was tied.

"Not a clue," said Jandra.

They climbed down the temple steps. There was a disturbingly large pool of red fluid where Shay's severed hand rested. Beside this was Jandra's bag. Shay was now more dizzy than he'd ever been in his life. Jandra's arm around him was the only thing keeping him on his feet. He dropped to his knees as they reached her bag.

He picked up Jandra's coat. She was naked save for her boots and her silver skull cap. Silver, he thought, really wasn't a good color on her.

"I kept this for you," he whispered. But as he tried to hand the coat to her, he fainted, tumbling face first into the pool of his own blood.

JANDRA WASN'T WEARING her skull cap when his eyes opened again. Her hair looked freshly washed. She was dressed in a tight-fitting green velvet gown decorated with elaborate patterns of yellow lace. She smiled gently at him. It was midday, judging from the light.

"How long was I asleep?" he asked, raising his hands to rub his eyes. He stopped in mid rub. He opened his eyes and stared at two unscarred hands.

"You're really good at this magic stuff," he said.

She shook her head. "You can thank Vendevorex. I gave him back the skull cap. It had been his far longer than it had been mine. He's much more experienced. I'm good with it, but he really is magic. He stitched your hand back on without any scars."

Shay sat up. He was in a large bed with white cotton linens in a room with large open windows draped with sheer curtains that fluttered in the breeze. He could hear waves crashing in the distance. The air smelled of salt.

"I'm glad he wasn't dead," said Shay.

"Just banged up," said Jandra. "I could never have escaped Jazz's control if he hadn't put my genie back in contact with my nervous system." She leaned down and gave him a brief, soft kiss on his brow. "I definitely couldn't have escaped if you hadn't been there to fight for me."

"Some angry ghosts helped," said Shay. "Bitterwood also played a significant role."

Jandra grinned slyly. "One day, when we tell our children this story, we can emphasize the parts that make you look good."

"Our children?" Shay asked. "Are you... um...?"

"No, silly," she said, rolling her eyes. "But one day. You're the first man who's ever made me feel joyous that I'm human. You're the one I want to spend my life with."

"Are you certain?" he asked.

"You held on to me when I begged you to let me go," she said. "Who else could there ever be?"

They started to kiss, but halted when someone nearby cleared his throat.

Vendevorex, Master of the Invisible, stood by the bed.

"I'm sorry to disturb you," he said. "I wanted to check in on the patient."

Shay held up his hand. "Good as new." He stopped to feel his pulse. "I guess you found all my blood, too."

"It was easier to grow new blood," said Vendevorex. "Your marrow is quite healthy."

"Didn't you have a hole to outer space to close?" Jandra asked.

"Done," said Vendevorex.

"You know how to open and close underspace gates?" asked Shay.

"Not yet," said Vendevorex, shaking his head. "I do know how to reconfigure the molecules of the roof of a marble temple into a ball with a radius larger than that of the gate. It makes an efficient plug. The earth is no longer in immediate danger of having its atmosphere sucked into orbit around another star."

"That's good news," said Shay, though he hadn't realized that was a danger until just now.

"Weren't you going to check on the boy that Zeeky rescued?"

Vendevorex tilted his head to the side. "Daughter, are you anxious to have me leave?"

She smirked. "Possibly."

"I'll go," he said. "You can open the gift later." The air shimmered and he disappeared.

"Is he gone?"

"I don't know," said Jandra. "He's really good at this invisibility stuff."

"I'm gone," said Vendevorex from the hall.

"Now for that kiss," said Jandra.

Shay leaned forward. But, as he closed his eyes he noticed a bright blue box sitting on the bed by his feet. It hadn't been there a moment ago.

"Now what?" asked Jandra, her face only inches from his, looking perturbed that he wasn't focused on her.

"That must be the gift he mentioned."

Jandra picked up the box and lifted its lid. Inside was a silver skull cap, a duplicate of Vendevorex's own.

"Do me a favor," he said. "Change it to a different color when you wear it. I don't want to see silver against your skin for a long time."

"Oh," she said, lifting the hair at the back of her neck and twisting so he could see the upper part of her back. A strip of silver metal ran along her spine, into her hair, where it clung to her scalp like a three fingered claw. The silver turned to jade before his eyes. "Done," she said.

"You're already wearing a genie?" he asked, puzzled.

"Ven's genie has always had the power to spawn new ones. He's simply been cautious in sharing."

"Then whose...?"

Jandra lifted the skullcap from the box. "It's your genie, Shay."

Shay took the skullcap, staring at his reflection. His hair was a hopeless mess.

There was a note in the box. "Thank you for saving my daughter," it read. "Study hard in case you need to do so again."

"He has nice penmanship," said Shay. He shook his head. "I adjusted to the wings, but I don't know if I'm ready to learn magic."

Jandra took the skullcap from his hands and set it back in the box.

"Learning magic can wait," she whispered. "Making magic is the order of the moment."

Her lips brushed against his. He closed his eyes.

And then there was magic.

VENDEVOREX FLOATED DOWN to the fishbowl garden. The fish, he noted, were still doing well. Jazz's antenna was dismantled, spread on the ground before the young boy who studied the pieces with ancient eyes. He was dressed in a white toga torn from the scraps of a larger garment.

Zeeky sat near him on the lip of a large flowerpot. Skitter foraged at a nearby tree, ravenously devouring the ripe avocados that weighed down the branches.

The boy looked up as Vendevorex's shadow fell over him.

"The jamming signal is gone," said Vendevorex.

"Yes," said the boy.

"But you still can't communicate with the nanites that populate the city?"

"No," said the boy. He looked toward the towering spires. "I can no longer hear the voices of my children." He looked back at the dismantled antennae. "I don't know how she managed it, but she's locked the parts of my mind that would let me talk to all the pieces of myself."

"What are you?" Vendevorex asked.

The boy smiled. "I'm Atlantis, of course."

Zeeky shook her head. "He knows who you are. He's asking what you are." Vendevorex looked at the girl. She shrugged. "I'm good at understanding what folks are really talking about."

Atlantis swept his hands across the garden, toward the spires, then gazed toward the ocean. "I am all that you see. I am the city."

"Again," said Vendevorex. "I am aware of that. Cassie told me you weren't from earth."

"Not from *this* earth," said Atlantis.

"That's an odd word to emphasize."

"There are many, many earths. More are created with every tick of the clock. Underspace is the medium in which these infinite earths float, each existing in a slightly different space than the others. You can't be blamed for not knowing. The earths are separated by dimensional membranes. Under ordinary circumstances, the only evidence of the other universes is their gravitational bleed. They create the illusion that there's far more matter in a universe than there truly is."

"I take it that these dimensional membranes can be crossed," said Vendevorex.

"Yes. The technology of this earth would have required eons to develop it, however. I come from an earth where the dinosaurs never died. They evolved into a tool-using civilization fifty million years before the clever apes of this world learned to master fire."

"You don't look like a highly advanced dinosaur," said Vendevorex.

"No," said Atlantis. "I arrived here as a seed. A tiny nugget of intelligence wrapped in a shell of nanites, programmed to serve the race of beings that had designed me, colonizers of other realities. I didn't find the race I was programmed to serve, however. Instead, the first intelligent being I encountered was a human. I sampled his genetic code and constructed this body in his image. I gleaned the myth of Atlantis from his memories. I was programmed to serve others in perfect altruism, providing for every need. So I allowed the children of this world to share in the bounty of my abilities."

"I'm not certain that your children have thrived under your guidance," said Vendevorex.

The boy's forehead wrinkled. "How can you say they haven't thrived? They're immortal, or at least they were. They had no reason to fear hunger or thirst or heat or cold, until I was crippled by the goddess."

"The fact that you have a city of six billion people who've forgotten how to feed themselves, or sew a garment, or start a fire, is rather convincing evidence that you've done your children a disservice."

Atlantis frowned. "It's all I know how to do. It's true, perhaps, that unlimited altruism has not been as successful an advancement strategy for humans as it was for the quinveris."

"The quinveris?"

"The race that long ago created my kind. You know them as earth-dragons."

Vendevorex was puzzled by this revelation. Earth-dragons could, plausibly, be evolved dinosaurs. They definitely weren't part of the genetically-engineered lineage that had produced sky-dragons and sun-dragons. But, as a race, they hardly seemed advanced enough to create the miraculous technology Atlantis commanded. However, if the quinveris had relied on this technology for millions of years, was it possible that their minds had devolved? Were they near-sighted, cannibalistic dullards when stripped of their technology?

"There are earth-dragons on the planet now," said Vendevorex. "Why didn't you assist them instead of humans?"

"Because they weren't here when I arrived. I was drawn to this world by a false signal. I arrived at the correct place, but almost a century earlier than my coordinates indicated. I didn't know this; I thought

I'd arrived on the wrong world, with no way of turning back. By the time the quinveris colonizers arrived, I was already imprinted on humanity."

Vendevorex shook his head. As clever as he was, he couldn't begin to fathom time travel. "How is it possible to arrive a hundred years ahead of schedule?"

The boy's white toga slipped on his shoulder as he shrugged. "I got lost."

"He's the lost city of Atlantis," said Zeeky.

Vendevorex knew the girl had said the words innocently. She didn't possess the cultural background to understand the joke. Vendevorex turned and said, "I'll leave you to your work."

"Thank you," said Atlantis.

He walked away. Zeeky hopped down from the planter and followed him. When they were far out of the range of the boy's hearing, she whispered, "You're figuring out if you should kill him."

Vendevorex looked down at the strange little blonde girl. As Shay was recovering, Jandra had filled him in somewhat on the powers of perception that had resulted from the goddess's genetic engineering.

"This is a curious notion," he said.

"You're afraid of what might happen if he gets his powers back. You think mankind—and dragonkind—are going to be better off without him. You already know how to use his tools. You think you can teach folks to use these tools in a less dangerous way."

Vendevorex stopped. "You seem to know a lot for a girl whose main claim to fame up to now was an ability to talk to pigs."

"I was born with some gifts," she said. "When I was a captive, Jazz gave me others." She bit her lip after she said that. "Don't tell Jandra. She'll be worried."

"Should she be worried?"

"No," said Zeeky. "Jazz was a bad woman. I'm a nice girl."

"I see. As a nice girl, tell me your opinion. Should I kill Atlantis?"

"Could you?" she asked.

He clenched his jaw and took a long breath. He knew she wasn't asking if he had the ability. She was asking if he had the coolness of thought to take the life of a being who had reverted, in appearance at least, to a five-year-old child.

"Yes," he said.

"Will you try to help the people here with their new lives?"

"Of course."

"Bitterwood wouldn't," she said.

"Did you have this talk with him?"

"No. I don't want him to have to make this kind of choice. He's been nice to me. He's really brave. But I've watched his face when he's sleeping. He doesn't need any more bad dreams."

"You should go find him now," said Vendevorex. "I have other matters to attend to."

"I don't think you do," she said.

He stared at her.

"You don't have to go back," she said.

"We both know what's at stake," he said.

"You don't need to do anything," she said.

"If I don't, who will?"

She shrugged. "I don't know." She shook her head slowly and started to walk again, with her hands clasped behind her back. "All I know is, if you don't watch a long-wyrm every minute, it's likely to eat just about anything."

CHAPTER THIRTY-TWO

MORNING MEDICINE

A NZA LED THE way as they came in low and fast from the east, the rising sun at their backs. Burke watched her with pride as she moved confidently through the air like some mythic creature.

Burke followed closely behind his daughter with Vance and Jeremiah flanking him. Far behind, almost hidden against the brightening horizon, Poocher and Thorny were mere specks. Burke didn't care about leaving the pig behind, but felt bad for Thorny, who complained that when they flew too fast he couldn't breathe. The flight that Shay had made in two hours had taken them all night. Still, that was far swifter than Burke had imagined possible.

Dragon Forge lay before them, the rust-mound surrounding it glittering beneath a sheen of morning frost. The trees beneath them were stunted parodies of healthy forests. Burke wondered if they suffered from a lack of light due to the brown clouds that normally hung over the area, or if trees no more enjoyed breathing smoke than men did. If he continued to run the foundry after this morning, he'd already thought of several improvements to the furnaces and smokestacks that would allow them to operate more efficiently. His intent was to make the atmosphere within the fort healthier; perhaps the forest would enjoy the benefit as well.

A mile from the town, they passed over the ring of encamped dragons enforcing the blockade. Several catapults had been brought into range. He wondered why Ragnar hadn't used the cannons to discourage this. The big guns had a far greater range than any catapult.

Below, a few bleary-eyed earth-dragons stood near a blue silk tent. He recognized the tent style as the work of the valkyries. The earth-dragons looked up, squinting, shielding their eyes as if trying to make sense of what they were seeing. He wasn't terribly worried. Earth-dragons were notoriously near-sighted. They probably would be mistaken for sky-dragons.

With the wind in his ears, Burke barely heard their shouts. He grimaced. Perhaps they hadn't been mistaken for sky-dragons. He saw the flap of a tent flutter open and a lone valkyrie poke her head out, craning her neck skyward. She looked only half awake, but alert enough to have thought to have put on her helmet.

Suddenly, the valkyrie's eyes popped open.

He hoped that Thorny and Poocher would be okay if the sky-dragon managed to summon her sisters to the air, but there was no time to slow down. The walls of the fortress were approaching fast. He scanned the battlements, looking for any sign that the sky-wall archers had seen them. He looked again, his heart sinking. No archers had seen him because none were on the walls. No living man could be seen anywhere within the city.

The same could not be said of dead ones.

As the walls flashed beneath them, he saw a severed human head in a state of advanced decay sitting on the wooden walkway inside the battlement, gazing up with crow-plucked eyes. All around the roof tops were other remains, legs and arms and torsos, along with whole bodies wedged up against chimneys or dangling limply from rain gutters.

His first instinct was that they were too late. The rebels had already been slaughtered. Logic kicked in and he understood what the catapults had been used for. The rain of corpses had been meant to soften up the rebels for an attack yet to come.

Again, he wondered why the cannons hadn't been used. Even before he left, the big guns had been rolling off the production line. By now, the construction needed to mount them on the walls should have been completed. Had Ragnar not read any of his battle plans?

Anza tilted her feet down, her long braid trailing behind her as she dropped toward the broad lip of the well at the center of town. She seemed to be going too fast, but in the final seconds her speed dropped as if a net had caught her, and she lighted on the stone rim as gently as a fallen leaf. Burke hadn't told her of the fate Shanna had suffered at the well, and the well made an inviting target for landing, given its central location and the way it rose up like a stage from the packed earth surrounding it.

Vance and Jeremiah landed beside her. Burke drifted down and then stopped, hovering above the center of the well. He nearly gagged at a human ribcage caught in the bucket that dangled a few yards down the shaft. Rats crawled over the tatters of its desiccated flesh. He hoped a lucky shot had placed it there. They were in trouble if the dragons possessed catapult marksmen capable of intentionally scoring a bull's-eye on the well. He didn't point it out to the others, who were looking around the city. There were more than enough horrors to gaze upon.

"Why hasn't anybody pulled those corpses from the roofs?" Vance asked, as he looked around the abandoned streets. "Where is everyone?"

Burke held the shotgun Shay had given him over his head. "Let's find out," he said, pulling the trigger. The bang echoed through the empty streets.

Seconds later, a few guards appeared along the city's walls. Had they been sleeping? He counted only seven. This, compared to the hundreds that should be at their posts.

Up and down the street doors creaked open. Shadowy faces with wide eyes peeked out. Slowly, voices began to call back and forth.

"Burke!" someone yelled.

"Burke," others echoed.

"Burke's ghost!" a voice shouted.

Burke grimaced. Convincing men he wasn't dead while floating a yard above the well could be tricky. But he still wasn't planning to land. He patiently reloaded the shotgun. Anza folded her wings back into the disk and drew her tomahawks. She stood in a stance that was both relaxed and impatient. Men began to cautiously step into the streets.

Vance followed her lead. He folded up his wings and drew his sky-wall bow, placing an arrow against the string and waiting, watching. Beside him Jeremiah drew Vulpine's knife, but kept his wings spread wide.

A moment behind them, Poocher and Thorny drifted down from the sky. Poocher let out a small grunt; all four of his cleft hooves touched the rim of his well at once. He stood next to Jeremiah. The pig also left his wings open. Burke wondered if he knew how to close them.

Thorny folded his wings in while his feet were still a foot above the well. He let out a loud "oof" as he landed. He looked up at Burke and said, "I'm your friend, and I'd die for you, but I'll be damned if I'm ever going to fly for you again. I'm giving my wings to Bitterwood next chance I get."

"I don't think he needs them," said Burke as he finished loading the shotgun.

"No man needs these things," Thorny grumbled.

"Is it my imagination, or are you in a bad mood?"

"I feel like a cranky baby. Sixty is too old to be teething again." To show what he meant, he pulled back his lips and revealed his gums. Where once there had been more gaps than teeth, there were now freshly minted chompers, ten times whiter than the old teeth that surrounded them.

By now, the square around the well was filling. The crowd was full of men shouting Burke's name—not cheering him, or greeting him: merely announcing his presence to others.

Burke looked down the avenue to the red brick house at the end.

He clenched his jaw as the door opened.

VULPINE WAS IN the habit of waking at dawn. In the quietness of the morning, he pondered the words he'd said to Balikan only a few weeks before. The world was in no danger of running out of days, or years. Yet, Vulpine was keenly aware that he was not the world. His body possessed a sluggishness in the chill of the morning that reminded him that his youth had long since vanished.

His kettle whistled upon the small oil burner. He picked it up, welcoming the warmth of the wire handle in his stiff fore-talon. He poured the oily brown contents into a tin cup. He sniffed it, savoring the complex sharpness of the odor. The soup was a mix of shaved barks, roots, and organs. The bark of the willow tree was especially bitter, but there was no questioning that it soothed the aching of his muscles. The root of the sassafras offset the bitterness somewhat with a medicinal tang and a touch of sweetness that prodded his thoughts into clarity on cool mornings. Alligator testicles, dried and powdered, ensured his continued virility and gave the whole mix a musky bouquet and salty aftertaste.

He crouched by a low table and sipped his morning medicine, reading the letter that had been delivered yesterday by Chapelion's messengers. He ground his teeth at Chapelion's incompetence. More of the aerial guard had abandoned the palace. Some new charismatic prophet had apparently established a base in the Free City and was drawing a following of both humans and dragons. Worse, Cragg, the beastialist who had inherited Rorg's abode, had announced that his tribe was seceding from the rest of the kingdom. There were reports that Verteniel, who oversaw the coastal abode that included the Isle of Horses, was prepared to do the same. This had always been the true danger of the empty throne— not that the other sun-dragons would try to conquer the kingdom, but that they would simply decide they could manage the affairs of their own small fiefdoms better without the interference of a king.

Faced with all this bad news, he welcomed the interruption when Sagen pushed aside the flap to his tent.

"Sir? May I speak with you?"

"Please come in," said Vulpine. He motioned toward the kettle. "May I offer you a cup of my daily elixir?"

Sagen's nose wrinkled as he contemplated the oily fluid.

"I promise it grows on you," said Vulpine.

"Breakfast can wait. I was awakened with news only moments ago. I felt it was important that I consult with you at once. There's been... activity... at Dragon Forge," said Sagen, sounding hesitant in his choice of words.

"So they've poked their heads out again after yesterday's bombardment?"

The skin around Sagen's eyes bunched up as if he were pondering how to say his next sentence. "There are reports that the blockade has been breached, sir."

Vulpine sighed. "Let me guess. The earth-dragons got so twisted on goom they fell asleep at their posts and let more refugees into the fort."

"No sir," said Sagen. "It was breached by the air. By angels."

Vulpine tilted his head, not quite certain he'd heard this correctly. "Angels," Vulpine said calmly. "Men with wings."

Sagen nodded. "And a pig."

"A pig?"

"Yes sir."

"With wings?"

"Yes sir."

Vulpine closed his eyes and rubbed his brow with his fore-talon. His scales felt especially dry this morning. Sagen, as a product of his bloodline, was designed to be among the most sane and intelligent dragons who'd ever flown above the earth. He was certain his son wasn't deranged. So, angels. And why not? He'd never believed in their reality, but the *Ballad of Belpantheron* spoke of them, and there had reportedly been an angel who'd come to the defense of the Nest during the recent nastiness with Blasphet. Perhaps that angel still lingered in the area, along with a friend or two.

"How many," he asked, opening his eyes.

"Counting the pig?"

"I don't see why not."

"Six. The pig, a woman, and four men, ranging in age from a boy to a wizened old man."

Vulpine took a sip of the hot elixir. He swished it around on his tongue for a moment, allowing the heat in his mouth a few extra seconds to warm his brain.

"Who reported the sighting?"

"Arifiel."

"Ah," said Vulpine. He didn't especially like the female, but she'd shown no tendency toward exaggeration or fantasy.

"Her sighting was confirmed by a score of earth-dragons, though given the weakness of their vision I'm not certain we can give much credence there."

"The word of Arifiel is enough," Vulpine said. "It's an odd development, I'll grant you, but we'll manage it. I'm familiar enough with human mythology to know they associate angels with death. Perhaps they're harbingers that the end is near."

"Is the end near, sir?" asked Sagen. "Many of the guard have noticed the lack of activity within the fort in recent days. The walls are practically undefended. We could be at the town center within minutes. Why must we tarry?"

Vulpine started to mention the wheeled-bows and the guns as good reasons, but held his tongue. He looked at the correspondence before him. Had he miscalculated the greater danger? He thought he was keeping chaos from spreading by containing Dragon Forge. But what if, by focusing on the few square miles of earth within the circle of the blockade, he was ignoring the greater danger at his back? What if they won Dragon Forge, but lost the kingdom?

"Summon Arifiel and Sawface," said Vulpine. "Let us hold a council of war."

"Why Sawface? You know his opinion. He will want to charge the walls of the city and rip the limbs from every living thing he encounters."

"True," said Vulpine. "And I'm intrigued to see if I can find any reason to argue against his doing so. Have them here in five minutes. I'm going to take a quick flight to survey the area."

Vulpine sat his tin cup onto the table, gazing at the gray and brown dregs at the bottom. His medicine looked no better than it tasted.

A CROWD OF at least a thousand men surrounded the well, their eyes fixed upon Burke. Most had rags covering their mouths and noses. The stench of rot and sewage grew as the morning sun climbed above the eastern wall. Steam rose from the skin of a corpse on a nearby roof.

No one said a word. Ragnar, prophet of the lord, was approaching.

Ragnar looked particularly wild this morning. His mane of black hair and chest-length beard clung to his leathery skin in oily, tangled locks. He carried the cross he'd had welded together from swords before him in both hands. The whites of the prophet's eyes glowed in the dark shadows beneath his bushy brow.

The crowd parted as Ragnar stalked forward. Behind him was Stonewall, also armed. He carried a mace and a heavy steel shield that Burke recognized instantly. It was one of the armored plates from the Angry Beetle. The giant wore a vest of chainmail and a steel helmet that covered most of his skull, but left his eyes and mouth exposed. Burke expected to see hate in Stonewall's eyes after their rather abrupt parting of ways. Instead, Stonewall looked more worried than vengeful.

Behind Ragnar were two more Mighty Men, Joab and Adino. They, too, wore chainmail vests and helmets, but carried flintlock shotguns. Burke felt a mixture of pride and consternation when he realized that the guns were both double-barreled and incorporated the back loading design he'd created for the Angry Beetle's weaponry. This meant someone had found and decoded his notes, or else extrapolated cleverly from the plans he'd already shared. His pride came not because the weapons were ones he'd designed, but from the realization that he wasn't the only smart man in the fort. These rebels who surrounded him were good men, brave, and clever. It would be an honor to die by their side in battle.

Of course, dying by their side had never worried him. Dying at their hands was what kept him awake at night.

The crowd drew back even further as Ragnar marched within a yard of the well. He glared up at Burke, studying him closely. The prophet's beefy hands squeezed tightly around the cross.

A thick vein beside the prophet's left eyebrow pulsed strongly enough that Burke could count the big man's heartbeats. Ragnar's mouth opened. Burke braced himself, certain that he was about to be condemned as a witch or a devil.

Instead, the prophet asked in a voice that was little more than a whisper, "Are you dead?"

Thorny glanced up at Burke, his eyebrows raised. The question had taken him by surprise as well.

Before Burke could answer, Ragnar continued, eyeing Jeremiah. "This was the boy sick with yellow-mouth."

Jeremiah nodded. "I'm not sick anymore," he said.

The hairy man studied Vance's face, then Thorny's.

"These were the men who fled town," he said, quietly. "You perished in the explosion."

Now Jeremiah, Vance, and even Poocher were looking to Burke to see what he would say next. Only Anza didn't look at him; she kept her eyes fixed firmly on the Mighty Men with the guns. For the moment, Burke felt bulletproof.

He shook his head. "We aren't dead," he said, firmly, making certain the crowd heard his words. "I know I could play upon your superstitions and claim we're specters, or angels. I could claim it was God who healed our wounds and gave us wings of silver. But these are all lies. I am a man who values truth.

"Our presence here has nothing to do with gods or magic. The wings that hold me in the air are machines, better machines than I know how to build. Jeremiah's yellow-mouth was fixed by machines, tiny ones, smaller than I can design. Vance can see because of them; Anza can talk. Thorny had lost most of his teeth over the years. Smile for the crowd, Thorny." Thorny gave a broad grin to the men who stood before him, displaying his restored choppers.

Ragnar's face twisted into a snarl. "Witchcraft explains all these things."

"Witchcraft explains a lot of things," said Burke, again speaking loudly enough for the crowd to hear. "It can explain how black powder ignites and pushes lead balls from an iron tube. You can explain how fire changes some rocks into metals by chalking it up as magic. And if you need to understand why crops sometimes fail, or why some men die in battle and others don't, or why plague besieges a city, it doesn't take a lot of thought. You can explain it all as the will of God."

He swept his gaze across the crowd, at the countless eyes fixed upon him. "All of these explanations have one thing in common," he said. "They're wrong."

"Blasphemer!" Ragnar barked. His knuckles turned white as he gripped his cross more tightly. He looked coiled to spring.

Anza shifted her stance, maintaining her look of casual readiness. Ragnar glared at her. "I do not fear your daughter," the prophet growled.

Joab and Adino lifted their guns to their shoulders, taking aim. Burke crossed his arms and patiently waited for Ragnar to make his move.

The prophet's eyes smoldered like droplets of molten steel. "Fly away," Ragnar said. "You are five against thousands."

Burke wondered who he wasn't counting. The pig? Jeremiah? It was time to find out if the prophet's math was fundamentally flawed.

"Perhaps it's the four of you against thousands," said Burke.

The prophet's mouth twitched.

Burked looked at the crowd. "I'm not here to take command of this fort by violence. I didn't come here for revenge against Ragnar, or to inspire you with wonderful words of how your struggle is part of God's plan. I'm here to offer to lead you in a struggle that's far more selfish in nature. I want to one day plant a garden on land I've plowed without some dragon king claiming the harvest. I want my grandchildren to live in a world where they won't be sold as slaves or hunted as prey. I want freedom. I'm willing to die by your side to earn it."

Ragnar looked at the crowd. His voice boomed like thunder: "Do not listen to this devil! Freedom is not the cause! We do not make war for land or riches! We fight for a greater glory! We are created in God's image, and the wrath of God is great and righteous! We struggle against serpents! We are the light in a world of darkness! Together, we will drive the dragons into the sea! Remember the Free City! Remember the Free City!"

As always, the utterance of these words was followed immediately by their repetition. Yet, it wasn't the crowd that cried out the words: it was the echo of Ragnar's own voice bouncing from the stone wall of the foundry behind Burke.

The crowd was silent. Some men watched Ragnar carefully, even fearfully. Some looked at Burke with the same fearful eyes. Others looked at the ground, as if they wished they were someplace else.

"You heard the man. He offers you wrath. He offers you a holy struggle. He offers you the promise of a wise and knowing God who will bring you victory in battle." Burke slowly shook his head. "If you follow me, no higher power will guide us. If we have a hope of winning, it will be because we go to war with better weapons and better tactics than our enemies. I was miserly with my knowledge before. Now, I vow to teach all I know to anyone who listens. I cannot offer you a god. I can only give you machines. The choice is yours."

"This isn't a democracy!" Ragnar snapped.

Stonewall placed his hand on the prophet's hairy shoulder. The holy man jerked his head toward his bodyguard. "Respectfully, sir," said Stonewall, his voice calm, almost gentle, "why isn't it?"

* * *

VULPINE HIMSELF HAD surveyed the fort and witnessed the winged men who stood near the well. He even spotted the pig. Though he kept his distance, he was certain the boy with wings was Jeremiah. He didn't know what to make of this. The timing was right; the boy could be dead by now. But he wasn't quite ready to accept the validity of human mythology regarding the afterlife. He was certain there was a logical explanation for the newcomers' wings. He was confident he could solve the mystery if he could examine their corpses.

It looked as if the entire population of the rebels had massed around the central square. They were, he thought, a wretched-looking lot, standing around with hunched shoulders and sagging heads. No doubt few men wanted to look up when the roofs were thick with corpses.

Thus, when the council of war was called, there was little time wasted in debate.

These men were bent. It was time to break them.

He stood by Sagen at the northern catapults as the sun inched higher in the sky. There was a pile of human bodies in various stages of decay nearby. The smell should have been horrible; save for buzzards and insects, there were no beasts that found the stench of rotten flesh appealing. Yet, Vulpine had been in the presence of so many corpses over the years, he was surprised to find that he barely noticed the odor. It was like the restorative tea he drank each morning; he'd grown so accustomed to the scent he sometimes forgot that others might find it unpleasant.

Beside the corpse pile was a larger heap of rusted scrap metal, salvaged from the gleaner mounds. Vulpine went to this mound and picked up a short shaft of iron about an inch in diameter. He couldn't begin to guess its former purpose. No matter. It was shrapnel now.

"Have you ever thought much about the year?" asked Vulpine. Sagen looked bewildered by the question. "Why do we number the years as we do? The earth is incomprehensibly older than eleven centuries. Do you ever contemplate the empires that rose and fell and vanished with barely a trace?"

"Occasionally, sir."

Vulpine dropped the scrap of iron and picked up a much bigger, heavier piece. It was an open box with rounded corners, mostly white, about two feet wide and a foot deep; the steel at its core was coated by a thin glaze of ceramic to protect it from rust. The glaze had failed. There was a hole in the bottom he could have stuck his snout through, and bubbles along the rim showed that the iron beneath the glaze had succumbed to rust in numerous spots. Still, it was a hefty object, mostly intact despite having been buried in the ground for centuries.

"The archeologists at the College of Spires would weep if they saw what we were about to do to these treasures," he said.

Sagen shrugged. "They strike me more as trash than treasure."

"They read trash as if it were a book." He rotated the white box in his hands. It weighed at least twenty pounds. The glaze on the interior had been crafted with greater care than the glaze on the outside. "No doubt, they would unravel the function this object served, long ago."

"I heard two of the guards debating this very artifact, sir," said Sagen. "They concluded it was a sink."

"Hmm," said Sagen, tossing the object back onto the pile. "That seems plausible. All that matters, I suppose, is that it will leave a nice dent in the skull of anyone it hits."

"I think a human would need an especially thick skull to only suffer a dent," said Sagen.

Vulpine looked across the rolling hills, over the jagged ravines carved into the red clay by erosion, to the fort beyond. "I want every scrap to land in the square. They're packed in so thick we'll kill half of them with our initial salvo. Sawface and his Wasters are ready to lead the charge. Let's finish this. We had breakfast in our tents. We'll cook our lunch in the furnaces of the foundry."

CHAPTER THIRTY-THREE

FREEFALL

BEFORE BURKE COULD say another word, Ragnar gripped the cross of swords with both hands and swung it with an angry grunt. Stonewall lifted his heavy steel shield to catch the blow with a loud *CLANG*.

Stonewall looked anguished as he gazed into the prophet's eyes. "Sir, I don't want to hurt you," the giant man said.

The wild-haired prophet released an incoherent cry of rage, spinning around, clearing a broad circle as men jumped back to avoid the arc traced by the sharp-edged cross.

The giant raised his mace and blocked the weapon again.

Anza glanced at Burke. Burke nodded. She leapt from the wall, raising her sword overhead as she dove at Ragnar's back.

A fraction of a second before she reached him, a large rusty cylinder that Burke recognized as the piston of an ancient engine flashed down from the sky and caught Anza on her left shoulder. The blow spun her in the air. Her sword flew from her grasp as she crashed into the center of Ragnar's back.

The broad-shouldered prophet barely flinched from the impact.

An instant later, the entire crowd began to scream. Countless bits of random metal, ranging in size from fingers to fists, rained down on them. Burke's heart froze as a hundred men dropped, victims of the falling debris.

"Don't panic!" he shouted, praying he could be heard above the din. "Don't panic! Grab the injured and carry them! Everyone into the foundry!"

With its sturdy brick walls, the foundry could withstand anything the dragons cared to throw at them.

Ragnar looked down at Anza, sprawled at his feet. "See the evil you have brought upon us with your blasphemy! The Lord strikes down all unbelievers!"

At that moment, a big white square of ceramic-glazed steel slammed into the back of the prophet's shaggy skull, bouncing off. The prophet's eyes narrowed as he remained on his feet. The sink clanged on the hard-packed earth behind him.

The look of perpetual rage on the prophet's face vanished as his brow and jaw went slack. His eyes rolled up into his head and he dropped to his knees, falling forward over Anza's legs. Anza kicked herself free and sprang to her feet, clutching her limp left arm with her right hand.

Panic spread through the crowd like a wave, even though the initial volley from the catapult was spent. The skies were empty for the moment.

Burke fired his shotgun into the air. "Listen to me!" he screamed so loudly he was certain he tore something in his throat.

Stonewall leapt over Ragnar to stand on the lip of the well. He shouted with a voice that rivaled the fallen prophet in both volume and authority: "Pay attention!" To Burke's great relief, it worked. The crowd turned their eyes toward Stonewall.

"You heard the man," said the giant. "Everyone into the foundry. Carry the wounded. No one gets left behind."

Anza looked up. "Fadder!" she shouted.

More shrapnel was darkening the sky.

"Take cover!" Burke barked out, though there was precious little cover to be had in the middle of the town square. The men nearest the foundry peeled off, vanishing into its shadowy reaches. Jeremiah flew toward the foundry and Poocher darted after him. Vance shot skyward, and Thorny hopped down and pressed himself against the wall of the well. Stonewall held up his shield like a giant umbrella.

Anza grabbed her fallen sword with her good arm and leapt into the air, her wings unfolding, as the second volley smashed into the crowd. Sparks flew as a large rusty bolt ricocheted from Anza's wings. She flashed toward Stonewall and pressed herself against him, pushing him over a few inches. Stonewall let out a loud grunt as a fist-sized chunk of scrap banged off his shield.

Men dove into any doorway available. Anguished howls of pain rose from those struck by the falling metal.

Luck alone spared Burke. "The foundry! The foundry! You'll be safe in the foundry!"

More men began to run for its darkened interior.

Stonewall looked up as the rain of metal died off. "What about the defenders on the walls?" Almost simultaneously, Vance, fifty yards above, shouted, "The earth-dragons are charging the gates!"

"Get the men off the walls," said Burke. "Let the dragons in."

"Come down from the walls!" Stonewall shouted. "Everyone into the foundry!"

"You too, Vance," said Burke. "Get down here."

"Someone has to go stop those catapults," said Vance.

"You won't stop them with a bow and arrow," said Burke. He glanced at Anza. "Despite what you're thinking, you won't stop them with a sword."

She grimaced.

Joab leaned over Ragnar's form. "He's still breathing!"

"Get him into the foundry. We only have a minute before the next volley."

"Seconds," Vance shouted down. "Here it comes!"

Burke didn't look at the sky. Instead, he shouted, "Take cover!" and he, too, darted for the foundry. As he zoomed toward it, he saw that the normally shadowy interior was bright as day. He remembered that the visor he wore allowed him to see in darkness.

He hovered above the crowd huddled into the foundry. "You men in back!" he shouted. "Get into the store room and bring out every gun you can. I know some of you have been trained in how to use them. I'm sorry more of you haven't. If we live through this, I promise that every single one of you will be given a gun and taught to use it."

"I've already got a gun!" a man shouted.

"Me too," echoed at least a dozen others.

Burke nodded.

Vance and Anza drew up beside him in the air.

"I could... break... a cat-uh-polt," she said, sounding out her words carefully as she held up her sword.

"I have no doubt you could do real damage to one if you got up close," said Burke. "But you're not getting up close. You and Vance are going to wipe out the catapults from the air. Thorny, too."

Thorny shook his head. "I can't fly again, Burke. I'm just not built for it." He reached behind his back and pulled the silver disk free.

"Give it to Stonewall," Burke said.

Stonewall was just entering the open door of the foundry. He carried two fallen men over his shoulders, and was helping a third man limp along on a bleeding leg.

"These are the same sorts of wings Shay used," said Stonewall, eyeing the disk he was offered. "Is he with you?"

"He had business elsewhere," said Burke. "You're now drafted to the air team."

"I don't—"

"You'll figure it out. The wings respond to thought. You seem good at thinking."

Stonewall placed the men he carried onto the ground. Thorny handed him the silver disk.

"Get the doors closed," Burke snapped as metal once again rained down onto the streets outside. He felt sick at all the bodies left behind. Aside from the dead and dying, the square was now empty.

Suddenly, the ground beneath them trembled as a loud *WHOOM*! rang from the northern gate.

"Battering ram," said Stonewall.

"Hammer," said Burke, remembering the beast that had broken the bridge.

Jeremiah moved among the wounded men and offered them the dragonseeds. Burke could think of no rational reason he should be afraid of the seeds, but he still couldn't help but wonder if this was all part of some greater scheme of Blasphet's. It was a bad moment to be having doubts.

Guns were handed out from the door in the back of the room that ran to the warehouse. Below him, the men gazed up with hopeful eyes.

"Gentlemen," he said, as a second WHOOM! rose from the northern gate, "Let's go over the plan."

"There's a plan?" asked Vance.

Burke allowed himself a small grin. "There's always a plan."

SAWFACE STRUCK THE northern gate a second time, with a shout that would have made an ox-dog flee with its tail between its legs. He didn't like to have to hit things a second time. It made him angry.

The gate tore from its hinges and fell, raising a cloud of dust.

The earth-dragons at his back let up a loud cheer.

"RRRRRRRAAAAAAAAAAAAA!" Sawface jumped onto the fallen gate and charged.

He ran down the central avenue toward the well. The footfalls of the army he led sounded like thunder. It enraged him that there were no living humans visible, only hundreds of freshly-slain bodies still bleeding in the dust.

"GRRRRRRREEEAAAA!" he cried out, as he smashed his hammer down onto the stone lip of the well. The wall shattered, sending shards of stone heavenward. He swung around and banged the shattered wall with his thick tail and watched as a long section of it tumbled into the black pit of the well. The collapse of the well brought him no satisfaction. He needed blood! He needed to see the fear in a man's eyes in the second before he crushed his skull!

On the second floor of the foundry, a window swung open. A short man with a wispy mustache fired an arrow that whistled toward Sawface. It landed at the exact tip of his boney snout, quivering between his nostrils.

Sawface tore the arrow free and charged the foundry. He slammed his hammer into the brick wall. Cracks ran up the mortar to the window where the man stood.

"Idiot," the man called down. "Too dumb to use the door."

"RRRRRAAAAAAAAAUUUUUHHHH!" screamed Sawface. The mammal dared taunt him! He spun around and looked into the eyes of the earth-dragon immediately behind him. The soldier was half his size, heavily armored in plates of thick steel. He snatched the soldier by the arm and said, "BRING HIM TO ME!"

He threw the soldier with all his strength at the window.

The man who taunted him turned pale and jumped back into the room.

The earth-dragon smashed into the wall a foot below the window with a loud crash, then dropped back to the earth at Sawface's feet. Blood poured from his mouth.

"EEERRRRRRAAAAAAAAAAAAAGGAA!" Saw-face screamed as he spun back to face the soldiers behind him. As one, they all jumped back a full yard. They stared at him with wide eyes.

"GAAAAAHHRRRR!" he cried out as he barreled toward them. The soldiers parted, and then quickly closed in behind him as he ran around the side of the foundry toward the great central doors. He swung his hammer with every fiber of rage he could muster. The double doors flew apart in a spray of splinters.

He leapt into the darkness beyond, halting for the briefest second as his eyes adjusted to the dim light. He was hungry to find a target as quickly as possible.

Behind him, he heard the clatter and clang of his Wasters as they, too, paused at the door.

Before him was a wall of men, at least a hundred, crouched down on their knees, pointing rods of iron at him.

Behind them were a hundred more men standing, also pointing iron rods. He recognized these pieces of metal. They were the bang sticks that had killed so many of his brothers at the battle near the river.

Above the twin rows was a man with wings.

"Now," said the man.

Sawface heard the *snick* of two hundred pieces of flint striking steel in unison. He heard the *ssss* and saw the dancing sparks as ten-score flash-pans sizzled to life.

"Raaar?" he whispered.

THE THUNDEROUS REPORT deafened Burke, but the visor protected him from the flash. He saw in crystal clarity the heavy iron head of Sawface's hammer drop through the pink mist where the beast had just stood. The anvil-shaped metal bounced in curious silence next to the claw prints on the stone floor.

Beyond, dozens of earth-dragons writhed in agony as their horrified companions looked on. The sky-wall team must have heard the guns go off—for that matter, the men on the moon must have heard the gun go off. But it was the sky-wall team that poured to the windows and roof and began to fire arrows into the dragons in the street. The arrows flew so rapidly they looked like flashes of light in Burke's visor. Above the ringing in his ears, he began to faintly hear the familiar song of the bows—*zing zing zing zing zing!*

The earth dragons screamed as a single chorus. Never before had Burke heard such music.

In thirty seconds, it was over. Not a single earth-dragon on the street outside the foundry was left alive.

"The sky-dragons will see this," Burke shouted. "They're free to use the catapults again. Bombers! Go!"

VULPINE LIFTED HIS head as he heard a thunder similar to the one that accompanied the explosion at the bridge.

Sagen said, "Did the humans have a second war machine?"

"Possibly," said Vulpine. "It sounds as if this one fared no better than the first."

Seconds later, wisps of white smoke rose into the air near the foundry.

Odd. With an explosion of this size, he would have expected black smoke.

He looked up at the sky-dragon spotters high overhead. All had their necks craned toward the city as they rode the wind. Suddenly, one broke off and dove toward them. It was a member of the aerial guard. The sky-dragon spread his wings fifty feet above the ground and parachuted to a halt on the red-clay earth by the catapult. "The earth-dragons have been massacred!"

"What?" said Vulpine, finding the dragon's exaggeration amusing. "In the three minutes since they knocked open the gate?"

The dragon shook his head. "In the thirty seconds after they reached the foundry."

"Are they in retreat?"

The sky-dragon sounded angry. "I mean, sir, that every last earth-dragon that followed Sawface has been killed."

Vulpine's voice caught in his throat. In the distance, he spotted the angels shooting into the air, straight up, one, two, three, four, five of them. They rose at an impossible speed until they vanished in the bright sky above.

Arifiel, who was with them at the command post, turned and said, "As of now, the valkyries are no longer part of this mission."

"What?" asked Vulpine.

"Has age dulled your ears?" Arifiel asked. "An angel came to the defense of the Nest. I'm alive because that angel saved me after I'd been badly burned. I was uncomfortable this morning when I saw the angels. They look different from the one who saved me, but their wings are the same. Now, the angels have come to the defense of Dragon Forge."

"And it's your duty to fight them!" said Vulpine.

"No, sir," said Arifiel. "A valkyrie's first loyalty is to the Nest. The Nest survives due to angelic intervention. Now, they have chosen to defend Dragon Forge. I do not know what their purpose is. But there are mysterious forces at work here, and I don't intend to leave those forces angry at the Nest."

"Arifiel!" said Sagen. "Such cowardice!"

"It's not cowardice that guides my judgment," said Arifiel. "It's—"

She never finished her sentence.

Vulpine's jaws closed around her throat quicker than she could react. He felt her swallow against his tongue. He whipped his head violently to the side, tearing away her windpipe.

She dropped to the ground, dying; bright red blood surged from the long rip in her pale blue throat. Vulpine spit away the bits of scaly hide that clung to his teeth.

"You're now in command of the valkyries," Vulpine said to Sagen.

Sagen looked pale as he stared at his father's bloody mouth.

"What if she's right?" Sagen asked. "What if there are forces at work here we don't understand?"

Vulpine's anger welled. "Of course there are forces here we don't understand! Wars unfold in a great fog, and any dragon who thinks he can see the grand picture is a fool!" He shook his head. "As I have been a fool," he whispered.

"Sir?"

"From the start, I've been advised to simply burn Dragon Forge and build a new foundry on the ash pile." He sighed. "In my arrogance, I believed I could control events to produce a more favorable outcome. I should have known better, Sagen. I should have known that the world is bigger than any one dragon can fathom."

"No one could have foreseen the intervention of angels," said Sagen.

"It's not angels that plague us," said Vulpine. He was certain of this, despite the evidence of his own eyes. "It's our unknown genius within the walls of Dragon Forge. All this time, I thought we had the luxury of waiting them out, as disease and dwindling resources depleted them. In truth, they were waiting us out... no doubt he calculated that the great empire Albekizan commanded would unravel before their food was exhausted."

At his feet, Arifiel convulsed briefly before her body went completely slack. Blood stopped spurting from her throat and slowed to an ooze.

"I learn from my mistakes," said Vulpine. "Load the catapults with oil and pitch. We may not eat lunch in the foundries, but it's not too late to roast our dinner upon the coals of the—"

Before he could finish, there was a clap of thunder from the southern side of the fort. He looked up and saw black smoke rising from the hill where the southern catapults had been stationed. An instant later, the ground beneath their claws trembled as if a giant fist had struck the earth.

He followed the trail of black smoke upward and spotted the five angels a mile above. "Load the catapults quickly," said Vulpine, kneeling to pick up Arifiel's spear.

"Where are you going?" Sagen asked as his father spread his wings and jumped into the sky, catching the spear in his hind-talons.

"I'm going to kill the angels," said Vulpine.

"You HAD TO hit it," said Jeremiah. His voice sounded odd. His ears were still ringing from the simultaneous firing of the rifles. Bombing the catapults below hadn't helped things.

They were up so high that Jeremiah was certain, had it been night, he could have tested his theory that Vulpine had carried him high enough to touch the moon. Even though the sun was out, the wind was piercing cold. He held the torch of oil-soaked rags closer, grateful for the heat.

Poocher hung beside him in the air. The pig was draped with a dozen quivers of arrows. Vance hovered nearby, sky-wall bow at the ready, eyeing the thick black smoke beneath them for any signs of dragons.

"I'm pretty sure you destroyed it," Stonewall said to Anza. Anza was about thirty feet down, tilted out parallel to the ground, studying the brief flashes of the dragon encampment that could be seen through the smoke. Stonewall was almost directly above her. He looked as at home in the air as Jeremiah felt. Except for Thorny, everyone who used the wings liked them. Jeremiah wondered if the wings did something to his mind to make him feel less afraid.

Stonewall was dragging a net filled with eight twenty-pound kegs of gunpowder. They'd already used two kegs. Anza's job was to pull them from the net and figure out the right spot to drop them from to hit the catapults. Jeremiah's job was to light the fuses. Vance was to protect them from any dragons who tried to reach them, and Poocher's job was to make sure he didn't run out of arrows.

Finally, Anza nodded and gave a thumbs up.

"West," she said, swinging around and darting off.

"West it is," said Vance.

The southern catapults had been taken completely unaware. They weren't going to be as lucky at the western station. There were at least thirty sky-dragons climbing toward them, straining to match their height. Jeremiah wondered if Vulpine was among them. It was hard to tell sky-dragons apart. They were all about the same size and color. Still, he didn't see any of them carrying whips.

They closed in swiftly on the thirty dragons. Jeremiah was a little nervous, but Vance said, "They carry spears, but they can't throw them far. They normally use them when they dive at people. We can be a few yards from them and not be in any real danger."

"I'd prefer not to test that theory," said Stonewall.

The dragons were now a hundred yards away and closing.

Vance lifted his bow. He began to fire, and dragons began to drop. Jeremiah eyed the dragons nervously as they grew ever closer. Poocher, too, focused his attention on the wall of enemies that approached.

Anza temporarily had her hands free, so she reached for her throwing knives.

Stonewall said, "Shouldn't we climb higher?"

"You guys are too nervous," said Vance, as his bow continued to sing.

As he reached the last arrow in his quiver, a dozen dragons were in freefall. The survivors wheeled, fleeing for their lives. He turned toward Poocher and grabbed a fresh quiver.

Jeremiah noticed how Vance's face went slack as he looked back. Before Jeremiah could turn his head, a blue shadow flashed across the corner of his vision. A long slender spear caught Vance dead in the center of his chest and pushed through. The impact of the weapon through his shoulder blades popped his wings off cleanly.

The sky-dragon who'd killed Vance released the spear in his hind-talons and snatched the loose wings from the air. He swooped up higher, flapping his wings to pause for a moment as he looked down to study the device.

A long whip of tan leather hung from the slave-catcher's belt.

"Vulpine!" cried Jeremiah.

Perhaps it was only a reflection of the silver wings, but Vulpine's eyes twinkled as he gazed at the boy. "A true angel wouldn't need machines to fly," said the slavecatcher.

Anza hurled her throwing knives at Vulpine, folded her body, and shot into a dive. Vulpine kicked up with the silver wings still in his hind claws and knocked the blades away. It was too late to save Vance, she knew, as she shot toward his body. But the sky-wall bow was caught in his limp fingers. If they were swarmed again, she would need it.

Vance's eyes were still open. He seemed to smile contentedly as she reached out, snatching the bow and jerking it away.

She slung the bow over her shoulder, which still throbbed terribly from the earlier catapult attack. If the blow had caught her on the ground instead of in the air, it would likely have broken her bones instead of merely bruising her.

She shot back toward the battle above. Poocher was being ignored by Vulpine at the moment, so the supply of arrows weren't in imminent danger. She could give her full attention to Vulpine.

Unfortunately, Jeremiah decided to give Vulpine his full attention first. He charged the slavecatcher, lashing out with his torch. Anza's battle-trained eyes could instantly see what was to come next.

Vulpine released the silver wings he carried and kicked out, knocking the torch from Jeremiah's grasp. The slavecatcher caught Jeremiah's slender throat in his left hind-talon.

With his right hind-talon, he caught the upper edge of Jeremiah's wings near the shoulder. He pulled, tearing Jeremiah free of his wings. The slavecatcher dropped the wings, which tumbled away in the wind.

Then, he let go of Jeremiah.

VULPINE SMILED AS the giant man released the net of barrels he carried and dove to save the boy. He was now alone in the sky with the pig—an absurd figure barely worth his attention—and the girl, who he'd seen in action at Burke's Tavern.

She rose in the air on her silver wings. Steel tomahawks dropped into her hands. He could tell as he studied her that her left arm was injured. She was more graceful in the air than her companions, but Vulpine had seven decades more experience in aerial combat.

She threw the tomahawks. The one from her left hand went wide of its mark. He caught the second one in his hind-talon.

"Care to try again?" he taunted as he glided in an arc around her. She did possess one mild advantage—she could hover. Vulpine had to keep moving to maintain flight.

In his experience, humans wore their thoughts on their faces. He often knew their next actions before they did. This woman was different. As she watched him move, her face grew blank, utterly devoid of emotion.

Suddenly, she shot toward him with an impossible burst of speed. Her right hand moved toward her shoulder and came back holding a razor sharp sword.

He twisted his torso, allowing the blade to slip into the thin flesh of his wing just beyond his ribs. It stung, but there were no major nerves or arteries there. He swiveled his jaws around and clamped them down onto her wings. The metal made his tongue tingle. With his hind-talon, he grabbed her ankle and jerked.

It took no more than a tenth of a second to strip her of her wings.

She fell, still with the look of utter dispassion on her features.

She reached out and caught the looped whip on his belt with her right hand. Her sudden weight tugged him down. He beat his wings to regain his balance. A knife appeared in her left hand. She thrust it over her head, sinking it into the center of his breastbone.

If this had been her good hand, Vulpine knew he would be dead. As it was, the blade caught in the bone. Pain radiated through his whole body, but the blow wasn't fatal.

"A good effort," he said, craning his neck toward her. "I suspect you might have won on the ground." He snapped his jaws onto her cheeks, sinking his teeth down until they rested on her skull. She let go of both the blade and his whip, and reached for his mouth. Her hands never reached their target.

He opened his jaws and gravity claimed her. As she slipped into freefall he saw, at last, fear flash into her eyes.

It was a most satisfying sight.

"So much for the angels," he said. "Where's the damned pig?"

There was a grunt at his back.

He craned his neck and saw the black and white beast gliding along behind him, his snout only inches from the tip of Vulpine's tail.

"You'll do nicely for dinner," said Vulpine.

The pig snorted. With the barest boost of speed, he shot forward the final inches.

Vulpine winced as the pig's jaws clamped down on the last vertebrae in his tail.

CHAPTER THIRTY-FOUR

DAWN OF A GOLDEN AGE

VULPINE'S TAIL WAS stretched straight as an arrow. He kicked, trying to reach the beast that held him, but his tail was much longer than his legs. He beat his wings harder. The bones along his spine popped. The pig simply wasn't flying as fast as he.

It finally occurred to him that if he slowed down, he would have the slack needed to reach the pig.

It occurred to the pig at the same instant to fold up the silver wings that held him aloft.

Vulpine was yanked from the sky as swiftly as if he had an anchor tied to him. His head whipped skyward as he dropped. In the space where he'd just been, several of his feather-scales floated in the air. He spread his wings, straining desperately to control their descent. They were falling toward Dragon Forge.

* * *

ON THE WALLS of Dragon Forge, Burke paid no attention to the battle overhead. He knew Anza and Vance could handle anything that was thrown at them, and would keep Jeremiah and Poocher safe. Instead, he focused his attention on the spy-owl. The catapults to the south were nothing but splinters. To the east and west, the dragons milled about in confusion, unsure of their orders.

The northern catapult didn't suffer from this lack of guidance. Here, the catapults were being loaded with barrels of pitch and oil. They were still a minute or two away from being able to fire, however. More than enough time to aim the cannon his men had just mounted on the wall.

ANZA SPREAD HER arms, turning to face the ground as she fell. The wind was like a giant invisible hand that held her in the sky. Of course, since the ground was racing nearer, the giant invisible hand wasn't doing a very good job.

The river was too far to reach. There were no convenient hay piles in sight. The sky-dragons who'd filled the sky earlier had gone into retreat.

She sighed. The world beneath her was beautiful. True, the hills around Dragon Forge were covered with decaying corpses and barren red earth cut through with deep gullies. The trees were twisted and stunted, and the whole area was so polluted it was as if giant buckets of ash had been dumped. But in her heart, she knew she would miss this world terribly.

A long, muscular arm wrapped around her waist. Her descent came to a sudden halt as Stonewall's momentum carried her parallel to the earth. She looked across at Jeremiah, who gave her a weak wave. She looked up into the gleaming eyes of her rescuer.

"I didn't mind catching Jeremiah, and I don't mind catching you, but I can't make any promises about the pig."

She nodded.

"You're brave," he said, as he wheeled to the north. "You didn't scream when you fell."

She smirked. The thought had never even crossed her mind.

IT TOOK ALL the strength left in Vulpine's wings to guide their fall toward the northern catapults. The pig still dangled from his tail, forcing his spine perfectly perpendicular to the earth. His wings were spread into twin parachutes, giving him some control, though they were still going to hit the ground hard. At least the pig would hit first.

He saw Sagen next to the loaded catapults, gawking at the odd sight of his father and the pig.

Vulpine was too winded to call out for assistance. No matter. When they hit the ground, he'd make short work of his portly tormentor.

There was a loud boom at his back. He couldn't turn his head to see the source of the whistling noise as it raced through the air toward him, then past him.

A black steel ball trailed smoke toward the catapult where Sagen waited. It landed at the base of the wooden war engine.

There was a flash of light and heat, and a clap of noise that made his teeth rattle. Dirt and smoke was thrown into the sky. Vulpine raced ever closer to where his son had been.

There was nothing left atop the hill but a smoking crater.

Before he could change his direction, he plunged into the smoke. Suddenly, the weight on his tail vanished, and the pig let out a loud squeal. Vulpine tried to flap his wings but the ground turned out to be only inches below him. He crashed onto the burning earth, rolling to a halt against a broad, splintered beam that had once been the arm of the catapult.

His left wing felt broken. He flapped his right wing to try to clear the smoky air.

Something moved in the smoke before him.

The pig?

It drew closer.

Jeremiah.

The boy held Vulpine's knife in his hand.

"We saw where you fell," he said.

Vulpine rose up, supporting his weight against the beam as he unlooped his whip. He coughed as the smoke choked him.

"That knife's too dangerous for you to play with, boy," said Vulpine. He flipped the whip back over his shoulder, intending to bring it forward and strike the knife away. At the far reach of his back stroke, the whip snagged and yanked from his grasp. He looked over his shoulder and saw the giant who'd dived to save the boy standing behind him, the braided leather wrapped in his enormous fist.

He turned back to face the boy.

Only now the dark-haired girl was in front of him. She had twin rows of puncture wounds along both cheeks that painted long stripes of blood down her face.

Unlike her earlier blankness, this time she smiled.

"We're... on... the... ground," she whispered. Her right hand closed around the knife still jutting from his breastbone. He trembled as she pulled the blade free.

BURKE WATCHED THE drama unfold in his spy-owl, frustrated by the smoke that obscured his sight. He let out a slow sigh of relief as Anza limped from the cloud. Jeremiah followed close behind, with Poocher trotting along beside him. The pig was covered in soot and had somehow lost all of the quivers that had been draped over him, along with his visor and the wings.

Finally, Stonewall stumbled out of the cloud. He had a large blue bundle tossed over his shoulder. Burke dialed the spy-owl to its sharpest focus and saw a limp sky-dragon, its jaws bound with what looked like a whip.

He stood up, stretching his shoulders. He'd folded up his wings after carrying the spy-owl onto the wall. The wings were so big, he'd been worried he might accidentally knock someone over the battlements. He grabbed his crutch and turned around.

Ragnar stood behind him. "I've killed five men to reach you," the prophet whispered. The big man wasn't carrying any weapons, but his chest was matted with blood. His hands shot out and grabbed Burke by the throat.

Burke's eyes bulged as the hairy man squeezed.

"Dragon Forge is mine!" the prophet hissed.

Behind Ragnar came the sound of rushing footsteps. The prophet turned his head just in time to see a large leather satchel swung at him. There was an explosion of paper as the bag caught the prophet across his face and ripped at the seams. Books flew everywhere. The prophet's fingers slipped from Burke's throat and the hairy man tumbled over the edge of the wall.

Burke looked down, wincing at the noise Ragnar's body made as it hit the ground.

Thorny knelt where the prophet had stood seconds before. He picked up remains of a very large book.

"*The Oxford English Dictionary*," said Thorny. Loose pages fluttered out of the ancient binding.

"Shay's going to have a fit when he sees what I've done to it."

Burke put his hand on his friend's shoulder. "He'll understand," said Burke. "He brought these books here because he knew that knowledge in the hands of mankind could strike a blow for freedom. You've simply taken the concept to a higher level."

THE WEEKS PASSED in relative quiet. With the blockade broken, it didn't take long for supplies to trickle back into the fort along with the news. The Dragon Palace remained empty after Chapelion had abandoned it and returned to the College of Spires, taking the remnants of the aerial guard with him. Albekizan's kingdom split apart at the seams as the patchwork quilt of fiefdoms he'd stitched together through decades of war came unraveled.

Among the news, there was one thread that remained constant: the story of a golden dragon who flew from castle to castle announcing himself the anti-king. He demanded no taxes or soldiers; he declared no law save for one: any dragon who dared to declare himself king beyond the border of his own small world could count on the golden dragon as a mortal enemy.

It was a warm spring day when the rifles began to bark out along the walls. Burke stood up on his newly-fashioned spring driven leg and walked to the window. Floating toward the center of town, landing near the rebuilt well, was a golden beast the size and shape of a sun-dragon. Sparks flew from the creature's hide as rifle balls bounced off its golden shell.

The glass in the window next to Burke shattered into a thousand pieces as a stray ball struck it. He stepped to the freshly opened window and shouted, "Hold your fire!"

Instantly, the order was relayed from man to man, "Hold your fire! Burke says hold your fire!" A moment later, all guns fell silent.

Burke walked to the elevator and rode it down into the foundry. The rumble of work carried on as usual. The machinery in the foundry was so loud that the workers hadn't heard the commotion on the streets.

Burke stepped out into the bright sunlight. As his eyes adjusted, he saw that the flowers in the window boxes on the building across the way were blooming. Now that more women had arrived, Dragon Forge looked less like a fort and more like a town.

He walked toward the dragon, who gazed at him with emerald eyes that shimmered amidst the gold.

"Burke," said the dragon. "You're looking fit."

Burke supposed he was. Some bit of good fortune had spared him from coming down with yellow-mouth, and in the weeks since he'd taken command of the fort he'd been sleeping well. Victory had a pleasant affect upon his constitution.

He shielded his eyes with his hands as he studied the gleaming dragon. "You're looking particularly robust yourself," said Burke.

"You recognize me?" asked the dragon.

"Hex," said Burke. "Bitterwood told me about your new look."

"Bitterwood has been here?"

"He's been here almost two weeks. He and Zeeky and Jeremiah took over an abandoned farm about five miles downriver. Once Shay and Jandra set up their school, he wants the children to learn to read and write."

"It's difficult to imagine Bitterwood behind a plow," said Hex.

"He won't be behind one for long," said Burke. "He had me design a plow harness for Skitter. With the speed at which that thing moves, I imagine he'll get his fields done in a few hours."

Hex nodded slowly, as if savoring the image.

"You aren't here to catch up on old times," said Burke.

"True," said Hex.

"You've come back from Atlantis as some sort of superdragon. You're strong enough to pull down a castle with your bare talons, I hear."

"The twists of fate have been kind to me."

"And now you're here to lay down the law as the new king."

"I shall never be king," said Hex.

"You're laying down rules. You're enforcing those rules with violence. It strikes me as kingly behavior."

"I have only one rule, Burke. I have explained it to all the sun-dragons. Now I'll explain it to you. If you send an army from this fort and attempt to seize neighboring land by force, you will find me opposing you. The age when disputes are settled by armies is at an end. There is nothing else that I care about."

"You used to care about ending slavery," said Burke.

"True. I still hope that slavery will end. But I'm keenly aware it would be possible for me to abuse my newfound power. In the end, I decided that enforcing a single law was all I could trust of myself."

"Even one rule has a way of growing," said Burke. "One day you'll realize that the world is too big for you to be everywhere at once. You'll decide to raise your own army, and you'll tax all the kingdoms where you keep the peace, because, after all, it's for our own benefit. Why shouldn't we bear the cost?"

"Your genius is no match for your cynicism, Burke."

Burke turned away. He saw Anza and Stonewall on the fortress wall, with the big cannon rotated to target Hex. While he was curious to see what the gun would do against the shell, he was also happy that Hex was doing what he was doing, at least for now. He would never admit it to the big lizard, but maybe what the world needed right now was an all-powerful idealist to let things calm down for a few years.

He waved his fingers back and forth under his chin, signaling Anza not to fire. She frowned, crossing her arms.

Dirt swirled on the streets as Hex's mighty wings beat down.

He watched as the mighty beast vanished over the eastern wall. He suspected Bitterwood was about to get company.

BITTERWOOD'S FARM WAS simple enough to spot from the air. Rows of fields plowed in perfect parallel lines radiated out for two or three acres from a simple log cabin. At the back of the cabin, the long-wyrm was curled up, napping.

There was a big gray barn near a stream, though it didn't look as if it would stay gray for long. Jeremiah and Zeeky stood before it with big broad brushes in their hands and buckets of red paint at their feet. Poocher rooted about at the banks of the stream. He was the first to look up at the bright slivers of light that reflected from Hex's shell and danced across the water before him.

The pig let out a sharp, short squeal and Zeeky and Jeremiah turned to face Hex. As he drifted to a landing, the figure of a man appeared in the barn door. Hex wondered for half a second who the old man was. His jaw slackened as the farmer stepped out into the light.

Hex had never seen Bitterwood without his cloak or the buckskin pants that clung to him like a second skin. Now, Bitterwood wore a pair of brown cotton overalls flecked with mud and dirt. His hair had been cropped close to his scalp. His skin was still leathery, but there was a subtle change in the man that Hex struggled to pinpoint. Finally, he understood.

Bitterwood was smiling.

"You still have the shell," said Bitterwood.

"I wouldn't know how to take it off if I wanted to," said Hex.

"Vendevorex or Jandra could probably help you with that."

"Vendevorex is going to stay in Atlantis to help teach the humans there how to survive in the absence of their god," said Hex. "And who knows how long Jandra and Shay will spend on their honeymoon? There's so much of the world they wish to see."

"I hear tell you've been seeing a fair bit of the world yourself," said Bitterwood. "The anti-king. I'm not certain I like the sound of it."

Hex shrugged. "You aren't in a position to judge me. You killed my father and brother. If I were a king, I would demand justice. But I'm no king."

"You're a big golden bully, then," said Bitterwood.

"And you're the Murder God," said Hex. "I would like to think, after the adventures we've shared, that we could call each other friends."

Bitterwood's frown returned. "I've never called any dragon friend," he said.

"I'm your friend," said Zeeky, coming up and placing her hand on Hex's wing.

"Me too," said Jeremiah. The boy had a big splotch of red paint on his cheek. Poocher trotted over and gave a gentle grunt as he set down next to Hex. The pig was a full-blown hog now, easily three hundred pounds.

"It's three against one, Bant," said Hex.

Bitterwood shook his head. "My feelings aren't up for a vote."

Hex sighed.

Bitterwood lowered his head, looking at the ground before him, weighing his thoughts. Finally, he said, "For what it's worth, I don't intend to kill you."

Hex nodded. "That's the nicest thing you've ever said to me."

"But if you ever do anything to hurt the folks in Dragon Forge, I won't hesitate to finish you off," Bitterwood continued. "I've hung up my bow. I didn't bury it."

"It might be interesting to see the tree that would grow if you did bury it, yes?"

Bitterwood didn't grin at the joke. Instead, he had his eyes fixed on Hex's jaws. "Did you know that the shell doesn't cover the inside of your mouth?" he asked.

Hex clamped his jaws shut.

"I've got a barn to paint," said Bitterwood.

"I've got a villain to bring to justice," said Hex.

"That's king talk," said Bitterwood.

"I've always been aware of my fundamental contradictions," said Hex, leaping into the air.

He glanced back down. It definitely wasn't a trick of the light. Bitterwood grinned as he watched Hex fly away.

He flew downstream another five miles to the agreed upon meeting place. As he dropped toward the bank, he saw his companions lurking among the trees. They walked out as they saw him. Their blue scales were especially bright beneath the spring sun. All two hundred of the valkyries wore armor. He wondered if they would need it.

* * *

JANDRA KNELT ON both knees as she placed the bouquet of yellow tulips in front of the rough stone pyramid. All along the valley, the rhododendrons bloomed, flecking the steep stony mountains with white. She carved the name "Lizard" into the largest stone with a flaming fingertip. She let the flame fade away and she stared at the word for a long, quiet moment.

"Even though I wasn't in control, I could still feel the warmth of his scales under my fingers."

Shay placed his hand on her shoulder.

"It's not your fault," he said.

She leaned her cheek against his arm. "I remember everything she did," whispered Jandra. "Do you want to know what the worst of it was?"

"Tell me," he said.

"She was so absolutely confident that she was right," said Jandra. "She thought the world was broken, and only she had the wisdom and courage and power to fix it."

Shay squeezed her shoulder. She knew he knew the significance of these words. "You're nothing like her," he said.

"I know," said Jandra. "But I've been thinking a lot about her journey. She started with good intentions. It's difficult to pinpoint the moment she went off the path from being a good person to being a monster."

"Perhaps it was around the time she decided it was okay to kill people to get what she wanted."

"I've killed," said Jandra. "Long before I'd met her I'd killed both dragons and men."

"You were acting to defend yourself and others," said Shay.

"She was acting to save the world," said Jandra.

She stood up, wiping the grit from her blue silk trousers. Shay already had his wings unfolded. He looked quite heroic in his red coat, with his shoulders pulled back. Vendevorex had repaired his muscles and scars. With the powers she commanded, she could have healed him herself... she could heal anyone and everyone. She could feed the hungry and give shelter to the homeless and strength to the weak.

"When we get back from the moon," she said, "I'm going to take off my genie."

Shay raised his eyebrow.

"I'll still help you train to use yours," she said.

"But—"

"I don't know if I have Vendevorex's level of self-restraint," she said. "He's always been sparing in the use of his abilities. He's far more powerful than he lets on. I never understood why he didn't do more good. For a while, I thought it was because he was afraid of the Atlanteans discovering he was using their technology. Now, I understand the truth—having been to Atlantis, he saw the effects of limitless altruism. Just because he has the power to fix the world's problems doesn't mean that it's always right to do so."

"You're afraid you might do too much good for the world?"

"I still want to make the world better," said Jandra. "But I want to do it following your vision. I want to help you start your school. We'll give people the tools they need to solve their own problems. I don't want people to become dependent on me."

Shay smiled. "It's a little late for that. I'm already dependent on you." He lifted into the air and held his hand toward her. "Without you near, I suspect I'd wither away."

"Flatterer."

"It's true," he said. "I think it's worth trying, by the way."

"What's worth trying?"

"When we get back, take off your genie for a year. I'll take off mine, since I can barely use it anyway. We'll discover if the world can last a year without our magic."

She took his hand as her wings chimed out to their full length. She rose into the air until they were the same height.

"With you," she said, "there will always be magic."

They tilted toward each other. Their lips met gently in weightless bliss. Shay wrapped his arms around her waist as they drifted in the flower-scented breeze. They floated for what felt like eternity, as her fears and doubts melted away.

When he finally broke from the kiss, she gazed into his eyes.

There was a question she felt embarrassed to ask.

"What?" he whispered.

"After we put up the genies, we're, um, keeping the wings, right?"

"Of course my angel," he whispered, stroking her cheek as they climbed into the endless blue.

IT WAS NIGHTFALL when Hex reached the Free City. In the weeks since he'd visited the population had swelled, rivaling Richmond in size. He suspected that the people in Richmond were enjoying the economic boom of selling an endless stream of building supplies to their thriving neighbor.

They landed by the barn that served as Blasphet's abode. A crowd of white-robed citizens gathered around him and the valkyries.

He noted with a certain satisfaction that humans outnumbered earth-dragons here fifty to one, and sky-dragons perhaps three-hundred to one. There were no sun-dragons to be seen. He wondered if this spoke to the differences in gullibility among the various species. Of course, it could also have reflected the degree to which the lives of the various races had been thrown into turmoil by the recent unrest.

The barn doors were open, allowing the warm spring breeze to flow through the place. The barn looked much as he left it, though the gate to Atlantis had been closed. Vendevorex had finally mastered that trick.

A silver mosquito landed on Hex's gold-plated ear.

It buzzed in a perfect simulacrum of Vendevorex's voice that only he could hear.

"I've been wondering when you would show up," the mosquito said.

"Are you near?" Hex whispered.

"I'm still in Atlantis," said Vendevorex. "There are machines here I need in order to do what you wish. But I have drones to serve as my eyes and ears."

Hex nodded, hoping Vendevorex saw the gesture. He walked into the barn with the valkyries at his heels.

Blasphet was on his canvas-covered podium. He looked pleased by Hex's arrival.

"You look worthy of worship, nephew," said Blasphet.

"No, my lord, no," whispered a robed woman near the black dragon's feet. She sounded distressed.

"My followers find the thoughts of worshipping any other dragon stressful, I fear," said Blasphet. "I believe it's because, despite my most fervent protests, they believe I am a god."

"You called yourself a god once," said Hex. "And, as a god, you're responsible for the deaths of eight-hundred and seventy-three valkyries, victims of your genocidal assault on the Nest."

"You speak of deeds I performed before I was reborn," said Blasphet.

"I speak of deeds for which you will be brought to justice. These valkyries are here to arrest you. You are to be tried for your crimes before a council of learned dragons. Should they decide you are guilty of the assault upon the Nest, you will face execution."

"I've already died for those crimes," said Blasphet. "My sins were washed away in my own blood."

"Perhaps this argument will impress your judges."

The woman at his feet sprung up.

"No!" she shouted. "You cannot take him! He's the life force of this city! He provides all food. He cures all ills. His wise counsel has united the races!"

"If his counsel is truly wise and you've learned from him, perhaps your city will thrive," said Hex. "I will not interfere with your development. If you've discovered a better path through life, I hope it spreads to all the corners of the earth. Blasphet, however, will be at the Nest."

The woman clenched her fists. Blasphet placed his fore-talon on her shoulder.

"Colobi, you are dear to me. I know you would die to protect me. I do not ask for your life, however. Listen to my nephew. Follow my example. Spread my teachings. Serve the world."

The woman looked up with tears in her eyes.

Blasphet sounded as if there were tears in his own voice as he said, "I ask that all of my children leave the room. I would have a moment alone with our guests."

The women who lined the walls glared as they filed out of the barn. The valkyrie at the back of the room drew the doors closed.

"Do you intend to come peacefully?"

"Of course," said Blasphet. He sounded smug. "I cannot guarantee, however, that my followers will allow our safe passage. They can be… zealous."

"We won't be leaving through the door," said Hex. "Vendevorex, it's time."

A circular rainbow opened in the air near the wall, yawning ever wider until it was large enough to swallow a sun-dragon.

"The Nest is on the other side," said Hex.

"I suspected as much," said the former Murder God. "I've been aware of the wizard's bug for days now. My eyes and ears are much keener than they once were."

"We know," said Hex. He pointed at the portal. Half of the valkyries were already passing through the gate. "Follow them," said Hex.

Blasphet rose. His eyes were creased with a look of satisfaction.

"Did you know that the humans have a myth?" he asked, just before he vanished into the gate.

Hex followed closely behind. They emerged in dim lamplight, in the dank, cool air of the Nest. They were in the thread room, the focal point of Blasphet's slaughter there.

Blasphet finished his thought. "They speak of a healer who some called a god. When he was alive, he would answer all queries about his divinity with riddles. The authorities of his day killed him. When he rose from the dead, his followers knew without doubt what he truly was. His worship has survived the rise and fall of civilizations."

"You won't be rising from the dead, uncle."

"Won't I?" said Blasphet. "I helped guide Vendevorex back from death. Not that I think I will die, mind you. When I called myself the Murder God, all I had at my command were a few poisons. Now, I control all matter. The building blocks of the physical world are my playthings. With my knowledge and powers, I expect I will enjoy a very long life. I may even be immortal."

Hex couldn't help but notice the smugness in Blasphet's voice. He said, "The valkyries will no doubt decide the span of your life. I suspect it may not be as long as you appear to think."

"I have nothing to fear from the valkyries," said Blasphet. "You won't let them harm me."

"Oh?" said Hex.

"Look at you," Blasphet said. "Gleaming like some temple idol come to life. You're an idealist, nephew. You want to make the world a better place. You dream you will be responsible for the dawn of a golden age."

"Perhaps," said Hex. "I assure you, no part of that dream includes you in it."

"My disciples have carried my dragonseed far across this kingdom," said Blasphet. "Twenty thousand and more have swallowed these small parts of my flesh. Some who've accepted my dragonseed are men you call friends."

"What of it?" asked Hex.

The thread room was now cramped with valkyries.

"Should I die, a signal will spread through all the tiny machines that linger in the bodies of those who've partaken of my flesh. When my heartbeat stops, so will theirs. You're a predictable do-gooder, Hex. You won't sacrifice twenty-thousand to avenge the deaths of a few hundred."

"You're correct," said Hex. "I wouldn't. However, I suspect the valkyries might."

One of the nearby valkyries said, "Those who have swallowed the dragonseed share in his guilt."

"I disagree," said Hex, thinking of Jeremiah. How could anyone plausibly argue the boy should bear the burden of this monster's sins? "In any case, his threat is an empty one."

"You think I'm bluffing?"

"I'm certain that you're not," said Hex. "I'm also certain that Vendevorex has far more experience with your machines than you do. He tells me that one of the first things he did upon regaining his awareness was to analyze your dragonseed. He informs me that they work as you say. On your last heartbeat, your genie will send out the death signal."

"Then it is your duty to see to my safety."

"Or my duty to take away your genie," said Hex. "Vendevorex assures me that if it's not in your possession when you die, the dragonseed can do no harm."

"Even with that golden shell, you still need to breathe." Blasphet moved with the swiftness that only those enhanced by nanites could possess as he tossed a talonful of silver dust across the room.

"Die choking in your own... own... um..." Blasphet's voice trailed off as the silver dust swirled and flew back at him, coalescing into silver chains binding his talons. "Curious," he said.

"Vendevorex says the genie you wear has never been locked. He can control the dust you command from half a world away."

"Ah," said Blasphet. He flicked off a black cap from the longest claw on his left fore-talon. The nail glistened with a tar-like black poison that smelled of almonds. He looked deep into Hex's eyes as he said, "I always knew, in the end, I'd have to fall back onto my familiar vices. These chains cannot bind me! These valkyries will never harm me. I am the Murder God!"

"I would be much more impressed if your claws had any chance of piercing my shell," Hex said, careful not to open his mouth too widely.

"You misunderstand," Blasphet said with a chuckle as dry as the rustle of dead leaves. "We're back to the ending where my heart stops and everyone dies."

He plunged the talon against his own neck. His face twisted into an expression of pure malice as the poisoned claw tore deep into his vein. Hex lunged, snatching at the genie that floated above Blasphet's brow. His talons closed on empty air. The tiara vanished like a popped soap bubble.

"It might be along his spine," Vendevorex buzzed into his ear. Hex's heart froze at the word *might*.

Blasphet shivered as he fell against Hex's chest. The Murder God's eyes glistened with tears as they rolled up into his skull. His last breath came out in a long, shuddering sob.

Hex sank his teeth into the flesh along his uncle's spine and ripped away the ebony metal he found there. He spat it out. It slid along the floor like a long black serpent.

Had he been fast enough?

Did the evil beast's heart still beat?

He held his breath. Blood surged out of the open wound as the Murder God's black heart pushed out one final pulse. He slid down Hex's golden chest, completely lifeless.

"We should have anticipated the poisoned claw," said Vendevorex.

"Did we stop him in time?" Hex asked, his throat tight.

"With at least a second to spare," said Vendevorex. "The genie never sent out a signal."

"So it's over. We've won. The world is finally free of the Murder God."

"Good riddance," said the Vendevorex mosquito as it flitted away. A few feet away it paused, before darting back to Hex's ear.

"Just to be certain," it buzzed, "burn the body."

DRAGONS

ON THEIR SPECIES AND LINEAGE

SUN-DRAGONS

Sun-dragons are the lords of the realm, possessing forty-foot wingspans and long, toothy jaws that can bite a man in half. Sun-dragons are adorned with crimson scales tipped with highlights of orange and yellow that give them a fiery appearance. Wispy feathers around their snouts give the illusion that they breathe smoke. Though gifted with natural weaponry and a tough, scaly hide, sun-dragons are intelligent tool-users who recognize the value of using spears and armor to enhance their already formidable combat skills. Politically, sun-dragons are organized under an all-powerful king, who, by rights, owns all property within the kingdom. A close network of other sun-dragons, often related to the king, manage individual abodes within the kingdom. Sun-dragons of note are:

ALBEKIZAN (Deceased)
The king of all dragons for 68 years, Albekizan conquered several small kingdoms to form his empire. When he perished at the hands of Bitterwood, his rule passed to son Shandrazel.

SHANDRAZEL (Deceased)

Albekizan's heir attempted to reform dragon government, intending to share power between all dragon species and even humans. His reforms were taken as a sign of weakness, and a full-blown rebellion of humans erupted under his watch, resulting in his assassination.

BLASPHET (Deceased)

Albekizan's older brother, Blasphet is legendary as the most wicked dragon ever to have lived. Also known as the Murder God, Blasphet built a loyal following of human worshippers who regarded him as the physical manifestation of Death. He was the architect of the Free City, a trap designed to slay all of humanity, and also was behind the assault on the Nest, an attempt at genocide against sky-dragons. It is said that he died during this final act of villainy, slain by Bitterwood.

HEXILIZAN

Albekizan's sole surviving son, Hex shuns all trappings of royalty and wealth and is, by most measures, a radical anarchist. Fearless in battle, and possessing a sly wit, Hex describes himself as a warrior-philosopher. He befriended the human sorceress Jandra, only to betray her, robbing her of her powers when he feared she was growing too powerful.

RORG

An old, fat dragon who keeps a harem of females, Rorg practices a philosophy known as beastialism that shuns the trappings of civilization. He refuses to build a castle to dwell in as is the fashion of other sun-dragons, instead feeling that the appropriate home of a dragon is a large cave surrounded by a field of bones.

SKY-DRAGONS

Half the size of sun-dragons, sky-dragons are a race devoted to scholarship. Most male sky-dragons dwell at colleges built around large libraries. Their leaders are known as biologians, a position that is part priest, part librarian, and part scientist. A tiny fraction of male sky-dragons serve the sun-dragon king as an honored aerial guard. Sky-dragons practice strict segregation of the sexes. The females of the species dwell on an island fortress known as the Nest, defended by fierce warriors known as valkyries. The scholars among the females tend to focus on more practical sciences, such as engineering. Sky-dragons of note are:

VENDEVOREX (Deceased)
Albekizan's wizard, also known as the Master of the Invisible. He raised from infancy a human girl named Jandra, who he treated as a daughter. He perished fighting to save mankind in the battle of the Free City.

ANDROKOM
A young biologian with a reputation for both genius and arrogance, Androkom served as High Biologian during Shandrazel's brief reign.

CHAPELION
Head of the College of Spires, Chapelion taught Shandrazel during his youth.

SARELIA, THE MATRIARCH
Leader of the female sky-dragons, the matriarch is charged with guiding the genetic destiny of all sky-dragons. All pairings of male and female sky-dragons are planned by her and her assistants to ensure the continued health of their race.

GRAXEN (Banished)

The matriarch's only surviving child, Graxen was a freak with a gray hide and stronger than average skills of flight. He was banished due to his inadvertent role in helping Blasphet invade the Nest.

NADALA (Banished)

A valkyrie who fell in love with Graxen. This love was then manipulated by Blasphet to give him access to the Nest. She was to be slain for her actions, but for mysterious reasons Sarelia commuted her sentence to banishment.

VULPINE

The Slavecatcher General, Vulpine oversees the small army of slavecatchers who are charged with regulating the slave trade within the kingdom and tracking and disciplining escaped slaves.

EARTH-DRAGONS

Wingless creatures, earth-dragons are humanoids with turtle-beaked faces and broad, muscular bodies. They are much stronger than men, but also much slower. As a race, they have few valuable skills beyond their enthusiasm for hitting things. This makes them excellent soldiers and decent blacksmiths. Except for the rare periods of time when earth-dragon females are in heat, it's nearly impossible to tell the difference between the two sexes of earth-dragons. They are the only dragon species to lay eggs instead of producing live birth. Few can truly be said to be of note. Two exceptions are:

CHARKON (Deceased)

The former boss of Dragon Forge, Charkon was a battle-hardened warrior before assuming leadership of the foundries where the weapons of the king's soldiers were forged. Unusually well-spoken for a member of his race, Charkon was fiercely loyal to the rule of sun-dragons and a strong ally of both Albekizan and Shandrazel.

SAWFACE

A giant of an earth-dragon at over six feet tall, Sawface is the embodiment of strength and savagery. He commands his loyal band of soldiers, the Wasters, through a mix of fear and awe.

HUMANS
THE LESSER SPECIES

A lesser species, humans live among dragon society as slaves, pets, and prey. The sun-dragons tolerate their existence primarily because of human's natural flair for farming; the labor of humans keeps the bellies of dragons full. Humans are generally peaceful in small, isolated groups, but quick to war with other tribes. Following the death of Albekizan, the prophet Ragnar gathered up a large army of men to do battle with their dragon oppressors, leading to the attack on Dragon Forge. Humans of note are:

BITTERWOOD

A legendary dragon-slayer whose long years of struggle against monsters have left him unable to feel any emotion but hate.

JANDRA
Raised by the sky-dragon wizard Vendevorex, Jandra knows the secrets of his magic and was herself a formidable power until her abilities were stolen from her by her former friend Hex.

ZEEKY
An orphan with a mysterious power over animals. Her only surviving relative is her brother Jeremiah, who has been missing since he fled from the battle of Dead Skunk Hole. Zeeky's best friends are her pet pig, Poocher, and Bitterwood.

RAGNAR
The charismatic preacher who has fanned the flames of revolution, gathering an army by marching from village to village with the ultimatum, "Join or die!" He has taken a vow never to wear clothes or cut his hair until the last dragon is driven into the sea.

BURKE THE MACHINIST
Ragnar's unlikely ally, Burke is the inventor of the sky-wall bows that doubled the range of human archers. Burke currently runs the captured foundries and is designing new machines of war to advance the human cause.

ANZA
Burke's mute daughter, trained since she could walk to master the warrior's arts.

VANCE
A member of the sky-wall bow team, Vance is a young man who ran from home with his brother Vinton to join the revolution.

SHAY
A runaway slave, formerly owned by Chapelion, Shay is one of the rare humans who has the ability to read. A true believer in the cause of human liberty, Shay believes that education is the best path toward a new age of human dominance.

JAZZ, THE GODDESS (Deceased)
A thousand-year old woman who still possesses all the technological secrets from the long-lost Human Age, Jazz has secretly manipulated events over the centuries to weaken mankind, since she regards her own species as the greatest environmental threat to the world. She was slain by Bitterwood.

OTHER SPECIES

OF NOTE

LONG-WYRMS
Fifty-foot-long serpents with fourteen pairs of legs and copper-colored scales, long-wyrms are a dead-end experiment created by the Jazz and pressed into service as defenders of her underground kingdom.

GREAT-LIZARDS
Often used as beasts of burden, great-lizards are twenty-foot long reptiles that closely resemble giant iguanas with a more upright stance.

OX-DOGS

The product of ten centuries of careful breeding, Ox-dogs are the largest species of dogs ever to exist, standing nearly six feet high at the shoulder. They are normally docile in temperament, but are frequently used by earth-dragons for hunting and tracking, and will fight to the death to defend their pack.

ACKNOWLEDGEMENTS

FIRST, SINCERE THANKS to five people who most assisted the development of this book: Laurel Amberdine, Cathy Bollinger, Suanne Warr, Bill Ferris, and Ada Brown served as my wise readers during the early drafts of *Dragonseed*. During my early drafts, I make no effort at winnowing out typos, so figuring out what I really meant to say requires hard work and dedication. I owe Cathy a special debt for brainstorming with me about the potential fates of various characters following the events in the last novel, *Dragonforge*. And, if you've ever laughed at a joke or a pun in any of the *Dragon Age* books, you can thank Laurel for marking all the places in the drafts where she found something funny. She's really helped me hone the subtle humor that runs through all my books.

SPECIAL THANKS AS well to Cheryl Morgan and Jeremy Cavin, who read the final draft before Solaris got their hands on it and gave me wonderful feedback on what was working well and what still needed sharpening. Since Cheryl lives near me, I get to discuss the books at length with her and find out what's holding her interest. Cavin is half a world away (Vietnam, as I write this), but his eye for detail and encyclopedic knowledge of darn near everything helps to keep me on my toes.

THEN, OF COURSE, there's the crew at Solaris: Christian Dunn gave me notes on the big picture, and helped me smooth out the last few rough patches remaining in the tale. The work then went to Alethea Kontis, who put in heroic effort as the line editor and helped create the illusion that I know anything at all about spelling or punctuation. Finally, artist Micheal Komarck has produced yet another eye-catching cover—both *Dragonforge* and *Dragonseed* are better books because I knew I had to work hard to meet the high expectations his covers would produce.

FOLLOWING THE RELEASE of *Dragonforge*, I traveled to Chattanooga to attend a gathering of the Codex Writers Group. This was hosted by Mary Robinette Kowal and her family, and organized by Codex's founder Luc Reid. The creative energy of the event was strong: acclaimed editor Ellen Datlow ran a series of critique sessions, and author David B. Coe dropped in to discuss the profession of writing. During the five days I stayed at the workshop, I worked extensively on the book. I'm grateful to have had the opportunity to bask in the creative light of so many fellow writers.

AFTER CHATTANOOGA, I drove to New Hampshire, where I gave a lecture on style to the Odyssey Writer's Workshop. I am greatly appreciative of Jeanne Cavelos for the invite, and to Susan Sielinski for her help in coordinating the visit. As a graduate of Odyssey in 1998, it was a real thrill to return 10 years later as a teacher.

TO CELEBRATE THE release of *Dragonforge*, I solicited dragon-themed poetry and art for my blog: *dragonprophet.blogspot.com*. I'm grateful to everyone who contributed work, including Kimberly Bea,

Eric James Stone, Shaun Duke, Meg Stout, Rebecca Roland, Danielle Friedman, Michael Livingston, Jeanette Jackson, Krista Hoeppner Leahy, Brian Dolton, Christina Crooks, Shawn Crawford, Scott Roberts, David Walton, Tysha Dawson, Nancy Fulda, Chris Coe, Lee Dixon, Giovanni Quinteros, Scott Mercer, Brian Waterhouse, Joseph Phillips, Dona Nova, and Kim Raginski.

IN MY ACKNOWLEDGEMENTS for *Dragonforge*, I was able to give thanks by name to the few dozen people who had written reviews of *Bitterwood*, since I was writing only a few months after the book's release. Now, it's been a year and a half, and hundreds of people have talked about the books on blogs and forums or reviewed the book on Amazon or Library Thing. Thanking everyone by name, would, alas, require more time than I have available. However, I'm deeply indebted to everyone who helps spread the gospel of the *Dragon Age*, and will continue to thank people on my blog as reviews appear.

CREATING A NOVEL is an interactive process. As the writer, I provide guidance, but it's the reader who actually builds the world in their imaginations and helps give life to the characters. So, I'll close this by acknowledging my most important partner in producing *Dragonseed*: You, the person holding this book. Thank you.

James Maxey
February 2009

ABOUT THE AUTHOR

JAMES MAXEY LIVES in Hillsborough, NC, USA. After graduating from the Odyssey Fantasy Writer's Workshop and Orson Scott Card's Writer's Boot Camp, James broke into the publishing world in 2002 when he won a Phobos Award for his short story, "Empire of Dreams and Miracles." In 2003, Phobos Books released his critically acclaimed superhero novel, *Nobody Gets the Girl*. In 2007, Solaris Books released *Bitterwood*, the first novel in the Dragon Age series, followed by *Dragonforge* in 2008. His short fiction has appeared in *Asimov's*, *Intergalactic Medicine Show*, and numerous anthologies. For more information about his writing, visit James at *dragonprophet.blogspot.com*.